MIDNIGHT SHADOWS

(SKY BROOKS WORLD: ETHAN BOOK 3)

EMERSON KNIGHT

MCKENZIE HUNTER

This is a work of fiction. Names, characters, businesses, places, events, and incidents are either the products of the author's imagination or used in a fictitious manner. Any resemblance to actual persons, living or dead, or actual events is purely coincidental.

McKenzie Hunter

Midnight Shadows

ISBN: 978-1-946457-00-4

ACKNOWLEDGMENTS

First and foremost, I'd like to thank McKenzie Hunter for allowing me to play in her world. What a fun place to be, with a rich mythology and full of complex characters I loved to spend time with. Midnight Shadows was a challenge! For the first time, Ethan has a significant story line that is unique from Sky's story. I don't know how I would've completed this book without my beta readers and Stacy McCright, who consistently kept me from straying off the path.

I'd also like to thank Gloria Knowles, C. Hindle, and the most supportive group of authors I could ask for: John P. Logsdon, Orlando Sanchez, Benjamin Zackheim, and Shayne Silvers.

Lastly but most important, my thanks to you, the reader. Fans of McKenzie Hunter and the Sky Brooks series have been very supportive of Ethan's POV, and I couldn't feel more fortunate. Without all of you, I wouldn't be able to do what I most love to do, write. You're the best!

CHAPTER 1

$\mathcal{T}$he wooden floor of the aging neighborhood ale house creaked as I walked the length of the bar and slid into a secluded booth.

"Scotch," I told the waitress.

Tim arrived at the same time as my drink. He was tall, with military-cut sandy blond hair and a chevron mustache. He was a pack member, a wolf who'd worked for the county police for twenty years and counting. Much of our ability to monitor supernatural activity in and around Chicago derived from a handful of pack members in law enforcement. At the moment, Tim was out of uniform, dressed inconspicuously in a tan jacket and pants. Among the blue-collar crowd the bar attracted, he fit right in. Because Tim's responsibilities with the pack sometimes collided with his official duties, he limited his appearances at the retreat to avoid drawing attention to our relationship. He'd arranged our meeting by text, which wasn't unusual. That he'd done so using an emergency phone that wasn't connected to either of us meant he had something significant to say.

He slid into the booth across from me and ordered a beer.

"Tim," I said, then sipped my Scotch.

"Ethan," he said, clasping his hands in front of him on the table. "How are Winter and Markos?"

Three months ago, Ethos, the most powerful purveyor of dark magic known to us, had sent his creatures to attack the pack using poisoned claws. Markos, Winter, and Joan had been among the most seriously injured. By the time I'd acquired the antidote, they'd been placed into medically induced comas in an effort to keep them alive. Once revived, the damage had been so pervasive that none of them had been able to participate in the final battle against Ethos. Winter had practically needed to be tied down to keep her out of the fight. It had been a difficult call, but the right one. It had taken two months for them to fully recover.

"You know Markos," I said.

Tim nodded, fishing peanuts from the bowl in front of us. "Winter?"

"Never going to let me live it down."

"I got a text from her yesterday informing me that our sparring session is scheduled for two o'clock this Saturday." He grinned. "Last time we sparred, she went full snake. I'd never been paralyzed before that. I don't mind saying, it had an effect on me. Gave me night terrors for a week."

His beer arrived and he took a long drink, then wiped the foam from his mustache. His expression was sober as he said, "We got a problem with the guy."

"The guy" was Dennis McDuffy, a private investigator Sky had hired months ago to locate any possible living relatives. Two years ago, she'd been a lone wolf living with her adopted mother. We'd saved her from vampires, and now she was part of the pack. Orphaned at birth, she'd never given up hope of finding blood relatives, even distant ones.

He'd found them, and I'd paid him to keep his mouth shut. I'd also put him to work tracking Chris, my ex-lover, who'd been trying to broker a truce between the pack and the vampires, her employers. He'd proved his skills, deftly avoiding her detection, but he hadn't been prepared to deal with Michaela, the Mistress of the Seethe and a notoriously sadistic killer even by vampire standards. I'd been careless with him, and it had cost Dennis his life when she'd caught him waiting for Chris outside the Seethe's home.

I took another sip of Scotch, washing down the distaste of my failure. The supernatural world was a dangerous place —were-animals rarely died of old age. It was a grim fact of life we'd become proficient at dealing with, but the death of a human like Dennis presented a number of complications.

Over the decades, the pack had developed a number of contacts within the medical profession that helped us keep our tragedies away from prying human eyes. My brother, Josh, one of the most powerful witches in the region and blood ally to the pack, used his magic to get rid of bodies and scrub the evidence from crime scenes when necessary, but hiding a death involved more than just the physical evidence.

When a body disappeared, it left people behind. Were-animals generally kept outside relationships to a minimum, but humans left long trails of workmates, friends, and relatives who noticed their absence. To make matters worse, bodies also left financial trails. It was hard to explain that someone just decided to move away and start life over somewhere else when their bank accounts sat untouched, their mortgages and car loans unpaid.

As the Elite—leader of all the packs in the country—Sebastian had directed each pack to have members infiltrate the banking system. After a few years, it had paid off, giving us a bank in Florida and a bank in Colorado that were willing to cater to our unique circumstances. Pack members were encouraged to use these resources. When a pack member died, the associated pack paid a hefty fee and our allies at the banks scrubbed the deceased's financial trail. It was a highly efficient system, but entirely useless in dealing with human collateral damage.

Fortunately, Dennis had been a loner. Tim had looked up Dennis's records and found he'd been divorced for twenty-three years. He'd remained estranged from his ex-wife. No children on record. Parents deceased. No siblings. A neighbor had reported him missing, but the curiosity stopped there. The vamps had ensured that his body never turned up, and the police hadn't shown much interest in looking for a down-on-his-luck private investigator who'd most likely skipped town because he was almost as behind on his office rent as he was on his mortgage. They'd let the case languish—until Dennis's daughter showed up at the precinct. That'd been a surprise.

It turned out Dennis's marriage had ended before he'd found out he was going to be a father. According to Caroline, the daughter, he hadn't known about her until she'd shown up at his office six months ago. They'd just begun to reconcile when he'd disappeared. So far, her pleas for an investigation of possible foul play had gone unanswered.

"It turns out," Tim said, "the daughter has a case of persistency. When the detectives brushed her off, she went straight to the chief. At his home. She mentioned the press once or twice and he folded for her like a wet noodle. Now he's holding a fire to the detectives' butts. They'll be launching a full investigation under the assumption that foul play might've been involved. Probably tomorrow."

"How bad?" I asked.

He gestured to my tumbler. "You might want to finish that Scotch so you can order another."

I scowled, then downed the rest of it in one gulp. The glass clunked against the table as I set it down.

Tim continued, "It's safe to assume that he kept records of his cases. Unless those records manage to disappear, you should probably be prepared to give an interview. And that can be problematic."

I caught the waitress's eye and raised my empty tumbler

4

to her, then shrugged to Tim, who was watching me closely. "I hired him to find out if my girlfriend was cheating on me," I suggested. "Then he took off with my retainer."

Tim shook his head as he fished his fingers in the bowl of peanuts. "They'd want to talk to your girlfriend."

I considered for a moment. "I hired him to try and locate a deadbeat client." It was a simple cover story, easy to maintain. Even in corporate law, which I practiced, there were clients who preferred not to pay their bills.

"Might work," Tim acknowledged. "Depends on what he recorded in his notes. If his story contradicts yours …" He let the thought trail off while he drank his beer. "I'm not going to be able to give you more on that situation, not for a while. I've already fished around too much."

"Okay. Is that it?" I asked, sensing it wasn't.

"Not quite." He took a folded manila envelope from the inside pocket of his jacket and slid it toward me on the table. Inside, I felt the shape of a USB drive.

"Some documents there, but you won't find much. The dashcam footage is the interesting part," he explained. "I stopped a biker—real badass-looking fella—with Indiana plates. I was just going to give him a shakedown, let him know he'd been noticed and that his welcome in the county was limited, but there was something about him. I could smell the darkness. He had that kind of magic that puts your hair on end, just by proximity."

A purveyor of dark magic, like Ethos.

"He goes by the name Lucas Reed. Maybe he's a guest of Marcia's, but I doubt it. He didn't have that I-play-well-with-others kind of vibe. I gave him the usual warning about pack territory, letting him know his life would be much less complicated if he didn't waste any time moving on, but I can't say he took me seriously. If it wasn't for the magic, I'd have bundled him into a jail cell for a few days, just to tenderize him. I figured I'd check with you before I pursued the matter."

"I'll look into it."

My Scotch arrived. I downed it in one gulp, left some cash on the table for the combined tab and then some, then left. Once home, I opened the manila envelope, which contained two pieces of paper along with the USB drive. The pages were printouts from a law enforcement database search on Lucas Reed. A copy of the driver's license showed a long, lean face with a crooked nose, hazel eyes, and dense red curls that flowed down to drape over his shoulders. His record was almost nonexistent. In fact, it seemed as if Mr. Reed had materialized out of thin air just a few years ago, when he'd purchased a commercial franchise selling motorcycles. Before that, there was nothing: no school, no traffic violations, no marriage license, no known addresses. He was a ghost, recently risen from the dead.

I loaded the USB drive into my laptop.

The dashcam video began just after Reed had been pulled over on his Harley Davidson Sport Glide. Beneath the leather riding chaps and a cut jacket, he was wearing faded jeans and a t-shirt. He removed his helmet as Tim walked into view, approaching from his car. Reed seemed amiable enough, handing over his documents. While Tim examined them, Reed glanced back at the police cruiser. His eyes flashed briefly and the image became static. I fast forwarded through the footage, but the static didn't clear until he drove off and Tim returned to his cruiser.

I called Josh. When I got his voice mail, I called the pack's nightclub, but he wasn't there. Most likely he was home. Up until a few months ago, home had been my condo near the club. He'd had a habit of practicing magic there—dangerous magic—but the physical damage hadn't started until he'd begun training Sky. After a few visits from the police and dozens of complaints from the other residents, the home-

6

owner's association had kicked him out, which was fine by me. By the time my brother had left, he'd cost me thousands of dollars in property damage. My insurance rates had tripled.

His Art Moderne ranch was a few miles outside the city. It was a good investment. More importantly, he could recklessly destroy it with magic as much as he liked. And *he* would pay for the consequences.

I picked up the keys to my tanzanite metallic blue BMW M6 and drove toward my brother's ranch.

The Creed, the governing witch council in Chicago, kept a close eye on visiting witches. Lucas Reed was obviously powerful, and Marcia, the Creed's leader, didn't trust anyone she perceived could threaten her dominance. While Josh couldn't ask her directly—she considered him a rival, and she didn't appreciate his relationship with the pack—he wasn't without his connections.

Just outside the city, I became apprehensive as a subtle, chilly wave of dark magic blew through the cabin of my BMW. Glancing around for a source, I spotted a dark sedan approaching from behind and driving significantly faster than the speed of traffic. I tensed, quickly assessing my options. On my right was a narrow shoulder, followed by a deep trench. If the sedan was looking to knock me off the road, it certainly had a great opportunity. My best evasive option, if needed, was to take the middle lane and push the sedan into the ditch. Traffic around me was light and spread out, but I didn't want to put anyone at risk. The only other option was to take advantage of the BMW's four-point-four-liter V-8 engine and leave the sedan in my wake, which might not be enough to escape a magical attack.

I slowly eased my foot from the accelerator, putting some extra distance between myself and the neighboring vehicles, while keeping my eye on the oncoming sedan, which showed no interest in slowing down as it came within half a car's length of my bumper. Inside, I saw a young woman glowering behind the wheel while her young male companion seemed to be vociferously complaining about something.

I didn't appreciate having the sedan on my ass, but the young couple wasn't the source of magic. After a moment, the sedan changed to the middle lane and sped past me.

The feeling of darkness within my cabin remained, a steady, disturbing flow of power that had a familiar feel to it. Like a fingerprint, every witch's magic had a distinct nature. The longer I felt the darkness around me, the more it felt like Ethos's magic, but that wasn't possible. Unable to determine more, I continued toward Josh's ranch. The closer I got, the stronger the flow of dark magic became.

By the time the ranch came into sight, I knew the source of power was there. Was my brother under attack? I tensed, prepared to race inside, but then I noticed Sky's Honda Civic in the driveway and realized she was the source.

I cursed under my breath.

In the final battle with Ethos, Sky had been trapped with him inside a nearly impregnable protective field. Despite the entire pack, supported by Josh's magic, throwing our full force against it, I was the only one able to break through, and Ethos had easily cast me back out. He'd been in complete control of Sky, able to do whatever he'd desired, yet he'd inexplicably transferred his magic to her until there was nothing left of him. I suspected the magic had been intended for Maya, the spirit shade that inhabited Sky's body. I didn't know what the relationship was between Maya and Ethos. Fortunately, Josh had been able to draw Ethos's magic out of Sky before we could find out. At least, he'd drawn most of it out. Before the last of Ethos's magic had been removed, Sky had stopped the ritual; she'd held on to a piece of the magic. Josh knew it, and so did I. I didn't know why.

Unlike other were-animals, she had the power to borrow magic and use it, but the magic always dissipated with use, like a battery. Knowing my brother's interest in dark magic, it was inevitable that he'd take advantage of her. I'd assumed the magic would be used up after one or two experiments.

Judging by the power emanating from inside the ranch, I was mistaken.

My jaw clenched as I parked on the side of the road in view of the house. As much as I wanted to charge through the front door, I knew a direct confrontation would only make Sky more determined. To my annoyance, I knew she'd listen to Josh. First, I had to convince him, alone. As the dark magic continued to pass through me, the wait only made me angrier. I was angry at myself for allowing them to maintain their secret, and I was angry at them for their reckless use of it. Didn't he realize they were broadcasting Ethos's magic for miles? Josh should've known better, but he was blinded by his ever-growing desire for power. Sky was no better at considering the consequences of her actions. Together, they were a powder keg with a lit fuse.

After a short while, the magic dissipated. Sky emerged from the ranch and drove off without noticing me. Once she was gone, I parked in Josh's driveway and walked inside without knocking. He was in the living room, straightening the furniture. Much the way he'd decorated my condo, his place appeared more like the living room of a frat house than the home of an adult. Nothing matched, in style or color. Odd accent chairs were haphazardly placed around the living room, none of them matching the dark blue sofa with the sunken cushions and more stains than I could count. The coffee table was scarred from boot heels resting on it, and there were water stains where he should've used coasters. The area rug beneath it all was worn in places to the point of being threadbare.

"By all means," Josh declared, "feel free to just walk in without knocking."

I shut the door behind me.

"I think my next lecture isn't scheduled for"—he frowned at his watch—"some other time."

I unclenched my jaw to speak. "What were you doing with Sky?"

He rolled his eyes dismissively, then went back to positioning his leopard-patterned chair as if there was some organization behind his chaos. "You know I'm training Sky to use magic. Honestly, Ethan, we've gone over this a dozen times. This conversation is getting rather old."

"What magic?" I demanded.

He paused to look at me, his eyes narrowing in suspicion. "I loaned her mine. We didn't break anything—other than a few drinking glasses. Come to think of it, those were from the set you gave me for Christmas."

I clenched my fists as I glowered at him, then slowly released them. "You were using dark magic—Ethos's magic. I could feel it. For miles."

He gave me a suspicious look. If anyone could fool me with a lie, it was Josh, but he didn't take the risk. Instead, he simply remained silent, watching me.

I said through gritted teeth, "I know that you let her keep some of his magic."

He dropped into the leopard-patterned chair and crossed one knee over the other. "It's powerful magic," he conceded, "but I've kept her practice confined to here."

"You just can't stop taking chances, can you?"

"What chances?" he snapped.

"Why did you let her keep it?"

He rolled his eyes at me. "It's a trace amount."

"It's dangerous, Josh. It's reckless."

He shifted onto the edge of the chair, his eyes bright with excitement. "She can create a field more powerful than anything I can make, Ethan. The pack values what I can do for them. Imagine having even a thimbleful of Ethos's power at our disposal. No one would even dare challenge us."

I saw it there in his eyes, the lust for power that drove my brother from one problem to another. He couldn't help himself. Forcibly relaxing, I strode to his couch, knocked some crumbs off the cushions, and sat. I let out a slow, steady breath before I spoke.

"How long until she completely expends the magic?"

"I'm not sure that she will," he said, surprised. "Every time we test her abilities, the magic remains as powerful as it was from the beginning."

"How is that possible?"

He shrugged. "Probably because Ethos is dead. I'm not sure."

I tried to rub the stress from my forehead as I considered the dilemma Sky represented. I didn't care for magic. At times, it was useful, but it was unpredictable and notoriously unforgiving. Sky didn't have the experience to handle that kind of power, and Josh was too willing to take risks to be trusted with her.

"Can it be removed from her?" I asked.

His mouth opened slightly as he stared at me in disbelief. "You've got to be kidding me. Are you that paranoid, or just that controlling?"

"Josh—"

"I can't do that to her."

Arguments between my brother and me were nothing new. It was my job to keep his head on straight—to keep it on at all. Normally we'd shout and throw things and occasionally throw punches at each other, but I was doing my best to hold my frustration at bay. Fighting with Josh was never productive. I needed him to listen.

"When she used Ethos's magic," I said carefully, "I felt it from two miles out. I tracked it all the way here—to her." He leaned toward me, concerned. "If I could feel that, so could someone else. Or some thing. It's too dangerous for her to have that kind of magic. She hasn't earned it. She has no idea what she's playing with, and no experience on how to control power of that magnitude." I ignored his scowl. "Just tell me if it's possible."

Josh sighed. "The Aufero could do it."

The Aufero was an orb with the power to absorb the magical abilities of others. It was one of five powerful artifacts that were protected by special supernatural beings known as the Mouras Encantadas. It was a responsibility that was passed down through the Moura's family. We had recently learned that Sky's mother had been the Moura in charge of protecting the Aufero. Something had caused her to carry it away from her family. When she'd died giving birth to Sky, that responsibility fell to her only daughter, but by then the Aufero had already fallen into someone else's hands. How or who, we didn't know, but it eventually ended up in Marcia's hands. She'd found it a convenient tool with which to neuter her rivals. Enlisting her help was out of the question.

I had another idea. "Could you use the same ritual you used to drain Ethos's magic from Sky?"

"With some modifications," he reluctantly admitted. "What we used in the field was pretty raw, and obviously not one hundred percent effective. But I can't do that to her, Ethan."

"Think about it," I said.

He stared back at me with narrowed eyes and said nothing, which was the closest I was going to get to a concession, for the moment.

Relaxing into the couch, my gaze drifted to the coffee table, where I noticed a printed drawing of three old book covers with simple but distinct lettering surrounded by unique symbols. The shelves in the pack's library were full of such books, but something about the covers in the drawing seemed unusually familiar.

Josh interrupted me. "Did you come here just to harass me, or was there a point to your visit?"

Remembering Tim's manila folder in my pocket, I drew it out and removed the contents. First I handed Josh the copy of the driver's license, followed by the USB drive. "We might have another problem. Tim pulled over an out-of-area witch who gave off a distinctive dark-magic vibe." Josh studied the driver's license closely, shook his head, then retrieved his laptop from another room and placed it on the coffee table. I pulled a lime-green accent chair next to him.

He watched the dashcam video three times, his gaze pensive, before he spoke. "I don't recognize him, but I'll see what I can find out."

"Is he a threat?"

"I just don't have enough to go on yet."

I rose and moved the chair back where I'd found it—not that it mattered.

"We need to talk about Maya and Ethos," he said. "I think I figured out their connection."

I listened carefully as he explained. By the time he finished, I needed a drink.

On the drive home, I couldn't help but question whether Sky joining the pack had been a smart decision. I'd initially objected to the invitation because it wasn't the kind of life she'd wanted. Once the vamps had discovered her unique traits, I'd realized that bringing her into the pack was the only way to protect her. Unlike other were-animals, her blood could stop a vampire's reversion, and there was still the mystery of how her blood could've been used in the ritual Demetrius had intended to perform with the Gem of Levage. Without the pack, it was only a matter of time before the vampires tried to exploit her.

Her inclusion in the pack came with its own challenges.

Together, Josh and Sky were a dangerous combination. When it came to magic, both of them were overly curious and reckless. By keeping some of Ethos's magic, she'd inadvertently put the pack in danger. Every time they practiced with it, they were lighting a beacon to the dark forces of the world, of which there were plenty.

I had a hard time shaking the anger.

I was halfway home when my phone rang, a unique ringtone assigned to my godmother. I placed the phone into the dash holder and put it on speakerphone.

"Claudia," I answered, smiling. "It's good to hear from you."

"Ethan, how are you?" she asked in her South African accent, which most people confused for British.

I caught a faint edge in her voice. "I'm well," I answered. "What can I do for you?"

"I'm afraid I have some difficult news. It's about your grandmother. The nurse said they've been leaving you messages but you haven't replied."

I pressed a button on my screen to see my missed alerts. There were two voice mails, left about fifteen minutes apart. I'd been so deep in my thoughts that I hadn't bothered to check my phone since I'd left Josh's house.

"I have not listened to them," I admitted.

"I'm afraid she's taken a turn for the worse. You may want to visit her soon, before it's too late."

The news was not entirely unexpected. Miriam was eighty-four and had suffered from dementia for years. Three years ago, she'd lit her apartment on fire by trying to cook oatmeal on top of the toaster. No one had been hurt, but I'd been obliged to move her into Twilight Harbor, a reputable home where she could receive the supervision and support that her condition required. Unless pack business intervened —which happened more often than I cared to admit—I visited her every Monday, though there were periods of time

14

when the pack was in crisis and it became necessary for me to remain out of contact, lest I draw the wrong kind of attention to her and the rest of the residents of Twilight Harbor.

I took the next exit from the interstate and changed directions. "I'm on my way now."

"Ethan, I have something important to speak to you about. Visit me when you can. There's no rush, but don't take too long."

I frowned. "I'll be there as soon as I can."

"My regards to your grandmother," she said, then ended the call.

Taking advantage of the pack's connections with the local police, I didn't worry about speeding. A short time later, I arrived at the home with a bouquet of daffodils and roses, Miriam's favorites. The nurse emerged from the room just as I arrived, relieved to see me. She offered me an empathetic smile.

"She's lucid at the moment," she informed me, her voice a gentle whisper. "I'm not sure how long that will last. She's been noncommunicative most of the day. Her body is shutting down and she refuses to eat."

The odors of impending death wafted from inside the room, just strong enough for my enhanced sense of smell to register. When the body shuts down, it begins to emit an odor, faint at first but progressively more prominent as death approaches.

The nurse continued, "I know this is a difficult time for you. Before you leave, we should discuss her no resuscitation order."

I nodded, then walked past her into the room. Miriam appeared to have fallen asleep, her comforter pulled up under her chin as she lay supine. Her once flowing brown curls were just a hint of their former selves, reduced to faint, white wisps. Her cheeks were pallid and her eyes appeared more sunken than usual. On the nightstand, the bouquet of daisies I'd brought two weeks ago were wilting in a vase.

Since Josh and I were only half-brothers on my mother's side, Miriam was alone except for me. Her husband had died under mysterious circumstances shortly after my father had been born, and she'd never remarried or had another child.

I sighed as I threw the wilted daisies into the trash, changed the water in the vase, then arranged the new bouquet. Afterward, I pulled up a chair to her bed and sat with her.

We'd never been close. She'd always been a decent woman to me, but she'd never been particularly maternal. It wasn't in her nature. She'd never forgotten a holiday or a birthday, often purchasing extravagant gifts, and she took an interest in the more measurable aspects of my life—my education, for example—but there was never an emotional connection between us. She'd never touched me—never touched anyone. As far as I could remember, she'd kept everyone that came into her life at arm's length.

Only once had I seen her emotional side. My tenth birthday party had been a large one, full of family and friends. After opening the gifts, Miriam had watched us at play for hours. A wistful look had come over her just before she'd left in a rush. My mother had insisted that Miriam hadn't felt well, but I'd seen the tears in her eyes. So had Josh.

She blinked rapidly before opening her eyes. She glanced around the room as if lost, until her gaze settled on me and her lips spread into a broad smile. "Ethan."

I smiled back. "Hello, Miriam."

"You've gotten so big."

Often when she remembered me, she thought I was still a teenager. After the first few times, I stopped reminding her that I was an adult. Drawing attention to her dementia only served to frustrate her. "Yes, I have."

"You were such a serious boy," she chided me.

I nodded, meeting her gaze and waiting for her to continue.

"You used to follow your brother around like a big guardian angel. He'd get into so much trouble, and there you were right behind him, always puffing out your chest and letting the other children know they'd have to answer to you if they touched him." She laughed, enjoying the memory. "It was so sweet." She shook her head, brushing her hair against her pillow. "You probably should've let him take a whoopin', at least once."

I laughed. "Probably."

Her smile quickly faded as her expression grew pensive. "I should've done better."

I didn't know what she was referring to, but that hardly mattered. I told her what she wanted to hear. "You did the best you could."

"It's awful."

Everybody dies.

"Not being yourself," she continued, her expression souring. "Always hiding. Always lying."

"Lying about what?" I asked dutifully.

For a long moment, she stared at the white wall on the other side of the room as she wrestled with something. As I watched a streak of tears roll down her cheek, I felt a stab of regret for her. I pulled a tissue from the box next to her bed and gently dabbed at the tears.

"I was afraid to touch him," she whispered.

"Touch who?" I asked gently, uncertain if she was lost in a memory or a delusion.

"My baby," she said, choking on the words. "I didn't have a choice. It's a curse."

"What curse?" I asked, my curiosity piqued.

She didn't seem to hear me. After a long, searching moment, she turned her head to me, a sudden desperate movement. The corners of her lips bent in a miserable frown. Tears welled in her eyes. "I'm sorry I did this to you. I never figured out how to take it with me. I tried, Ethan. I held on as long as I could, but it's on you now. I'm sorry."

I edged closer to her until I was on the edge of my seat. "Held on to what?"

"I don't think I have much time left. There's something I need to tell you. I—"

"Knock knock," a woman said at the door, walking in with a tray of food. "Time to eat, Miriam."

"Give us a few minutes," I insisted.

Reading my intensity, she mouthed an apology and left, closing the door behind her.

"Miriam," I said, gently encouraging my grandmother to continue. When she turned to look at me, she appeared puzzled. Her eyes searched my face, confused. When she glanced about the room, her gaze fixed on the fresh flowers, then returned to me with a weak smile.

"Was my grandson here?"

Intuitively, I reached out for her hand. She jerked it away, scowling at me.

"Who are you?" she demanded, her gaze shifting to my attire. "You don't work here. Nurse," she called over her shoulder, as if afraid to let me out of her sight. When no one appeared, she turned to the door to shout, "Nurse!"

The nurse rushed into the room, assessing the situation quickly.

"There's someone in my room!" Miriam cried.

"I'll leave," I announced, rising.

The nurse tried to calm my grandmother. "It's okay, Miriam. It's your grandson." The effort only agitated her further.

"That's not my grandson. My grandson is a child."

I slipped past the nurse and into the hall. I was nearly to the front door of the building when she caught up with me.

18

"Mr. Charleston, can I speak to you in my office for a moment?"

I sighed, then turned toward her. "Of course."

"I'm sorry about that," she said, after closing the door for privacy.

"No need to apologize. You're not responsible for her condition."

"Dementia is always tough on the people closest to the patient. It can be very challenging to cope with."

"It is not challenging," I said stiffly. "It just *is*."

She hesitated, taken aback by my frankness. It wasn't easy seeing my grandmother—always a strong woman—become something so fragile, but I wasn't about to share my thoughts with her nurse.

"As you know," she said carefully, "Miriam has a no resuscitation order on file."

"Yes."

"At times like this, we think it's important to reassess such requests. Obviously she is not in a mental state to properly evaluate the consequences of such an order. As her legal guardian, if you have any reason at all to believe that Miriam would have changed her mind, you can vacate the order. It would just take your signature."

"No," I said, perhaps more harshly than intended. Artificially extending her life would only prolong her suffering. "Unless you can reverse the effects of her dementia, the order stands."

"There is no cure," she said. "Even if we could, her body is still shutting—"

"You've done a great job taking care of her. Is there anything else?"

After a moment to take in the bluntness of my response, she shook her head. "No. I guess that's it."

"Thank you," I said, then left.

CHAPTER 2

I stopped for dinner at one of my favorite restaurants, but the best steak in Chicago couldn't ease the sourness in my stomach, or the weight on my thoughts. Helplessly watching someone else's suffering was never easy. Our emotional distance didn't spare me in the slightest.

Miriam wasn't supernatural, but she understood our world, having married a were-animal and raised another, my father. Was her concern about a curse figurative, or literal? Based on my observations of her over the years, I found the latter hard to believe, but her fear had been genuine. I shook my head as I cut my steak, watching the blood ooze from the tender meat into a pool on my plate. I resolved to visit her again, tomorrow. If she was lucid, I'd ask her about the curse.

While I ate, the shapely brunette waitress returned to my table more often than necessary, giving me long, meaningful looks. She had green eyes, mahogany hair, and an intriguing intensity. She was exactly the kind of distraction I needed— at least, I thought she was. Her shift conveniently ended when I paid my tab. We met at the bar for drinks, and a few hours later I took her home.

That morning, I dreamed of Dennis sitting in his blue Cutlass, completely oblivious to the danger as he watched Michaela, the Mistress of the vampires' Northern Seethe, saunter toward him. He even admired her physical beauty, anticipating his conversation with her. From behind a glass barrier, I yelled and screamed for him to run, but he couldn't hear me. All I could do was watch the horror of recognition that came over him the moment before she reached through the open window, gripped his head by the hair to expose his neck, and ripped out his throat with her teeth. She laughed at me, bathing in his blood as it washed over her in scarlet waves.

I woke up with a start, my body drenched in sweat. I sat for a few minutes catching my breath before I realized my guest had already left. *Probably for the best.* I took a long hot shower. As I dressed, I noticed the woman's necklace on my dresser—a silver necklace. I retrieved a tissue from the bathroom, scooped up the necklace, and dropped it into the waste bin.

After a quick breakfast, I settled onto my couch with a laptop and did some quick Internet searches for Lucas Reed. His bio on his company's website was bland and useless and probably a lie. Other than some promotional images of him on his motorcycles, there was nothing useful to me. He had no other online presence, but that wasn't surprising. Most supernaturals steered clear of social media, where it was too easy to draw the wrong kind of attention.

I had more to worry about than Lucas Reed. I closed my searches and started over, looking for anything on Dennis's daughter, Caroline McDuffy. Her Instagram was mostly a collection of artistic wallpaper and glass chandeliers, which told me nothing useful. Her Facebook page was entirely private, but she ran a large, public group that focused on criminal justice podcasts and cases of wrongful conviction. I scowled. She liked a good cause, and she knew how to organize.

I ran my hands over my face, trying to wipe away the stress that stubbornly clung there. Closing the laptop, I stripped and stepped out my back door into the brisk morning. At my bidding, my wolf rose to the surface. A cool comfort spread through my body as it elongated, my bones cracking as they adjusted to my wolf form. Gray fur burst through my skin. Once transformed, I sniffed at the air, taking in a dozen subtle scents; something small and earthy, like a mole, had been close recently—a cat, as well, possibly in pursuit. From the next block over, the pungent smell of freshly cut juniper carried on the breeze. Eager to stretch my legs, I trotted into the woods behind my house and ran for a couple of hours.

Reluctantly, I returned home and changed back to my human form. As much as I wanted to give the day to my wolf, there was too much to be done.

I drove my BMW to the city and parked a couple of blocks away from Dennis's former office on North Ashland Avenue. Walking the rest of the way, I found several MISSING posters bearing his image stapled to telephone poles. When I finally arrived at the nondescript, tan brick commercial building, I found a young woman with windblown raven hair, wearing black jeans and a matching jacket, was handing out copies of the poster to anyone and everyone passing by. I recognized Caroline from Tim's description. Judging by the number of posters in her hand, she was nearly finished.

"Have you seen my father?" she repeated over and over. Most simply took the poster without breaking stride. A few crammed their hands in their pockets and shook their heads as they passed by.

I sighed, questioning my plan. As an attorney, I advised

myself against it, but my need for information outweighed the risks. I took a deep breath, steeling myself, then walked toward her as if I, too, just happened to be walking by. I didn't even make eye contact with her, because I knew she would open the door for me.

"Have you seen my father?" she asked, extending her last poster into my path.

I took it and took two steps past her, gazing at the poster, before I stopped and turned to face her. "Is he lost?" I asked, wearing a concerned look.

Her eyes brightened as she walked to me, eager to engage. I noticed a silver pendant resting over the collar of her t-shirt, a Celtic knot wrapped around a black crystal. "You've seen him?" she asked.

I glanced at the poster once more, then shook my head. "He looks familiar, but I'm not sure. I frequent this area. There are a lot of people around here during the workday. Perhaps if I knew more about him," I suggested.

She brushed back her hair as it blew into her face. "He's a private detective." She held my gaze, intently watching for some sign of recognition. "He worked … works"—she corrected herself—"in that office building over there. A couple months ago, he just stopped responding to my calls or e-mails. I live in Boise," she explained. "At first, I thought he was just blowing me off…." She glanced away, embarrassed. "That's a long story, I guess. When I came looking for him, I found out he hadn't been seen since I'd lost contact with him."

I glanced about the area. "No witnesses? No clues as to where he went?"

She hesitated just for a moment before answering. "Not a one. Everyone just looks at their shoes around here. No offense."

"The police?" I asked.

She frowned. I saw the bitterness in her russet eyes as she said bluntly, "They don't actually care."

The breeze picked up, and I saw her shiver. "It's chilly out. You've probably been out here for hours."

She shrugged the observation aside. "I'm picking up more posters in half an hour and I'll be back at it." She looked me dead in the eye as she said confidently, "Someone around here knows something. Sooner or later they're going to walk through this intersection. I just need to put a poster into their hand."

I nodded to a café across the street. "Why don't you join me and warm up while you're waiting for your posters? I'll buy you lunch and you can tell me more about your father. I talk to a lot of people in this area. I can ask around." I smiled. "I might even get a tip for you."

"What is it that you do?"

"Insurance broker," I said quickly.

She grinned as she looked me up and down. "You look like an insurance broker." She glanced to the café, then back to me, seemingly weighing the decision, but I sensed she'd already made up her mind. "Sure. Why not? Thank you."

I requested a table at the front window, giving her a view of the street to put her at ease. While she studied the menu, my gaze was drawn once more to her necklace. The black crystal radiated a low but surprising level of magic.

"That's an interesting necklace you have there," I said, watching her reaction closely.

Her heart rate accelerated slightly, but only for a moment as she lifted the pendant with her finger and looked down at it with a wan smile. "It's ugly. I know. It was my mother's. She claimed it had some special power. She was really into that New Age stuff. She said it would come in handy someday." She rolled her eyes as she let the pendant fall back against her chest.

While I wasn't sure what power the medallion possessed,

it was more than was typically found in a New Age magic shop. On occasion, magical items of actual value ended up there, usually unwittingly sold by family members of a deceased witch who had no idea what they were selling. Did Caroline know more than she was admitting to?

Staring at the crystal, I felt a slight dizziness come over me, just for a moment.

"Are you okay?" she asked.

Before I could answer, the waiter arrived with coffee.

"Thank you," Caroline said, reaching for the sugar packets.

After the waiter took our order and left, I asked her, "Your father was a private investigator?" She nodded. "Is it possible he's out of town on a job that requires some secrecy?"

Her smile thinned as she slowly stirred her coffee. "I doubt he would've stopped paying rent."

"Were you close? Did he talk about his work?"

Her gaze lowered to the spoon as she continued stirring. "I wasn't particularly involved in his life until recently."

"I'm sorry to hear that."

"I didn't know he was my father until six months ago. To say the news was a surprise to him would be an understatement." She chuckled. "We've mostly been getting to know each other by phone and e-mail. I don't think he liked his work. I thought it must be glamorous, but he said he mostly got paid to track down cheating spouses and people who didn't want to be found. He made it sound so bland. He never talked about his personal life, either. Truth is"—she nodded toward his office across the street—"the only reason I know that's his office is because that's where I first showed up at his door. As far as I know, he lived there, because he's never given me another address." She frowned. "That's sad, isn't it?"

The waiter arrived with our sandwiches. What little appetite I'd brought with me was gone. Keeping the secret of

Caroline's father's death gnawed at me. I had the answers she needed, but I couldn't give them to her. The best I could do for both of us was to bring the investigation to an end as soon as possible. She would never get the closure she deserved, but she might at least move on with her life once the hope of closure ended.

"Have you been to his office?" I asked, deliberately calming my voice to disguise the importance of my question. Without Dennis's body or his car, which the vampires also disposed of, the only possible evidence linking me to him would be in his office.

"I tried," she said, setting her sandwich down on her plate. A hard look came over her as she said, "The detectives, in their professional opinion, didn't consider it a crime scene, so the landlord cleared it out. He's quite happy to hand over my father's belongings as soon as I pay the three thousand dollars in back rent." A mischievous look came over her. "He's in for a surprise, though. He doesn't have to give me access, but I'm this close"—she held out two fingers, making a show of them almost touching each other—"to getting the detectives to at least take a look. He has to let them look at whatever they want. If one of my father's clients had anything to do with my father's disappearance," she said darkly, "I'll find out, one way or another. Assuming someone hasn't gone through his stuff and removed any evidence first."

She glanced at the time on her phone. Her eyes widened. "Time to pick up my posters. I'm sorry," she said, suddenly blushing. "I'm rude. I never even asked you your name. I'm Caroline."

"David," I said, shaking her extended hand. She had a strong, confident grip.

"David the insurance broker," she chuckled, rising. "Listen, I really appreciate your help. Do you have a card? In case you get me that tip."

I made a show of patting my pockets. "All out, it seems."

The check arrived on a tray. She picked up the pen, selected a clean napkin, wrote down her number, and handed it to me. She shook my hand once more, then left in a hurry.

I brought out my phone and texted the address of Dennis's office building to my legal assistant and researcher, Stacy. "I need the landlord's name and number."

From what Tim had told me, the detectives could contact the landlord at any moment to get a look at the contents of the office. I needed to get there first, and I needed those contents to disappear.

By the time I walked back to my BMW, Stacy had replied with the landlord's contact information. His name was Leon Walker. I fished an untraceable burner phone from the glove box, then called him.

A raspy male voice—probably mid- to late fifties—answered on the first ring. "Yeah?"

Judging by the skepticism in his voice, he'd been in business long enough to get jaded—exactly what I'd hoped for. Most likely he'd accumulated rental properties for decades. He could tell at a glance who he wanted to rent to and who he didn't want to rent to, and he didn't like being told by the city how to run his business. There were strict rules about how landlords could deal with the belongings of a tenant. Fortunately, he was exactly the kind of landlord who didn't give a crap about rules.

"Mr. Walker," I said, "my name is Webster Fields. I represent a group of buyers who purchase the contents of abandoned properties or storage units."

He grunted.

"I'm sure you run a tight ship," I continued, "but we both know the kinds of tenants the city forces you to accept, and how unreliable they can be."

"Damn section eight waivers," he grumbled. "They're doing drugs and who knows what else."

"Exactly. If at some point in the future you find yourself stuck with abandoned property, I'd be happy to bid on it as a lot. That way you can at least recoup some of your losses and unload unwanted property at the same time."

"Just so happens I have a deadbeat right now. It's mostly just junk. What's in it for you?"

"There's always something of value to someone. I sift through it, sell what I can at auction, then donate or throw out the rest."

He sniffed. "He just walked off and left his entire business behind. I'd hoped the family would pay to get it back, but they don't seem to think it's worth much. I guess you might think differently. How much are we talking?"

"I'd need to see the lot before I could make an offer."

I waited a moment while he thought it through. "Yeah, why not? Sooner I get that off my hands, the better." He gave me the address, which wasn't far away. "I can meet you there in a half hour. It's then or not at all."

I smiled. He probably knew Caroline was stirring up trouble. If detectives informed him they were investigating a missing person case, Dennis's belongings would be evidence, which Mr. Walker would be obligated to store until the case was closed, which might never happen.

"I'm on my way," I said.

"See you then," he answered, then disconnected the call.

Turning the phone over, I exposed the blank, white label stuck to the back. All of my burner phones had such labels. Fishing a pen from the glove box, I wrote the name Webster Fields on the label and pocketed the phone. From that point, the phone was exclusively dedicated to the persona of Mr. Fields. I'd use the phone and the name for nothing else until I'd obtained what I'd wanted, and then I'd destroy the phone and dispose of it.

The address belonged to a rundown brick apartment building with three floors. I parked across the street. As I walked up the porch, he opened the door from inside.

"Mr. Fields?" he asked.

I smiled, sincere but strictly professional. Some people responded well to enthusiasm, but others found it suspicious. He belonged to the latter category. "Yes, Mr. Walker. It's a pleasure."

He accepted my offer to shake hands, establishing our relationship with a strong grip. I suppressed a laugh. With a simple squeeze, I could've broken every bone in his hand.

"This way," he said, gesturing as he led me to an elevator in the center of the hall. "You're in an interesting business," he mused, still skeptical while we waited for the elevator to arrive.

I figured he was a man who valued family business. "I took over for my father a few years back," I said.

He nodded appreciatively. The elevator dinged, then opened. A moment later we were standing in a dingy room that reeked of rat poison and stale air, at least to my senses. He led me down a narrow path between two rows of storage units defined by walls of chicken wire.

"Good thing I had the extra storage," he said, gesturing to the two units at the end, on either side of the path. "But I'm going to need those units soon."

The unit to my left contained the furniture from Dennis's office: a desk, a chair, a filing cabinet, and a couple of empty bookshelves. The other was stacked with sealed boxes. I made a pensive show of evaluating both storage units, then made a disappointed clucking sound with my tongue.

"Not a lot of value there."

"That's what I told you," Mr. Walker snapped.

I gestured to the boxes. "I assume that's all the paperwork from the filing cabinet, the desk."

He nodded as if the answer were obvious. "And books. Lots of books. That should be worth something."

I gestured to a neighboring storage unit that contained some outdoor gear and an old computer monitor, among more mundane items. "That's closer to what I'm looking for."

He scowled at me for wasting his time. "That's not for sale."

To say Mr. Walker was disappointed was an understatement. He didn't have much to say as he escorted me out of the basement and out the front door. I doubted I'd hear from him again. As I walked toward my BMW, I noticed Caroline walking past it, cradling a bundle of posters. I ducked into the next doorway, peering around the entryway as she stapled a poster to a telephone pole, then walked around the corner.

Remaining in the doorway, I called Josh. He answered quickly.

"I'm going to need your help tonight," I said. "I need the contents of a couple storage units to disappear." There wasn't any point in leaving the furniture behind—Dennis was exactly the kind of nervous man who would squirrel away something important under the upholstery. Josh would only need a few minutes to get rid of it all. Now that I could describe the location and layout of the storage room, he could transport himself inside and send the contents to the same place he sent dead bodies, bloodstains, and any other inconvenient evidence that threatened to expose the pack to outside scrutiny.

"I can do that," Josh answered. "What's it about?"

I sighed. Of course there were going to be questions. My brother didn't know about Dennis. Up to that point, he hadn't needed to know. Before I could answer, my phone vibrated. I pulled it from my ear to read the screen.

A text from Artemis read, "Would you like to know if a dark witch is in the neighborhood, looking for trouble?"

I put the phone back to my ear.

"Ethan?" Josh asked.

"I got a lead on our biker witch. I'll call you back." I disconnected the call, then called Artemis. Before she answered, Josh materialized next to me. I glanced around quickly to make sure no one was paying attention, then scowled at him for his recklessness. He didn't seem to care. Typical.

"That was quick," Artemis answered, pleased.

"Where is he?" I asked.

"Excellent. I should probably inform you that my rates have recently increased," she said speculatively.

I don't have time for this. "Double the usual finder's fee," I said. "One time only. If you want more than that, I can come over to your house to talk with you about it." Artemis took considerable pride in keeping her home a secret. I'd found it a few months ago, but only because she'd left me no choice.

"You drive an unnecessarily hard bargain," she complained. "He's strolling through the farmer's market at Lincoln Park."

"Let me know if he leaves before I get there."

I disconnected the call and turned to Josh. He could transport us there instantly, but the market at Lincoln Park was one of the busiest farmer's markets in the city. Magic in a crowd was a gamble. Often people in a crowd weren't paying attention to anything not immediately around them, but a miscalculation could cause a stir and draw far more attention than we could handle. I could see by the look in his blue eyes that he was ready to risk a transport. I gestured to the BMW, unlocking it with the fob.

Speeding as much as I could without risking an accident, it wasn't long before we parked across from the bustling market and walked in. Hundreds of people were crowded into three rows of market stalls, where local craftsmen and farmers sold their goods from tents pitched beneath the silver maple and green ash trees. Josh and I walked together, weaving through the crowd as we looked for Lucas Reed. At just over six feet tall with a pile of red curls on his head, he wasn't hard to miss as he purchased a bag of roasted nuts from a vendor. If that wasn't enough, he wore the same leather jacket and chaps he'd worn in Tim's dashcam video.

An oppressive dark magic wafted off of him.

Josh tensed, his gaze focused intently on the crowd around us. The market was no place for a fight—too many eyes, too much potential for collateral damage. If I had my way, I'd grab him by the jacket collar and haul him away to have a quiet chat that ended with him racing out of town, but I couldn't be sure he wouldn't put up a fight. As a rule, supernaturals didn't want to be noticed by the outside world, but that didn't mean Reed was going to let me manhandle him.

Beyond the vendors was an open area that was clear of bystanders. Our witch was already close to the end of the row. I got Josh's attention and nodded toward the clearing, but he'd already seemed to figure out the same plan.

The last tent was occupied by a vendor who made and sold scented candles—obnoxiously scented, to my senses. Reed lingered there. That's when I knew he'd made us.

Scowling, I strode to his side, gripped his elbow tightly, and walked him away from the tent. He chuckled, but didn't resist as I escorted him into the clearing. He reeked of sage, lemongrass, and some kind of obnoxious perfume.

"Nobody told me there'd be a welcome wagon," he said, smiling. When I stopped and turned him to face me, his expression had only grown smugger. His heart rate remained calm as he glanced between Josh and me. "As I live and breathe, witches and wolves walking hand in hand— metaphorically speaking. An amazing if unlikely accomplishment. If you gentlemen stopped me to join you in a round of Kumbaya, I should warn you—the reports of my golden pipes and gentle disposition are greatly exaggerated."

"Just a courtesy greeting," Josh said, the tightness in his voice matching the tension in his body as he anticipated a magical confrontation.

"Why are you here, unannounced?" I demanded.

"I do apologize for the break in decorum," he said, brushing a dangling curl from his face. "If I missed the markings on the trees, it's probably because I didn't give a shit. Still, there's no need to be alarmed. I'm just here to take in the sights, like the rest of the tourists. If you're worried about me digging up the bones you've got hidden around here, I promise to leave them undisturbed. Not that that wouldn't be entertaining, but chew toys aren't really my style. I'm more of a consume-your-soul type of guy."

I growled as I stepped up to him, giving him a close look at the wolf in my eyes as it rose to just below the surface. Judging by the intensity of the dark magic that radiated from Reed, Tim had considerably underestimated his power, but his magic was useless against my wolf, and I had Josh beside me. As much as I wanted to teach Reed some manners, I needed to get my message across without causing a scene, if possible.

"Does Marcia know you're here?" Josh asked.

"The Creed?" he said with a sneer. "Unless they've opened a tourist office and are offering discount tickets to Second City, I have no business with them. Last I heard, Marcia wasn't too fond of dogs. Safe to say, you're not here on her behalf." His smile broadened as he glanced between Josh and me. "No, I believe this is an official visit from the Midwest Pack. And I have the misfortune to draw the attention of Ethan Charleston, the pack Beta, and his witch brother. It's your tattoos that give you away." He winked at Josh, then turned his full attention to me, his gaze locking with mine. "If you have some not-so-subtle threat to give me, something about Chicago being the pack's personal fire hydrant, I do hope you'll get on with it. The art museum closes in six hours."

The muscles in my neck grew taut. My fists clenched as I fought the urge to knock the witch's smug smile from his face in a memorable fashion. Josh stepped closer to me, sensing I was on the cusp of losing control.

I stared unblinking into Reed's mocking hazel eyes as I issued my final warning. "I suggest you take in as many of the sights as you can today, because by noon tomorrow you're going to be on your way back to your business in Indiana. Cause any trouble, or return unannounced, and there will be consequences."

He nodded slowly, his lips bent into a crooked smile. "Message received. I assume we're done here?"

Josh pulled at my arm and I took a step back, allowing Reed to walk back into the marketplace.

"I've felt his magic before," I said, staring after the witch. "He's one of Ethos's followers, like Pala."

Two years ago, Josh had enlisted Pala's help to find the Gem of Levage. Instead, she'd tried to steal his magic. Like all of Ethos's followers, they'd offered servitude in exchange for some of his magic. Supposedly he'd reclaimed it all before we'd killed him, but that obviously hadn't been the case. There could be only one reason for a follower of Ethos to be in Chicago; he'd sensed his master's magic and he'd come looking for it, which made Sky his target.

I was considering how we could set a trap for Reed and kill him, away from public view, when Josh said, "He doesn't know who he's looking for. He's just tracking the magic. As long as Sky doesn't use Ethos's power, he'll have nothing to track. I'll stop her training sessions for a few days."

I rounded on my brother with a hard look. "That's not enough."

"We can't just take it from her," he snapped. "You can't just do what you want to people. I'm not going to help you do that. If she can be talked into giving up Ethos's magic, then I'll help remove it."

"And when she refuses?" Which she would.

His brow furrowed, weighted with worry. "Then I'll help her find a way to hide it."

I shook my head in disgust, but that was the best I was going to get, for the moment. At least Josh understood the immediate risk, but allowing Sky to keep Ethos's magic for any length of time was unacceptable. I'd need his help to take it from her, which meant I needed to give him some time to come to the same conclusion I had. For the moment, he would keep his promise not to train her, and without a footprint of magic to track, Lucas Reed would give up and leave town by morning—or I'd kill him.

For the time being, I needed to keep Sky safe, which was problematic. For anyone else, a simple warning would suffice to keep her home and under our protection. Sky was too independent and too stubborn for her own good. If I warned her she was in danger, she'd go looking for trouble. If I put a guard on her, she'd do everything imaginable to escape.

I ran my hands over my face, trying to wipe away the tension.

For the first time since Steven had left town to help his adopted mother, Joan, rebuild the Southern Pack, I'd regretted his absence. While I found his relationship with Sky suspect, and I didn't approve of the way he'd inserted himself into her home, making himself a virtual roommate, he was the only pack member who could get that close to her without raising her suspicions. She trusted him more than Josh. More than me.

I frowned as I drew out my phone and texted a description of Reed to Markos, my sixth. "If he gets within two miles of Sky, let me know." I pocketed my phone and said to Josh, "Let's take care of the storage. Then we'll talk about Sky."

Josh rolled his eyes but followed me back to the BMW.

. . .

A short time later, we stood across the street from Mr. Walker's apartment building. While we waited for the street to clear, I described the general layout of the storage unit. All we needed was a window of time where Josh could disappear and reappear without being noticed by the trickle of pedestrians that used the block.

Just when we thought we had that window, a blue Crown Vic turned onto the street. I frowned as the vehicle, notoriously used by plainclothes police, parked in front of the building's entrance. A bored-looking woman emerged from the driver's seat, joined by her male Latino partner from the passenger side.

"I'll do the talking," she informed her partner.

"By all means," he answered.

As they climbed the steps, Walker emerged from the building to hold the door for them. The woman flashed her badge as a courtesy.

"You have to go now," I whispered. When I turned toward Josh, he was already gone.

To avoid looking conspicuous, I put my phone to my ear, pretending to be in conversation as I paced the sidewalk. All I could do was wait and worry. If Josh was discovered in the storage room, he'd be unable to transport himself out—not in plain sight of two police officers.

A few tense minutes passed before the front door of the building opened and the officers emerged, visibly irritated, followed by an angry, apologetic Walker. The officers wasted no time entertaining his excuses. Instead they returned to their Crown Vic and drove away. Walker shook his head as he watched them go, then went back inside, grumbling to himself.

Josh appeared in front of me, grinning as he brushed

clingy foam packing peanuts from his shirt and pants, then his hair.

"That was close," he said. "I had to transport into one of the other storage units and hide in a box of packing foam."

"Did you get it all?"

He nodded.

"Both units on the end?"

Josh tilted his head to give me a puzzled look. "There were two storage units?" he asked, then watched my anger rise before he chuckled. "Relax. I got both of them."

I let out a slow breath, feeling my shoulders drop as the tension left my body. It had been a long, stressful day. "Come on," I said, directing him to follow me down the alley to the next block. "I'll take you back to your place."

That evening I was at home, alone with my thoughts and a bottle of Scotch, when I got a call from Markos.

"Is he gone?" I asked before he could speak.

"I had him in my sight all afternoon up to now, and then I lost him." There was a sigh on the other end. "I hate to say it, but I think I got rope-a-doped."

My hand clenched around the phone until I thought it might break, then I forced myself to relax.

Markos continued, "He must've known I was there the entire time, because he never went to his hotel or to visit anyone he knew—just tourist stuff." He growled in disgust. "I got complacent. When he wanted to dump me, he did it easily."

"Get to Skylar's, now."

"I'm on it, but I'm a ways out. If anyone else is closer, you might want to call them as well."

Next, I called Sky. When she didn't answer, I threw my phone across the living room. It bounced off the back of my desk chair and landed on the floor with a clatter. Growling as I walked across the room, I picked up the phone and examined it. Relieved that it still worked, I called Winter.

"Hello," she answered, sounding bored.

"How close are you to Sky's?" I asked.

"Closer than I'd like to be. You need me to babysit?"

"I need you to get eyes on her until Markos gets there. Make sure she's home and alone."

"Should I knock on the door, or am I playing stalker?"

"Keep it quiet. There's a new witch in town. A biker. If he shows up, he doesn't get inside."

Her interest level rose at the prospect of a fight. "I can do that."

I killed the call, picked up the keys to my BMW, and was halfway to Sky's when I got the call from Winter. I placed the phone in the dash cradle and answered on speakerphone.

"She's fine," Winter said, sending an immediate rush of relief through me. "She's alone, watching some crappy movie on television. No biker witch to speak of, unfortunately."

I eased my foot off the gas, slowing down to the speed of traffic. "Wait for Markos, then go home."

"Okay," she said with a sigh. "If you need me for a fight, don't hesitate to call." She ended the call.

I found a turnaround and drove back toward home. Despite my relief, my heart was still pounding.

I can't wait for Josh to come around.

Every minute Sky remained in possession of Ethos's magic put her in danger. It put the pack in danger. The longer she possessed it, the greater the risk. Josh's promise to halt her training wasn't going to stop her from experimenting on her own.

I'd talk to her first, try to get her to give up the magic voluntarily. She was stubborn, but I could appeal to her sense of obligation to the pack. As long as I kept my temper and my impatience in check, I might be able to convince her. If she couldn't see reason, Josh was going to help me take it from her, whether he wanted to or not.

Once home, I texted Markos to send me updates every half an hour until Sky was asleep. As long as she was conscious, there was a chance she'd get bored and start experimenting with Ethos's magic. Unfortunately for him, it wasn't unusual for her to stay up well past midnight watching crappy movies. Unfortunately for me, I couldn't sleep until I received the final update, just before two in the morning.

I woke the next morning, exhausted. After a shower and breakfast, I decided the best course of action was to show up at Sky's unannounced, before she got her day started. I was en route to her house when the nurse from the assisted living home called. I put the phone on speaker and answered.

"This is Ethan."

"Mr. Charleston," the nurse said in a soft, empathetic tone. "I'm sorry to inform you that Miriam has taken a turn for the worse. I encourage you to visit her today, the sooner the better."

I frowned. "I understand. Is she lucid?"

There was a brief silence before she answered. "No. I'm not sure that she will be again before she passes."

I sighed. The issue with Sky couldn't wait. As long as she possessed Ethos's magic, she was in danger. We all were. And there was nothing I could do for Miriam, especially if she couldn't recognize me, but that didn't absolve me of my obligation to her. "I'll get there when I can," I promised.

I continued toward Sky's house.

Within a mile of her home, I felt a faint ripple of dark magic pass through me, a gentle, oppressive wave of power. *Skylar.* She was using Ethos's magic. I shifted anxiously in the driver's seat and pushed down on the accelerator.

I started to call Markos, then realized I'd sent him home. *Just a few hours,* I fumed, cursing myself for trusting Sky to last just a few hours of the morning without using magic she had no business possessing. Disgusted, I tossed my phone onto the passenger seat.

The closer I got to her house, the stronger the wave of power. I tried to calm myself. *If he isn't nearby, he won't have time to track it to her before I put a stop to whatever she's doing.* I held my breath as I turned onto her street, until I saw that her driveway was clear—no sign of Lucas Reed or his Harley —and let out a sigh of relief.

After parking in the driveway, I slid out of the BMW and walked toward the front door. Before I reached the porch, I caught sight of movement through the bedroom window. The curtains were wide open. Walking a few feet across the yard for a better look, I saw Sky lying on her bed, her entire wardrobe dancing and gliding about the room as she conducted the clothes like a symphony.

Frustration rose in me, coloring my cheeks with anger. *How could she be so careless?* I strode toward the front door, intending to barge in and put a stop to her gross display, when I heard the violent rumbling of a motorcycle engine approaching from the street. A moment later, Reed appeared on his Harley, drawn by the same subtle sense of power that had drawn me.

Glancing back through the window, I saw the clothes still dancing. She had no idea the danger she was in. Reed intended to take Ethos's magic from her, and I doubted he cared if she survived the process. As long as she remained inside the house, protected by Josh's magical ward, she had a chance, but I wasn't kidding myself; Reed was powerful enough to break that ward eventually. If I failed to stop him, at least my effort bought her some time to react, assuming she stayed inside. Once she realized what was happening on her lawn, I knew she would come running out to help me. I couldn't have that.

Over the last few months, I'd picked up a few spells and rituals from the books in Josh's library. Recalling one of them, I turned toward Sky's bedroom window. Muttering a quick chant, I gestured with an outstretched hand, my fingers splayed. A translucent shimmer spread across the windows, then extended out over the nearby wall, forming a thin barrier that was impenetrable by sound.

The Harley's engine rumbled and boomed as Reed slowly turned into the driveway and parked next to my BMW. My hand slipped into my pocket for my phone. Once I texted nine-one-one to Josh, he'd transport to me, ready for a fight. Between the two of us we could put an end to the witch, but my pocket was empty.

I remembered leaving the phone in my BMW and growled. Calling my wolf to the surface, I tore open my shirt in anticipation of the change. It was my only advantage against his magic, which would be useless against me while I was in animal form. If he was arrogant enough to fight a wolf hand to hand, I'd kill him easily. My bones cracked as the transformation began. My muscles and tendons began to elongate, until a force struck my chest and quickly engulfed me, suppressing the transformation. I fell to my knees, straining to force the change. Inside me, my wolf snapped and snarled as it fought to escape, to vent its fury in Lucas Reed's blood, but it couldn't escape the oppressive spell that constricted around me. I panted, struggling for breath as the force steadily compressed my chest.

He grinned at me as he swung off his Harley and swaggered toward me. "Bad doggie."

Concentrating, I tried to break the magical hold, but my own abilities were no match for his. *Stay inside,* I pleaded to Sky.

Reed stood over me, gloating. "You know, the more you

41

fight it, the faster it'll kill you. I suppose that's not particularly comforting. I mean, sure, you could suck in another half breath or two before you die, but is it worth it?" He shrugged. "By the way, I know you killed my master. It's okay. He wasn't exactly well liked. But you don't get a gold sticker. And you don't get to keep his magic." He grinned. "That little nugget is my legacy, and I'm going to take it." He turned toward Sky's bedroom window. "I don't have the best view of her from here, but she looks like a pretty little wolf. Did you make her? Ah, hell, you can always make another." He paused, lifting a finger as if he had just remembered something. "Except you'll be dead in about a minute. Oops."

I felt my rage build inside of me like an explosive force, pushing at the magic that suffocated me, but I couldn't break it. For the first time in my life, I felt completely helpless as Reed swaggered onto her porch. He was reaching out to break the ward when he suddenly stopped. His head tilted as if sensing or hearing something, then he turned back to me with a look of pleasant surprise.

I felt it then, a dark, cold power striking down like a javelin as it pierced through the magic that held me and struck me at the back of my skull. My vision went white as every nerve in my body fired simultaneously, sending searing jolts of pain like shards of glass through my brain. For a moment, I lost myself in agony. When the pain finally receded, I realized that I was still alive. Only a moment had passed, and Reed was once more standing over me, his smug smile melting into a concerned scowl.

My body radiated power it struggled to absorb. I didn't know what had happened, or how, and I didn't care. I shrugged off his magic with a thought, then rose to my feet.

"You should be dead," he snarled.

"About that." I growled, extending both hands toward him. He attempted to raise a field, but it didn't matter. Angry blue tendrils of electricity shot from my hands, tearing down his half-constructed field in a shower of blue sparks. He tried to wrench free as the tendrils wrapped around his chest like an electric serpent and squeezed the breath from his lungs.

As he struggled, I made a flippant gesture, flinging him through the air and slamming him down onto his back on the driveway. Lost in rage and power, I tightened the tendrils around him. I listened to the beat of his heart as it struggled, slowly failing until it finally gave up. Still, I continued to squeeze until eventually the rage receded. Realizing Reed was dead, I released the magic, then stared at my hands as ripples of electricity continuously rolled over them. Glancing down I saw the ripples traversing my entire body, drawing waves of pain that were quickly escalating. Without a target, the magic seemed to be turning against me.

Josh.

My phone was still in the BMW. Glancing back toward Sky's bedroom window, I saw that the silencing spell had disappeared. Lucas Reed dead, I could call to her for help, but I didn't know what the magic would do. Would it attack her? I couldn't take that chance.

Grimacing, I stumbled toward the BMW to retrieve my phone. I made it as far as the witch's body before the undulating waves of pain became too much.

Looking down at Lucas Reed, I knew I had one hope to get help.

A fresh wave of pain reached its crescendo. I dropped to my knees, then twisted onto my back, gasping for breath until the pain subsided. A few more waves and I'd be completely incapacitated. Time was running out. Grunting and growling with the effort, I reached across the witch's body and hauled him to me. Once close enough, my fingers plumbed his pockets until I fished out his phone. Luckily, it wasn't locked.

I called Josh's number from memory. When he picked up, I didn't wait for him to speak.

"Nine-one—" I grunted, folding over as a new wave of pain hit me. The phone fell from my hand. I writhed on the concrete until the wave eventually subsided, and I saw my brother's concerned expression as he crouched over me.

"Don't touch me," I gasped, but he needed to get me out of sight before the neighbors took notice. It was very possible that an ambulance or the police were already on their way to investigate the dead body and the man with lightning still crackling over his skin.

Josh began to mutter a chant. Slowly, steadily, I felt the waves of pain recede. The visible electricity diminished and died, and then I felt a rush of relief that left me panting for breath.

"I'm going to get you out of here," he promised. Worried that I still wasn't safe to touch, I jerked from his hands, but he managed to touch my leg before I could stop him. My senses reeled for a moment, then I found myself on his couch.

He quickly pulled a blanket over me. "I'm going back to get rid of the body," he said.

"Move my car," I groaned, tossing him my keys from my pocket. "And get rid of the motorcycle."

"I got it," he insisted, then disappeared.

I lay there for a few minutes, slowly bringing my breathing under control as the echoes of pain diminished, but I couldn't shake the faint film of darkness that clung to me. Feeling stifled, I threw off the blanket, but the sense of darkness remained.

When Josh reappeared a short time later, he looked relieved to find me sitting up. "It's taken care of. Ethan, what happened?"

"Sky?" I asked, wishing I'd remembered to tell him not to upset her.

"She's safely tucked inside the ward around her home. She has no idea." He scrutinized me for a moment, his eyes roaming my body for signs of injury. "How did you kill that witch? He didn't have a mark on him."

I shook my head. "I can't answer that."

His lips pressed together in a tight frown. "Can't, or won't?"

"I have no idea," I said sincerely. "Something came over me, like a bolt of lightning. He had me on the ground. I was suffocating, and then I had this ... power." I stared at my palms. "Maybe it controlled me. I don't know, but I somehow used it to kill the witch. He put up a field, but I broke through it easily."

I looked to him for answers.

He ran a hand through his already tousled hair. "When I found you, you were overflowing with magic. Now it's subtler. If I wasn't looking for it, I'm not sure that I would notice."

I sighed, relieved. "It's dissipating."

He shook his head. "More like it's settling."

"Do you recognize it?"

"No. How do you feel?"

"Different."

Josh took a step back from me and a translucent bubble shimmered to life around him—a magical protective field. "Try and break it down."

We both knew I could, even without the strange magic inside me. "No."

"We need to test this," he insisted.

I scowled. "When I killed Lucas, I didn't have control over what I was doing. I'm not going to test it on you."

"This is important," he insisted.

I rose on wobbly legs to face him. "It's reckless." He rolled his eyes, triggering a spark of anger in me that seemed to excite my newfound magic. "Did you see what she was doing, how he found her?"

Josh frowned but didn't answer.

"She was making her wardrobe dance. She used Ethos's magic. To make her clothes dance. Tell me, Josh, what would've happened to her if I hadn't been in the area and gotten there before Lucas Reed?"

"She was safe inside the house."

"He could've broken in easily, and you know it." Josh reacted as if stung, but I continued to press him. "You two have been playing with magic even you don't understand. Do you think Lucas Reed was the only witch out there that is attracted to Ethos's magic? And Sky is clueless. You both are."

"I'll talk to her," he said, avoiding my direct gaze as he soaked in the blame, trying to mitigate it.

"No. She's just as reckless as you are. No matter how much you warn her, one or both of you will come up with another excuse to use Ethos's magic."

"Ethan—"

"What if Maya has access to that same power? What could she do with it?"

He chewed absently on the bed of a fingernail while he considered the possibilities. Finally, he admitted, "I don't know."

"Sky doesn't have the training or the experience to deal with it. Until she does, it's too dangerous for her to have."

"She's not going to understand if we just take it from her."

"You just don't want to give up your chance to study Ethos's magic," I snarled. "Grow up. Forget about power and make the right decision for her, for the pack."

He clenched his teeth and walked a few steps away before he turned back to me, angry. "What do you want me to do?"

"Teach me the ritual to extract Ethos's magic from her."

He struggled for a long moment before he answered with an almost imperceptible nod. I realized it wasn't the loss of power that hurt him the most; he couldn't bear the guilt of taking something from Sky that she valued. For once, he understood the kind of decisions I was frequently forced to make as the pack Beta.

"I need a drink." He turned and shuffled his way into the kitchen. "You?"

"Yeah."

I dropped down onto the couch and waited until he returned with two tumblers of whiskey. I'd give him a few minutes to relax before I pressed him for the ritual. For Sky's sake, the job needed to be done soon. At least he didn't have to bear the brunt of her anger after it was done. I could at least spare him that.

CHAPTER 3

We sat quietly for a moment, sipping our whiskeys, until Josh asked, "Is there anything you can think of that might explain where the magic came from?"

I shook my head. Considering I'd used the mysterious magic to kill Lucas Reed, I doubted he'd been the source. He'd felt it coming before I had, and he'd been just as surprised. The memory of all that power suddenly coursing through me, inflaming every nerve of my body, made me shudder. Thanks to Josh, the magic had been reduced to a faint, dark vibration that hummed in my body like a ringing in my ear, a constant reminder that something in me had changed.

"Someone sent you that magic, or you somehow intercepted it," he said with a wary look. "Your body didn't know how to absorb that much raw magic, at first."

"How did you get rid of it?" I asked.

He considered for a moment, frowning at his whiskey. "I helped your body absorb it. I didn't have time to do anything else," he added in a defensive rush, closely watching my reaction.

I swallowed my suspicion, for the moment. "This wasn't an accident."

"No."

"I'm being set up," I stated.

He lifted his tumbler in semblance of a shrug, causing the ice to clink against the glass. "I suspect we'll hear from your anonymous donor soon enough. I'll ask around and see what I can come up with. Do some research. In the meantime, it wouldn't hurt to figure out the potential of your new abilities."

I scowled. "Playing with Ethos's magic isn't reckless enough for you?" I downed the last of my whiskey and set the empty tumbler on the coffee table. "You're going to teach me the ritual to take Ethos's magic from Sky, and then you're going to demonstrate it on me."

He leaned back into his chair. "I'm not sure that's a good idea."

I grunted. "Which one?"

"Both, but for different reasons. I'll teach you the ritual, but I think removing this magic from you is a mistake."

"Of course you do."

His lips bent into a disgruntled frown. "What do you think will happen when the owner of that magic comes looking for it and finds out we've destroyed it?"

"A convenient rationale," I said bitterly.

Josh gestured broadly as he said, "I'm just considering all the angles. Isn't that what you do?"

I suppressed a growl as I scrutinized my brother. If his theory was correct, having the magic in my possession gave me a bargaining chip—or made me a target. Giving the magic up might make me a target as well. As much as I didn't like the conclusion, he was making sense. "Teach me the ritual."

Josh gave me a long, sideways look, then set his tumbler aside and began gathering the items needed. While the ritual wasn't complicated, it took me several dry runs before I felt confident. The more I focused, the more aware I became of the mysterious magic inhabiting my body, as steady and annoying as a ringing in my ear. After the last run-through, I gathered the necessary items into a bag and Josh transported me to my BMW parked a block away from Sky's house.

Behind the wheel, I picked up my phone from the passenger seat and discovered two voice mails. The first was from Claudia, reminding me to visit her. Though she didn't press the matter, I could feel the subtle urgency in her voice. The second call was a somber one, from the nurse at Twilight Harbor.

Miriam was family. I should've been there when she died. I shook my head, reminding myself, *If I'd been with Miriam, Sky would be dead.* But Lucas Reed should've never been a problem. If I hadn't allowed her to keep Ethos's magic, there wouldn't have been a crisis in the first place. I couldn't shake my anger at Sky, but I shared the responsibility.

I called the nurse, instructing her to contact the funeral home where Miriam had previously made her arrangements. The home would handle everything. Judging by the shocked tone of the nurse's response, I presumed that she found my seeming lack of emotion offensive, but we didn't share the same frame of reference. The supernatural world was a dangerous place. People around me died all the time, often by violent means and while at the peak of their potential. With Miriam, I felt the small absence in the world of a face I would never see again, a voice I would never hear, but we'd never been close. She'd made sure of that.

Claudia's gallery was a large brick building just off the city's main street. Noticing Sky's Honda Civic parked outside triggered a rush of anger. At one time, her recklessness had been easily attributable to her lack of familiarity with our world.

Her mother had died giving birth to her, leaving her to be raised by an adopted mother with no knowledge of the supernatural. Sky had grown up believing that her animal was a lonely curse, to be suppressed and shunned. But she'd spent the last two years with the pack—enough time to absorb the pitfalls and dangers of our way of life, enough time to appreciate just how dangerous magic could be.

Still, I couldn't escape my own culpability, and the sinking feeling in my stomach as I schemed to take Ethos's magic from her. *It has to be done,* I reminded myself. *The sooner the better.* Lucas Reed wasn't the only threat out there; he'd just been the first to find her. *She'll understand it was for her protection,* I decided. *Eventually.*

I let out a slow breath, forcibly suppressing my anger and frustration and replacing it with a facsimile of calm, then went inside.

Claudia's gallery showcased Chicago's most sought-after artists. Exquisite modern and abstract art dotted the textured white walls. Sculptures and installations were generously placed throughout the gallery, intermingled with uniquely styled benches and sofas placed for optimal viewing.

As I walked in, I noticed Sky standing in front of her favorite painting. It was the one piece of art Claudia refused to sell, and Sky was obsessed with obtaining it. Her home was tastefully decorated with the fruits of her failure, as Claudia had skillfully converted each plea into a purchase of some other piece of artwork. I smiled. My godmother was a beguiling salesperson as well as a gifted artist. She claimed the painting was inspired by the relationship between my brother and me, but I only saw a passing resemblance.

Sky was so engrossed in the painting that she failed to notice as I stopped just behind her. I found myself scrutinizing it over her shoulder, wondering just what it was that fascinated her. The smaller of the two boys, with short ruffled hair, appeared angelic as he slept peacefully, while the other boy knelt protectively nearby. His brown hair was flecked with gold. His gaze was somber and intense, displaying a wariness beyond his years as he watched over his sleeping brother, unaware of the looming shadow behind them.

The shadow remained an inexplicable curiosity of the painting. Perhaps Claudia had attempted to convey something she'd seen of my future—aside from being a powerful empath, she could also see the potential future of someone she touched. I'd never asked her for an explanation. Josh and I were careful not to press her about her abilities, or to take advantage of them. If she'd seen something I needed to know, she'd tell me.

"Why this one?" I asked, surprising Sky.

She turned slightly, taking a quick breath as she noticed my proximity to her, then shrugged. I moved to stand close beside her, silently observing the portrait with her as I considered my options. To perform the ritual, I needed to be with her alone, in a space where interruption was unlikely. I needed her to be comfortable and to let her guard down.

Her house, I decided.

"Let's have dinner tonight," I announced.

She scoffed, turning from the portrait to give me an indignant look, as if the answer should've been obvious. "No."

"No?" I grinned. "Why not?"

"I don't like being lied to or threatened, and every time we're together you do one or both. So, no, I don't want to have dinner with you."

"You're the one who wanted to talk," I said indifferently, noting the increase in her heart rate as I sidled closer to her. "I am giving you an opportunity to do that and I will answer any questions you may have."

She scrutinized me, her curiosity piqued. "You will

answer them truthfully and promise not to give me any of those silly lies of omission that you are so fond of?"

I nodded. I'd give her whatever honesty I could, but there were limits, lines I wouldn't cross. She remained skeptical, but I knew she couldn't resist the opportunity.

"I'll see you at eight," I stated.

She countered quickly. "I will meet you at Gigio's at six."

I raised an eyebrow. Was she that distrusting of me? Before I could ask why she insisted on a public meeting, I noticed Claudia approaching. "I will be at your house at eight with dinner," I stated softly, then turned to greet my godmother. She appeared impeccably dressed, wearing long, elegant gloves that matched her peach pantsuit. Her delicate brown curls, usually up in a tight bun, were now loose, just brushing the top of her shoulders.

"If I am going to be subjected to your inquisition," I explained to Sky, "I do believe privacy is necessary."

"Ethan, I'm so glad to see you," Claudia said in her metropolitan South African accent.

I smiled, greeting her with my customary air kiss over each cheek. Given her empathic abilities, it would be considered an intrusion to touch her skin without permission. While her abilities made physical affection challenging, she'd never been emotionally distant, like Miriam.

"You have to promise to visit more. Brunch Sunday, okay?" she suggested.

"Sunday will be great." I made a quick mental note to rearrange my schedule.

Claudia smiled at Sky. "You should join us."

"Of course," she answered with a cloying smile; she'd no intention of attending. If Claudia noticed, she didn't appear to be offended.

"Wonderful," she beamed, then leaned forward to offer Sky an affectionate half embrace. Surprisingly, their cheeks pressed together. At first I thought it was a mistake on Sky's part. Instinctively, I started to intervene, but Claudia purposely held their contact for a moment—a rare courtesy for her. Was she expressing her affection for Sky, or reading her? My godmother rarely used her abilities, except in times of great need. It was hard on her. To offer herself willingly was unusual.

After a moment, she broke the embrace, beaming as she gathered Sky's hands into hers. "Your lovely friend is becoming one of my favorite patrons," she informed me. "Her curiosity is inspiring. I see why you're so fond of her, she is quite charming."

Sky's eyes widened in surprise at me.

"I am quite fond of her," I repeated. "And her curiosity, if nothing else, is quite … *charming*." My sardonic tone was met with a slight flare of her nostrils.

"Ethan," Claudia said, "I'd like a word with you in my office, if you have a moment."

"Of course." I said, following her. I grinned over my shoulder at Sky, taking pleasure in her vengeful smile.

Claudia's office was a private continuation of the gallery. Original artwork overlooked an antique cherrywood writing desk complete with an old-fashioned pen and inkwell, a mother-of-pearl chaise couch, and a pair of hand-carved wooden chairs on either side of a tea table. Claudia turned in front of her desk, observing me with an empathetic look.

I closed the door behind me.

"I'm sorry about Miriam," she said.

"Thank you."

We waited for each other to speak further. It was a game we both played with others, using silence to draw them out. She scrutinized me, as if searching for something. Could she feel the change in me?

"Did you have a chance to talk with her?" she finally asked.

"The dementia made conversation … challenging."

She gestured an invitation toward the table. When we were seated across from each other, she leaned toward me, clasping her hands in front of her. "The distance she kept from you and from others was harder on her than you realize."

That wasn't a conversation I needed to have. I'd long since come to terms regarding Miriam's emotional distance. Still, I listened patiently out of respect for my godmother.

"She didn't tell you," she realized, disappointed.

"She was not coherent."

Claudia sighed. "As you are aware, our world is full of secrets, some more dangerous than others. I never told you because it wasn't my secret to tell. But if she wasn't able to, then I am the only one who can." She reached out and placed a gloved hand on mine. "You've probably noticed something different about yourself since her passing."

I straightened in my chair, a dozen questions racing through my mind at once, all of them doubtful that the mysterious magic inside me was connected to my grandmother. *She must be referring to something else.* Rather than worry Claudia, I didn't want to bring up the incident with Lucas Reed. "I'm not sure what you mean."

"Miriam had abilities that she didn't want anyone to know about."

Had she been an empath, like Claudia? That would've explained a great deal about Miriam but had nothing to do with my present.

She continued, "As her only descendant, those abilities, along with the risk and the responsibility that come with them, are now yours. I wish there was some way to prepare you for this news. Miriam waited too long, and now you don't have the luxury of a careful introduction. You're in danger, Ethan—more than you know. Your grandmother was not entirely human."

I raised an eyebrow.

Claudia gave my hand a light squeeze as she said, "She was a dark elf."

I felt my jaw start to drop, then closed it.

Dark elves were extinct. Unlike their elvish cousins, whose powers were limited largely to moderate trickster magic or localized manipulation of the weather, dark elves had been formidable. Their greatest power, the one that had made them such a threat that the elves and vampires and were-animals had joined forces to exterminate the dark elven race, had been the ability to kill with a touch.

"That's not possible," I insisted, but Claudia wouldn't involve me with unsubstantiated rumors. The timing of Miriam's death made sense. The magic that had saved me from Lucas Reed had been hers, escaping her breathless body and transferring undiluted to her sole living relative. I hadn't been set up. I'd been cursed.

Miriam had spent her entire life under a death sentence, as afraid of her powers as she was of revealing her true nature. I wondered how she'd hidden her magical abilities for more than eighty years. I'd never noticed if she wore iridium. For nearly all supernaturals, iridium suppressed magical abilities, but I doubted it had been effective on dark elves or it would've been offered to them as an alternative to death.

I thought about the way she'd avoided ever touching me, or anyone. She must've struggled with control. Perhaps she'd discovered her abilities just as I had, without any preparation or guidance. Had she spent her entire life withdrawn from friends and family out of fear that a single, casual touch could kill?

Instinctively, I drew my hand from beneath Claudia's and stared at it. My mind flashed to images of my hand squeezing Josh's shoulder as he rescued me, of carelessly brushing against Sky just a moment ago in the gallery.

I could've killed them.

"Ethan," Claudia said, distracting me. "You're stronger

than Miriam was. To find yourself with such unanticipated power is a tremendous burden, but I'm confident you will find a way to control it." She rose and retrieved something from the surface of her desk, then placed it in front of me on the table as she slid back into her seat. I stared at the thin, silvery metal. Iridium. "I'm afraid it won't fully suppress your abilities, but it will help. Josh can be of great help to you, as well. I wish I had more to offer you. I'm afraid there is no one left who truly understands the power you now possess."

I stared at the band, an unpleasant reminder of my own childhood. Eventually, the practicality of it won over my distaste. It would only take one emotional outburst to lose control and kill someone I cared about. I swept the band off the table and attached it to my left wrist, where it was less likely to be noticed.

"Thank you," I said.

She studied me for a moment before asking, "Are you going to tell Sebastian?"

Can I trust him, you mean. There was more at stake for me than just the unexpected revelation of new magical abilities; a death sentence hung over me. If I told Sebastian, he'd be obliged to kill me, or turn me over to the other supernatural factions for extermination. If he protected me, the entire pack would be at risk. I couldn't let that happen.

My mind reeled as I absorbed the complications of the new reality that had been forced on me. As long as I kept it a secret, the risks were mine alone. "I understand," I said as I started to rise.

"There is one more thing I'd like to ask you," she said.

I sat back down, eager to change the subject. "Of course."

"I'm fond of Skylar, but if she had to choose between her personal safety and the safety of the pack, could you count on her to make the right choice?"

I scrutinized my godmother, wondering what she'd seen when she'd touched Sky. It was a futile effort, of course.

Claudia was far too wily to give away more than she felt necessary.

"I have a request," I said, taking her question as rhetorical. "If your offer of the painting of the two boys is still valid, I accept."

She smiled, pleased. "Of course." She'd been waiting years for me to accept it.

"I would like to give it to Sky," I explained. My promise to answer her questions intrigued her, but I needed something more; the painting would put her completely off her guard. I also wanted her to have it. Perhaps after the ritual was done, the painting would help her to forgive me, eventually.

By the time I emerged from Claudia's office, Sky had already left. Sitting in my BMW, I drew out my phone to call Josh, but stopped myself. Once he knew I was a dark elf, he would suffer the same dilemma that Sebastian would—turn me in, or suffer the consequences. I couldn't put either of them in that position.

I pocketed my phone and drove the couple of miles across town to the Law Firm of Wendell, Harper, and Holmes, where I spent the afternoon burying myself in work. Like most of the pack, I worked professionally. Over the last five years, I'd managed to make a name for myself in corporate law, working exclusively with large, often international corporations. Clients frequently asked for me by name, which afforded me the ability to work whatever hours I saw fit—as long as the clients were happy, and I made sure they were. But there were times when I had to choose my responsibilities as pack Beta over those of my career. Twice I'd turned down an offer of partnership with my firm, leaving my employers baffled, but it wasn't a difficult choice for me to make. Work was an entertaining necessity, and at times a welcome distraction, but the pack was my life.

I enjoyed corporate law because the stakes were strictly financial. Life and death weren't part of the equation, as they were in pack life. This time, burying myself in the linguistic minutiae of a hundred-page international contract wasn't enough. My thoughts repeatedly returned to my newly discovered heritage and the elf magic.

If Josh's ritual could be used to remove Ethos's magic, it could be used to remove mine, but the ritual wasn't selective. I'd inherited some witch magic from my mother, and I had no intention of losing it. The Aufero seemed my best chance, though I wasn't entirely certain it would be selective, either. Unfortunately the Aufero was in Marcia's possession. I doubted it would just be in her office, sitting on top of her desk like a paperweight. No, the Aufero was too powerful to leave lying around; it would be hidden and protected by magic.

Frowning at the clock, I realized my appointment with Sky was growing closer. I'd enough to worry about now. I considered calling her to reschedule, but I reminded myself that her safety depended on the ritual. Still, I dreaded it. My emotions quickly ran the gamut from regret, to empathy, to anger in a seemingly endless loop. *It needs to be done,* I reminded myself, dreading the repercussions.

If she could control it... I heard Josh's voice pleading. Having Ethos's magic at the pack's disposal could prove invaluable, but I didn't think she was capable of controlling it or of using it responsibly, for all the same reasons I'd previously given Josh.

Perhaps I owed it to her to at least find out.

After I left the office, I stopped at a store to pick up a bottle of Sky's favorite red wine, then stopped by Dr. Baker's house to pick up a small vial of clear, odorless liquid. He didn't bother to ask what it was for, and I didn't volunteer. Once home, I rehearsed the ritual until I felt confident, then packed up the articles required into a black bag. I carefully tucked the wrapped portrait into the back of my SUV and slipped behind the wheel. After a moment's hesitation, I frowned and backed the SUV out of the driveway.

On my way to Sky's, I made a brief detour to her favorite restaurant, an Argentinian steakhouse. By policy, they didn't offer orders to go, but I was a regular. A generous gratuity helped.

When I pulled into the driveway of Sky's quaint two-bedroom home, I noticed David, her nosy neighbor and more-than-casual acquaintance, giving me a look that I could only describe as hungry suspicion as he strolled on the sidewalk. I scowled back at him and he quickened his step, trotting away as quickly as he could manage without putting his fear on display. Her relationship with David and his partner needlessly put them at risk of dangers they couldn't possibly anticipate. When she'd purchased her home, I'd counseled her to limit her interactions with neighbors to just the amount necessary to avoid suspicion. She'd rolled her eyes at me, much the way Josh did when he thought I was being overly cautious.

I carried the black bag to the porch and placed it against the house, out of sight next to the door, then returned to my SUV to retrieve the portrait, the dinner, and the wine. I took a slow, calming breath in front of the door, then knocked. After a long moment, I was about to knock again when the door opened.

Sky greeted me with wary reserve, but then her green eyes were drawn to the wrapped portrait, brightening in surprise as she eagerly accepted the gift. I followed, passing her on my way to the kitchen while she carried the portrait into the living room to admire the wrapping. I assumed she was trying to guess which painting I'd brought her.

I placed the wine and the bag of takeaway onto the

counter next to her iPad, then began searching the cupboards for plates, glasses, and utensils. Next to the wineglasses, I found one of Steven's coffee cups, bearing the logo of his university. I scowled as I glanced around the house, noting the curious absence of his belongings. He'd been virtually living with her before he'd left to help his mother rebuild the Southern Pack. I guessed that his belongings were still there, temporarily stashed in the so-called guest room. I didn't approve of their living arrangement, but I let the matter drop —for the moment.

I retrieved a corkscrew from a drawer and opened the wine. "Open it," I encouraged her. Her lips spread into a delighted, childlike smile as she began gently sliding her fingers along the seams of the wrapping. While she was distracted, I drew the vial from my pocket and tipped out three drops of a translucent liquid into her wineglass, then returned the vial to my pocket and poured the wine.

I heard a slight gasp as she lifted the framed portrait just far enough out of the box to recognize it. "How did you get this?" she exclaimed. "She said it wasn't for sale."

I divided the steaks between the plates, giving Sky the best cut. "It wasn't."

"But she sold it to you?"

"No," I said as I plated the potatoes and asparagus. "I asked her if I could have it so that I could give it to you." I smiled back at her, enjoying her happiness. "You seem to really like it. I wanted you to have it."

Her grin broadened as she gingerly drew the portrait the rest of the way from the box and held it in front of her, beaming as she examined every detail. Incomprehensibly, she reached out with a finger and gently touched the canvas, as if proving to herself that it was real. I remembered the gold sign that had hung next to the portrait on the gallery wall that had read PLEASE DO NOT TOUCH THE ART, and chuckled.

"Thank you," she said, genuinely pleased as she gently leaned the portrait against the living room wall, then backed away several feet to examine it.

Once everything was ready, I plated the single piece of red velvet cake and brought it to her. She was nearly as delighted by the cake as she was the portrait.

"You seem like a dessert-first type of woman," I explained.

She accepted it with a coy smile, then retrieved her iPad from the counter and sat at the dining room table, eating absently as she scrolled through what appeared to be a long list of questions. I placed her glass of wine close to her plate, then sat across from her.

"You are able to break wards," she read as I placed both of our dinner plates on the table. "How?"

"Can I at least take a bite before you start questioning me?" The longer I took, the fewer questions I'd have to answer before the drug took effect.

She nodded agreeably as she forked another bite of cake. When I pushed her glass of wine closer to her, she brushed it aside, giving me a wary look as I sat across from her.

"It's a gift from Claudia," I lied, reaching across the table to slide it back in front of her. Lying came easily to me, such that I didn't have to think to moderate my voice, respiration, and heart rate to avoid detection. "Just take a couple of sips. I can assure you the next time you see her, she will ask for your thoughts about it. She will consider it an insult if you haven't tried it."

Sky took an obligatory sip, raised her glass as a testimonial, then set it down. Her attention returned to her iPad as she scrolled through the questions, already searching for the next one. I remained quiet, watching. After a moment, she reached absently for the glass and took another sip.

Relieved, I relaxed into my chair and began cutting my steak.

She repeated her question.

Waiting until she met my gaze, I took a long draw from my wineglass. She took another sip of her own, unconsciously mirroring my behavior. "My mother was a witch," I answered. "I inherited it. In skills that Josh falls short in, I seem to excel. I shouldn't have been able to do anything because I'm a were-animal, but things never happen as they should. When my mother noticed that I was able to do magic, she suppressed it."

"Suppressed it?"

"With iridium." I drew my left arm back, conscious of the iridium bracelet on that wrist. "I spent most of my childhood with either an iridium cuff or iridium injected into me." The latter had been the most uncomfortable and had been forced upon me. I hadn't understood at the time, but the constant presence of iridium cuffs would've been noticed.

"Injected into you?" she repeated, appalled. "Couldn't that have killed you?"

"It wouldn't be any worse than if Marcia or the others found out. She is a purist. Since she has taken over the Creed, she's done an exceptional job at eliminating any anomalies that she is aware of. A wolf with the ability to use magic would have been a target for her."

Sky gaped in abhorrence.

"Agendas do not discriminate based on age," I explained. "Anomalies grow into adults that become problems. Delaying it because of a soft spot for children doesn't make the problem go away or be any less dangerous." It was a cruel but practical policy.

I was raising a bite of steak to my mouth when she asked, "What is the fifth protected mystical object?"

Surprised, I hesitated—an unconscious tell—but I quickly recovered. "I don't want to answer that."

"You said you would give me the truth."

"That is the truth," I calmly stated. "I don't want to answer it. Next question."

She scrutinized me over the lip of her glass as she drew a long drink of wine. *Won't be long now,* I thought.

Sky didn't bother addressing her iPad when she asked, "Did you really love Chris?"

I paused with my knife and fork over my plate and glared at her. "That is neither relevant nor your concern."

"I want to know," she stated matter-of-factly. "You promised you would answer my questions. You already avoided one. If you aren't going to answer my questions, then you need to leave."

I let out a long, resentful sigh as I set down my utensils and crossed my arms over my chest. "Yes. I did." *Once.*

"You let her die."

She'd been brutally, methodically beaten nearly to the point of being unrecognizable, most likely by Michaela. While the pack and the rest of the Seethe had been fighting Ethos's creatures, she'd taken advantage of the chaos to attack Chris, hoping that Demetrius, in a jealous rage, would blame me for her injuries. Michaela wanted a war between the Seethe and the Midwest Pack. She almost got it. Unfortunately for her, Chris hadn't died right away.

Sky and Kelly, Dr. Baker's human assistant, both believed I should've changed Chris into a were-animal to save her, but they didn't understand the process or the complications involved in transforming a human. Even for a healthy child, the transformation was dangerous. Transforming an adult carried much greater risks and was rarely successful. Chris's injuries had been too severe for me to change her; the process would've been a cruel torture, and then it would've killed her.

The transformation of a human into a vampire was a much simpler process.

When Demetrius had offered to change her, I'd refused to allow it. Chris had worked for him, even traded blood with him, but she'd never wanted to be his slave. In siring her, he would've owned her for eternity. But Kelly had intervened. The choice hadn't been hers to make. Defying my explicit orders, and violating the trust of the pack, she'd locked herself in the hospital room with Chris and Demetrius. She'd even allowed the vampire to feed from her in order to rejuvenate him from the fight, enough to enable him to change Chris into a vampire and transport her away from the pack's retreat.

Despite Kelly's best intentions, she'd failed to save Chris. She was dead. She was a vampire. As far as I was concerned, the creature in her body was an evil, murderous beast, an enemy of the pack, just like any other vampire. There was nothing left of the Chris I'd known and had tried to protect.

"So?" I demanded, answering Sky's accusation.

She frowned. "I couldn't let someone I love die without doing everything possible to save them, even if it meant letting her be changed to a vampire."

She held my cold, unblinking gaze for a long moment, hoping for some form of capitulation on my part. In the world of predators, unbroken eye contact was a challenge. Sky didn't understand that, but her wolf did. Eventually, her wolf instincts took over and she averted her gaze.

"Well," I said, stifling my irritation, "that is one of the many differences we have. I wasn't going to be responsible for making a vampire, especially one created by Demetrius with the ability to be as dangerous as Chris. Next question."

"But—"

"Next. Question."

She took a sip of wine as she scrolled through her iPad once more, preferably searching for a question that was less invasive about matters that didn't apply to her.

"How long have you known about me and what I am?" she asked.

My lips spread into an amused smile. Her depth of distrust surprised and impressed me. Judging by the slightly glazed look of her eyes, the drug was beginning to take effect, which meant it was time to begin a test of my own.

"I said we would have an honest conversation," I started, "and I plan to honor that. You might as well have a neon sign on your face flashing everything you are thinking because it is that easy to read. When we took you to Claudia, it wasn't the first time you had met her. You may not remember. You may have been eleven or twelve when she met you in a store. Do you remember her?"

Sky shook her head, her curiosity piqued. "And what did she think of me?"

"You were still young, but she found you to be peculiar. She could tell you were a were-animal that hadn't emerged and suggested that we keep an eye on you. So we did. You didn't really prove to be a danger, so we checked in periodically. It was quite a boring job for whomever was tasked with it. It wasn't until Josh came to us with the request that you needed to be protected that you proved to be remotely interesting."

"Then why didn't you want me to join the pack?"

"Sebastian sees you as an asset. I still disagree and you haven't shown me anything since we've met that has changed my opinion," I lied, testing her reaction. If she couldn't control Ethos's magic, it would rise to the surface on an intense emotion, like anger. According to Josh, I would see the magic in her eyes—that same black vapor that had turned her eyes black when Ethos's magic had overtaken her body. I continued, channeling my own anger, embellishing it. "You're impertinent and irresponsible. Before, the only person who had to deal with your screwups was your mother, and given what she had to work with, she did an exceptional job. Now your carelessness is our problem. We are now tasked with the immense responsibility of protecting your life. I don't think it is worth the risks."

Her cheeks flushed with anger.

Good.

I leaned toward her at the other end of the table, noting that her pupils had begun to dilate, but there was no sign of Ethos's power. Not yet. I needed to push her closer to the edge. "As a Moura, you have your benefits, but I am not sure if the cost-benefit is really worth it. Those responsible for guarding things of such power must possess some of their own. At all times it should be controlled, never the other way around. I have not seen anything in you that would prove that you have the ability to possess or control anything of power, even your wolf half. At best, you're an endearing mess; at worst, you become an obligation that could hurt this pack. You're witty," I admitted. "It's good fun for a laugh or two. You're kindhearted, which means you will be trampled by those in this world. You blush when you're upset, you make unwise decisions when you are scared, and you are incapable of getting people to see a reality you wish them to believe. These are not the qualities of one fit to survive in this world. I figure far too many pack resources will be wasted trying to keep you alive."

I leaned back in my chair and waited for the fireworks.

"'Incapable of getting people to see a reality you wish them to believe'?" she spat back at me, incensed. "You mean lie? I am sorry I do not possess the qualities of a deranged psychopath and haven't perfected the fiendish art of lying. Please, let me apologize for being sane and not an unconscionable degenerate. You of all people should know that you can never mistake kindness for weakness; they are not mutually inclusive."

"Of course they are, but in your case they aren't. Your ability to manipulate magic can be an asset; however, of the many people I have encountered, I do believe it is a gift wasted on you. I still think taking on the responsibility of being your babysitter, and honestly that is what we will be for you, was one of the few unwise choices Sebastian has ever made."

For once, she bit her tongue, responding with only a malevolent, plastic smile before returning her attention to her iPad, swiping her finger down the screen in long, aggressive strokes until she saw a question that surprised her.

"Why are you such an ass?" she asked. "I am sure you've already won some type of award for it. Why keep at it?"

"Is that really on there?" I asked, genuinely curious.

She turned the iPad around to show me and tapped a finger on the screen, next to the question. I smirked, impressed. If I hadn't needed her angry, I would've laughed.

"Do you really want to waste time on silly questions?" I asked.

She turned the iPad around to examine it once more. I watched as her eyes roved the screen. "Okay, here's another," she announced proudly. "What happened in your life that caused you to be such a jerk? Are there any mood-altering medications that you aren't taking enough of or too much of that make you act like this?"

I chuckled unexpectedly. "You said you wanted the truth and I gave it. I'm not one to coddle people or to temper my words because of sensitivity. I advise you to toughen up, because that is more likely to happen than me changing. If you don't want the answers, then don't ask the questions."

She sucked in an indignant gasp, blatantly resisting the urge to go on the offense before she asked her next question. "The Tre'ases were afraid of you, and your presence sent Ethos into a violent rage. What is it about you that causes them to respond like that?"

"I don't know," I answered honestly. "I've often wondered the same thing, but I don't know that answer. I am an anomaly; there are many that simply hate me because of it. I guess we are alike in some ways." Judging by her dark glower and the tension in her shoulders, I had pushed her to the borderline between anger and fury. I leaned over the table toward her. Gazing directly into her eyes, I saw the telltale black mist of Ethos's magic gathering, aroused by her anger. I masked my regret, reminding myself that the chances that Sky could've kept such power under control had always been slight.

I would perform the ritual as planned.

"You know what I wonder?" I said. "Why Ethos was so lenient on you. He could have forced you to do whatever he wished—but he *asked*. When you stabbed him, he could have just as easily killed you—but he didn't. Do you ever wonder why, Sky?"

Her jaw twitched as she clamped it shut. She'd wondered the same thing. While she struggled with her emotions, I scooped up her wineglass along with mine and carried them to the kitchen counter, next to the bottle. While she stared at the table, contemplating my question, I surreptitiously drew the vial from my pocket, tipped three more drops into her glass, returned the vial, then poured wine into each of our glasses. With the glasses in hand, I walked past her into the living room, drawing her attention as I set them onto the coffee table next to a vase filled with decorative water beads, then dropped onto the sofa. At first, she simply stared at me, stubbornly refusing to join me.

I scrutinized the portrait, waiting for her. I wondered if the shadow looming over me in the painting might be my own darkness.

Sky joined me a moment later, her expression sullen and defiant. I lifted both glasses and handed one to her, intending to make a toast, but she set her glass onto the table next to the vase. For a moment, I wondered if she knew what I was up to, or if she simply thought I was trying to get her drunk.

"You are aware of Maya's story?" I asked. It was a rhetorical question. When Sky had been in a coma over a year ago, she'd spent four days communing with Maya. I only had

Sky's word as to the context of those conversations. I was sure she knew more about Maya's history than she let on. "I am not sure how accurate the information is," I continued. "Perhaps it is a tall tale or some twisted variation of the truth, but it is my understanding that Emma had another child, a son. She kept him hidden to keep him from Maya's fate, and he grew up to be who we now know as Ethos."

Her pupils were mostly dilated as she stared back at me, trying to focus. The black mist there dissipated with the cooling of her temper. Distracting herself from my story, she scooped up her glass and sipped her wine.

"Wouldn't it make sense?" I asked. "After all, when he was reunited with his sister, he asked for her help in controlling the vampires and the were-animals. She could've taken control of you and joined him, but she didn't. Even after her betrayal, when she stabbed him in the middle of battle, he never retaliated. Instead, he relinquished his power to her. Unfortunately, the fragile body that hosted his sister wasn't able to contain it."

I watched her take another long drink of wine; for the first time, she seemed to notice the bitter taste, pausing to look into her glass.

"What are you able to do?" I asked, distracting her.

"Wh-what do you mean?" she slurred, surprising herself.

"The magic that you kept—or should we keep pretending you didn't?"

For a moment, she considered lying, then shrugged. "Not much." At a wave of her hand, the napkin on the table rose and danced about on the surface before flying toward me. I didn't flinch as it rose over my head at the last moment. More objects around us began to rise, joining the dance.

"Impressive," I said. "Besides making napkins bounce around—and I assume all your clothes in the morning as you make them dance around the room—what else can you do?"

She gave me a groggy, speculative look, wondering how I

knew. When I offered her no visual cues to glean from, she gave up her speculation. Her gaze softened as she concentrated, conjuring a defensive ward around her—a thin golden aura of magic that felt significantly stronger than I'd thought her capable of. Even sitting just outside the protective barrier, I felt the pressure of it pushing against me. When I pressed a palm against it, it repelled my effort with equal force. Testing its strength, I pushed harder at the barrier's boundary, which responded by pressing me back into the sofa. Impressive. It also interfered with my plans.

"Drop it," I said politely.

Her head tilted as she considered me for a moment before the field dissipated in a collapse of gold sparks that briefly illuminated the room.

"What else can you do?" I asked.

Her eyes shifted from mine to stare absently at the vase on the coffee table. "Nothing."

I doubt that. "Josh hasn't allowed you to do any spells?"

She shook her head, as if not verbalizing the lie would somehow mask the betrayal of her heartbeat, or the sudden shortness of her breath. She seemed about to collapse into sleep, her body slumping, when she caught herself. Startled, she glanced around the room for an explanation and settled on the wineglass.

"I think I'm drunk," she whispered, surprised.

The sedative I'd put in her wine was taking longer than anticipated as she stubbornly resisted its effect. Needing to distract her, I decided to test just how powerful she was with Ethos's magic. I drew my phone out of my pocket and sifted through magic spells I'd copied from some of the older books in the pack library, searching for one in particular. Once I located it, I handed my phone to Sky.

"Read this," I said. While she examined the document with a confused expression, I took a few beads from the vase, gently opened her hand, then placed the beads in her palm.

"Change them." It was a tall order. Rearranging the molecules of one object to create another required a great deal of power, even to create simple objects.

"Sure," she said with a wry smile. "What do you want? A bunny? Bird? Lizard? Kitty?"

"You can't produce something organic from an inorganic," I explained. "No one can. But you should be able to change the form."

I waited patiently as she concentrated on the beads. After a long moment, I was about to abort the test when the beads began to vibrate. Slowly, reluctantly, they rolled toward the center of her palm as if drawn to each other, melting into a single, misshapen ball that then formed into a small basin. My eyes widened in genuine surprise. It was an impressive feat, but she wasn't finished. A tiny, remarkable fire sparked to life within the basin, crackling orange, blue, and claret embers. I felt the heat rising from it as the fire began to spread toward the basin's edges.

I glanced anxiously at Sky. Her eyes were entirely black, indicative of the power she was using. As the fire threatened to overwhelm the edges of the basin, she seemed oblivious to the danger. Should the fire escape its confines, it would burn through whatever other material it touched and quickly start a fire that would be very difficult to extinguish.

"Sky, stop it," I urged, but she didn't appear to hear me.

I hurried to the kitchen and returned with a damp towel just as she yelped and dropped the now glowing-hot basin. I caught it in the towel—ignoring the heat of it as it tried to light the towel on fire. While Sky ran to the kitchen to run her hand under cold water, I quickly smothered the fire with the rest of the towel.

Examining my hand, I found a mild burn. It hurt, and it would blister, but the damage wasn't significant. With my natural healing ability, the wound would completely disappear within a matter of minutes. Retrieving an ice cube from the freezer, I gently took Sky's hand from beneath the cold water and held it in mine as I slowly massaged her palm with the ice cube. Her burn was worse than mine, but already healing. She stared at the cube as I gently slid it over her wound. After a moment, she gave me a confused look, but didn't object to my touch.

The first cube quickly melted, and I retrieved another. The power she'd displayed was far beyond what I'd thought Ethos's magic could grant her. The potential of such magic was difficult to contemplate. I understood then the intoxicating effect that magic had on my brother, but the risks couldn't be denied. Had Sky attempted that same spell without my brother or me present to stop her from carrying it too far, she would've burned her house down, and probably the entire neighborhood with it.

After the third cube melted into a useless stub, I tossed it into the sink and asked, "More?"

She shook her head.

I gently led her back toward the sofa. Once seated, I handed her her glass of wine, then picked up my own. A smug smile settled on her lips as she basked in the vibration of powerful magic that still thrummed in the room. The sooner I completed the ritual, the better.

"I do believe I've underestimated you," I said sincerely. "You are becoming very powerful. Impressive." I sighed, resigned, and raised my glass to her. "To untapped power."

She gently tapped her glass to mine, then hesitated a moment before finally drinking the rest of her glass in a single tilt. I waited for the additional sedative to take effect as she contemplated the empty glass in her hand. After a moment, her eyelids fluttered and she began to sway.

"Are you okay?" I asked, gently taking the glass from her and setting it on the table.

She could barely keep her eyes open. "Too much wine," she muttered, blinking. "It always makes me sleepy."

I slid off the sofa to make room. "Lie down."

"No." She waved me off. "I just need some water."

"I'll get some. Just relax." Nodding slightly, she lay supine, closed her eyes, and stretched out.

While she made herself comfortable, I retrieved the black bag from outside her front door. As the spell required, I placed six candles around her; one on the couch at her head and one at her feet, two beside her on the coffee table, and two more on the back of the couch. While I lit them in turn, her eyelids fluttered as she tried and failed to keep them open. By the time I finished, she was completely asleep.

The air in the room thickened as the pungent redolence of herbs and cedar diffused from the candles, irritating my nostrils. Looming over Sky, I began the memorized chant. Once complete, I patted her cheeks—just enough to draw her from her drug-induced slumber. When her eyelids flickered partially open, she seemed unaware of her surroundings.

"Sky, open your eyes," I said, lifting her chin slightly. "Look at me."

She tried. Her lids fluttered open, but then slowly closed as she drifted back toward sleep. I patted her face again, progressively harder until she was finally able to keep her eyes open. Cradling her face in my palms, I whispered into her ear, "Repeat this." I gave her the four key words, carefully pronouncing the sounds that were from an old dialect. When she repeated them, they were jumbled, breathed out in a reluctant sigh as she tried to go back to sleep.

"No Skylar, you have to say them exactly as I did."

I repeated them again, breaking the sounds into syllables. After she repeated them correctly, I bent over to brush my lips over hers and inhaled, drawing Ethos's magic from her until I felt the cold of it numbing my body, then turned away from her and exhaled the black vaporous mist into the room, where it dissipated. We repeated the ritual three more times. When I pried open one of her eyelids, her green eyes appeared disassociated, but they were clear. The black mist was gone. I sighed in relief, experiencing just a moment of satisfaction before I imagined the confrontation that would ensue when she woke up. But she was safe now.

"What's happening?" she muttered.

"Go to sleep," I whispered softly. A moment later she was snoring. I quietly blew out the candles and gathered them into the bag. I rinsed any trace of the wine from our glasses, emptied the bottle down the drain, and left.

CHAPTER 4

Once home, I changed clothes, then went for an evening run, hoping to wear myself down enough to sleep. Hours later, I returned home exhausted, showered until well after the water went cold, then went to bed without checking my phone. Despite my exhaustion, I couldn't sleep. I wasn't sure if it was the dark elf magic buzzing through my body—keeping me perpetually on edge —or my conscience. *It was the right call,* I reminded myself, a useless refrain that couldn't save me from a downward spiral of guilt and anger. I harangued myself for not intervening sooner, and I harangued Sky for creating the situation that required my intervention.

The battle continued inside me until it finally exhausted itself with the early glow of dawn. Instead of rising, as was my ritual, I fell into a restless, short-lived slumber. After only a few hours, I woke wondering just how long it would be until Sky showed up at my door to confront me.

I was making a breakfast of steak and eggs when her car lurched to a halt in the driveway. She slammed the car door and was on the porch a moment later, knocking with a loud urgency. I turned off the stove with a snap of the control, set aside the frying pan, then strode to the door. For a moment, I just stared at it, expecting it to melt from the heat of her anger.

When I opened the door, I found her glaring up at me, a molten fury in her eyes, her lips twisted into a hateful scowl. Her body was rigid, leaning toward me, with her fists clenched at her side. Frowning, I stepped aside for her to enter. She slammed the door behind her and stood speechless inside the entryway.

If looks could kill. I leaned against the wall, patiently waiting for the volcano to explode.

She tried to calm herself, taking a few breaths before finally asking in a restrained voice, "What did you do to me?"

I rolled my eyes. *Do we really have to go through the obvious?* "You know what was done. Don't ask silly questions. Why don't we get on with it? Throw your tantrum, yell, and tell me how hurt and violated you feel. Call me whatever creative insults you've come up with and when you're finished with your little show—go ahead and let yourself out."

I had no illusions of being forgiven.

"Why?" she demanded through clenched teeth.

"Why do you think? If you can't stop indulging every childish urge that overtakes you, then we have no choice but to intervene. If it is any consolation to you," I added softly, "I do not enjoy cleaning up your messes."

"What you did was cruel and unnecessary. You could have just asked."

"Would you have agreed?" I asked, challenging her.

She hesitated, knowing I was right but still clinging to her righteous indignation.

"That's exactly why I didn't," I added.

Her cheeks burned crimson as her anger came flooding out. She shouted, punctuating her accusations by stabbing her finger toward the floor, "You had no right to do that to me! I know that somewhere behind that monster you put on display at every given moment, there has to be a real person. A person who balks at the way you treat people."

I frowned at her. I didn't create problems. I solved them. "Josh's affection for you has compromised his reasoning. It is unfortunate, because there is no way in hell you should have ever been allowed to keep that form of magic. So I had to clean up his mess and yours before things got out of hand. A situation that should have been avoided in the first place. You need to get over it."

I should've seen the punch coming. As often happened with Sky, I underestimated her. The blow struck the side of my mouth, snapping my head sideways. She wore a thin, triumphant smile as I turned back to her. *Satisfied?* Before I could ask, she punched me again. I spat out blood, wiping a smear of it from my mouth. My wolf rose to the surface, drawn by the violence. When she reached back to strike once more, I stepped forward, grabbing her fist while it was still cocked back. I drove her back against the wall, pinning both of her hands next to her head and pressing my body against hers to keep her from wriggling free. Her lips pressed together as she tried to sweep my leg. I blocked her, shifting my hip. Glaring down at her, I resisted the primitive impulse to strike back.

My eyes locked with hers. I turned my head to spit out the blood building in my mouth, then ran my tongue over my front teeth to confirm they were intact.

The fury burning in her eyes was fueled by pure, righteous hate. "You hide behind the false dogma that your actions are necessary to protect the pack," she said. "That's a load of crap! You do cruel things simply because it brings you pleasure. You are a sadistic, cowardly, self-absorbed asshole that enjoys behaving this way simply for the hell of it. And you are too much of a coward to admit it to yourself."

After everything I've done for you—I scowled, shaking my head—*you don't even know me.*

She sucked in a breath and continued her verbal onslaught. "You aren't controlled by your wolf and your commitment to the pack. You are ruled by your narcissism and malice, and there isn't anything humane about you. We might as well keep you in the zoo with the other animals."

I waited for her to continue, listening to the furious beat of her heart and the sharp, rapid breaths of her lungs. "Are you finished?" I finally asked.

She glared back at me, lips defiantly pressed together.

"I asked a question. Are. You. Finished?"

She tried once more to slip away from me, but couldn't. When she glanced down at my hips, I knew she was searching for a vulnerability.

"If Ethos is actually dead," I explained, "you didn't think it wasn't going to throw up flags each time you used his magic? It's so strong I can feel it miles away. Whatever is going on between you and Josh has made him complacent regarding your careless whims and irresponsible behavior. I do not have that problem. I will not allow you to destroy this pack because you lack impulse control."

I stared into her eyes, waiting for some form of recognition. Was she so angry that she couldn't see the truth? Disappointed, I frowned as I shook my head. "But you are too naïve and self-indulgent to understand the repercussions of your stupidity. There isn't anything entertaining about it— it's pitiful. You're pitiful. Don't worry, I won't be pulling your ass out of the fire anymore. The next time you fuck up, and undoubtedly you will, I will let you burn for it."

"Let me go," she spat, but I saw fear beginning to take hold in her.

I'd let my anger get the best of me. My wolf fought to unleash itself and I found myself battling to keep it at bay. Every muscle in my body clenched with the effort. I struggled to relax, trying to breathe slowly, to unclench my jaw, but I'd reached a boiling point and was teetering on the edge of control. Growling, I pressed a hand to her chest and pushed her back into the wall, harder than I'd meant to. "Do you really understand the effects your actions have on things?" I shouted. "The problems aren't just yours anymore. You are … no, *we* are dealing with things that we have never encountered, and the only thing you can do is screw up!"

Sky opened her mouth to spit back a retort, but something surprised her. She flinched, as if shocked. The beat of her heart suddenly slowed to the point it struggled to beat at all, and her breath became a gasping struggle. Her gaze wandered, confused, as panic set in.

Sky?

"Get … off … me," she gasped, weakly trying to brush me aside.

Her heartbeat became almost inaudible.

In my own panic, my eyes roved over her, desperately looking for something wrong, then settled on my hand pressed against her chest. I knew with a sudden, dark realization that I was killing her. I snapped my hand from her and stepped back, eyes wide with fear as I gaped in horror at her. The moment I broke contact, the beat of her heart strengthened.

What've I done? "Sky," I pleaded, "I'm sorry."

She pushed me, stumbled backward, then ran out the door. By the time I emerged from the house, her Honda Civic was backing out of the driveway in a rush. It stopped suddenly, then lurched forward as she sped off.

Both of my hands pressed against my temples, I tried to contain my self-directed fury as I stormed back into the house. I'd lost control, and the dark elf magic had nearly killed Sky. *I* had almost killed her. I lost myself to blind, self-directed rage.

. . .

Eventually I came to my senses to find myself standing among the remnants of my living room, my chest heaving as I caught my breath. Several jagged, fist-sized holes dotted the walls. Bookcases and tables were flipped over, contents spilled across the floor. The couch was on its end, leaning against the wall, its upholstery sheared away in rough strips. Turning, I saw the damage extended to the dining room. The table was broken in two, with a fist-sized hole at the epicenter. The chairs were reduced to long, jagged splinters.

Glancing down at the iridium band on my left wrist, I snapped it off and hurled it across the room. After a moment of fuming, I begrudgingly retrieved it. Iridium couldn't contain the dark elf magic—that was obvious. But I couldn't be certain it didn't inhibit the magic. Without the bracelet, would I have killed Sky outright? I couldn't take the chance. Taking a deep breath, I snapped the band back onto my wrist.

I sighed at the damage I'd done, but it wasn't important, just wood and fabric—replaceable.

Looking for my phone, I picked through the rubble until I found it beneath the overturned couch. No calls from Sky. I called her, impatiently waiting through the rings, only to reach her voice mail. I hung up and called again. And again. When she didn't answer, I threw my phone against the brick hearth of the fireplace, where it shattered into pieces.

Furious with myself, I sifted through the pieces and found the sim card intact. Retrieving a spare phone from the desk, I inserted the card, activated the phone, then downloaded the latest of my hourly backups from the cloud. Since most flashes of temper began with a phone in my hand, I'd streamlined the recovery process until it came as naturally as changing my clothes.

I can't lose control again, I thought, taking a slow, deep breath.

I called Sky once more, cursed when it went to voice

mail, then called Josh. "I'm on my way over," I said, then killed the call.

I strode into Josh's ranch without knocking and found him waiting in his leopard print chair, wearing a concerned expression. He rose to greet me as I walked into the living room.

"What happened?" he asked.

I stopped in front of him and whispered, barely able to believe my own words, "I nearly killed Sky."

His expression hardened. "Be specific."

"I specifically need you to figure out how to control this damn magic!" I shouted, then paced the living room while he remained unmoving, like a statue, observing me. "I got angry," I admitted, irritated. "It just happened."

"Ethan, if you can describe *exactly* what happened, it might help to identify the magic's source."

"You mean it might help you figure out how to use it for your own ends." I sneered at him, instantly regretting it.

As much as I wanted to, I couldn't tell him. Only dark elves had the power to kill with a touch. If I described what I'd done to Sky, he'd recognize the magic, and then my death sentence would hang over him, as well. I couldn't allow that. "I don't need to understand it," I stressed. "I need to get rid of it, or at least shut it down."

He suppressed his own temper, aware that I was withholding important information from him. He nodded, shrugged. "Iridium, then."

I raised my left hand, displaying the bracelet on my wrist. "It didn't stop me from nearly killing Sky."

His mouth slightly opened in surprise. "Iridium suppresses all magic," he insisted.

"That was the prevailing theory," I snapped. Since dark

elves were supposed to be extinct, I guessed no one had thought it worth remembering that their magic wasn't entirely subject to the rules that applied to other magical creatures.

Josh pursed his lips and ran a hand through his tousled hair as he looked down at the floor. The longer he thought, the tighter his expression became. He didn't have an answer, and I couldn't tell him anything more without putting his life at risk.

I only just stopped myself from reaching down and flipping his coffee table across the room. *Control,* I thought, taking a slow, ragged breath. At the bottom of my exhale, I noticed on the table the copy of the drawing I'd seen there the other day, a sketch of three mystical books. A memory nagged at me.

"Is she okay?" Josh asked, distracting me. His voice was thick with concern.

I nodded, drawing out my phone. "She won't return my calls." I dialed once more. A few rings later, it went to voice mail.

"She's upset," Josh said. "Eventually she'll calm down and she'll understand it wasn't intentional. If she can describe what she experienced …." His voice trailed off under my glare. Rather than challenge me, he retrieved his phone from an end table and called her.

I watched with anticipation as he waited through the rings. After a moment, I knew she wouldn't answer him, either. She'd assume he was calling on my behalf. At the moment, I doubted she'd talk to anyone. Judging by the anxious look on his face, I knew I was right.

"Go to her," I said as Josh pocketed his phone.

"I will."

"Now," I insisted.

He frowned. "She's upset," he said carefully. "If I show up now, or the rest of the pack just happens to converge on her, she'll know it's you trying to smother her. Give her some time and space to process what happened."

"Then I'll go myself."

He stepped in front of me as I walked toward the front door, reaching out to grip my arm. I instinctively flinched from his touch, drawing a wide-eyed look of surprise and hurt from my brother, until he remembered why and took a step back. I took one more deep but ragged breath. He was right. Confronting Sky was only going to drive her further away. In my emotional state, it was also dangerous, but I couldn't just wait for her to confront me about what had happened. I'd nearly killed her. I needed her to understand that it was an accident. I couldn't force her to talk to me, but I couldn't just wait for her, either.

Without meeting Josh's gaze, I said in a strained voice, "Go to her when you think it is appropriate."

He nodded. "In the meantime, I'll keep working on a solution for you."

I was halfway to the door when he said with an accusatory tone, "It would help if you told me everything you know about the magic."

I hesitated in stride, but only for a moment before I walked out the door without answering him.

As I approached my BMW, I felt a sudden dizziness. I paused, steadying myself, but the moment quickly passed. As I reached for the car door, I saw a man in a cheap blue suit staring at me from the copse of trees across the street from Josh's driveway. Blood covered the chest of his white dress shirt, but he seemed unaffected as he stared at me.

"Are you in need of assistance?" I called to him.

He didn't answer.

First glancing about for signs of trouble, I walked toward the man, then stopped in the middle of the street as I recognized Caroline's father, Dennis.

Impossible.

84

"Was it worth it?" he asked from the side of his mouth, his dark glare unblinking.

Had Michaela lied? Had Dennis escaped? Both seemed unlikely. Something about him wasn't right. I sniffed the air, expecting the smells of cheap booze, cologne, and blood, but found only the scent of pine trees and recently cut grass. As I started toward him, he turned and walked into the copse. By the time I reached the trees, he'd disappeared from sight. I burrowed through the dense foliage trying to pick up his scent, which was inexplicably absent.

Had I imagined him? I slowly massaged the stress from my temples, then returned to my BMW.

I sighed in relief as I turned onto the winding, secondary road that led to the pack's retreat. We kept a number of homes in various locations, but the retreat was our primary gathering place. In times of trouble, it was our fortress.

After parking in one of my reserved spots in the garage—leaving my M6 next to my white Audi R8—I walked inside, intending to change and hit the basement gym when Sebastian called me into his office. Winter and Gavin were already there. I closed the door behind me and waited, ignoring his perpetual scowl.

After a nod from Sebastian, Gavin laid three photographs on the end of the Alpha's desk and gestured to them. His gray eyes watched me closely as I stepped forward to examine the images of three young women, each of them eerily similar to Sky in appearance, with oval faces, full lips, and wavy mahogany hair. All three of them were dead. Two of the photos I'd seen before, but the third was new. My jaw clenched as I resisted the urge to punch my fist through a wall. It wouldn't be the first or the last part of the house to suffer from all-too-common violent outbursts. A portion of the pack's annual budget was set aside for *unanticipated* structural repair and furniture replacement, but Sebastian's office was out-of-bounds. He'd never declared it so, but the pack had made it an unwritten rule.

"The Lost One has killed another one," Gavin said heavily, referring to the vampire Quell. "He's a threat. I think we should treat him as one."

Kill Quell, you mean. Since they'd first met, he and Sky had shared an inexplicable bond. When Ethos had staked Quell a few months ago, Sky had intervened, feeding him with her own blood to stop the reversion. It shouldn't have worked. For as far back as our histories remembered, were-animal blood had never been able to sustain vampires, but somehow she was an exception. I understood she felt a sense of obligation to him, but were-animals didn't feed vampires.

The thought of her presenting her neck to him sickened me. I did my best to swallow my anger. I'd come to the retreat to set my temper aside and regroup. The last thing I wanted was another of her problems to solve. Killing Quell would be the simplest solution, assuming Demetrius didn't take offense and start a war. It would be one more thing Sky would never forgive me for, one more time I'd been forced to save her.

"I agree," I said, surprising Gavin. I explained to Sebastian, "He is unable to control himself, and he's escalating." Murderers always followed a path of progression, their crimes growing bolder and more gruesome. Natural killers, vampires were amoral and driven by a powerful bloodlust, but Quell was unique. From the moment of his creation, he'd seen himself as being above feeding on humans, or perhaps he'd simply despised them. Instead of indulging his natural instincts, he'd chosen instead to feed from the Hidacus, a rare plant with a bloodlike juice—until Michaela had destroyed his plants and forbidden him from obtaining another.

While the plant had offered sustenance, it had only been through a sheer act of will that he'd suppressed his bloodlust.

But with his plants destroyed, he'd had no choice. When he fed at all, he'd often killed his victims—except when he'd fed from Sky. Somehow she'd remained immune to his blood-lust, for the moment at least. So of course she'd volunteered to become his food source, predictably to save others. After a warning from Sebastian, she'd tried to help Quell find a volunteer he could feed from without killing. So far, she was oh-and-three. Had Dr. Baker not intervened, there would've been a fourth victim.

He was no longer just Sky's problem. He was the pack's problem. We couldn't have a vampire feeding on one of our own, and we couldn't have him wantonly killing humans, either. Despite their cruelty, the vampires were aware of the risks of exposure and did their best to hide their activities. Most of the time they fed from the members of their garden —human volunteers who for some deranged reason gained satisfaction by submitting to the vampires. Other victims were often left dazed, confused, and weak from blood loss, but alive.

The only reason Quell could stop himself from killing Sky was that he claimed to love her. I stifled a chuckle. Vampires approximated love, a weak semblance of a remembered emotion that belonged to their former lives. At least his claims of love were protecting her, for the moment.

I scowled at the photos. Eventually, look-alikes weren't going to be enough for him.

"Why should we solve Demetrius's problems for him?" Winter said.

Gavin bristled. "If he can't control his own, it's up to us. It wouldn't be the first time we've put down a rabid vamp."

Sebastian sighed, then looked to me. "Sky needs to learn to clean up her own messes."

Over the last two years, Sky'd become a capable fighter, proving herself on the field of battle against Ethos, but she wasn't prepared for a one-on-one fight with an experienced vampire. As Demetrius had once pointed out, Quell's distaste for human blood had nothing to do with the idealization of humans. On the contrary, he despised them.

"He'll kill her," I stated.

Winter shrugged. "If we kill him for her, she'll just find another vamp, or maybe a stray fae, to take in."

"She won't learn anything if she's dead," Gavin added.

Sebastian considered for a moment before announcing his decision. "So far, each of us have survived our mistakes, but we've known many were-animals who haven't. We'll do what we can to help Sky, but this situation is her creation. Whether or not she survives to learn from the experience is up to her."

Until she realized that Quell was already dead, she was in danger. She was stubborn, and she believed that there was something redeemable in him. It wasn't in her nature to give up and turn her back on someone she cared about, even a vampire.

I suppressed a growl as I left Sebastian's office. I'd already failed Sky twice in less than twenty-four hours. While I couldn't directly ignore Sebastian's instruction and proactively kill Quell, I could put someone close enough to Sky to intervene when he finally broke and tried to kill her. If we killed him in the act, there would be no retaliation from the vamps.

I spent the next few hours working out my frustrations in the retreat's gym, interrupted more often than I cared to admit by glances at my phone. At this point, I'd settle for an angry text telling me Sky never wanted to speak to me again. Anything was better than silence. On several occasions, I found myself dialing her number and disconnected before the call went through.

Josh was right, I reminded myself. Pressing her would only make her angrier. Eventually she would respond to him, if not me. I just needed to be patient.

I alternated between cardio and weights until I exhausted myself. After a shower and a meal, I went to work reviewing the various intelligence reports that had come in over the last week. We kept tabs on a number of potential problems, most of which would likely never materialize, but it paid to be proactive. When that was done, I remotely logged in to my work files and buried myself in contracts until I finally tired enough to sleep.

CHAPTER 5

*F*riday morning, I woke at sunrise and checked my phone. Still no word from Sky. After another long workout, I showered and dressed for work. Once in my Audi, I started the engine, but remained parked in the garage as I stared at my phone in the dash holder. Calling her was as much of a mistake now as it had been the previous day. Even if she answered, I couldn't expect much; it was too soon for forgiveness, but she might at least hear my explanation. After several minutes of internal debate, it occurred to me that she might answer a number she didn't recognize as mine. I retrieved a burner phone from the glove box, the one designated for Webster Fields. She didn't answer that number, either.

Irritated, I returned the burner to the glove box. On my own phone, I opened the tracking app Stacy, my legal assistant and part-time hacker, had installed for me. A stealth version of the same program was running in the background on Sky's phone; as long as it was on and able to obtain a signal, I could track her location. After a moment, a street-level map appeared with a blinking blue icon. Not recognizing the neighborhood, I zoomed out until I realized that she wasn't in Chicago. She was in Virginia. My stomach balled in worry as I recognized the small, historic town. I'd driven through it a few months ago, just before Ethos had launched his attack on the pack; the Nunes family lived just a few miles outside of town—Sky's family, the one I'd warned to never contact her. I guess they didn't get the message.

Zooming back to the street view, I saw Sky was in a coffee shop, which gave me some relief. If she was with the family, she was at least in a public place, for the moment.

From my brief encounter with them, I doubted their intentions toward Sky were altruistic. They'd known who and what I was, and what I'd do to them if they contacted her. The question was, what did they want from her that they felt was worth my wrath and the enmity of the Midwest Pack? It could be the Aufero, but I doubted they'd risk contacting Sky without doing enough research to know that it was in Marcia's hands.

What else does she mean to them?

Closing my eyes, I relived every word, every visual detail from my previous visit with the family until I remembered Senna, the young woman who looked so much like Sky, sweeping a pair of old books from the family's dining room table. I'd barely had a chance to notice the runes and ancient symbols on the covers, but the titling had been unique. I'd seen those books recently, in a drawing on my brother's coffee table.

I called Josh, who waited several rings to answer. I was sure he did that to aggravate me.

"I haven't talked to her yet," he greeted with an annoyed tone.

"That drawing I saw on your coffee table. What is it?"

"What does that have to do with anything?"

"What. Is it?"

"I've been researching the Clostra."

I let my head slowly drift back against the seat. The

Clostra was a set of three powerful spell books. Together, they were one of the protected objects.

Josh continued, "The drawings are a representation of the covers, but I've no way to know if they're accurate."

I swallowed hard before answering. "Pretty damn close. I've seen two of them."

"Ethan, where—"

"There's no time to explain," I said, massaging the stress from my forehead with the fingers of one hand as I held the phone to my ear. "We're leaving for Virginia just as soon as O'Dowd can file a flight plan. I'll meet you at the airport."

"Okay," he said.

Aidan O'Dowd was a charter pilot the pack kept on retainer. We didn't use him often, but we paid him enough for him to be ready in an emergency. If he was out of the area on a charter, he had a network of pilots that could provide immediate and discreet service.

The moment I ended my call with Josh, I texted O'Dowd, "911."

Next I started to dial Sky's number, then hesitated. Once she realized I'd interfered with her efforts to find her family, I doubted she would heed my warning. More likely, I'd drive her toward them. Cursing, I pocketed my phone, then returned to the house.

I found Sebastian at the kitchen counter, eating the prior evening's leftovers. "The Nunes family have two of the Clostra books." He already knew about my previous visit. "They have Sky, as well."

He calmly wiped the corners of his mouth with a napkin, then dropped it onto his plate. "Is there a connection between the two?"

"Yes, but I don't know what. I've already put O'Dowd on alert. Josh will meet us at the airport."

He nodded, his expression determined. "Then let's go."

Within minutes, we were in a black SUV as I drove us

toward the small, private airport just outside of Chicago. Halfway there, I received a text message from O'Dowd.

"Fueling now. How many?"

I gave my phone to Sebastian, who answered. "Three en route. Returning with four, possibly more."

The drive to the airport was tense and quiet. I cursed myself for ever visiting the family in the first place. If I hadn't, they'd likely have never learned about Sky. I'd practically laid out a road map for them to find her.

We passed through security quickly, then drove to the hangar, where we found Josh and O'Dowd waiting for us outside his Gulfstream G650ER jet. At our approach, O'Dowd took a final drag from his cigarette, flicked the butt to the ground, and pressed it into the concrete with the toe of his shoe.

Josh greeted me with an inquisitive look while O'Dowd shook Sebastian's hand. A moment later, we were inside the jet.

By design, the Gulfstream sat nineteen passengers, but O'Dowd had modified his jet to suit the needs of his mostly corporate clientele. Several of the seats had been removed to accommodate a modest oak desk bolted to the floor at the center of the cabin, along with two chairs on each side. The remaining eight seats lined the sides of the cabin in pairs, with generous spacing.

"Ethan," Josh started as I buckled into a seat next to him.

"Not until we're airborne," I said brusquely.

He continued to stare at me until I finally turned to meet his gaze. "You're in my space," he said.

Admittedly, I was large enough that even with the generous spacing of the seats, the tip of my elbow just reached over the armrest of his chair—only just. He answered my scowl with a wan smile. With an exaggerated sigh, I drew my arm away from his chair and closer to my side.

Drawing my phone from my pocket, I checked the time: four o'clock. Updating Sky's location with the tracking app brought a snarl to my lips. She was on her way out of town, heading directly toward the Nunes family home, and we were about ninety minutes away from landing in Virginia, with a half hour drive ahead of us. Suppressing a growl, I called ahead to the airport to arrange for an SUV rental to be waiting for us on the tarmac when we disembarked from the jet.

Next I called my fixer, Marion James.

"Ethan," she answered with an amused tone. "I thought I might hear from you soon. It's been months. What can I do for you?"

"Living room," I said softly, aware of Josh listening next to me. "There are some holes to patch, as well."

"How many?"

"At least five."

Josh shook his head in disappointment. "Is that Marion?"

I scowled, gestured for him to back off. "Preferably today," I said to her. "Use your key."

"I'll take care of it," she promised, ending the call. By the time I returned from Virginia, Marion and her team would have patched and painted the holes in my walls and replaced my broken furniture with like or similar pieces. I didn't know exactly how Marion did her work, or anything else about her. She was a referral from Claudia.

Glancing out the window, I saw we were still rolling toward the runway. Impatient, I unhooked my belt and walked up to the flight cabin, where O'Dowd and his copilot were going through their preflight routine.

"Everything okay, Ethan?" he asked.

"Best possible time," I said.

He nodded. "Already on it."

Returning to my seat, I had nothing left to do but wait impatiently for takeoff while Josh absently bit at his nail beds next to me. A few minutes later, the jet was airborne. Once it leveled out, Josh and I joined Sebastian at the desk, sitting across from him.

"What does Sky have to do with the Clostra and why are we going to Virginia?" Josh asked.

Avoiding my brother's gaze, I started at the beginning. "Last year, she hired a private detective to determine if she had any family that she wasn't aware of." I hesitated for just a moment. "He located six family members—an uncle, three aunts, and two cousins—living together in a house in Virginia."

Josh smiled, surprised. "She never told me."

I glanced down at my hands clasped together on the desk as I said, "She doesn't know. Didn't," I corrected myself.

My brother's smile faded, his expression an accusation. "What did you do?"

"I intercepted the information. After interviewing the family, I determined that a relationship between them and Sky wasn't in her best interest."

He slowly shook his head as if he'd never believed I could be so callous. I met and held his gaze. *This is what caution looks like,* I thought, but kept the rebuke to myself.

"The detective?" Josh asked coldly.

The image of Dennis and his blood-soaked suit flashed through my mind before I answered. "Dropped his existing cases to work exclusively on my retainer."

"Of course." Josh leaned back in his chair, splayed out his legs, and folded his hands in his lap. His ocean-blue eyes glared at me. "So why are we racing to Virginia to intercept her? Are you planning on prying her from her family's arms?"

I sighed before continuing. "There are two possibilities. First, the family considers the Aufero to be their heritage. They believe Sky's mother stole it from them."

"Sky's mother was the orb's Moura," Josh insisted. "Unless Sky has an older sister, the Aufero is her responsibility."

"They were searching for the orb when I found them."

Josh's disappointment deepened. "They didn't know she existed until you told them, did they?"

"Josh," Sebastian said before I could answer, "allow Ethan to give his brief."

My brother gave a reluctant nod and I continued, addressing him directly. "I made it clear to them that she was under the protection of the Midwest Pack, and that they were never to make contact with her, or to respond to any contact made by her."

Josh shrugged. "She doesn't have it. Let them deal with Marcia." His expression quickly soured. "If they kill Sky, the next female in line becomes bonded to the Aufero." That bond gave the Moura influence over the orb, which would make it easier to capture.

I nodded.

Sebastian sat back in his chair, folding his arms across his chest. "What's the second possibility?"

"They have two thirds of the Clostra and they think Sky has the third," Josh answered for me, his gaze fixed on mine as he awaited the final confirmation.

I nodded once.

Sebastian asked, "How did they come by the Clostra?"

"I don't know," I said, "but while I was there, I saw two of the books in their possession. I didn't know what they were at the time."

"You're sure they only have two of the three books?"

"I only saw two. They could have the third book, which means they're after the Aufero, as well. Either way, we can't leave the books in their possession."

"The question is, how did the Nunes family become involved with two of the protected objects?" Sebastian turned to Josh. "Is it possible for one family to be the Moura for multiple objects?"

"No," he answered, adamant. "If they have part of the Clostra in their possession, it's been stolen."

"Can they use it?"

Josh's expression grew sober. "If they can read it, maybe. Are any of them witches?"

"I didn't feel magic from them, but there were plenty of charms around their home, and a handful of books on their bookshelves that are similar in appearance to what we have in the pack library."

"The books would be worth a great deal of money, especially with the complete set."

Sebastian was quiet for a moment. His lips bent into a determined frown. "Our objectives are to rescue Skylar and retrieve the Clostra. The family was previously warned. If they choose more than a token resistance, they will have to be eliminated."

I proceeded to describe first the surroundings of the family property, then the exterior of the house, including entry points, followed by a detailed description of the house's interior. "Our aim should be to overwhelm the family before they can put up a defense."

Josh looked doubtful. "If they know we're coming for Sky, they could take her somewhere else."

I debated whether to reveal that I was able to track the location of Sky's phone, then decided against it. "The family will bring her to their home."

"You seem pretty confident about their location," he said with a speculative look. "If we're wrong, we won't get a second chance to find Sky before they kill her."

"It's the logical place to start," I explained. "They'll want her in a secluded location. From my previous research of the family, they own only the one property." While Josh accepted my logic, he held on to his suspicions. If Sebastian cared how I obtained my information, he didn't ask.

The discussion came down to specifics. Once the plan was decided, there was nothing to do but wait.

Shortly after six o'clock, we landed at the small airport in Virginia. As O'Dowd steered the jet toward a hangar, I saw our rental SUV waiting. I drew out my phone and checked Sky's location; she was still at the Nuneses' family home. Josh watched me with a curious, suspicious look as I returned the phone to my pocket. Ignoring him, I cracked my knuckles in anticipation as the jet rolled to a stop next to the SUV.

The drive to the house was tense. I sped as much as I dared, but the pack had no influence with the local police. I couldn't risk a traffic stop. Assuming Sky was still alive, she couldn't afford the delay. I found myself repeatedly pulling back on the accelerator as I caught myself unconsciously racing toward her. The drive was agonizing. Regardless of her recklessness, if she were harmed, I'd have no one but myself to blame.

I watched the minutes tick by on the dashboard clock, the miles stack up on the odometer. By the time I saw the familiar white cottage in the distance, my fingers were white around the steering wheel and my jaw ached from clenching. I felt my brother's eyes on me as I leaned forward in the driver's seat, my eyes locked on our target.

The family lived in a pastoral neighborhood where the homes were separated from one another by several acres. As I approached the turnoff onto the Nuneses' property, it took every ounce of control I could muster not to race up the long dirt driveway. I wanted to reach Sky as quickly as possible, but rushing up to the house was sure to draw the family's attention. A stealthy approach had its risks as well, but Sky's best chance of survival depended on an element of surprise.

The tension in the cab thickened as I eased the SUV up the driveway, each of us watching the house closely for any revelation of exposure. Each of us prepared for the fight to come; Sebastian radiated a cool, unrelenting power, while Josh's magic filled the cab with an electric charge.

I rolled the SUV to a stop behind a blue compact rental car. There were two cars next to it. From one, I smelled the oily heat of the engine still cooling, which gave me hope that we weren't too late. Three of the SUV's doors opened almost simultaneously as we emerged from the vehicle. Without a word, we followed the plan. Sebastian walked around the side of the house toward the back while I climbed the steps of the porch. Behind me, I felt the rise of Josh's magic. Glancing over my shoulder, I saw him standing at the bottom of the steps, hands open and slightly held out from his hips and his eyes black as he called forth powerful magic.

I scowled as the screen door creaked, but the front door wasn't locked. It opened easily and I strode inside, my eyes darting about. The house was exactly as I remembered, a cluttered space spotted with brass lamps and small talismans. Vintage art hung on pastel walls. Sky's scent intermingled with the scents of the family that permeated every object and every piece of furniture, making it difficult to track.

I glanced into the kitchen and found it empty, which left three closed doors in the hall.

Sky's primal scream cut through the quiet. From behind the door at the end of the hall, I heard voices chanting. As I raced toward the door, Josh's magic flowed through the house, filling the empty spaces with his power.

The hall light flickered as I kicked in the door with the heel of my boot and stepped into the room to find Sky struggling supine on a bed, her wrists and ankles handcuffed to the bedposts. The stunned family rose from the floor where

Josh's magic had dumped them. I recognized Sky's uncle William, her aunts Caitlyn, Beth, and Madalena, and cousins Suri and Senna. All of them appeared shocked and defeated, except for Senna, who eyed me with an intense hatred.

Assured that they had no intention of putting up a fight, I turned back to Sky. Her forearms were slashed crosswise, seeping blood. Her heart beat furiously, but she was safe, impatiently waiting for me to release her. Judging by the crystals that were placed at her head, sides, and feet, we'd stopped the family in the midst of a ritual that seemed surprisingly similar to the one Josh had used nearly two years ago to exorcise Maya. They must've figured if Sky wouldn't help them, Maya would. Either they didn't know the separation would kill Sky, or they didn't care.

I leaned over the bed and swatted the crystals away from her. Shoving William aside, I knelt at the bed next to Sky and examined the handcuffs, careful not to touch them. Silver. Somehow, she was uniquely immune to the burning effect of silver, but I wasn't.

"Unlock her," I commanded. When no one moved to obey, I shouted, "Now!" I rose, glaring at each of the family members in turn as they steadfastly refused my order. My gaze locked on William's as I gripped the nearest bedpost with both hands. The wood cracked and split before the post snapped off, and Sky pulled the cuff free. They watched as I snapped each post until she was able to sit up, frantically trying to break the cuffs that bound her ankles.

William barely held on to his bravado as I walked up to him, glaring down into his face, and growled. If I had to make a bloody example of him, I'd happily do so. "Unlock the damn handcuffs."

I could smell the fear rising from him, but he was in control of himself, calculating. He only needed a moment to realize that even if they could somehow contain me, Josh was more powerful than all of them put together. His jaw twitched, then he cautiously drew a key from his pocket and reached over the bed to unlock the cuffs, ignoring Sky's murderous glare. After the last cuff fell from her wrist, I growled to back him off, then knelt and gently lifted Sky's arm to examine the cuts, which should've healed shut within seconds of the injury. A thick liquid was smeared over the wounds, seemingly interfering with her natural healing ability. When she winced at the pressure from my hand, I remembered just how dangerous my touch was and immediately released her.

"Sorry," I said.

Josh entered the room, followed by Sebastian. While he took in the scene, staring the family down, I picked up the books from the nightstand and handed them to him.

"Where is the other one?" Sebastian asked the family.

Confused and angry, Sky scooted across the bed. As she did, her shirt shifted and I saw at least half a dozen small burn marks on her lower torso, the kind of marks left by Taser weapons. I barely suppressed a violent rage. Once on her feet, she rubbed at her raw wrists. Her attention was fixed on Sebastian as he towered over William.

"*Where* is it?"

William's silent defiance lasted only for a moment before he submissively lowered his gaze. "All three were stolen from us by her mother," he said, throwing a disgusted glance toward Sky. "We only managed to recover those two."

"When were they taken?"

He took a quick breath. His lips spread into a plastic smile as he tried to ease into the folksy comfort of his well-practiced charm, but he couldn't hide the rapid pace of his heartbeat, or his shallow breathing. "Thirty years ago?"

"And you are just now noticing?"

"Not at all. We've been looking for them all this time."

"Why?" Sebastian demanded, his suspicion piqued. "Can you use them?"

101

Senna shifted slightly, her defiant stare suddenly softening as she self-consciously eased herself behind William.

"No," he answered.

Sebastian detected the lie as easily as I did, but took a moment to scrutinize William, agitating him before pointing it out. "Lie."

"We know someone that can," he admitted reluctantly, then folded his arms over his chest in a futile act of defiance. In a childish show of solidarity, the rest of his family mimicked the gesture. Each one of them pressed their lips together, communicating they had no intention of answering another question.

I know how to change their minds. I growled, drawing an anxious glance from Aunt Caitlyn.

Sebastian scrutinized the family, then spoke to Senna directly. "We are taking these"—he gestured with the books held together in one hand—"because you shouldn't have them and aren't in a position to keep them safe. However, if it is found out that you can read them, your family will not be able to protect you. You are welcome to call me." He drew a card from his pocket, pinched between two fingers, and held it out to her. Her arms tightened around her chest as she stubbornly refused to look at the card.

"Take it," he said. "I can assure you that one day you will need it."

Reluctantly, she snapped it from his grip. "Thank you," she muttered.

Sebastian nodded, then walked out of the room. Sky followed, then Josh, leaving me alone with the family. I glanced down at the broken bed, the posts and cuffs laid in the center, then turned a baleful glare to William.

"I warned you, and then I left you alone. You're pack business now. Contact Skylar again, or interfere with the Clostra in any way"—I met every one of their bitter gazes—"and I'll kill you all."

I strode out of the room and caught up to the others just as they approached the vehicles. Sky fished in her pocket while Sebastian had his phone to his ear.

"Cole," he said, then gave the address of the cottage and a description of Senna to the Alpha of the East Coast Pack. "Keep an eye on the girl, but let me know if the family does anything out of the ordinary."

Sky's visage was a dark cloud of anger, relief, and embarrassment as she unlocked the doors of her rental car with the key fob. I gently took the keys from her hand and gestured toward the backseat. She bit back a retort but obeyed. While Josh and Sebastian returned to the SUV, I crammed myself into the driver's seat of the compact rental. Even after pushing the seat as far back as it could go, I was still hunched over the steering wheel.

I glanced over my shoulder toward the house, then followed the SUV back to the road.

Sky fumed in the backseat, arms folded over her chest. She caught my gaze in the mirror, then quickly turned away, her posture stiffening as if she expected me to scold her. She'd spent her entire life with only an adopted mother for family. When she'd finally discovered she had a biological family—aunts, cousins, an uncle—they'd tried to kill her. As much as I empathized with her, I couldn't help being angry that she'd once again put herself and the pack in danger. In her need for a familial connection, she had run off without telling anyone, without researching who she was dealing with, and put herself in the hands of strangers. If we'd arrived a few minutes later, the family would've exorcised Maya and killed Sky in the process.

And I led them to her.

There was plenty of blame to go around. I focused my eyes on the SUV ahead of us, trying to calm my anger while we drove toward the airport where O'Dowd's Gulfstream was waiting.

. . .

A short time later, Sky watched with a bemused expression as we drove through the gate of the private airport and parked on the tarmac outside the waiting jet. I gave the concierge the keys to both vehicles, along with a sizable tip to deliver Sky's compact to the appropriate rental office, then motioned for her to follow me up the steps to the jet.

Once inside, she took a moment to absorb the unexpected surroundings, then chose an inconspicuous seat at the back of the cabin and proceeded to distract herself with the activities outside the window.

Sebastian sat at the desk, sliding the books to Josh, who sat across from him. He eagerly scooped up one of the books and began flipping through the pages. Ignoring his perplexed look for the moment, I retrieved the first aid kit from the flight attendant's cabin and knelt in front of Sky.

"Let me look at your arms," I said as softly as I could manage.

The flight attendant appeared to help, but I brushed his offer aside. Sky showed me her forearms with the enthusiasm of a rebuked child. The cuts were still seeping blood, which led me to wonder what the substance was that kept the wounds from healing. Fearful that I might once again hurt her with the dark elf magic, I considered calling the attendant back, then thought better of it. I took a slow, careful breath to check my temper, then reached out to gently brace one of her arms.

The soft, cool feel of her skin against mine helped to calm me. Still, I avoided her gaze as I picked the antiseptic and gauze from the kit and began to gently wipe away every trace of the sticky substance.

"I just wanted to meet my family," she whispered in an apologetic rush. "I didn't expect—"

"Please," I said, glancing at her as I carefully bandaged her wounds, "don't talk."

"If I thought this would happen, I never—"

"What part of that request are you having difficulty understanding?" I snapped. Fearing the sudden rise of my anger, I quickly released her arm and walked to the other side of the plane to get myself under control. After a long moment of pacing and chastising myself, I managed to calm myself enough to return to Sky and finish wrapping her wounds. Without meeting her gaze, I quickly gathered up the first aid kit, handed it to the flight attendant, then locked myself in the bathroom to catch my breath.

The fear of what I could do to her—to anyone—when I was out of control was unbearable.

Several minutes passed before I could bring my heart rate down to something resembling normal. As long as I avoided contact with her for the rest of the flight, I was fine. *Most likely she'll stay out of the way,* I assured myself, then opened the door to find her standing there, her bandaged arms folded over her chest, waiting for me with an indignant look. Startled, I took one step back and nearly fell over the toilet.

"Do you think," she started, "that if I suspected anything like this was going to happen, I would have come here?"

The anger came rushing back. *You didn't even consider that you were walking into a trap. You just walked right into it without a second thought.* My mouth clamped shut. I stepped around her. As I walked back into the main cabin, I could feel her following close on my heels.

Unable to contain myself, I snapped over my shoulder, "I don't care to try to figure out what actually goes on in your head. I do believe there are children far more responsible and equipped with better survival skills than you. Sky, your —" I held back, pressing my lips together until they hurt. Sebastian and Josh had stopped their conversation. They had no choice, as I'd practically led her to them. With nothing else to say, I shook my head and took a seat at the desk next to Sebastian.

The three of us sat in sullen silence, sharing our displeasure with her until she took the hint and retreated to her seat. The flight attendant was quick to take her order: water, a turkey sandwich, and chips.

How can she eat after what she's just been through?

"Jack and coke," Sebastian ordered.

Josh nodded. "Make it three."

After our second round of drinks, we turned our attention to the books. The first was a plain earth tone, with simple but distinct black lettering on the cover, surrounded by a handful of esoteric symbols. The second book was midnight blue, with similar lettering but in gold, and a different array of symbols. Both books smelled of blood, sage, metal, and sulfur—the scents of witchcraft accumulated over a long history of use.

Josh pushed the first book to me. Handling it carefully, I opened it to a blank page. The next was blank as well, and the next. Flipping through the book, I found all the pages were empty.

He frowned as he tapped the second book with a finger. "The same," he said softly.

"They're not the Clostra?" I asked.

"If anything, this convinces me that they are. They're obviously protected. By what means, I don't know, but I suspect the Moura responsible for the books can read them."

Sebastian frowned. "We have to assume that the Moura is dead."

I leaned back into my chair as I pushed the book toward Josh. "Then they're useless."

"Not necessarily," he answered, though his expression suggested little confidence that he could crack the magic that concealed the pages.

I nodded. If it could be done, he would find a way. "If

you're going to try to crack them, which book should you start with? I assume each one has a different focus."

Josh shook his head. "According to my research, the books read as one, line by line, maybe even paragraph by paragraph—I'm not sure exactly how, but they work together. Without all three books, the spells inside will be useless."

"Maybe the text appears once all three books are together," I suggested.

"It's possible." He considered a moment before continuing, "The family must've known we'd come after Sky sooner rather than later. I don't think they'd risk the pack's wrath without a plan for how to use them."

"Senna," I said, remembering how she'd tried to make herself invisible when Sebastian had asked if they could read the books. "The young girl."

Sebastian said, "If Senna can read the Clostra, then perhaps Skylar can as well."

"It's worth a try," Josh agreed, looking to me.

I nodded once.

He caught Sky's attention just after she'd taken a bite of her sandwich. Chewing quickly, she wasted no time joining us. *The curiosity must've been killing her,* I thought, suppressing a smile as she sat next to him.

He placed both of the books in front of her, instructing, "Open them both to the same page."

"Any page?" she asked, accepting his nod with a skeptical look.

After glancing around for a napkin, she chose to wipe her fingers on her jeans, then opened the first book near the middle. I saw Josh wince as she pressed down on the spine, flattening the book, then turned her attention to the second book. She flipped through the pages until she stopped and looked up at him expectantly—as if awaiting further instruction.

I rose half out of my seat as the three of us leaned over the books. The pages in both were blank. She watched our confused excitement with a puzzled expression.

Josh gestured to the books. "Read the first two lines of each page."

She frowned at the pages. "I don't understand it."

"It doesn't matter," I encouraged her. "Just read."

Starting with the first book, she traced an invisible line across the page as she fumbled through the words only she could see. I recognized the language was Latin, but my vocabulary was limited—not enough to provide a useful translation. Josh, however, knew the language well. When she transitioned to the second book, the language was the same.

Once finished, she looked up, pleased and surprised by our obvious enthusiasm.

"Read the next two," Josh instructed.

She did.

"Absolutely amazing." He grinned.

I scowled when he inexplicably kissed her on the cheek.

"Yeah, yeah. I'm great," she blushed. "The best there ever was. The cat's meow. Now tell me what's going on."

When Josh gingerly took the open books from her, her eyes widened at the pages as if they had suddenly changed.

"They're protected," he explained, "and there doesn't seem to be a rhyme or reason about who can and cannot read them."

It was a smart lie. Until we learned what her connection to the Clostra was, there was no reason to feed her speculation.

"That will be all, Sky," Sebastian coolly dismissed her.

She bristled at his tone. "Well, since so few people are capable of reading the damn things, it seems like you would be a little nicer to the one person you know who will be willing to do so. I can almost guarantee Senna will not be as easily coerced into helping you. Either you all tell me what this is and what's going on, or I will wish you good luck with your adventure finding someone else, because I will not do anything with these books until I know what is going on."

Apparently she'd noticed Senna's reaction, as well.

Sebastian smiled broadly, a rare and dangerous sight. "I strongly advise you against pulling this card again. First, so that we understand each other, I am giving you this information because I don't see any harm in you knowing it. Second, if I were you, I wouldn't underestimate Senna's willingness to help us, which kind of makes you superfluous. Am I correct?"

Her confidence faded. "What are the books?" Sky asked, deflecting his challenge.

He answered coolly, "Two-thirds of the Clostra."

Sky blinked. "Someone else is a Moura Encantada in my family?"

"No, the best I can tell, your family took it. I am not sure what their goal was in doing so. I assume to sell it. They can easily command a high seven figures."

"And the Moura for it?"

"I am sure she is dead."

"You don't know that," Sky insisted. "I haven't had the Aufero in my possession, ever, and I am still alive."

I growled, "For now."

"Great." She glared at me. "Just what this story needed—a narrator." She turned back to Sebastian. "How did my family get it?"

"That is a great question," he answered. "I wish I knew the answer. Did your family say anything to you?"

Sky thought a moment, then shook her head. "They just wanted to know where my mother put the third book."

Sebastian considered for a moment. "I suspect she took it because she knew that no one should have all three in their possession, even a Moura."

"What's in them that is so important?"

Josh and I answered together, "Spells," then looked to each other in mild surprise.

Josh elaborated for her. "As long as I can remember, there have been rumors about these objects being so strong they could do things that sheer magic couldn't. We always wrote them off as fables. But once we discovered the Gem of Levage existed, and then the Aufero, we started to speculate that maybe the Clostra existed as well. The idea that there were books of magic so powerful that they were guarded by a ward that would only allow a select few to read them brought out our curiosity. When the rumors persisted along with those stating that Marcia was trying to find them, we made it our goal to try to find them first. Apparently, the spells are very unique and dangerous, unlike anything witches, fae, or elves can do."

I added, "The one that concerns us is one that can 'lay the beast to rest.'" The spell had long been rumored to exist, but no explanation was known. We'd have to translate the Clostra to know for certain.

"Is that what this is about?" Sky asked, her heart beating rapidly with excitement. "You want to use it to cure us?"

My lips twisted into a scowl. After two years with the pack, she still believed that she was somehow separate from her wolf, that she could live without it. She wanted to live without it.

Sebastian responded before I could, lecturing her. "The beast will be laid to rest along with the person who shares its body. If the rumors are correct, the spell exists to kill us all."

After we returned to Chicago, I picked up my Audi from the retreat and gave Sky a ride home, occupying the space between us with my favorite jazz album played at a high enough volume to discourage questions. She already knew more about the Clostra than I was comfortable with, and I preferred not to lie any more than necessary if she pressed the issue.

Now that I finally had time alone with her, I wanted to explain that stopping her heart had been an accident, but I couldn't find a way to apologize that wouldn't lead to more questions I couldn't answer.

When I finally turned onto her street, I felt a wash of relief until I noticed Quell impatiently waiting at her door. She noted his presence with a look of concern, triggering a fresh wave of anger in me. *Is she ever going to learn?*

"Your vampire is here," I remarked dryly as I parked in the driveway.

She gave me an annoyed look that hardened when I got out of the Audi to follow her inside; I had no intention of leaving her alone with a vampire.

As we approached Quell, I noted the orange quarter ring in the corner of his right pupil, a terait, the telltale sign of bloodlust. At times, Sky's green eyes were marred with the same defect. She was an innate were-animal, but while in the womb her mother had been bitten by an insane vampire that had tried to turn both mother and unborn child. Were-animals couldn't be turned. The process should've killed her. It would have, if not for Maya. While Sky's wolf remained her dominant supernatural trait, she did have the misfortune of inheriting the vampire's bloodlust, but to a minor extent. It didn't drive her to kill, and an occasional medium-rare steak appeased both the bloodlust and her wolf.

Quell's lifeless black eyes shifted to the bandages on her forearms, then turned on me. His eyes narrowed in anger. His brow furrowed. I realized his uninvited presence might prove therapeutic. He was on edge, caught in his bloodlust. With a little prodding, he might lose his temper and attack me, providing all the justification I needed to kill him. But I had to be careful. I couldn't overtly goad him, not in Sky's presence.

She acknowledged him with a slight nod as she walked past him to the door, then stopped. Her lips spread into a smirk as she defiantly waited for me. It was always a game to her, to test my magical abilities. This time, I was too annoyed to bother playing. Beside her, I whispered the key word that allowed us to pass through the protective ward, then followed her inside. Quell entered close behind me, following Sky into the living room. She dropped onto the couch with a sigh while he positioned himself between us.

His body tensed as his gaze shifted from her bandages to me, glaring. "Did you do that to her?"

I leaned back against the wall, folding my arms over my chest.

"I asked a question," he spat, gesturing angrily toward Sky. "Did you do that to her?"

I stared back at him. When his lips curled back, exposing his fangs, I pushed off from the wall into a defensive posture. *Too easy,* I thought, waiting for him to strike first.

Sky's tone was bored as she explained from the couch, "He had nothing to do with my injuries."

His glare lingered before he walked to Sky and knelt in front of her. "Are you okay?" he asked softly.

She nodded.

"Who did this to you?"

"I don't want to talk about it now. Maybe later." Her tone softened, suddenly concerned. "Have you fed?"

I rolled my eyes in disgust.

"I can wait," he said bitterly, shooting me another dark glance from over his shoulder.

"No," I said, stepping into the room. "She'll do it now. The responsibility she takes on doesn't stop because she had a rough day. Isn't that right, Skylar?"

Her eyes locked stubbornly with mine as she pulled at her

shirt collar, exposing her bare neck to him as though she were a servant, a member of the Seethe's garden.

"Go ahead," she said to Quell.

He leaned toward her hungrily, then hesitated, throwing a hostile glance in my direction. "Are you sure?"

She nodded slightly, pulling her collar farther.

My body tensed as he bit into her, eliciting a sharp hiss of pain. Her defiant gaze remained fixed on mine as her neck slowly rocked in tune with the sucking sounds of his feeding. I wouldn't give her the satisfaction of my anger, barely constrained, but I made no attempt to hide my contempt as I stared her down, daring her to look away. As Quell drank, she seductively slid her hand down the nape of his neck and pressed him closer. He responded greedily.

Anger spread through my body like a wildfire, but I somehow held my ground. Observing my discomfort, her lips slowly twisted into a vindictive smile. Eventually, the tension became too much. Making a show of my disgust, I pushed myself from the wall and walked into the kitchen. My eyes darted about for something to destroy, but I refused to give her the satisfaction. I closed my eyes, but the eager sucking sounds of him drinking from her haunted me.

After what seemed like an eternity, the feeding finally ceased. Gathering myself, I emerged from the kitchen just as Quell walked out the door, closing it behind him without meeting my gaze.

I frowned at Sky as she lounged exhausted on the couch. "You do manage to get yourself in some very compromising situations, don't you? Michaela's favorite is enthralled with you—how cute. It will be interesting to see how this will play out."

"It can't be any more interesting than you sleeping with Chris when she was obviously Demetrius's mistress," she shot back. "I can assure you, it was quite interesting watching that train wreck."

I slid my hands into my pockets as I took a calming breath.

"Are we going to talk about the elephant in the room?" she asked.

I smiled. "Should we talk about how you held on to dark magic? Or discuss how you were attempting to run away to be with your family—or anywhere just to get away from us? Perhaps the topic should be Quell and how your actions will adversely affect this pack when Michaela decides to take notice. Yes, let's discuss the elephant in the room."

She blanched, then went on the offensive. "No, I would rather discuss what you did to me the other day. What the hell *are* you?"

I didn't want to lie, but that wasn't a subject I could discuss with her or anyone without putting them in danger. "Do you really think your panic attack is discussion-worthy?"

She gaped at me. "Do you really believe I don't know the difference between a panic attack and what happened to me at your house?"

I frowned, disgusted by my use of such an obvious misdirection. It worked, for the moment, but the shelf life was limited. I said on my way to the door, "I don't care to try to figure out what goes on in your mind. It is simpler that way."

"I don't trust you," she barked, giving me pause.

Good. Trust will get you killed if you're not careful. I held her gaze for a long moment before answering. "I don't trust you, either," I said, then left.

CHAPTER 6

For the next few days, Sky seemed determined to avoid me, which suited me. I'd had enough of being angry at her. The dark elf magic had me on edge, and her recent actions weren't making it easier to control my temper. Until I got that magic under control, I was a danger to her, to Josh, to everyone around me. Finding a way to rid myself of the magic, or at least get it under control, was my priority.

With any luck, the Clostra might provide an option, but that would take some time to translate, and without the third book, any spell we discovered would remain useless. My only other option was the Aufero. I'd have to find a way to steal it from Marcia that wouldn't bring the wrath of the Creed down on the pack.

First, I'd have to find it. Marcia would never keep such a powerful object in an obvious location, such as her home, but she also wouldn't entrust it to one of the other members of the Creed. She'd keep it close, and there was a good chance she'd use magic to hide it.

As a start, I had Stacy research any properties Marcia owned. As it turned out, she was an ambitious real estate investor. Two of the properties were currently unoccupied, which made them possible hiding places, except that they were located on the other side of town from Marcia, too far out of her reach to hide the Aufero. The other three properties were occupied by tenants, as confirmed by a check of the utility usage. She wouldn't leave the Aufero in a location where it might be found, and where she couldn't guarantee immediate access to it. The only other options were the two magic shops she owned and operated. She was actively involved with both of them, seemingly in equal measure.

While the shops mostly served the non-witch community with a variety of New Age ridiculousness, they did provide some under-the-counter supplies to actual witches, which meant there was a fair chance I'd be recognized if I walked in to take a look around. Word of my interest would reach Marcia, and it wouldn't take her long to figure out what I was searching for. She'd move the Aufero to a place I'd likely never find.

Breaking in after-hours was an option, but there was a risk of getting caught. Before I went to that extreme, I preferred some stealthy reconnaissance. For that, I needed someone the witches wouldn't connect to me, someone I could trust to keep quiet.

"I'm not a fan of this plan," Artemis complained from the passenger seat of my parked Audi, her cognac eyes fixed on the magic shop across the street. Her copper hair, with symmetrical layers of loose waves, framed her fair, heart-shaped face.

I sighed, exasperated. "What part?"

"The part where I'm out in public with the Beta of the Midwest Pack," she answered matter-of-factly, "where everyone can see me."

As a clever purveyor of information, she'd spent a great deal of effort cultivating a reputation for discretion and impartiality. An orphaned were-fox, she'd learned her trade on the street from a young age, gathering whispers and selling them to the various supernatural factions; a dangerous game, but so far she'd managed to walk a delicate line. She'd proven her value to me on numerous occasions. I'd no intention of creating a problem for her.

I gestured to the neighborhood, which was quiet except for the light vehicle traffic. "There's no one here."

Her eyes narrowed as she leaned forward to glance up one side of the street, then the other. "Someone's always watching," she whispered.

"Then the sooner you get this done, the sooner you can go home. You know what you're looking for?"

A sly smile twisted her lips. "Secrets."

"Powerful magic," I clarified. If the Aufero was hidden in the store, it would be protected by magic significantly stronger than the usual weak charms found on the shelves. While Artemis didn't have my ability to sense magic, she was an astute observer. If Marcia was hiding anything supernatural in her shop, I was confident that Artemis would pick up on the deception.

She opened the passenger door and had one leg out before she turned back to me, as if something had just occurred to her. "If I'm recognized, it will appear strange if I don't make a purchase." She blinked at me, waiting with a determined innocence as I sighed and fished out my wallet. The only cash I had was a pair of hundred-dollar bills, one of which I owed her when she completed the job. She wet her lips as I handed her the other bill.

"I want change," I insisted.

She tapped a knuckle to her forehead as if she were doffing a cap, then slipped on a pair of sunglasses and stepped out of the Audi. I watched as she gracefully strolled across the street and disappeared into the magic shop. From my vantage point parked in an alley across the street, I had an easy view of the shop, though the tinted windows prevented me from seeing inside. I kept the car running, assuming she would return in a few minutes.

After what seemed like an hour, I glanced at the time on my phone. Twenty minutes had passed. *What the hell is she doing?* For a moment, I wondered if she'd been discovered, but that didn't make sense; even if someone there recognized her, there was no reason to link her to me.

A sudden dizziness washed over me. I cradled my forehead in my palms, focusing on the pressure until the sensation passed a few seconds later. When I looked up, I was startled to see Dennis standing in front of my Audi. He wore the same cheap blue suit I'd seen before, but instead of a bloody shirt, four deep slashes as if from claws cut across his face, beginning at his forehead and ending below his cheek. The wounds looked fresh, seeping blood.

Beneath the gore, he glared down at me in furious judgment. "Why?" he demanded.

Aside from the fact that he was dead, something about Dennis wasn't right. I sniffed the air. Just as before, there was no scent to accompany him, not even the distinctive metallic smell of blood.

His lips contorted into a snarl. "You can't just do what you want and get away with it."

Seeing the pistol rising in his hand, I put the car in gear and stabbed the gas pedal with my foot. The Audi leapt toward Dennis. I braced myself for the impact, expecting him to roll up the front end and crash into the windshield. Instead, he seemed to disappear. The Audi jumped into the street and was struck by an SUV as it tried to veer away.

Somehow, I'd missed him at point-blank range. *Impossible!*

Anticipating gunshots, I threw open the Audi door and leapt out, still reeling from the shock of the collision. People were emerging from the local businesses and cars were already backing up, but there was no sign of my dead detective. Had I run him over after all? Where he'd stood in the entrance to the alley, the concrete appeared impossibly free of bloodstains. I grimaced; even if he'd escaped the collision, which I doubted, his wounds should've left an obvious blood trail.

I turned my attention to the SUV, where a woman emerged in a panicked rush from the driver's seat. "You flew right in front of me. What were you thinking?"

I calmly drew a card from my wallet and handed it to her. "I accept fault," I said, putting her at ease. The damage to her SUV was minor, but the front corner of the Audi was completely smashed. It was going to cost a fortune to fix. "You should go to the hospital and get checked out. I insist. I will cover all of your expenses."

She glanced between the card and me. She hadn't been in an accident before and didn't know what to do, I guessed.

"Do you have your phone?" I asked. When she showed me, I explained, "You should take pictures of the damage to both vehicles, and be sure you get one that includes my license plate."

She blinked at me, then set about following my instructions while the light traffic flowed around us. Once she was satisfied, I took her contact information before she drove away.

Frowning at the crushed front tire, I called roadside assistance for a tow. As I pocketed my phone, I watched Artemis stroll out of the magic shop with two seemingly full shopping bags in her hands. Only when she stopped in front of me did she acknowledge the accident with a sardonic frown. "I thought you wanted to be discreet."

My gaze drifted to the bags in her hands. An obnoxious potpourri of perfume and floral fragrances wafted from one of them.

"I assure you that every one of these items was entirely necessary to avoid detection," she whispered. "Especially the bath fizz thingies."

I sighed, then asked, "Did you find anything?"

Her gaze flicked over the crowd before she answered in a low voice, "Nope. I gotta go. Pay me later." She saw a cab approaching and waved it down.

There was still the other magic shop to check out, but that would have to wait for another day, most likely without Artemis.

"Do you have enough?" I asked.

"I have the change," she winked at me, then slid into the back of the cab. The driver received her instructions, then drove away.

Waiting for the tow truck gave me plenty of time to scowl at the gawkers and wonder what I'd witnessed. I'd never actually seen Dennis's body. Michaela had informed me, gloating, that she'd killed him, and I'd no reason to doubt her. Regardless of his skill as a detective, he'd have been no match for her, and Michaela wasn't one to show mercy. *Dennis is dead,* I told myself, and I didn't believe in ghosts, which left only magic. As far as I knew, it wasn't possible to raise the dead, but I wasn't fool enough to believe I knew all of the types of magic that were out there.

Hours later, I parked a powder blue Prius in my driveway. The mechanic had offered me the loaner. The Prius was all they had available and I wasn't in the mood to wait for a cab. I'd have Markos return the loaner for me in the morning.

Once inside my house, I slipped off my shoes, poured myself a Scotch, then sank onto the couch, my mind still fixated on Dennis. I couldn't explain why he seemed devoid of any scent, and there was something about his wounds that I couldn't quite put a finger on. I started to call Josh, then thought better of it. Once he learned that I'd gotten the detective killed by Michaela, I'd never hear the end of it—not that I didn't deserve the rebuke, but I needed his full attention on the Clostra.

When it came to Dennis, there was only one person I could think of who might provide answers. I found the napkin with Caroline's number in my jacket, retrieved a burner phone from my desk, and arranged for us to meet for a drink that evening.

I chose a popular nightspot that appealed to the burgeoning tech crowd. No one knew me there, a precaution against the inevitable moment when David would simply cease to exist. Should Caroline come looking for him, I didn't want to leave her with any avenues into my world. At the center of the open floor, a gas fire burned hot in an oversized brick hearth. Small round wooden tables dotted the floor, flanked by plush, high-backed armchairs and cushioned benches. I arrived early to find Caroline was already seated next to the hearth. Her raven hair was straight, and she'd changed her black jeans and jacket for a clingy black sheath dress that fell mid-thigh, complimented by elegant blood-red heels. The pendant with the black crystal graced her cleavage. She'd dressed to be noticed, I realized, a temptation I'd have to avoid.

She seemed preoccupied, withdrawn into anger, even. When she noticed me standing in the doorway, her expression softened, almost as if she'd flipped a switch. She smiled as she gave a slight wave to catch my attention.

As I approached the table, she rose and offered me her hand. We exchanged some minor pleasantries, sat, then ordered drinks.

"Thank you for meeting me," I began, having already mapped out the rest of our conversation. I'd allowed for some minor variance, but I wouldn't allow the conversation to drift any more than necessary to give it the semblance of spontaneity.

Smiling, she folded her arms over the table in front of her and leaned forward slightly, displaying her interest. Her deep russet eyes blinked. "I admit I was surprised to hear from you," she said. "I assume you learned something when you were asking around about my father?"

Manipulating Dennis's daughter didn't give me pleasure, but I was out of options. First I needed to gain her trust. I leaned toward her, mirroring her movement. My gaze fixed on hers. "I'm part of a group of enthusiasts who enjoy investigating unsolved crimes," I explained. From my previous research, I knew of her own interest and involvement with similar groups.

Her eyebrows rose skeptically, but her curiosity was aroused. "You didn't mention that before."

"Because we have active law enforcement members, my group prefers to operate under the radar. We work strictly pro bono. Of course, we cannot promise results, but when we accept a case, we commit all of our resources to it. With your permission, I'd like to present your father's case to the group."

"As it happens, I'm pretty active in the cold-case community online. Maybe I've heard of your group. What's it called?"

The best lies were built on brittle details. There was no point giving her a name she wouldn't find through a Web search, which she would do the moment she returned to her hotel. "As I said, we prefer to keep a low profile. I'll understand if you're not interested in our help, but we could be a resource to you."

She leaned back, folding her hands in her lap as she made a show of consideration, but I knew by the spike in her heart rate that she was going to accept. "I guess I've got nothing to lose, right? The police have already given up. Again." She

122

explained quickly, "The only hope they had for a lead was the contents of my father's office, but the landlord claims that the contents were stolen. Disappeared, as if by magic, he claims." She laughed. "More likely it's buried in the municipal dump, or he sold it to some scavenger."

I nodded, showing a proper look of concern. "I appreciate your trust. I know these are trying times for you."

She brushed off the courtesy. "What do you need from me?"

"Is there anything you can share with me about your father that you haven't already told me?"

"Like what?"

"Did he have any social or activity groups? Anything unusual or fringe? Something that might seem easy to dismiss in other circumstances?"

She shook her head.

"Any unusual beliefs?"

"Like what?" Her gaze darkened as she said, "You mean, did he believe in werewolves?"

I clamped my jaw shut and barely stopped my eyebrows from rising reflexively, then wondered at her smug smile. Had I betrayed my surprise in some other fashion? It was an offhand comment that was meaningless to anyone but me, anyone who wasn't a werewolf. *Is she baiting me?* I wondered, but quickly decided that she must've meant the question as a joke. Holding her gaze, I waited for her to commit further or change the subject.

Like most people, silence quickly made her uncomfortable.

"He didn't really believe in anything or anyone," she said. "He'd laugh if he knew that I went to a witch to find out who'd killed him."

I chuckled, showing just the right amount of mirthful incredulity. "A witch?"

She explained in a rush, "I'm not saying the witch was real

or anything. I just needed to do something besides hand out fliers."

"I understand. There are stories of psychics successfully helping to solve crimes. But there are many more stories of vulnerable people being taken advantage of by unscrupulous con artists."

While I waited for her to continue, Caroline reached out to her wineglass, slowly turning it with her fingers gliding across the stem. She smiled coyly as she said, "I suppose it's telling that she threw in a curse for an extra twenty."

Most street witches were con artists or New Age wannabes, but there were a few legitimate witches who plied their more modest skills to the general public in order to earn a living. Under normal conditions, I would've dismissed her witch out of hand, but a curse could explain a great deal. Had she stumbled into the den of an actual witch?

"A curse?" I asked in an appropriately mocking tone.

She nodded, explaining dramatically, "Whoever was responsible will be haunted by my father's ghost until driven to their death."

"Do you remember the witch's name?"

"I'm not sure I asked."

"Do you remember where the witch's office was?"

She answered with a sideways look. "You're asking a lot of questions."

"I don't like seeing someone taken advantage of."

She grunted, her skepticism set aside but not broken. "I found a card in some New Age shop and called the number. Honestly, it was a relief just to take some action. I don't feel cheated, but if you really want the number, I'll get it for you. I still have the card at home."

"Thank you."

"I have to admit, I like the idea of my father's ghost stalking his killer, getting into his mind, and driving him mad until he makes a mistake and gets what he deserves."

I couldn't deny her that. "Revenge is a powerful motivator. Sometimes, that's all we have left."

She sipped from her wine, studying me over the lip of her glass. "Your interest in my father's case surprises me."

"As I said, it's a passion of mine, and your story is compelling." I'd learned everything I could. It was time to extricate myself before she turned the questions on me, which was inevitable. I glanced at my phone, affecting surprise.

"Tell me about your group," she said, leaning toward me. "What was it that got you involved in the first place?"

With a perfectly weighted sigh, I returned the phone to my pocket. "I'm afraid I'm needed at work."

"An emergency auto claim?" she asked, raising an eyebrow as she took another sip of wine.

"I'm a fraud investigator," I said, rising. I put enough cash on the table to cover the check and the gratuity. "My apologies. If you could forward me the contact number, I have some questions for your witch."

"Do you have a card this time, David?"

I padded my pockets, shrugged.

"You're a terrible businessman," she teased.

"The number I called you from is a direct line. It was a pleasure meeting you again," I said.

I left the bar in a hurry to continue the charade. Once home, I wrote "David" on the back of the burner phone and set it on the coffee table in front of me. There was nothing to do but wait for her to forward me the contact information of her witch.

CHAPTER 7

*S*ometime in the middle of the night, I woke with my head spinning. Only when the dizziness passed a few seconds later was I able to blink my vision clear and see Dennis glowering down at me from the foot of my bed. His once white shirt was torn open, revealing a gaping gory wound, as if something had latched on to his throat and shredded his torso with razor-sharp claws, rending bone, flesh, and viscera into tatters.

"Tell me why," he said, his voice broken with anger.

His hands were clenched fists, but there was no sign of a pistol. I glanced about the room, noting the bedroom door was closed. My nearest weapon was the knife sheathed to the headboard of my bed, just above the lip of the mattress, but I wasn't sure it would be effective against whatever Dennis had become. He certainly wasn't among the living.

"You'll tell me why you killed me," he moaned. "And then you'll die."

I caught the slight dip of his hips just before he leapt. Tossing the top sheet aside, I spun off the bed, swiping the knife from the sheath in the process. My foot caught in the sheet, pulling it with me as I landed. I stumbled awkwardly on my feet, immediately dropping to a defensive posture with the knife raised, but Dennis was gone. Still on guard, I jerked my foot free and walked around the bed. No sign of blood anywhere. No scent left behind.

The bedroom door remained closed.

I slowly pushed open the bathroom door with the fingers of one hand. Empty. Glances at the floor revealed no sign of blood there, either. As I turned back toward the bedroom, something bright in the waste bin caught my attention. Tipping it with the point of the knife, I saw the waitress's silver necklace I'd tossed there previously.

I spent the next several minutes searching every corner of the house and found no sign that Dennis had ever been inside. The front and back doors remained shut and locked, as were the windows. Believing I'd missed something, I searched once more. Finally assured, I returned to my room, dropped the knife onto the end of the bed, then sat next to it.

I don't believe in ghosts, I thought, leaning forward as I slowly ran my hands through my hair and caught my breath. How else could I explain the lack of evidence that Dennis had ever been in my house? For the first time, I wondered if I was losing my edge. His wasn't the only death I'd caused in my life, and no matter how careful I was, his likely wasn't the last. Guilt was dangerous. Until that moment, I'd efficiently kept it at bay. Had it finally caught up to me? My mind drifted to the dizziness that afflicted me just before each encounter with the dead detective.

That's not my imagination, at least.

Unable to manufacture an answer, I glanced at the clock on my nightstand. It was three in the morning. My body vibrated from adrenaline. I doubted I'd get back to sleep before sunrise. Unsure what to do, I sat there with my conscience, trying to wipe the vision of Dennis from my mind. It clung stubbornly, etched in vivid guilt. Unable to shake it, my gaze drifted toward the open bathroom door and the waste bin just inside. Uncertainly at first, I rose and walked over to stare down at the delicate silver chain laying haphazardly there.

I scowled.

Turning my attention to the counter, I drew a fresh tissue from the box and reached down to pinch the silver between my fingers, then raised the chain to dangle at my eye level. Like all were-animals, I'd spent my life fearing silver. The mere touch of it seared flesh, causing nearly unbearable pain while simultaneously inhibiting our natural healing ability. *Nearly.*

Carrying it back to my room, I returned to the edge of the bed and dangled the chain once more. The image of Dennis, his torso torn open, remained vivid in my mind, refusing to leave me in peace. Without thinking, I extended my forearm, then slowly rested the end of the chain onto my skin. Searing pain erupted in my mind, burning away Dennis and guilt and anything else. As I slowly piled the chain onto my arm, there was nothing at all but cleansing pain.

I endured it, clenching my teeth and forcing myself to breathe. In. Out. In. Out. Pain was a weakness I could control. Burning. Searing. In. Out. When I thought I couldn't endure more, I took one more breath, then slowly lifted the chain, leaving a winding, blistering, black-and-red tattoo where it had lain across my flesh. *Keep breathing. In. Out.* I closed my eyes and endured the aftermath, resisting the urge to get up and treat my wound. Slowly, steadily, the biting pain dulled and faded as my natural healing ability took over.

I sat silently, enjoying the comforting clarity of mind as the pain receded. After a long moment, I transferred the necklace to my left hand and repeated the process on my right forearm.

. . .

By midmorning, I'd still not received a message from Caroline. After a run and a shower, I donned a long-sleeved t-shirt to cover the fading wounds on my forearms, then met Josh at the retreat's library. From the look of him, he'd already been at the walnut table for hours. His hair was more disheveled than usual, and he had a focused intensity as he glanced up from a book to greet me.

Without formality, he gestured to two books that were farthest away from him. "Dive in," he said. I slipped into the chair across from him, picked up one of the books, and started skimming for anything that might help us understand the Clostra. While I focused on a single text, Josh's attention wandered from one to the other and then back again in some sort of logical flow that only made sense to him. While I could help with the research, the bulk of the work fell to Josh, and he was tireless in his drive for answers.

After hours of quietly poring through books, I sat back in my chair, rubbing the strain from my eyes. Lack of sleep was getting to me. My mind drifted to the memory of Dennis standing in my room. While I wasn't willing to discount him as a figment of my guilt, I thought to pursue another possibility.

I watched as Josh turned his head from one open book to another. "Have you ever encountered a type of mind magic?" I asked, not entirely clear how to word my inquiry.

He paused and blinked at me. "Why do you ask?"

I couldn't explain, not without revealing my role in the detective's fate. I held my brother's gaze evenly, waiting as if he hadn't asked the question. Eventually, he gave up and answered.

"It's out there, but it's rare."

"Why rare?"

He sighed, anticipating a prolonged disruption to his study, then leaned back in his chair. "It would be difficult to detect if someone was under the influence of that kind of magic, which makes it dangerous. A talented mind witch could wreak a lot of havoc. Plus it's a specifically hereditary talent, which means it would be easy to eradicate by cutting off the bloodlines that carry it."

By killing off the bloodlines, just as we killed off the dark elves. "They've all been eliminated?"

Josh shrugged. "There are probably a few bloodlines that went underground. I've never encountered a practitioner, or their magic."

"Any idea how it works?" I asked.

"No." His eyes narrowed as he scrutinized me. "If you tell me why you're asking, I could probably be of more help."

Frowning, I glanced out the nearest window. When I'd arrived at the retreat, it had been a clear day, yet a heavy rain angrily battered the pane.

"Coffee?" I asked, rising.

His lips thinned as he shook his head at me. "Why do I bother to ask?"

"Precisely."

In the kitchen downstairs, I found the pot empty and growled. *Josh, probably.* I changed the filter, added the grounds and water, then wandered out of the kitchen while I waited for the coffee to percolate.

I found Gavin pacing angrily in the entryway of the house, glaring at the door as if waiting for someone. He saw me and stopped.

"The Master of Mischief is here," he said with a sardonic tone. "And his sister."

"What?" I asked, baffled. The Master of Mischief could only mean Gideon, but there was no reason for an elf to be in the pack's retreat, not without my involvement, a damn good reason, and plenty of negotiation beforehand.

Gavin returned to pacing, his mood darkening. His tone was full of accusation as he stated, "Winter brought him."

Before I could demand an explanation, Dr. Baker came

through the door, removing and hanging his wet coat in a hurry. He was a tall, slender man with silver hair. *Mercury rises tonight,* I remembered, noting his normally calm demeanor was replaced with an agitated look. *He should be home, preparing.* As a were-tiger, he was like all felidae, subject to Mercury in the same way that canidae were subject to the moon, but the anticipation of Mercury affected each differently. For Dr. Baker, the anticipation put him on edge, sometimes severely.

"What happened?" he asked both of us as he strode toward the clinic.

"Skylar is fine," Gavin called after him.

Dr. Baker turned, confused.

"She called you here to treat Gideon."

"She said Sky was injured."

"That's because she knew you wouldn't come to treat an elf."

I unclenched my jaw. "Abigail?"

Gavin nodded. If Winter had a weakness, it was her some-time lover, Gideon's sister. As the son of Darion, one of the elves' most beloved leaders, he would have no trouble receiving the best treatment that their kind could provide. While Dr. Baker's reputation as a miracle worker was well deserved, he had minimal experience working with the other supernatural races. If Abigail wanted his help, something was amiss—or afoot; she was ambitious, and cunning.

The rain, I realized, frowning. As an elemental elf, Gideon was able to manipulate the weather in a localized area. If he were injured or sick, he might do so unconsciously.

Dr. Baker's brow tightened into a knot as he glanced between us, then he turned with a scowl and continued on toward the clinic. I followed him while Gavin remained behind.

Dr. Baker pushed through the double doors with me close behind. Inside, we found Gideon laying supine on one of the beds, his eyes closed. His twin sister anxiously stood over him. The pair were tall and thin, with blond hair that Abigail wore longer. Like most elves, they were unusually attractive, with handsome narrow faces, aquiline noses, delicate lips, and long lashes over expressive violet eyes.

Winter stood close to Abigail, deliberately avoiding my gaze. Sky was there as well.

There's a surprise.

She seemed pointedly determined to ignore my presence.

Dr. Baker took in the situation at a glance. "He shouldn't be here," he insisted, directing his attention to Gideon.

Winter tried to explain. "I know but—"

"No," he snapped, jarring her. "There are no excuses. He shouldn't be here. What you have done is unacceptable, and you know that." His voice softened as he added, "You've never been able to deny her, which has always been your problem. That weakness cannot become our problem, and you promised it wouldn't."

"He's here now," she said gently. Her expression was pleading as she asked, "Will you please just look at him?"

He patted her shoulder comfortingly. "I will see what I can do."

Abigail's violet eyes watched with an anxious intensity as he gently lifted one of Gideon's eyelids, then the other. "When did this happen?"

Who did it was the question on my mind. Gideon had been expected to take the leadership role after his father's demise, but he'd refused. As the story went, he preferred his free-living ways to the constricting demands of leadership, but I suspected he feared the incredible expectations of responsibility. Instead, the mantle of leadership fell to Mason, but an election was on the horizon and there were rumors that Gideon was considering putting himself on the ballot. Abigail was the most likely source of those rumors, in my opinion.

Does he know that his sister might've gotten him killed? Though Dr. Baker had yet to determine what afflicted Gideon, it was clear that he had been the target of an assassination attempt. Abigail thought so, or she wouldn't have brought him to us.

Mason had recently drawn the elves into an alliance with the witches. If he saw Gideon as a threat to that alliance, Gideon's survival might be of value to the pack.

"It's been about two days," Abigail answered as Dr. Baker continued his exam. "We were supposed to meet for lunch, but he didn't show up. You are aware of my brother's reputation." Gideon never seemed to tire of booze and women. "It isn't unusual for him to sleep in and miss our lunch if he had a very active evening the night before. But when the hard winds and rain started in our neighborhood, I knew something was wrong with him."

Sebastian entered behind Dr. Baker as he asked, "Your doctors have no idea what's wrong?"

"We've already lost four to similar symptoms," she explained. Her voice cracked, but in a forced way. "They were only alive for five days once it started. No one seems to be able to help him. Some didn't even try. I just couldn't sit back and wait for him to die." She wiped tears from her eyes, smearing her mascara.

At least her concern for her brother is genuine.

Sebastian walked up to the table to scrutinize Gideon's limp form. "The four that died, were they potential candidates for leaders?"

Abigail appeared stunned by the question.

Does she think we're stupid? We were often underestimated by the other supernatural factions, which gave us an advantage over them.

She sidled closer toward Winter, taking her hand. Abigail answered with a reserved tone, "Three of them would be ones I would consider potentials."

"You don't think this is a coincidence?" Winter asked Sebastian.

"Coincidences do not occur as often as people would like to believe," he explained, "and almost never in situations like this."

I didn't envy Sebastian, to be thrown into such a critical choice without any forewarning. There were several political factors to consider. The ramifications of our intervention depended on an accurate assessment of who was responsible for the assassination attempt. We would be putting the pack at risk, but the potential rewards might be worthwhile should Gideon survive to become the next elven leader.

Sky's desire was plain. Her chin was up and she was watching Sebastian with expectant eyes, almost willing him to protect Gideon. Once again she would make a rash decision without fully comprehending the stakes, but I begrudgingly acknowledged that for all she'd seen with us, she'd yet to become jaded. She still believed in a moral high ground. I could appreciate that, but she needed to also learn that someone who appeared helpless might in fact be a poisoned dagger waiting to strike.

After a long, pensive moment, Sebastian asked Winter, "You are aware that last month the witches and elves became allied?"

She nodded, expecting the worst but ready to accept his decision. Abigail's mouth opened as she read the fatalism in her ex-lover's expression. Sky appeared about to interject herself into the conversation when Sebastian turned to Dr. Baker.

"Examine him," Sebastian directed. "Do what you can, but we cannot be involved for more than twenty-four hours. If he cannot be helped within that time, then please accept my condolences for the loss." He turned to leave, but hadn't made it out the door before his phone rang. He frowned as he glanced at the number, then answered the call. "Yes,

Mason," he said, allowing just a hint of annoyance in his voice.

"You should worry about yours, and let me deal with mine," Mason said in his raspy Australian brogue. With our enhanced hearing, phone calls were rarely private. "Aren't you tired of poking your nose where it never belongs? Send her away."

Sebastian smirked. "Obviously, if she is here, you aren't taking care of your own."

"As usual, you have found your way into business that isn't yours. I am asking this time. But if I were in your situation, I would consider the request thoroughly and do as I ask."

I bristled at the elf's insolent tone. Since Mason had formed his alliance with the witches, his arrogance had become brazen.

"Of course," Sebastian said coolly, his broad lips spreading into a bright and dangerous smile. "I will give it as much consideration as I give you." He disconnected the call, then turned to Dr. Baker. "Take as much time as you need. I want Gideon alive."

Abigail visibly relaxed against Winter, who responded with a comforting kiss on the lips, then gently stroked Abigail's cheek.

I followed Sebastian out of the room as he walked toward his office.

"What's your assessment?" he asked.

My answer was immediate. "Abigail's involved, somehow."

"See what you can find out."

I nodded and started up the stairs toward the library to brief Josh when I heard Gavin downstairs.

"I have better things to do than babysit Winter's girl-friend's brother," he grumbled.

Sebastian answered, his tone casual, "If I cared, that

135

would be a different story, now wouldn't it? You're here. If Mason decides to act on his threat, I need you, but most importantly, you'll do it because I requested it."

I heard the front door open and the click of a woman's heels on the hardwood floor. Backing down a couple of steps, I saw Kelly in the entryway. Instead of her usual medical smock, she appeared dressed for a date. A cream wraparound dress clung to her curves, and her face was framed by a thick corkscrew halo. Dark mascara and liner shaded her walnut-colored eyes. Her lips and cheeks were highlighted by a deep coral color.

"Why are you here?" Gavin asked, suppressing his agitation.

She smiled, ignoring his harshness. "Dr. Jeremy called me."

Leaving them, I walked up the stairs to find Josh where I'd left him, bent over several books, seemingly reading them all at once. As I joined him, he gave me a forlorn look while slumping in his chair.

"This is pointless," he sighed.

"So take a break. Get your head straight and then come back and start over."

He gestured broadly at the contents of the library. "There's nothing here that's going to shed light on the contents of the Clostra."

"Ask London," I said.

His gaze shifted away from mine as he scowled. "She's not talking to me. I burned that bridge in our hunt for Ethos. We need Sky's help."

"No."

"She can read the books," he explained as if his argument was both undeniable and obvious.

"We're not getting her any more involved than necessary. Without the third book, the spells are useless. When we have all the books, we can consider using her help, but only as a last resort. Until then, there's no point."

"We can't cast the spells," Josh agreed, "but we can figure out what they are. With Sky's help, we can determine if there is a spell that lays the beast to rest."

All we knew about the spell was rumor, that it had the potential to somehow kill the entire were-animal species. We needed to locate the spell, determine its actual purpose. Could it be cast by any witch, or did it require a witch of high skill?

Josh continued, "We can at least get an idea which other spells might present a danger to us. It's also possible that somewhere in these books is a clue to the location of the third book."

I scrutinized him for a long moment. After their shared recklessness regarding Ethos's magic, I didn't trust the two of them with another magical secret; I understood enough Latin that I'd be able to follow along with the translation, but I'd have to rely on my brother for a deeper understanding of the text. When it came to power, his track record for self-control was manifestly poor. With Sky involved, could he stop himself from drawing her into his experiments to test the spells once he had access to the third book?

Sky couldn't be trusted when it came to Ethos's magic, so I didn't see why giving her access to the Clostra would be any wiser. Josh was right, though. There was too much at stake not to utilize every advantage we had.

"There are nearly two hundred pages in each book," I said, "and she doesn't speak Latin. You're going to have to interpret her terrible pronunciation. This will take a long time."

He shrugged, helpless.

While I considered the option, his gaze shifted to my hands. "Coffee?" he asked.

I'd left the pot brewing in the kitchen. "I was distracted." I filled him in on Gideon's presence in the clinic.

"What is your assessment?" I asked him.

He was about to answer me when something in the doorway caught him by surprise. His eyes brightened. A broad smile spread across his lips. I knew before I looked that Sky was standing there.

"Just the person I wanted to see," he proclaimed. "I was about to come get you." He pulled out a chair next to him and patted the seat for her. She obliged, acknowledging my scowl with a dismissive look while going out of her way to return Josh's smile.

He slid both of the Clostra books in front of her, pressing them both open to the first page. "Please," he gestured, "start reading."

She blinked at him. "Read what?"

"All of it. We need to translate it."

While she waited for the punch line to an imagined joke, he leaned down to the messenger bag beside his chair and retrieved a digital recorder and a tablet. Only when he was ready and gave her an expectant look did she seem to realize that he was serious. Glancing at the pages, she shook her head. She gave him another look, then began reading. As expected, her pronunciation was terrible, frequently leading Josh and I to instinctively lean over the pages to read for her. Each time we did, Sky would make a disgusted sound as the pages apparently went blank for her. She didn't appreciate when Josh frequently stopped the recorder to clarify her pronunciation, either.

To make matters worse, the information from the missing third book proved consistently critical to understanding the spells, but that didn't stop Sky from asking at the end of nearly every entry, "What does that spell do?"

After a few torturous hours, we were all on edge.

"Do you understand any of this?" she asked Josh, exasperated.

"It's Latin; I understand most of it, but the rest we will figure out later." He gestured for her to continue, which she did reluctantly.

After a while, my thoughts began to drift toward the visions of Dennis until I heard Sky utter *"bestia"* as she read through one of the spells.

Beast.

I leaned forward, stopping myself from hovering over the book. Josh was paying particular attention, as well.

Sky stopped reading as she stared at the page, her brow furrowed. "What is *ripiso?*"

Josh and I answered together, "Rest."

"The beast will lay to rest," she whispered, then continued reading.

I raised an eyebrow to Josh, who gave me a frustrated look and shrugged. Like most of the spells, there just wasn't enough information to be sure what they did, but I saw him highlight the translation on his tablet.

Eventually, she read another phrase that caught our attention, *Magia rescet.*

Magic will wither.

Josh's color melted to a ghostly white as he stopped the recorder. "Why don't we take a break?" he said, putting on a cheerful smile for her. He rose to leave the library. When I rose to join him, he waved me off. Whatever the text meant to him, he needed to think about it.

The silence between Sky and me quickly grew awkward. Judging by her occasional cold glances, she remained angry. I couldn't apologize for depriving her of Ethos's magic; she'd made that decision for me when she'd chosen to keep the magic in the first place. As much as I wanted to, I couldn't explain how it was that I'd stopped her heart and nearly killed her; that knowledge was too dangerous for her.

We sat like teenagers, looking at our hands, our nails, our clothes, and every piece of furniture in the library in an effort to not look at each other. I was relieved when she placed her phone in front of her on the table and began browsing the Internet. I brought out my phone as well. For lack of a better idea, I slowly swiped through my settings. We remained like that for several minutes until Josh finally returned, balancing three cups of fresh coffee in his hands.

Our project had taken on a greater sense of urgency. I doubted we would stop before the texts were fully translated.

He gingerly set the three cups on the table, then slid one to each of us before taking his seat. Sky took a tentative sip, watching him closely as he turned on the recorder, picked up the notepad, then looked at her expectantly. After another sip, she set her coffee aside, cleared her throat, and continued reading from where she left off.

After two more tedious hours, her Latin wasn't much better than when she'd started. Her already limited pronunciation began to slip, leading to more interruptions from Josh. She paused, rubbing the strain from her bloodshot eyes as she leaned back into her chair.

"Do you know who can do these spells?" she asked Josh.

"There seem to be numerous safeguards for the spells. Not only do you have to be able to get past the ward; you also have to be strong enough to perform them." He looked down at his tablet. "These seem to be very strong spells. I wonder if even I could perform one."

I scowled but remained silent. There were few witches more powerful than my brother, but none of them could be trusted with such power. *A bridge for another time,* I decided, sipping my coffee. I turned to Sky as her body sagged in her chair. Her expression was dull. *This is exhausting for her,* I reminded myself, suppressing my impatience.

"Shall we continue?" I asked softly.

She nodded begrudgingly as Josh turned on the recorder.

The next hour was an exercise in diminishing returns as exhaustion caught up to each of us. After several cups of coffee, my head was ringing but I could barely keep my eyes open. It occurred to me that I could slip out of the library for a short rest, but I didn't want to leave the two of them alone with the Clostra for long.

When Sky eventually asked for another break, I finished off my cup and excused myself to get a refill. Only a few minutes later, I returned to find the books on the table but Josh and Sky gone. I scowled and left my cup on the table as I went looking for them. Had he been waiting for a chance to get her alone? Was there something about the Clostra that he didn't want me to hear?

Both of their rooms were empty. They weren't in the main room, either. After checking the game room, then the porch, I felt a rising surge of anger. Only the gym was left, and there was only one reason for Josh to take her there; they were practicing magic. Descending the stairs to the basement, I could feel a sudden, powerful pulse of magic from the gym.

There was a thud, followed by Sky's anxious exclamation, "Sorry!"

I stopped in the doorway to find them kneeling together next to the far wall, near the cardio machines. For a moment, I thought Josh was hurt, but he was simply collecting himself.

"Try another protective field," he said.

She concentrated and a vaporous barrier formed close around her, but it lacked strength. Without Ethos's magic, she was once again limited to whatever magic she could borrow. The pulse I'd felt from the stairs had used up most of what Josh had given her.

"Offensive magic requires a lot of power," he said apologetically. "You will have to use it sparingly."

Offensive magic? My arms folded over my chest. Teaching

Sky offensive magic was only going to get her into more trouble. *You just couldn't help yourself.*

Her shoulders slumped as grief came over her. She was feeling the loss of Ethos's magic, I realized. He comforted her as she leaned forward and rested her head on his shoulder.

"I know," he whispered.

Did she know it was Josh who'd shown me how to take the magic from her? "Playtime is over," I snapped. "We need to go back to work."

He glared at me as he released Sky. "Okay," he said with the tone of a spoiled brat who had no intention of obeying.

"Now," I insisted.

He sighed, exasperated, as he watched her rise and walk past me.

"Come on," I said, nodding toward the stairs.

A mischievous grin came over him. At his slight gesture, an invisible force pushed me back against the wall, then dissipated. It wasn't a strong spell. Josh was just letting me know he wasn't to be trifled with. I had every intention of trifling with him when Sky inexplicably laughed. We stared at her, confused, before she stifled her laugh and went on her way up the stairs.

I scowled at Josh, letting him know this wasn't over, then started after her. There was too much work to do to waste time on my brother's insecurities. After a few minutes, he followed.

Another hour passed in the library, with little progress to show for it. I could tell by Josh's growing impatience with me that he still didn't have answers to his questions. He'd figured out just enough to scare him, and that pissed him off. When it came to magic, my brother didn't accept failure. He rarely found someone or something that could defeat his curiosity, and the frustration was getting to him. The frustration was getting to me. The longer we spent together, the further back into our childhood our relationship seemed to regress.

Does he resent me now for taking Ethos's magic from Sky?

Sebastian walked into the library. "Anything?"

Josh slouched back into his chair, his legs spread. He frowned as he gestured to his notepad. "This is a riddle within itself. There is absolutely no way to tell what the spell is for without the third book. Like this one: The first book reads, 'I will that the undead walk among'—then it continues in the second book—'The living will hear my request—'" He shoved the notepad toward the middle of the table. "And freaking what? Then do *what*, a dance? Bake me a cake? Sing me a ballad? What will they do?"

Sebastian stroked his chin thoughtfully as he walked to the table and opened one of the books, flipping through the blank pages. "Senna," he said to Sky, "what's her deal?"

Her tired expression became bitter. "With how meticulous and obscure this world is," she answered, "I am surprised that someone else in my family would be so closely linked to an object of power."

He paced slowly along the side of the table. After some consideration, he announced, "I don't think she is true family."

"We look just alike," she said, surprised. "She's a teenaged version of me."

"She's a dark-haired, olive-colored woman; other than that, there wasn't anything that similar in your appearances. I don't believe she is a Moura Encantada. There has to be a link between you and her as to why you two can read these things. I need to find the link."

"Why, so you can find others?"

"Yes." He smiled. "Do you see something wrong with that, Skylar?"

Sky defiantly puffed out her chest. "Yes. If they are as dangerous as you all say. I don't think *we* should have these books at all, let alone try to find the other people who can read them."

"I prefer to know those that are in a position to hurt this pack, and handle things as necessary. As far as the books are concerned, I would love to destroy them."

Sebastian crossed to one of the small cabinets where Josh kept some of his magic supplies, and removed a lighter. Josh tensed as Sebastian returned to the table, bent the lighter to the edge of the blue book, and struck a flame against it. The book burst into orange, blue, and red flames that burned furiously, though the fire didn't seem to consume the material. As the Clostra called on more magic to defend itself, the temperature in the room dropped dramatically. A frigid breeze licked at the flames, while ice rose up the leg of the table, spread across the surface to envelop the book, and snuffed out the flames. Once extinguished, the breeze died. The ice receded and disappeared, and the temperature quickly returned to normal.

Sky appeared horrified as Sebastian lifted the unblemished book to examine it. "As you see," he said, unsurprised, "they can't be destroyed. I want to know as much as I can about the Clostra. I prefer to go on facts and not rumors. Once you have translated them, they will be separated."

He was on his way out of the library when we heard a crash downstairs, followed by Kelly's scream, "Get it off of me!"

Sebastian rushed out of the room, with me directly behind him. We arrived at the clinic just behind Dr. Baker to find Kelly on the floor frantically clawing at her leg. Medical tools and a tray lay spilled beside her.

"Get it off of me!"

Dr. Baker knelt beside her, running his hands over her legs, then arms. Failing to find what frightened her, he ripped open her scrub pants and felt along her skin while Kelly continued to panic. He cursed and tore the pants higher.

There was an anxious tension in his voice as he asked, "What am I looking for?"

"It looks w-weird," she stammered, "a bug, small legs ... tan, no, brown."

"I found it."

I knelt and saw beneath his fingers the form of a camouflaged creature that revealed itself as it tried to match the color of Dr. Baker's skin. Within a few seconds, it succeeded and became invisible once more, but he maintained his grip on it. Holding it in place, he retrieved a pair of tweezers from the spilled tray and used it to pry the creature from Kelly's skin. Holding it carefully, he rose to the counter and found a jar of tongue suppressors. After dumping the contents, he dropped the creature inside and sealed the lid. It quickly adapted its camouflage, but imperfectly, leaving thin, light brown legs exposed.

Sebastian knelt beside Kelly. "Are you okay?"

She grasped at her legs that were splayed to one side. Biting her lower lip, she fought back tears as she slowly shook her head. "I can't move my legs," she said, trying to shift into her clinical voice. A thin stream of tears broke free, streaking down one cheek.

Sebastian carefully straightened her legs, but once he released them, they bent back into a splayed position. She gasped at the sight, her respiration quickly accelerating toward panic. He gently lifted her into his arms and laid her on one of the beds.

"What happened?" he asked.

"I found it on Gideon, at the nape of his neck," she said, grimacing as she tried to move her legs. "It jumped on me when I tried to remove it. The next thing I knew it was biting and clawing its way up my leg. I couldn't get it off me." She closed her eyes and took a ragged breath. "And then I fell. I tried to stand, but my legs wouldn't move."

Sebastian stepped aside as Dr. Baker pushed a wheeled

stool to the edge of the bed. He set a tray of tools next to her and proceeded to test her reactions as he touched her skin with heated and cooled instruments. As he progressed from her feet up her legs without a reaction, I saw deep concern creep through his normally calm bedside manner.

Only when he touched her abdomen with a chilled tool did she report any sensation. I felt a rush of relief until I saw his frown deepen. From a box of microfilaments, he touched one of the tools to her skin and again looked to her for a reaction.

She barely shook her head, the color draining from her visage.

Dr. Baker pushed up his glasses, then picked up the jar to examine the mysterious creature inside. After a long moment, he announced to no one in particular, "I've never seen anything like this." Removing the lid, he tipped the jar onto a petri dish, then retrieved a camera from a cabinet drawer. After taking several pictures, he loaded the images into his computer and began searching his database for a match.

I knew by his deepening frown that he found nothing.

Gavin appeared next to me, examining the state of the room, then slipped past Sebastian to stand beside Kelly, gently resting a palm on her leg as he examined her. "What happened?" he asked, the usual edge in his voice absent. When she didn't react to his touch, he moved his hand from her leg to her arm, gently stroking his thumb across her forearm.

He listened attentively as Dr. Baker explained.

"Are you in pain?" Gavin asked her.

Winter and Abigail slipped into the room as he adjusted the pillows, then the position of the bed until Kelly appeared at least somewhat more comfortable.

She shook her head.

He asked more questions, which she continued to answer

with shakes and nods of her head. Was she conserving energy, I wondered, or too frightened to speak?

"We will fix this," Sebastian promised her.

Gavin approached the petri dish, scrutinizing the creature within. After a moment, he picked up the dish and dumped the creature into his palm. I scowled. Dr. Baker objected, but Gavin ignored us both as he calmly watched the creature scramble up his arm. It stopped a few inches from his palm, then camouflaged itself against his skin. A few seconds later, I barely saw the shimmer of the creature as it crawled back down to his palm, where it remained.

He raised it to the level of his eyes to examine it more closely. "It's a sleeper," he proclaimed.

"I've never seen one before," Dr. Baker said, awed. "I assumed it was a myth. Weren't they supposed to have been destroyed?" He rubbed his temples as he thought. "The elves created this creature...."

The elves can provide the cure.

Gavin explained as he gently returned the creature to the petri dish, "They created it as an undetectable elimination tool. It releases venom that paralyzes the body, eventually infecting the organs, rendering them ineffectual. Once you're dead, it slithers away, taking along all evidence, leaving the cause of the person's death inconclusive and the murderer blameless." His body stiffened. The muscles in his neck tightened like cords, and his fists clenched. His anger filled the room as his panther rose to the surface. "Why is an elven creature that should have been destroyed in our house, Abigail?" He turned to her, glaring.

"You all created this thing that causes death," Sebastian said, deliberately controlling his temper, "but don't have a problem killing your own people who happen to be capable of the same thing?"

He meant the dark elves. The *Makellos*, the elven elite and purists, had led the charge to commit genocide on their powerful, dark brethren, and here they were using the very same magic on their own kind.

Kelly had gone from pale to a shade of green. "If it released venom," her voice tightened, "even if you can make or find an antivenin, whatever damage is done will be permanent."

"That's for snakes," Winter lied, but Kelly knew too much to be fooled.

Sebastian turned to Abigail. "When is your election?"

Her attention drifted back toward her brother. "In four months."

"And they will select the candidates in probably a month. What happened to your brother wasn't a coincidence, nor was what happened to the other potentials."

Abigail's skin blanched as she began to fidget and pace the small area next to Gideon's bed. "As I said before, my brother has no interest in leading," she said unconvincingly. "That was my father's dream for him, not his."

"Eventually he will mature and will accept his responsibilities," Sebastian stated, scrutinizing her. "Maybe not now, but sometime in the future, he will want that position, and due to your father's legacy, it will be his without opposition. This"—he gestured to Gideon's paralyzed figure on the table—"is not a coincidence."

Abigail seemed aghast, so struck with horror that she leaned against the bed for support. "Someone tried to kill my brother," she gasped.

"Is there an antidote?" asked Dr. Baker, his expression hopeful.

"Not that I know of," she answered, distracted, "but we need to find one."

He turned to Sebastian. "We should call Mason to see if he knows anything that can help."

Fat chance.

Sebastian agreed with me. "He will not offer us assistance."

"Call him anyway," Dr. Baker pleaded.

Before Sebastian could respond, a low moan drew our attention to Gideon. Every one of us stared, disbelieving, until we saw his foot jerk. His legs shifted before he eased himself up, slowly turning to sit on the edge of the bed, groggy as if waking from a deep sleep. He ran his hands over his face as he looked up to take in his surroundings. Realizing he was trapped in a room with several angry were-animals, his body tightened. I doubted he had the strength to flee, but I was prepared to stop him. He calmed at the sight of his sister as she moved to his side and took his hands in hers. He offered her a weak smile.

His gaze fixed on Sebastian as he spoke softly to her in their language. She responded in kind, and at some length, while Gideon occasionally nodded. My suspicion was immediately aroused. It wasn't polite for guests to conspire in front of their hosts. I turned to Josh, who only shook his head. He couldn't translate their conversation.

"She's bringing him up to speed," Gavin whispered, surprising me. Sebastian was surprised, as well. "She left out the part about someone trying to assassinate him," he added.

When Abigail finished speaking, the two remained locked in silent communication.

"Abigail is afraid of us," Gavin whispered.

She should be. My hostile gaze shifted toward Winter, who wore an uncharacteristic look of guilt. She'd broken protocol to bring them to the retreat. It wasn't our responsibility to treat every supernatural that took ill. We kept to ourselves, and for good reason. Now Kelly was paralyzed from the waist down, and we were quickly becoming embroiled in an elven affair we didn't fully understand.

They shouldn't be here.

"May I use your bathroom?" Gideon asked, meeting my gaze for the first time.

Dr. Baker was the only one who moved, helping Gideon off the table and guiding him to the bathroom at the back of the hospital.

The moment her brother was out of the room, Abigail turned to Sebastian. "He can't find out that someone tried to kill him," she said, half pleading, half insistent.

I frowned, skeptical. "You think it is wise to keep such information from him? He can't protect himself from an enemy that he doesn't know exists."

I ignored the irritable, perplexed look that Sky gave me.

"At this time it would be best. He will respond irrationally." Abigail sighed. "Right now is not the time."

"I don't care what goes on with the elves and what truths you hold from him," Sebastian snapped. "You keep whatever secrets you like. We need to find a way to fix Kelly."

When Dr. Baker returned with Gideon, Kelly asked, "If he's awake, then I should get better, too, right?"

The brightness in her eyes dimmed as he hesitated to answer. Finally, he frowned as he gave her a half-shrug. He didn't know the answer, and apparently he didn't want to lie to her. Seeing the collapse of her hope, I wasn't sure he made the right choice, but that was between them.

He promised her, "If you don't, we will find a way. You will not stay like this."

One hour and we'll know.

From the time the creature was removed from Gideon's body to the time he emerged from his coma, one hour had passed. No one wanted to say it out loud, to get her hopes up, but we were all waiting.

CHAPTER 8

*E*ach of us counted the slow, agonizing minutes. We stayed close to Kelly, one or more of us always by her side. Gavin was glued to the chair next to her bed when he wasn't bringing her water or something to eat, even though she could barely bring herself to do more than nibble at what he brought. I suspected she did so as a courtesy.

As the hour finally approached, each of us found our way into the hospital room under one pretense or another, but we weren't fooling her. When Dr. Baker repeated his exam and she still couldn't feel or move her legs, hope drained from her expression, leaving her desolate. She blinked away tears until they overwhelmed her.

Still, we waited for something to happen. Perhaps the effect of the creature took longer to wear off with a human. Unlike the rest of us, Kelly didn't have magic to help her heal. Perhaps she'd need a few more minutes. Perhaps it would be hours, or days, or years. Or never. I didn't want to contemplate her future as a paraplegic. Not yet.

Frustration tightened in Sebastian's expression as he turned on Abigail, demanding, "Why isn't she better?"

Just a few months ago, he'd had Kelly removed from the

retreat house for defying his orders and enabling Demetrius to convert Chris. Instead of contrition, Kelly had stubbornly doubled-down on her moral defiance. His anger then matched his concern for her now. Had her defiance made her more endearing to him?

"I'm not sure," Abigail answered carefully, avoiding the roomful of accusatory glares. "Is she wholly human?"

Sebastian nodded.

"Hmm, usually you all are fanatical about limiting exposure. Why is she different?"

"That's not your concern," Sebastian snapped. "Concern yourself with things that matter. How can we fix this? What do you know about this sleeper?"

She pursed her lips as she considered. "It is new to me, just as it is to you."

Gavin said coolly, "It is an elven creature."

"No," she corrected him, "it's a *Makellos* creature."

"To me, it's the same thing. Whether they consider themselves elite to you all or have skills and powers stronger than yours, at the end of the day they are still elves. You all knew they were creating creatures foreign to us. Things that are so vile they keep them hidden, and when they manage to escape, no one can fix the problem."

"They are not the same," she insisted. "They consider themselves pure-breed and do not associate with the likes of us. We know as much as you do about what goes on with them."

Dr. Baker stepped closer to her. His eyes narrowed and anger filled the worry lines in his face. "Then you need to play nice," he growled, "and find someone to help her."

"We will see what we can find out," she promised meekly, her hand searching for Gideon's. When he took it, they gave each other a meaningful look before starting together toward the exit.

Sebastian barred their way with his body, looming over them. "No. He stays. You will work better without him."

Holding on to Gideon was the only way to guarantee her cooperation.

"People will respond better to him," she said softly.

Sebastian answered with a sly smile, "Then during your drive, you should work on your people skills."

Winter said, "I'll go with her."

"No," Abigail said apologetically. "It will be difficult to get information with any outsider, but it will be even more difficult with you present." To numb the blow, she gave Winter a soft kiss on the cheek, then turned to her brother. Another silent communication.

"I'll go with her," Josh volunteered.

Abigail considered him for a moment before making up her mind. "Okay."

I frowned, unsure why he would put himself in the hands of elves who were likely to be hostile to any outsider. Who knew what he would be walking into?

"I'll go, as well," I announced.

She took longer to consider me, studying the determination in my face. Apparently, she didn't understand it wasn't a request. "That will be unnecessary," she politely apologized. "Josh will be just fine."

Before I could object, I caught the slight shake of his head as he stood behind her. Where my presence tended to illicit fear and resistance, Josh's was more charismatic. He was admired for his power. The elves were much more likely to want to encourage my brother's favor, and without their help, Kelly didn't have a chance for a cure.

As much as I didn't want to admit it, Josh was much better able to deal with Abigail and the elves if she betrayed him. And if they harmed him, I would kill them all.

. . .

Left with my concern for Josh and Kelly, and the ever-present concern over Dennis's appearance and what that said for my state of mind, I spent the next few hours working out in the basement gym. My gaze frequently drifted toward my phone, but after three hours, my brother still hadn't given me any indication that they had made progress, or that he was safe. I frowned as I jogged on the treadmill. *Typical.*

My wolf lurked just below the surface, eager for release. I needed the cool comfort my animal nature provided. It might clear my thoughts about Dennis, allowing me to gain a fresh perspective, but I'd need to leave my phone behind. As long as Josh was with the elves, I didn't dare take that risk. If he needed me, there would be no time to waste.

I found myself considering the mind magic theory once more, deciding to research the subject. After exhausting myself, I showered and grabbed a quick bite of leftovers before making my way to the library. Sky was there, pulling books off the shelves, quickly flipping through them, then promptly returning them.

"What are you looking for?" I asked.

She spun around, startled, but quickly recovered. "My glass slipper, have you seen it?" she quipped. "What do you think? The Clostra. I want to finish translating."

I closed the library door, then folded over a corner of an area rug, exposing the hardwood floor beneath. I'd used the secret storage area so many times that I could find the panel with my eyes closed, but I went through the ritual, feeling for the indentation with my finger, then sliding under the lip and lifting the panel to reveal a rectangular steel lockbox that sank deep beneath the floor. Using the combination only Josh, myself, and Sebastian knew, I removed the brown-and-blue books of the Clostra and handed them to Sky.

"Sheesh, it's just us," she teased as she took a seat at the table, placing the books down in front of her. "Don't you think this is a little over the top?"

I felt a flush of anger heat my cheeks, but suppressed the urge to snap at her. It wasn't her fault. The constant hum of dark magic in my body had me on edge. Concern for Kelly and my brother only increased my irritation. I returned the box, then the panel. "Apparently we are now running a shelter for misfits," I said as I restored the rug to its usual state, then took a seat at the table across from her. "We have enough carelessness here. I will not add to the problem."

Ignoring the rebuke, she pressed both books open side by side, then retrieved a tablet from a nearby shelf and laid it on the table. If she thought I was going to trust her alone with the translation, she was incorrect. Eyeing her, I pulled the tablet toward me and detached the pen clipped to the binder.

"Start," I said.

"You know Latin?"

"You don't have a mother who's a witch without learning Latin."

"And yet you made Josh do all the work," she said.

Once again, she was quick to misjudge me, but I didn't owe her an explanation. "Josh is the only one who finds your little quirks entertaining. Can we start?"

She answered me with an exasperated sigh, then focused her attention on the books. Once she warmed up to the translations, we made steady progress. After hours of reciting Latin, she'd picked up many of the standard pronunciations.

Without the third book, much of what she read remained mysterious, but an obvious pattern began to emerge. The bulk of the spells dealt with magic and magical beings, such as the fae and the elves, but we still didn't understand why.

Sky stopped for a moment, staring at the place on the page that she marked with her finger. Before I could ask what had piqued her interest, she read aloud, "*Et non consurget a umbra spiritu militia* ... What does that mean?"

I had her repeat the sentence as I wrote it down, then

examined it. "The spirit shade will rise from its host and no longer …" I frowned. As with the other clues, there was just enough information to cause worry.

"There are spells for spirit shades," she said, the pitch of her voice rising with excitement, "which means that there has to be more than just the one in me. Ethan?"

"I don't know," I said.

Her eyes narrowed as she leaned toward me. "If you are lying to me, then stop it. Despite what you seem to think or believe, we are on the same team." She brushed the books aside, overstating her point.

I glowered back at her. We didn't have time for childish games and sensitive feelings. "If I knew the answer, I would give it to you. For now, we are on the same team; but I am under no illusions that you will be anything but the undoing of this pack. Unfortunately, the feelings people have for you will cause them to ignore affronts and tolerate things longer than they should and only deal with them once there is irreparable damage."

I regretted the outburst immediately, but couldn't take it back. She wasn't the only one making mistakes. Winter's decision to bring Gideon to the retreat might well have cost Kelly the use of her legs for the rest of her life. *We all make mistakes,* I reminded myself. *I got a detective killed and now I'm misleading his grieving daughter to cover my tracks.*

"I'm sorry," Sky snapped, her temper rallying. "Are we talking about *this* pack?"

I frowned as I settled back into my chair, scrutinizing her. "People make mistakes," I admitted, softening my tone. "It happens. No one sets out to do anything to jeopardize this pack."

"If I am not mistaken, your relationship with Chris compromised this pack quite a bit. You sleeping with the Master of the Northern Seethe's mistress wasn't good for the pack. Yet, you continued to do so without reservation."

The hair on my neck bristled with a sudden rise of anger. The frequent accusations regarding myself and Chris were tiresome. Since our relationship had ended, we'd gotten together once. It had been a mistake, never repeated, but Sky couldn't seem to let it go. "She's not his mistress," I growled. "My relationship with Chris was never a question of compromise when it comes to this pack. We had no illusions about our roles and the boundaries of our loyalty to each other. If she was a problem or ever became one, trust that she and the situation would have been handled without hesitation."

"Oh, you were handling the situation just fine. You seemed to *handle* each other every possible moment you could. So you can take your hypocrisy and shelve it, and while you're at it, put the attitude and the arrogance there, too."

The longer we glared at each other, the more emboldened she became. After a long moment, I'd finally had enough and returned my attention to the notepad in front of me, turning to a blank page.

"Go through the book and read off all the spells with spirit shade in it," I instructed. A short time later, I counted twenty-eight spells out of three hundred, a considerable amount considering we'd only found three spells that dealt with were-animals. Frustratingly, reading the spirit shade spells together provided no insight into the purpose of the spells.

Sky eased back in her chair. "Twenty-eight spells. There have to be more spirit shade hosts than just me out there."

Scrutinizing her, I wondered what was behind her obvious excitement that left her fidgeting in her chair. Her attention remained fixed on me, as if waiting for something she preferred not to voice. The longer I stared at her, waiting, the more she squirmed, but remained silent.

Eventually, I laid my arms on the table and leaned toward her. "And?"

"Don't you wonder if there are, and their purpose? For years Maya remained dormant, and all of a sudden she is making a grand appearance. I can hold magic, manipulate it into dark magic, feed vampires and—" She stopped abruptly.

"And what?" I asked.

"And I feel like something is off," she said, diverting from her original thought. I knew it by the short, sharp intake of breath she took before speaking, by the sudden shift in her gaze before her eyes once again met mine.

I folded my arms over my chest and leaned back into my chair, scrutinizing her. "I guess you are more dangerous than we even speculated."

"Just different. There are twenty-eight spells for spirit shades," she repeated, stabbing a finger onto the table in emphasis. "We are nearly a third of the way through the translations and there are only three regarding were-animals. Are the were-animals so innocuous that so few spells are needed for us, or are the spirit shades so complex that more than three spells are needed to subdue them?"

It was an astute question. "There isn't any way we can find out if there are any more spirit shades. Maya is hundreds of years old and just now coming to light. It would be difficult to find another one, especially if they are hosted."

"Well, it would be limited to a smaller number than the masses. They can only exist where magic does, so the host will either be a mage, witch, were-animal, elf, or fae. That definitely brings down the numbers."

"Not enough; there are millions of us."

"Then we follow the origin and talk to Tre'ases."

Only the trickster demons could create a spirit shade. "That is an idea," I admitted. *A good one.* "The problem is we only know of one; she is dead and so is her son. We have no way of finding out if other Tre'ases exist."

Sky rose, taking in the entire library with an exasperated look, as if the answers to all our questions were just a book away, if only we could find the right one. I knew the feeling.

I said, "I am more concerned with the link between you and others that can read the Clostra."

She walked along the shelves, tracing them with a finger that occasionally tapped a spine as she paused to examine it. "We need to determine if it is just my family lineage, being a Moura, or hosting a spirit shade that allows me to read the Clostra. If it's because I host Maya, then that can be a start. I suspect it has something to do with my family since Senna can read them, too." She drew a book from its place and flipped through the pages, frowning.

Sebastian spoke from the doorway, surprising us. "It's not your family. Senna isn't a blood relative. Her hair isn't naturally dark like the others in your family; I could smell the chemicals in her hair. When she speaks, her Portuguese isn't fluent. She stops too often to think about her words before she responds, which means she learned it at a later age. The small cleft in her chin is another sign. There was a picture on the fireplace mantel of her and a woman who claims to be her mother, along with a man, who I assume is the alleged father. A cleft chin is a dominant trait; one of them should have one—they don't. They are not her parents."

Sky's expression darkened as she snapped her book closed. "If they raised her, then they are her parents."

Sebastian brushed her criticism aside. "Semantics. The issue still remains; she isn't related to you. Her ability to read the Clostra isn't linked to your lineage. Your family are low-level witches, but since she is the only one able to read it, I assume it isn't linked to that, either." He pulled out a chair next to me and sat. "There has to be a link between you and Senna since you two can read them."

His gaze turned to me, a heavy scrutinizing look. When he spoke, he chose his words carefully, a show of respect

159

rather than fear. "Chris knew a lot about Gloria," he suggested.

I nodded, wary of his intention.

"She knew about her son, as well?"

Another slight nod.

"She seems to be privy to information that we aren't. Sometimes ahead of us by steps."

He wants me to use her. My expression tightened, but I withheld the bulk of my disdain. The Chris I'd known was gone. Michaela had brutalized her and left her for dead, just to spark a war between Demetrius and the pack. Against my wishes—against Chris's—Kelly had allowed him to turn her into a vampire. That had been three months ago. I didn't know what I'd find, or if she was going to be willing to cooperate. If she was, it was going to cost us. Plenty.

"She is good at what she does," I stiffly admitted. "Or rather, what she did."

"We should see what she knows."

Reaching out to her was the last thing I wanted to do. "Of course." I couldn't deny Sebastian, but there were a couple of sources I would try first. With any luck, visiting Chris wouldn't be necessary.

"I'll go with you," Sky said.

I gave her a raw look, but didn't bother to object. Did she have some insight to the questions we needed to ask Chris, or did she just want to watch a train wreck up close? The two were hardly fans of each other. When we'd first found Sky, almost two years ago, Chris had contracted with the vamps to kidnap Sky for them—just another day at the office for Chris, but Sky had plenty of reasons to dislike her.

From the passenger seat of my BMW, she appeared confused as I drove into the city, glancing over both of her shoulders to identify the locale. "This isn't the way to Chris's house."

"It is not," I stated.

She gave me a sideways look. "You lied to Sebastian?"

I turned into an affluent neighborhood that was popular with young professionals who had money to burn. "Chris is not the only hunter in town. I'd prefer to exhaust the possibilities before relying on a vampire."

After a moment, I parked on the street behind a gaudy, camouflage-painted Ram Macho Power Wagon. Sky scowled at the vehicle, then eyed the cluster of luxury townhouses that surrounded an opulent fountain in a small courtyard.

"Where are we?"

"Somewhere else," I answered, then turned off the ignition and opened the driver's side door.

Still skeptical, she followed me through the courtyard. If I'd forgotten which townhouse belonged to Sean, the loud techno-pop music vibrating the front windows of the farthest condo was a strong reminder. Walking up the porch, I knocked loudly on the door, then waited. After a moment, I knocked again. The volume of music quickly faded until it was just audible. A barely discernible shadow passed over the peephole. A moment later, I heard heavy, excited breathing on the other side of the door.

Sighing, I knocked once more.

"Who lives here?" Sky asked.

The door snapped open, revealing a wary young man wearing combat fatigues and a pistol holstered at his right hip. A knife was sheathed at the right side of his waist, the pommel tilted for a left-handed draw. His lips spread into a condescending smile as he glanced between the two of us. "Oh, baby girl and big boy," he said, slowly shaking his head, "you can't afford me. Ann does the discount work. You should call her. Bye bye."

I blocked the door with my foot.

He blinked rapidly at me, his smile frozen on his lips. "Are you here for trouble, big man?" he asked, incredulous. His hands lowered to his hips, conveniently close to his weapons, as he stared up at me.

I towered over him by at least a foot.

"You don't remember me," I said dryly, not entirely surprised. After Chris's demise, he'd stepped out of the shadows, announcing himself as the go-to hunter in Chicago. Before then, he hadn't even been on the radar. As a test, I'd given him a fictional target to locate, then had Artemis leave two trails of clues for him to follow; the longest route to the target was the easiest, while the shorter required more skill and experience. Chris would've solved the latter within days. After three weeks, Sean had stalled after barely making headway on the former. Instead of admitting his failure, he'd submitted a lengthy receipt for expenses and doubled his fees to continue. I'd fired him on the spot.

"Have we?" Sean asked dryly. "I meet so many people."

Sky gaped at his ignorance. "Ethan Charleston?" When Sean's eyes narrowed into thoughtful slits, she added, "Beta of the Midwest Pack?"

Recognition dawned in his expression as he snapped his fingers. "You're the wolf guy. Right. Maybe you can afford me—if I'm available, that is."

This is a waste of time. Regrettably, he remained my best chance to avoid a meeting with Chris. "We need information," I said gruffly, my unblinking gaze fixed on his.

"Yeah? Okay," he said, stroking his boyish wisp of a beard. "I'm best at racking up kill counts, but information is good. That can take a lot of forms: stolen disks, secreted papers, exhaustive reports. My going rate is one hundred bucks a noun. You think you can handle that?"

Mortified, Sky looked him up and down, then turned to me while hooking a thumb in his direction. "Is he for real?" She turned back to Sean. "Do you even know what a noun is?"

The boyish humor quickly faded. "It's a four-noun minimum," he stated, "payable in advance."

Before Sky could retort, I said, "I need the names and locations of any Tre'ases in the area, other than Gloria and her child."

"Who's Gloria?"

Sky shook her head at him.

"Whatever." He bristled. "I take cash, cash, or cash." He expectantly held out his hand. "But if you're in a real pickle, I'll take cash instead."

As I drew out my wallet, I noticed the way he wet his lips in greedy anticipation. Sky scowled until she saw that I drew out a business card and returned the wallet to my pocket. Sean blinked at the card as I placed it in his palm. He turned it over, frowning.

"Prove you're worth something," I stated, "and then we'll talk price."

His eyes narrowed as he studied me. "Okay. I'll give you two pieces of information for free. After that, you pay." After an annoyingly long stare down that was over-timed for effect, he said, "The routing and account numbers for my bank account. You'll need them to make that deposit by EFT."

I made a disgusted sound as Sky gestured to him, asking with a voice thick with disbelief, "You're a Hunter?"

He stared down his nose at her. "The best there is."

"I'm not the biggest fan of Chris," she told me, "but she's got miles on this guy."

"She's also dead," he snapped, "so there's that. Right now I'm the only show in town, honey. I mean, there's Ann, but she couldn't track two halves of an Oreo to a dab of frosting." He bit his lower lip while giving her what was surely meant to be a meaningful look, earning only a mocking chuckle in reply.

"I'm done here," she informed me, then turned and

walked off the porch. I followed her, an amused smile on my lips. I didn't need to look over my shoulder to know that Sean watched us all the way to my BMW.

"Is this Ann going to be any better?" she asked from the passenger seat.

"No." I considered for a moment, searching aimlessly for any reason to delay the inevitable.

"We should just go to Chris and get it over with," Sky said, giving me a meaningful look.

I sighed and started the engine.

CHAPTER 9

By the time I stepped onto Chris's porch, I already knew she was standing behind the door, making up her mind whether she would open it. The sweet redolence of her floral perfume wafted through the seams of the doorway. There was no heartbeat on the other side, not even the faintest hint of breath, proving a stark reminder: *She's dead. I tried to protect her, but she belongs to Demetrius now.*

Swallowing my regret, I reached up and knocked on the door.

After a long wait, I felt relief lighten the tension in my neck as it seemed she was going to deny us an audience. Just as I turned from the door, it creaked open to reveal Chris. At first glance, she appeared as I remembered her, wearing her typical tight black tank top and jeans. A closer inspection revealed her toasted almond skin, once glowing, was now tainted by a deathly hue.

She stood back inside the doorway, just far enough to avoid the sunlight that reached over the threshold. She studied me with a harsh indifference before stepping aside for us to enter.

Crossing the threshold, I caught the earthy scent of

Demetrius, the Master of the Northern Seethe. I tensed immediately, my wolf rushing to just beneath my skin in anticipation of violence. From his seat on the couch, he stared back at me with a dark, malignant gaze. It was our first encounter with each other since he'd stolen Chris from the retreat's medical clinic, right from under my nose.

As we glowered at each other, each tensed for violence, I weighed the ramifications of killing him outright. He'd disobeyed me. In my home.

Chris glided toward him, scrutinizing me from over her shoulder. "What do you want?"

He rose to take a protective stance at her side. I noted the aggressiveness of his posture, his right foot slightly forward and his weight shifted onto his toes. *He wants to kill me.* I smirked at the thought. He appeared about to try when Chris stepped between us to address him.

"I need you to leave," she requested.

I chaffed at the softness of her tone, the implied subservience. *She's a vampire,* I reminded myself yet again. He was her maker and she owed him such subservience—which was what he'd wanted, and what she hadn't.

Demetrius balked at the request, his lifeless black eyes fixating with a predator's intention on mine. "I'm not going anywhere."

"This is business," she said soothingly, then turned to me for confirmation. "Right?"

After a brief struggle, I unclenched my jaw enough to speak, but didn't bother to mask the disgust in my tone. "Yes. I need to ask you something."

"It will be quick," she promised him.

His chin rose defiantly. "Then you will not mind if I stay."

"He will not speak to me in front of you," she said carefully, irritation creeping into her voice.

"Then he should leave."

I faced him squarely, fists clenched at my side. *Make me.*

"Please," she said. "It is not his request, it is mine."

The Master of the Northern Seethe seemed stymied by the request. Beneath her obvious subservience, Chris retained a semblance of her willful independence. He wasn't used to his spawn pushing him away.

She's not entirely gone, then, I thought, surprised.

After a moment, he reluctantly acquiesced. "I will be back in half an hour. It will be best if he is not here when I return."

She offered her cheek to him as he leaned down to kiss her. In a grotesque demonstration of control, he lingered there, watching me with a belligerent stare. His lips brushed against her neck as his hand swept over her shoulder, tracing a delicate line down her spine to linger in the hollow of her lower back. A growl nearly escaped my lips, but I wouldn't give him the satisfaction. They could play their games for all I cared, but this was a show for my benefit. I'd accepted that she was gone, but to watch him flaunt his control over her galled me.

She acquiesced to his control, leaning into him as he kissed her forehead. The hint of a deadly smile brushed his lips before he vanished. She turned to me with her hands on her hips, her head slightly tilted. "What do you want, Ethan?" she demanded, impatient.

Her eyes, once brown, were as black and lifeless as Demetrius's. The absence of a terait meant she didn't have a problem transitioning to drinking blood for sustenance. I wondered, did she torture her food as well, like Michaela? Did Chris hunt the innocent strictly for food, or for sport?

She's dangerous, I reminded myself. *More now than ever.* If the situation became violent, I needed to anticipate her newfound speed and agility. It wouldn't pay to underestimate her.

Glancing around the large, open living room, I noted that not much about the room had changed since my last visit. Despite Chris's newfound abilities, there was still a pistol in the desk, I was sure; another one or two under the cushions of the couch; more in the ottoman, with knives attached underneath; melee weapons and at least one shotgun in the closet. It was safe to assume the four drawers of the V-shaped television stand contained a number of threats as well, and I noted the hilt of a sword largely concealed among the umbrellas in the umbrella stand. As a human, she'd always relied on weapons out of necessity, but she was just as dangerous now without them.

"How many Tre'ases do you know of?" I asked.

"Hmm." Her lips twisted into a sly smile. "I am sure I am not your first stop. Who did you go to first, Ann or Sean?"

"Sean," I admitted.

"Did he know anything? Or did he just flounce around like a self-entitled twit, demanding payment upfront for information he didn't likely have? He's a piece of work, isn't he? A true shyster. He considers himself to be my replacement since rumors have it that I'm dead." She scoffed.

"Well, technically—"

"Don't," she hissed sharply, flashing a finger at me like a switchblade. There was no mistaking the anger in her tone. Did she blame me for her situation? Even before Demetrius had turned her, she'd thrown in her lot with the vampires, trading blood in order to gain an advantage. From a human perspective, it was understandable. Hunters were at a distinct disadvantage from their supernatural prey, which was why they usually died young. I'd tried to steer her away from Demetrius, tried to convince her to retire. She'd made her choice, but she blamed me for it. Before Demetrius, I'd denied her request for me to change her into a were-animal.

Soothed by my silence, the flash of anger dissipated. She continued, slowly pacing in front of us. "Sean is absolutely useless. More arrogant than competent." She turned an assessing gaze on Sky. "Terait, odd magical ability, a connection with Ethos, unusual ability to stop a vampire's reversion, and let's not forget the connection you had with the Gem of Levage. You are a *unique* little wolf."

"And?" I demanded.

Chris shrugged. "Usually an anomaly like her would have the Midwest Pack siding with others to rid us of a potential problem that could get out of hand. I guess times have changed. I always thought the fall of your pack would be something far more cataclysmic than a doe-eyed brunette."

She strode to her desk and opened a laptop. While she worked, I noticed the floor-to-ceiling windows in the side room where she used to enjoy the sunrise were now draped with blackout curtains. As if I needed another reminder of what she was, the screen on her laptop flashed with the speed of her work, browser tabs opening and closing at a rate that tested the limits of the laptop's processor.

I glanced at Sky, wondering if it had been wise to bring her. Did Chris blame her, as well?

"Ethan," she said with her back to me, typing and scrolling and clicking, "you don't need to worry. Your little anomaly has no effect on my life, and until she does, she is safe from me. But I would make sure she is never my problem."

"Oh wow, thank you," Sky shot back. "You mean you aren't going to kidnap me and try to give me to the vampires to be murdered? You're so sweet. Do you like gift baskets? I should send you a gift basket. Such largesse should be rewarded."

I frowned, but Chris only chuckled as she worked. "So, Bambi, is it safe to assume they need this information for you?"

"It's Skylar, and no, I am just here with Ethan."

If she was trying to get under Chris's skin, it didn't work.

"I really would prefer to stay out of things like this, but I kind of feel like I owe you, Bambi."

Sky laughed. "It's Skylar, not Bambi. Do you really think

our past—you know, the whole thing with you trying to kidnap me to give me to the vampires—will be squared by this information?"

"You don't like me," Chris said, stopping her work to turn and give Sky a plastic, cordial smile. "I get it. It isn't undeserved. Now if only I could find it in me to care. Like I said, I feel like I kind of owe you. But whether or not you like me just isn't something I can care about. It's probably better if you don't."

When she was done taunting Sky, Chris wrote something on a piece of paper and handed it to me. "This is how much this information will cost you."

I scowled at the figure, then handed it back to her. "Try again. I asked for addresses and names, not for you to organize a meeting with them on a private island."

"That's what the information costs. If you aren't willing to pay, that's your problem. You can let yourself out."

"You're being unreasonable."

Her visage contorted into sudden, hot anger. "You want reasonable from a person you chose to let die!"

I bristled at the accusation. "I didn't have a choice!" I shouted back, tired of shouldering the blame for her choices. Had she forgotten how much she'd hated the idea of Demetrius controlling her? The Chris I remembered never wanted to become a vampire.

"You had a choice," she growled. Her eyes followed me as I stepped closer to Sky. "It just wasn't the choice you wanted. You can't always have things your way!"

She slapped the paper to my chest, hard enough to push me back on my heels. If the paper tumbling to my feet was meant as a distraction, I refused to take the bait. *She's fast,* I reminded myself. My eyes remained fixed on hers, my hands free and ready to counter if she acted on her anger.

"You want the information; this is how much it will cost. This isn't a rummage sale. We aren't going to haggle."

"No, it is more like extortion."

She gestured toward the door. "You are welcome to leave."

We glared back at each other. "Do you need an apology?" I snarled. *For trying to save you from Demetrius?* "If you need one, I will give it to you." *I'll give it to you for the pack, and because you might yet prove useful, once you get over yourself.* "Either you take the apology or deal with it."

I heard Sky sigh in relief beside me, but didn't dare take my eyes from Chris as anger rippled through her expression. Vampires were quick to anger and prone to violence. She was struggling with her new nature. She'd never understand that it would be worse had I changed her into a were-animal, assuming she'd even survived the process. If her desire for revenge overwhelmed her, she was welcome to try and take it. I had no desire to end her existence, such that it was, but if she forced my hand, I wouldn't bemoan one less vamp in the world. Demetrius could take the blame for that, for making her his slave instead of allowing her the humble human death that had been her right.

After a brief struggle, she chewed her lip. Her shoulders sank as tension left her body, but I remained on guard, wary of deception.

"Why don't you deal with this?" she said slyly. "This is my fee for the information. Either pay it or get the hell out. If you don't make a decision in the next minute—yes, I mean sixty seconds"—she glanced at her watch—"starting now, the price doubles."

I released a slow hiss of breath as I drew my phone from my pocket. She was the only source of information I had, and she knew it. If money was the price of her revenge, so be it. "Is the account the same?" I asked as I opened the banking app on my phone and selected the appropriate account for extortion.

She nodded.

I bit back a protest as I tapped in the amount, then completed the transfer. "Done," I muttered as I returned the phone to my pocket.

She turned back to her laptop. After a few key strokes and a double-click, she removed a fresh page from the printer tray, then handed it to Sky. "This one," she said, marking a name with a pen. "If you tell him I sent you, he will be a lot more amenable." She marked a few other names. "They will help, but there will be a price and it may not necessarily be money. And these two—well, I can't help you on this, but I strongly advise you to leave my name out of it, or they will never talk to you and will likely try to kill you."

She followed us to the door. "You should hope that Ann or Sean get better at their jobs, because I won't help you or your pack again, so please don't ask. We are done."

Sky blurted before Chris could close the door on us, "What do you know about spirit shades?"

I tensed at the revelation. The less she knew about our objective, the better, but it was too late.

"Is that what you are looking for, Bambi?" She took the paper from Sky's hand and circled two names, then handed it back to her. "Then you will only need to speak with them."

Sky glanced at the page, then asked, "What do you know about protected—"

"No, Bambi." Chris pressed a finger to Sky's lips. "You are part of the Midwest Pack, so *you* have no more business here with me." Removing her finger, she turned to me with a stern expression. "Don't come here again. Don't challenge my request. I mean it. That includes you, too, Bam—Skylar."

Once on the porch, I watched her disappear behind the door as she closed it between us. Sky remained silent until we were in the BMW.

"I guess that is one source we no longer have."

I glanced over my shoulder as I backed out of the driveway. "For now."

"You can't seriously believe she is going to change her mind?"

"Yes, but out of necessity. She was created by Demetrius. People will assume she has an intrinsic loyalty to him. No one will hire her again."

I glanced once at Chris's house in the rearview mirror as we left it behind.

"And you don't believe that blind loyalty exists?"

"Did you see how she responded to him?" I said. "A new vampire would never do anything to displease its creator. As they age, it becomes more obligatory than compulsory. Did you sense any of that between her and Demetrius?"

"I don't think she is capable of fealty, and displeasing people seems to be her thing."

I smiled at the thought that there might yet be some small part of Chris still there, untamable.

"Hmm, so that is the way to your heart? A person who actively tries to displease you?" Sky speculated, then returned to studying the names on the paper. "Pardon me for considering that the behavior of an insane person."

"She gets the job done." I shrugged, smirking. "Whether she makes enemies or friends in the process has never been a concern. I don't know of any job given to her that she didn't complete."

"The number of maimed, murdered, and betrayed that she leaves in her wake doesn't matter?"

"It matters that she always completes the job," I insisted, adding emphasis.

Sky sighed as she glanced at the paper. "Who do we visit first? There's one nearby. A couple more are close—four hours away, probably." She frowned. "One of the Tre'ases that knows about spirit shades is in Texas. Are we going to Texas?"

With any luck, that won't be necessary. "We'll visit the nearest one first."

She nodded.

"When do you want to leave, tomorrow?"

She fidgeted, giving me a sideways glance. After a moment, she explained awkwardly, "I don't want to leave until tomorrow when Kelly is better."

If she's better. It was entirely possible that she would never regain the use of her legs, but I wasn't going to rob Sky of her hope. I signaled to turn toward the retreat.

"I really don't like being chauffeured around." She frowned, shifting in her seat. "Can we go by my house so I can pick up my car?"

I gave her a skeptical look, wondering what she was up to, but I had no reason to object. "Sure."

A few minutes later, I pulled into her driveway. Before I even stopped the car, she blurted, "I want to go visit the Tre'ase with Josh instead of you."

"Just because you and my brother can't stay away from each other for longer than twenty-four hours, you will not put him in a dangerous situation. I am going with you."

"My relationship with Josh has nothing to do with it," she insisted. "Each time you encounter a Tre'ase, they respond poorly to you. One of them already isn't going to be friendly, why agitate them or the situation any more by bringing you?"

The leather cover of the steering wheel squeaked in my grip as I squeezed it with both hands. "Fine, if I need to stay outside, I will, but I will be close and Josh can come as well."

She rolled her eyes as she climbed out of the car, taking the paper with her. "Thank you, your majesty. Whatever would we have done without you granting our approval to leave the city?" She shut the door harder than necessary. I glared at her back as she strode to her front door and then went inside.

· · ·

Fifteen minutes later, I watched from my vantage point as Sky backed her car out of the driveway and drove off. "Predictable," I grumbled as I activated the tracking app on my phone, nestled it into the holder on the dash, then pulled out to follow her from a discreet distance. Had she meant what she said about wanting to take Josh with her, or was that just a ploy to get me out of the picture? Once again, she was blindly waltzing into danger.

I knew which Tre'ase she intended to visit, but hadn't paid much attention to the address. Without the piece of paper, I was obligated to follow her, which grew increasingly difficult as we put the city behind us. Long rural roads, where a new BMW M6 stood out, made it necessary to fall back a half mile, leaving me to rely almost exclusively on the tracker.

After an hour, I began cursing at the gas gauge as the needle approached empty. The nearest station was a mile behind me, and I'd no idea how much longer the drive was. Minutes? Hours? If I was forced to divert for fuel, I could find Sky again with the tracker, but I'd be giving her a private audience with the Tre'ase. If I ignored the gauge, I risked stranding myself on the road before she reached her destination. My fingers tightened around the steering wheel as I watched the miles tick on the odometer. I was calculating how long I had until a decision was forced on me when I noticed on the tracker that Sky had come to a stop.

A moment later, the paved road became gravel and quickly narrowed. A little farther and Sky's Honda Civic came into view, parked at the end of the road. She remained in her vehicle, glaring at me through her rearview mirror as I parked behind her. In front of her, the gravel continued as a path, but a barrier blocked the way, a sign stating, "Private Property." Beyond that, the path twisted, and any view of what lay beyond was obscured by a dense forest of high grass, shrubbery, and willow trees.

I got out of my SUV, walked up to the Honda, and opened her door.

She greeted me with a sardonic cheerfulness. "Hi."

"Hi," I said, imitating her. "You're so predictable it's not even a challenge anymore."

Her eyes rolled as she emerged from the car and started on the path, skirting the barrier. Given the slight stiffness of her walk, I assumed that she was carrying a pistol, but there was no telltale bulge beneath her thin jacket. Her arms swayed smoothly at her side, without the slight arcing curve required of a hip-holstered weapon. *A waist holster, then,* I decided.

I closed the Honda door with an exaggerated gesture, then jogged to join her, matching her stride. Her lips pressed into a narrow crease as she prepared for my rebuke. "Skylar," I said, trying to check my temper, "I am only going to say this once, so I need you to listen carefully. For whatever reason, Sebastian wants you alive. I couldn't care less if the Tre'ase rips you to pieces the moment you walk through the door. But for now, our responsibility is to keep you alive. Your behavior is making it more difficult to care whether or not we succeed. Perhaps we may find it easier if you weren't alive." I wrapped my fingers around her forearm and stopped her, obliging her to meet my gaze. "Do you understand me?"

She yanked her arm free, matching my anger with a hateful look. "I don't need a babysitter, and I'm sorry you feel that I do. I need answers and I am going to do what it takes to get them. You've made 'babysitting' me your job; no one gave it to you. Either you learn to love it or quit. I hope you quit. Regarding the pack no longer caring to keep me safe or alive—big deal. If I don't get the Aufero, I am as good as dead anyway; so you won't have to make that decision."

She walked faster, the gravel crunching beneath her long, belligerent strides in front of me. As we walked deeper into the woods, the forest slowly strangled the winding path, threatening to swallow it. Visibility was limited to mere feet as the overhanging foliage thickened, pressing down on us. Despite broad daylight, we were walking into a gloomy, oppressive darkness.

After a few minutes, the path ended suddenly at the door of a small, brown cottage buried beneath a canopy of interweaving tree branches that obscured the sky above. Thick foliage grew to within inches of the walls, forming a protective barrier.

Sky stopped at the bottom of the porch, licking her lips as she stared at the door. I'd expected her to walk straight up and barge in, but she was showing caution. *Good. She might have a chance to survive, after all.* I gently placed my hand at the small of her back, reminding her that she wasn't alone. "I'm ready when you are."

She smartly inventoried her weapons, revealing a Ruger LCP holstered at her waist beneath her jacket, and a sheathed knife on her right calf beneath her pant leg. I smiled approvingly, but she didn't notice.

Finally she took in a deep breath and stepped up to the door. Her hand was raised in a fist to knock when a deep, welcoming voice spoke from the other side.

"Come in. I was wondering how long it would take for you to get to the door."

Sky turned to me and swallowed. I nodded, walking up behind her. After a moment's hesitation, she took in a breath, then pushed the door slowly open and stepped inside.

I'd only met two Tre'ases before. With the ability to change her appearance at will, Gloria had presented as a seemingly harmless old crone. Thaddeus, her son, had lacked that ability. As a hideous half man, half horned demon, he'd been forced to hide in the woods, much as this Tre'ase did. I'd prepared for the same disgusting sight, but found a man with broad shoulders, light brown skin, and short wavy brown hair watching us with a curious, pleased expression from the edge of the kitchen, just beyond the entryway of the small cottage. Tattoo sleeves wound up thick arms and disappeared beneath the short sleeves of his tan t-shirt.

Lavender eyes seemed to look right through us.

If he felt any unease at our presence in his home, he didn't show it. I assumed he had the magical means to monitor anything that followed his path.

His chin turned up slightly in my direction. As he approached me, his lips bent into a curious half-smile. I wondered what it was about me that drew his attention. So did Sky. I waited, patiently annoyed, as he observed me with a disassociated gaze. Was he listening to my heartbeat? My breath? Did he sense my wolf? After an uncomfortable moment, the smile on his lips broadened. He eased out a hand to touch me, as if I might be an illusion, then changed his mind, deciding instead to slowly circle me.

I didn't appreciate the objectification.

"Remarkable," he whispered.

I shifted uncomfortably, clearing my throat.

"Logan?" Sky asked.

"Yes," he answered pleasantly. "How may I help you?"

Without waiting for an answer, he turned back to me, gently passing his fingers between us as if he were tracing the edge of something intangible. *Does he sense the dark elf magic?* If Logan was a witness to my curse, he was a threat, but was he a threat I could do anything about?

He raised a palm toward my cheek, then stopped. "May I?"

My answer was immediate and unambiguous. "No."

"Just for a moment. Please. I will be a better host if my curiosity is satisfied."

I scowled. According to Chris, Logan was the closest and most likely source of information on her list. We needed his cooperation. If he'd sensed the dark elf magic, then the damage was already done. I'd have to assume that every Tre'ase we met could sense the magic as well.

If I declined, would he deny us the information we sought? If I accepted, would it make him more pliant, or was he just playing a game? There could be an ulterior motive to his request. There were some spells that required touch.

I glanced at Sky, who gave me an imploring look.

My eyes narrowed to discerning slits as I met his unfocused gaze. There was a harmless innocence about his curiosity, but he wasn't harmless, I reminded myself. Finally, I decided the potential reward was worth the risk.

"Okay," I said, a hint of harsh warning in my tone.

Logan eagerly stepped closer to me, his forehead unexpectedly inches from my chin. Anticipation and excitement played over his countenance before he finally pressed his warm palm to my skin. Something about him flashed, causing me to blink. *A glamour*, I realized. He was wearing a disguise, after all. Though the flash was too short to reveal his true nature, I suspected it was similar to Thaddeus's.

He abruptly withdrew his hand from my cheek and stepped back, rubbing the tips together as if checking for damage. Once satisfied, he lowered his hand and walked into the living room. His gait was awkward, as if unfamiliar with the shape of his glamour. I suspected he'd chosen it for my benefit, but couldn't decipher the purpose.

"Please have a seat," he said, gesturing before he eased himself into a tuxedo chair and then casually slung his legs over one armrest. He waited patiently, listening as we crossed the room and sat together on the red couch. The rest of the cottage's decor was equally mismatched.

Josh would be right at home here.

"Do you want something to drink?" he asked.

"No," Sky and I said simultaneously, with her adding, "thank you."

Logan smiled politely. "How may I help you?"

"You don't want to know how we found you?" Sky asked.

I opened my mouth, but cut short my rebuke. Her interview skills needed refining. We were there to obtain information, not to give it. There was no point in drawing Logan's attention to the peculiarities of our visit. Doing so could only make him uncomfortable, or inquisitive, and would get us no closer to the answers we sought.

He shrugged, unconcerned. "Very few people know I am here. The ones that do, I know and trust that they wouldn't send harm my way. And if they did, I am confident I can protect myself."

"Chris sent us."

"Ah, Chris." He smiled. "I adore her. She's a delightful little misfit with a temper to match. It is a pleasure to watch her. How is she faring these days? Still causing trouble?"

Before I could dismiss the question and get to the point, Sky blurted, "She's a vampire."

"Really?" He straightened in his chair, swinging his feet to the floor in front of him. He seemed more curious than concerned, as if he were asking about the characters of his favorite television show. "How did that happen?"

"A long story," she said. "She thought you would be able to answer some questions for me."

"Of course," he answered, his hands and forearms draping over the armrests as he eased back into the chair. "I will do my best. May I ask that once I answer your questions, you offer a favor to me in the future?"

I gasped reflexively as a vibrant electricity filled the room, a rush of magic that took my breath away. It took Sky's as well. Logan grinned at our reaction. Though he sat entirely still, I saw movement on his arms. His tattoos had come to life, morphing as they slid and rolled along his skin. After a moment, they stopped. The tattoos had changed, become more archaic. Only a few of the symbols were familiar to me, not enough to comprehend the magic he'd just made available to himself.

Tre'ases loved traps hidden in bargains. Flicking my eyes to Sky, I saw the sharp intake of breath that indicated she was about to speak, but she'd no idea of the danger she was walking into. One poorly worded phrase and she might spend the rest of her life at his mercy.

"No," I declared first. "If you answer our questions, there will be no debts, no favors. We will pay you cash if necessary, but nothing more."

He seemed to grow suddenly bored, turning his head aside and smacking his lips in disappointment. "I don't require your money," he said with a reserved politeness. "Just a remembrance that I helped you when you offered nothing to me."

I chose my words carefully. "We acknowledge the assistance, but offer nothing more."

He sighed. "Very well."

I felt Sky edge closer to me. In her eyes I saw the growing awareness that she'd underestimated the danger of this encounter. I gave her a reassuring smile.

Tired of waiting, Logan splayed the fingers of one hand in an impatient gesture as he inquired, "What information do you seek?"

I nodded to Sky to answer.

"Spirit shades," she said. "What do you know about them?"

Another bored sigh from Logan. "They are nothing more than unsettled souls cursed to walk the earth without a body. Nothing special."

"Do you know how many there are?"

"I am sure there are still spirit shades, but not nearly as many as there were in my youth. We are becoming extinct, maybe less than a thousand of us exist, and most do not live here in the States. No one really requests that we create spirit shades anymore. It is such a taxing effort that the offerings for us to do it are considerable. I assume those that do know of our abilities aren't willing to pay the cost. Perhaps it is better that people do not request that of us. I have not created one, and I doubt that I will."

"And why is that?" I asked.

"Except for a few humans who were made shades as punishment, it is far crueler than death for them—"

"Because of being immortal," Sky said.

"No, because they are alive but unable to live without a body to experience life through. They usually have a problem finding hosts. No shade with great powers would consider a human because humans have nothing to offer. Most shades were killed for a reason. To give them a chance to exist again is a very unwise decision. I am sure there are many types of powerful shades: witches, elves, mages, and even demons. Of course, no one could change a vampire for obvious reasons, and your kind"—he grinned—"back then weren't the pretty little things you are now. Then you were more animal than man: gruesome, vile creatures." He gave a slight shiver, then stated what he felt should be obvious to anyone, "Animals can*not* become shades."

I snorted derisively. "What about the fae?" I asked, ignoring a pressing glance from Sky. *Caution doesn't require us to embrace his insults.* "Are they immune to such a fate?"

Logan smiled. "It was mutually accepted that we would never help them, but of course there are some of my kind that enjoy the anarchy and destruction that only a fae can deliver."

"Really?" I asked, surprised. "Fae?"

He laughed gently. "Yes, you all call them fae now, which is quite fitting since they are mere fractions of their ancestors, the Faerie. What this world considers fae"—he rolled his eyes—"are what I consider demi-Faerie, if not quarter-Faerie. Their mere tricks and poor execution of their pitiful little spells are just a minuscule representation of what Faeries can do. Oooh"—he gesticulated, comically mimicking the casting of a spell—"my magic can make you fall in love with me. Look at me, my magic can force truth with a kiss." He waved off his disgust. "Whatever little spells they manage is nothing compared to those of their Faerie ancestors."

Placing his hands over his knees, he rose and walked into the open kitchen to pour himself a coffee. When he gestured with the pot, I declined. I gave Sky a warning look, but she declined before noticing. *She is learning,* I thought appreciatively. *Never accept anything from a Tre'ase. Anything.* For them, everything was a bargain, and it was possible to unwittingly accept their terms before the terms had even been announced. *Buyer beware applies to magic, as well as used cars.*

The smell of French vanilla coffee steamed from a mug in Logan's hand as he returned to his chair. "Where was I? Oh yes. Faeries, the original, were powerful beings, masters of chaos and violence. They were so powerful in strength and magic that they were feared by most in this world. No one bothered them. The only thing that stopped them was the limited number of them that existed. Too few to be the threat that they could have been. They possessed the strongest and most nearly unstoppable form of magic that I had ever seen. They had the ability to manipulate the world with the same ease with which we blink our eyes. They reproduced with one another, but their progeny were so few it was only a matter of time before they mated with humans. You want to retain power, you don't reproduce with the weakest.... It never turns out well." He offered us an apologetic expression. "Well, sometimes it works out. Were-animals were dreadful creatures. I still find it difficult to believe they found willing human mates. Perhaps they weren't all willing," he added suggestively. He seemed to be waiting for a reaction from me. Finding none, he conceded, "Or maybe they were; we all have our own little perversions. Faeries made us look like

183

docile little peddlers of magic. No, you definitely didn't want to make a Faerie a shade. Doing so would likely ensure your death."

"Why?" Sky asked.

"We all like magic and power." He smiled at me. "Even death has its appeal. That is why I am enjoying this visit so much. It can be cleansing, whether it's yours or someone else's, and it settles well on the palate."

"How does creating a Faerie as a shade ensure the death of a Tre'ase?"

"You create a shade, you are linked to it indefinitely, which has its advantages. But as I stated before, usually shades were formerly powerful beings, and that craving to have possession of it again doesn't die with the loss of their body. They are very selective of their hosts, seeking ones with the ability to use magic. They pick hosts that are weak enough that the idea of hosting them is a benefit. The longer it is hosted, the closer the bond becomes, and then one begins to wonder if the actions of the host are truly their desires or that of the hosted. I can imagine that it can become quite the dilemma. The hosted lives past the life of its host. Once the host dies, it moves on to find another one. And they will continue to live until the Tre'ase that created them dies."

I swallowed, my worried gaze flicking to Sky. Josh had believed that Gloria had created Maya, but that wasn't possible. Gloria was dead, but Maya still lived, still kept Sky alive. Somewhere out there, among a thousand Tre'ases scattered around the world, was a ticking time bomb. It could go off at any moment, without warning. When it did, Maya would die, and so would Sky.

She wasn't the only one who was vulnerable.

Logan continued. "Now you see why I don't want the hassle. What if the shade is a terror and needs to be stopped? Well, you can kill the host, but the shade lives on and will just find another body to inhabit. You kill the Tre'ase and you correct that problem."

I heard Sky swallow her fear, even while she tried to keep a calm expression as Logan appeared to absorb her anxiety as if it were expected, as if he sensed the shade in her. He seemed to expect the same anxiety from me.

"This visit has been quite nice for me." He rose, signaling the end of our conversation. "Please come again, under a different agreement."

As we walked the path back toward our cars, my mind raced with a new worry. The Tre'ase that created Maya had to be found, but what could we do to protect it? If Logan was a reasonable example, the demons were too powerful to safely imprison. Even if cooperative, what was the normal life expectancy of these demons? Logan had said that creating a spirit shade required a significant investment of power, which meant Maya's creator wasn't young. Even if every precaution were taken to keep the demon safe, nothing could stop the normal course of its biological existence. At some point, it would die. It could die at any moment, and I couldn't do anything to stop it.

I shook the thought from my mind, replacing it with another concern about Maya. If Logan's prediction was accurate, Maya was steadily exerting greater influence on Sky. At some point, she might take control entirely. What if—

"What was that about?" Sky asked, startling me.

"What?"

"The Tre'ases, either they love you or hate you. The one that claims to have an obscure fondness for death was quite intrigued by you."

"Make up your mind," I snapped. "Are you concerned that they like me or dislike me?"

"I'm concerned with both. Why is one who professes an adoration for death so intrigued by you?"

185

"As with you, I try not to concern myself with what goes on in the mind of someone that I will never understand. It makes life simpler that way."

So much for questions.

We walked the rest of the way in silence. Behind the wheels of our cars, a brief standoff ensued as we each waited for the other to leave first. While I thought Sky now understood the danger of dealing with a Tre'ase, I wasn't about to give her the chance to prove me wrong. It didn't take long before she gave up with an exaggerated sigh and drove off. I waited a minute before following her, my eyes stalking the gas gauge as I looked up the nearest gas station.

*a*s I pulled into the garage at the retreat, I noticed the absence of Josh's Jeep. I frowned at my phone. No calls. No messages. We hadn't agreed on a timeline, but I wasn't going to wait much longer before I tore apart the city looking for him.

There was a general agitation in the house as those affected by Mercury impatiently waited for it to rise.

I was on my way to the clinic to check on Kelly when Sebastian called me into his office. I sat in front of his desk and filled him in on our visit to Logan, then waited as he took in the information, weighing his thoughts.

Eventually, he leaned back into his chair and said, "Maya will have to wait until this matter with Gideon is resolved."

"Finding the Tre'ase that created her is going to be expensive, perhaps impossible."

"We might be able to use the link between them to track the Tre'ase."

I nodded. Josh might be able to trace the link, or at least use it to narrow down the search. "Have you considered how you want to deal with Abigail?" I asked, changing the subject.

He brought his fingers together into a pyramid, gently

tapping the tips together. "You're certain that she is the one who turned the creature loose on her brother?"

I saw by the determined line of his jaw that he'd already made up his mind but wanted independent confirmation. "A number of candidates for the elven leadership have died under mysterious circumstances, but somehow Gideon miraculously survives the attempt. There are already rumors circulating among the elves that it was his virility that enabled him to survive." Sebastian and I shared an appreciative smile at the blatant but effective propaganda. "He doesn't have the ambition for such machinations, but she does. As a female, she is ineligible to lead the elves, but she's not above using her brother as a proxy. Assassinating the other candidates eliminates the competition. Poisoning Gideon eliminates any suspicion against him. It also gives him the motivation for revenge, and it will galvanize his already considerable public support. If this isn't Abigail's plot, then there is another power seeking to put Gideon in charge, but we've no sense of that. My money's on the sister."

Sebastian tapped his fingers together a few times, then leaned forward, resting his forearms on his desk. "We'll continue to protect them as long as doing so is to our advantage. If there are signs that he may lose the election, we'll need to revisit our support."

"I agree."

His eyes held mine, searching for something. I saw there the same caution he used whenever there was a delicate matter between us. "I haven't had a chance to offer you my condolences for your grandmother," he said cautiously. "I'll understand if you need to take some time."

"That won't be necessary," I said stiffly. "We weren't close."

As he chose his next words carefully, I wondered why the cautious dance. His amber eyes were steady, empathetic, as they studied me. "The pack relies on your steadiness," he stated, leaving the rest unsaid.

Between the dark elf magic and the unsettling appearances of Dennis, I'd been off, and it had been noticed. I shifted in my seat, frowned, debated how to answer. Revealing my newly discovered lineage would put Sebastian in a dangerous position. I couldn't do that to him, but I'd never lied to him, either. I could tell him about Dennis and conveniently leave out the story of my newfound magic but was loathe to mislead him.

In any other pack, I would be the Alpha. I didn't challenge Sebastian because I recognized the strength of his leadership, and he recognized my value as his second. It was an arrangement of mutual benefit and respect.

"There are some *unexpected* challenges," I said carefully.

He frowned. I felt his searching gaze probing deeper through my facade. "Is there a threat to the pack?"

I took in a breath and let it out in a frustrated gasp. "Only if I describe it. This is something I need to handle alone, outside the pack."

He nodded, folded his hands in his lap. After a moment, he informed me, "Our house on the North Side was broken into last night."

I pushed to the edge of my seat. The security of our properties was my responsibility. Under normal circumstances, I rotated pack members randomly through the properties, checking security, taking out garbage, picking up mail, rotating lights to give an impression of use. I'd been too distracted since my encounter with Lucas Reed. "Who? How?"

"A pair of vampires that were wandering through Chicago, picking out vacant properties on their way to New York. Tim caught them in the middle of dinner."

A growl rumbled from my chest.

Sebastian waved off my obvious assumption. "They're not

Demetrius's. A pair of wanderers taking a joy ride from coast to coast. Tim checked them out."

"They're destroyed, I assume." If not, I'd kill them myself.

Sebastian gave a slight sigh. "I gave them to Demetrius for punishment."

I frowned, but it was a reasonable choice. He didn't tolerate interlopers, and it saved us the task of cleaning up the mess. If any vamps came looking for their pals, they'd be Demetrius's problem as well. Still, the situation left a sour sense in my gut. What seemed an inconsequential incident could quickly blossom into a much bigger situation. I'd thought my problems were contained, isolated from the pack, but I was wrong.

Feeling the tension in the office as Sebastian waited for an explanation, I glanced at my palm.

"If there is a risk to the pack . . ." he said, allowing his voice to trail off.

I swallowed before answering. "Knowledge is risk. If I tell what I know, the risk is extreme."

"Between us, then."

"I can't put you in that position."

"I take responsibility for my own choices."

"Sebastian—"

"I have a responsibility to every member of this pack, including you. It is a responsibility that goes beyond issues of my personal safety."

I took a deep breath, then filled him in about my grandmother, Lucas Reed, my newfound magical talents, and my hunt for the Aufero. He listened soberly, keeping questions to himself.

"If you feel it would be best for the pack," I finished, "I will leave." Aside from my brother, the pack was my life. Imagining a life without it was difficult. I'd likely leave Chicago, though I'd stay close to my brother, unless he chose to join me.

"Can you contain the magic?" he asked.

So far. Since I'd nearly killed Sky, I'd managed to keep the dark elf magic in check. "It is under control, but it remains unfamiliar. My understanding of it is limited. The risk of an unexpected encounter is significant, but will reduce over time."

"Have you considered keeping the magic?"

I assumed he was testing me. "I do not share my brother's ambition for power. There is no upside to this magic."

He nodded, thinking. "The Aufero is the best option. The pack needs plausible deniability, but if there's something I can do to assist, tell me."

I nodded, then left his office, grateful and guilty for having shared my burden.

In the clinic, I found Gideon and Kelly looking uncomfortable as Gavin paced the room. His panther was steadily rising closer to the surface in anticipation of Mercury's rise, when he and his were-animal would be more intertwined than any other time. Unlike the others, he resisted the need to change. Whether he was keeping Kelly company or protecting her from the elf, I wasn't sure, but I could see by the tension in her body, the wary look in her eyes as they tracked his movement from one end of the clinic to the other in a repetitive cycle, that he was unnerving her.

Seeing me in the doorway, she gave me a pleading look.

"Gavin," I said, gesturing for him to follow me out of the room. He scowled at me, then at Gideon, before joining me in the hall. As I walked toward the living area, he was obliged to follow. "Gideon knows that he and his sister will be held responsible for anything that happens to Kelly. He's not going to harm her."

Gavin's eyes darkened with anger. "I'll be the judge of that."

"She's on edge," I said, softening my tone. "Your agitation

191

is affecting her." A sullen acceptance came over him. He nodded. "You should change."

"When it's time."

I was going to insist when he glanced out the window. His shoulders tensed. A dark look came over him and he strode out the front door.

Before I could follow him, Sebastian appeared, getting my attention to discuss his concerns regarding Dr. Baker. He, too, was defying his natural instinct in deference to Kelly. Where Gavin's agitation had long surpassed his usefulness to her, Dr. Baker's attention was critical. How long would that last? At what point would we have to force the doctor to change?

We were discussing the issue when Gavin returned to the house with Sky close behind him. His agitation was worse than before he'd left. Gold sparks flashed in his eyes, indicating his panther was just below the surface. Lost in some thought, he ignored us. Turning toward the clinic, he ran a trembling hand through his hair as he walked by.

"Gavin," I said, infusing my voice with command.

He stopped. In his glare I saw just how close he was to losing control.

"Mercury is rising," Sebastian cautioned. "You need to change. Shouldn't you be outside preparing with the others?"

"What do I need to prepare for?" Gavin snapped. "It peaks. I change. Then I run around in panther form for a couple hours, and then I'm back. Preparation isn't needed. I'm not going to leave her here alone while *it* roams through this house unchecked."

"We will make sure she is okay," Sebastian said.

He rolled his eyes. "Of course, because you all did such a great job before."

"She'll be fine," I promised. "He's more of a nuisance than a threat."

His eyes narrowed as he leaned toward me. "She can't

move her legs. He's not just a nuisance; he's a problem. It is because of him she is like this."

"It was an unexpected event," Sebastian said, his tone betraying thin patience.

"And that makes it okay with you?"

"No, it's not okay, but you not changing and being an irrational ass isn't going to help, either. You want to protect her, so do we—"

"If you really wanted to protect her and this pack, we wouldn't have gotten involved, damn it! So what if Gideon had died? He's not the ruler and probably never will be. What did saving him do for us?"

I tensed, exchanging a meaningful glance with Sebastian. Gavin was a caustic personality by default, but the influence of Mercury couldn't be underestimated. Patience was required, but there were limits. Engaging in his argumentative nature would only encourage him.

"I don't think I am going to change this time," Gavin decided.

Denying the call of Mercury was akin to denying his true nature.

Sebastian tried to reason with him. "Just because you *can* do something doesn't mean you should. She's scared and you seem to comfort her. She needs you at your best. You're a jackass when you don't change. Go change so that you can be there for her, because she needs you better than you are now."

"I'll be fine," he snapped.

Sebastian took one step toward Gavin, glaring down at him. "You will change," he commanded, "and you will do it now. There will not be any more discussion about it. Do you understand me?"

He held Sebastian's gaze for a moment, challenging him until he saw the amber fire in the Alpha's eyes. Gavin was going to change, or he was going to leave the grounds, but he wasn't going to be allowed near Kelly. Faced with a brick wall of determination, he slowly lowered his gaze in reluctant submission. After a moment's hesitation, he turned and walked out of the house, presumably to change.

Sky's gaze flicked between Sebastian and me. When neither of us entertained her unspoken questions, she rolled her eyes and slipped between us on her way to the clinic.

I drew my phone from my pocket and examined it.

"Any word from Josh?" Sebastian asked.

"No." It was nearly eight.

I was going to ask Sebastian a question when Gavin's panther padded into the house, his clothes gripped in his teeth. He uttered a casual growl as he padded between us, following Sky.

Later in the day, I was on my way to the gym when I noticed Sky and Winter leave together. For a moment, I considered following them, then thought better of it. Whatever mischief Sky was up to, she couldn't get in much trouble with Winter along. The were-snake was already chafing under the burden of guilt for Kelly's condition; she'd stop at nothing to protect Sky, even from herself.

I spent the next few hours in the gym, watching my phone and plotting what I would do to Gideon in order to leverage his assistance in finding Josh and his sister. I doubted she would leave her brother in our grasp while double-crossing us, but it didn't hurt to plan.

It was close to nine when Sky called down to me from the stairs. She'd returned, and so had Josh and Abigail. I changed quickly and found them in the clinic with Sebastian. The tension in the room was oppressive. *They failed,* I realized, noting my brother's dark look. I glanced to Kelly and found her supine on the table, propped on her elbows, her expression crestfallen. Abigail faced Sebastian's angry glower with an assumed casualness, but the way she fidgeted with her braid betrayed her anxiety. She stood protectively between him and Gideon, who appeared disappointed.

Whatever the cause of their failure, the creature that poisoned Kelly was an elven creation. Only the elves possessed the cure, somewhere. Until the cure was obtained and Kelly walked again, one of the twins would remain in our possession at all times. Their devotion to each other was our only leverage.

Sebastian frowned down at her, his tone weighted with judgment as he said, "So you have nothing?"

Before she could answer, Winter walked into the room, her obvious relief at seeing Abigail quickly fading to concern as she read the tension in the room. Sky slipped in beside her, trying to remain unnoticed.

"Mason didn't take my request for assistance to help you at all well," Abigail said, trying to sound exasperated. "And he must have put the word out because no one would give us any information."

Josh ran a hand through his tousled hair. "Most people claimed they didn't have any idea what it is. I have a hard time believing that so many people were killed by this thing and no one knows anything."

"Even if Mason could help, he will not," Abigail explained delicately, imploring Sebastian to understand. "Now that there is an alliance with the witches, he has a renewed sense of power. He feels invincible and no longer fears you as an enemy."

Sebastian's rising anger filled the room. "Invincible? It will only be a matter of time before he no longer has any control; he has foolishly rendered Marcia too much of it. Your people will not be any better off. Instead, they will become victims of her thirst for even more power. She will destroy you from within."

"I know," she admitted, allowing a weighted amount of

exasperation, "but he was chosen to lead and most follow him blindly. I share your feelings and have voiced it so many times, that now, I have lost favor with him and most of my people." She lowered her gaze, making a display of shame for Sebastian's benefit.

Is she playing for his sympathy? Is this part of her plan, to use the pack in her efforts to gain power? Unlikely, I thought. To gain leverage, she would've had to anticipate the creature infecting one of our own. She was intelligent, ambitious, and clever to some degree, but her machinations appeared to be two-dimensional, playing only a step in advance. To intentionally infect Kelly and use her situation to manipulate the pack into enhancing her position with the elves required multiple levels of cunning. Few played the game that well, and she would have to walk a fine line indeed to navigate her people's inherent distrust of were-animals if word of such an alliance became known.

No, I decided. She would see any association with us as a risk to Gideon's chances of becoming the elven leader. She'd used us as cover for her brother's recovery. That was to be the extent of our involvement. Kelly's infection was unplanned, but that didn't mean Abigail wasn't fishing for an advantage, a way to manipulate the current circumstances in her favor.

Sebastian scrutinized her carefully. His anger felt like a pressure in the room, pushing against everyone. Amber flashed in his eyes as he drew a phone from his pocket.

"There will be no reasoning with him," I cautioned. Without the possibility of agreement, appealing to Mason only enhanced his position, while weakening ours.

Sebastian asked Abigail, "Who else will have any information on elven creatures?"

"Maybe the witches." She shrugged. "I doubt they would enter any alliance with anyone blindly. They will know enough about us, maybe more."

Josh stopped chewing his nails to glance at Kelly. She was doing her best to appear hopeful, but his failure to return with a cure had left her dejected. His features softened into resigned empathy as he declared, "Marcia will not help without an offering."

I understood exactly what he intended. She had only allowed his alliance with the pack out of spite, assuming that he would struggle and eventually crawl back to her. That he'd developed into one of the most powerful witches in the country represented a challenge to her authority. She'd take any advantage to pry him from the pack and reclaim dominion over him.

Glancing at Kelly, I understood why Josh would consider such a sacrifice. She was one of us. As she cared for us, it was our job to ensure her safety, yet one of us had brought a danger to her that she should've never faced. That was Winter's mistake, but Kelly was our responsibility. The pack took care of its own.

"No," I stated, drawing my phone from my pocket. Josh thought Marcia was our last option, but he was mistaken. "Give me a minute." I walked into Sebastian's office and closed the door. On my phone, my finger hovered over Claudia's number. If I asked, she would help. I wasn't sure what form that help would take, but she was a woman of many unexpected connections, respected by all of the factions. If there was someone who could help Kelly, Claudia would know, but I couldn't help the sinking feeling that I was betraying her by asking. Whether she used her abilities or her connections, there was always a cost to her. Out of respect and appreciation, I'd always been reluctant to draw her into my world.

I grimaced at the phone, trying hard to think of some other avenue to explore first, but there was none. It wasn't just about Kelly, either. After seeing Josh's expression in the clinic, I knew that if I couldn't find another way, he'd go to

Marcia on his own and make whatever bargain she required in order to enlist her help—another expression of his recklessness, but it was also selfless. I couldn't allow him to make that sacrifice. Claudia wouldn't allow it, either.

She answered after several rings. I knew by the singing of birds in the background that she was in her garden. "Ethan, how are you?" While she pitched her voice to sound casual, I knew by the slight strain in her tone that she was worried, seeking confirmation, but that was a different conversation. "Ethan?" she repeated, her concern more apparent as I struggled to find my voice.

I forced air through my throat as I answered, "I need your help."

There was only a slight hesitation, just enough for both of us to weigh the significance of those few words.

"Tell me everything," she said. After I finished, she informed me, "Wait there. Give me two hours."

Precisely two hours later, she arrived at the house with a man I'd never seen before. He was tall and slender, dressed professionally in dark slacks with a matching jacket, a gray vest, and a black tie. He wore expensive sunglasses that hid his eyes. A tightly trimmed goatee emphasized thin, mirthless lips framed by permanent frown lines. Two large men—bodyguards—followed him into the house. In contrast to his grim professionalism, Claudia appeared relaxed and casual in dark slacks, a white short-sleeved button-down shirt, and a multicolored scarf draped over her shoulders.

As he stood in the entryway, the man ran nervous fingers over what little brown hair he had left.

Claudia gave me a slight smile before directing her attention to Sebastian. "He is one of the Creed's assistants. I think he will be helpful."

"Claudia, thank you. I owe you."

She waved off the gesture. "No debts. It was my pleasure." She directed a maternal smile toward Josh as she slipped off one glove, and then the other, then took Sebastian's hand into hers. It was a surprising gesture, a rare use of her gifts that left me puzzled as to her intentions. Was this a price paid, or was there some other purpose involved in her gesture? Sebastian tensed, but accepted her gift without resistance.

The room remained respectfully quiet for several minutes until she smiled at him. Relief washed over Sebastian's face. He bent to kiss her lightly on each cheek, then whispered something so softly that I couldn't make it out, even with my enhanced hearing.

As she released his hand, he said, "It is good seeing you again."

"And you, too." On her way out the door, she hesitated, turned back to Sebastian with a curious look. She gave him a faint smile, then turned and walked out of the house, leaving the assistant and his bodyguards behind.

Once the door closed, the assistant claimed our attention by clearing his throat. With slow deliberation, he pushed his glasses higher onto his nose, then drew his satchel close to his chest. "You are in need of my assistance," he said, his tone curt and professional to the point of arrogance. "What can I help you with?" His brows raised slightly when he noticed Abigail. He frowned, then turned back to Sebastian.

"Yes," he said. "Follow me."

As I followed our guest to the clinic, I wondered what the connection was to my godmother that brought this reluctant servant of the Creed to our aid, and just what aid he could provide.

We found Dr. Baker hunched over a microscope on his desk, a stack of seemingly obscure medical books in disarray next to the microscope. At our entrance, a glint of hope lightened his tired mood. He rose to greet the assistant with a shake of his hand, which was politely accepted. Gideon nodded from his chair in the corner—the farthest corner from Kelly's bed, where Gavin stood close. At the sight of our guest, a bitter recognition flashed in his eyes.

He sidled closer to Kelly as he greeted the assistant with a twisted sneer. "Bernard."

She glanced between the two, skeptical.

The assistant smirked back. "Gavin. It is good to see you here. The new city must be a welcome change."

A nasty retort was on Gavin's lips until a look from Kelly stopped him. He remained silent, but the resentment in his glare spoke volumes. I wondered what it was that had previously brought these two men together.

Disrupting the tension between them, Sebastian described just how Kelly had become afflicted, and by what. Bernard listened with apparent indifference.

Once Sebastian had finished, Dr. Baker added with an uncomfortable gaze toward Kelly, "The paralysis is progressing. It appears to have a different effect on her than it did on Gideon." He gestured to the elf. "It left him comatose, but once the creature was removed, he regained consciousness after about an hour."

Bernard turned to Gideon. "It was on you first?"

The elf nodded.

Bernard's expression became puzzled. He turned back to Kelly. "Madame, did things happen as they report?"

"Yes."

He walked to the table near Dr. Baker's desk and examined the jar with the creature trapped inside.

"It's a sleeper," Gavin stated.

"Yes, a Tod Schlaf," Bernard said admiringly. He glanced over his shoulder to Gavin. "But the boorish translation would be *sleeper*." Ignoring Gavin's indignation, Bernard straightened, drawing his hands together at his waist. His thumbs worked over and around each other while he considered the details of Kelly's situation.

The room was still, silent, as we waited for him to provide answers.

When he finally spoke, his tone was perfunctory. He addressed Kelly without bothering to meet her gaze. "Madame, you are not cursed, are you?"

She looked to Sebastian, confused.

"No," he answered for her, "she isn't a were-animal."

"But you consort with the cursed," Bernard said, his gaze roving over each of us from above the rims of his glasses. "Would it be too much to ask why?"

"I work here," she explained, as if the answer were obvious.

"Are you indentured?"

"No."

"If you work here, I doubt your skills are substandard," he remarked, pushing his glasses back up onto his nose. "Could you not find employment among the civilized?"

I tensed, suppressing an irritated growl.

"I chose to work here," she snapped, "because I like them and I like my job."

Bernard's lips spread into a thin semblance of a sympathetic smile. "You seem wise, but your choice in associates has shown a true lapse in judgment. I hope once this is over that is remedied and you find that your love of this job isn't worth what you will endure by sheer association"—his eyes flicked toward Sebastian—"with certain people." He sniffed obnoxiously, then continued before she could respond. "And your connection to Claudia, may I ask the particulars?"

"Does it matter?" she asked, barely hiding her dislike behind a joyless smile.

"Yes. I am curious why a woman of such power and means, who chooses a position of abject neutrality, is so interested in your survival. Why have you been given such favor?"

If not for my godmother, and for Kelly's need, I would've cuffed his head and schooled him on proper courtesy. Whatever sway or obligation she held over Bernard, he wasn't here willingly. I wondered if his provocative, insulting manner was an attempt to draw a reaction that would justify his leaving us without fulfilling his obligation.

I glanced at Sky, noting her particular interest in the reference to my godmother. That was going to lead to questions, eventually.

Realizing he wouldn't get more than a harsh stare from Kelly, Bernard turned to Abigail. "Do you know how to get to Elysian?"

She blushed as she shook her head.

"You've never been considered worthy of an invitation?" he asked, surprised.

Shamed, she glanced down at her hands.

Bernard sighed as he drew a piece of paper from his vest pocket and handed it to her. "These are the directions to Elysian, along with the required supplications. There, if granted admission to the dark forest, you should find what you need to help her. I can't offer any more than this, but it should help you. Whether or not you will be allowed entrance will be up to you. It would be in the interest of both parties that you choose the one among you all that would be considered least offensive to ask for admission."

"I will go with her," Gavin insisted.

Bernard chuckled. "If you wish to receive cooperation, I advise you not to flaunt the more unflattering aspects of their history to them. He would not be a good choice."

Gavin's Brooklyn accent was apparent as he snapped in anger, "Why didn't they just get rid of me instead of sentencing me to the bowels of the world and holding a grudge that will outlive my existence?"

I rolled my eyes at his histrionics.

Bernard blinked rapidly as he smiled. "You hate it here? Perhaps the intended justice has been served."

"Screw. You." On Gavin's way out of the room, he made a point to bump Bernard's shoulder.

"So eloquent and refined. I see why Jessica was so enthralled by him," Bernard explained to Sebastian. "Worth the shame her betrayal and infidelity caused Conner."

"Yes," Dr. Baker growled, "Gavin should have been penalized for the loose morals of the New York council head's wife. Gavin is truly responsible for him not choosing a more suitable and monogamous spouse. And it definitely is Gavin's fault that elves are so simple that the actions of their spouses reflect upon their ability to remain on the council. No, it's not their flawed system that should be held accountable, it is definitely Gavin's libido that is responsible for the crumbling government of the New York elves. Are you going to offer assistance or continue to pass judgment, Bernie?"

The smug grin faded from the assistant's visage. "Bernard," he corrected haughtily.

"Okay." Dr. Baker sneered. *"Bernard."*

With a sniff, he raised a hand to Sebastian. "Your phone, sir." Receiving it, he placed his satchel on the table and withdrew a binder. After flipping through a few pages of photographs, he took a picture with the phone, then handed it back to Sebastian. "Find this and you will find the cure. It often camouflages itself among the trees, but will find shelter behind what it perceives as the vilest predator. This is how it survives because its defenses are weak in comparison."

He removed a pen and notepad from his satchel and scribbled a note for Abigail. "I wish you success in this endeavor." He packed up his satchel and turned to Kelly. "It was a pleasure meeting you. I hope you maintain your favor with Claudia; it will serve you well in the future."

She summoned a gracious smile. "Thank you for your help."

The rest of us couldn't do better than scowl at him as he left.

Dr. Baker arranged a bed in the clinic for Abigail, while I put Marko in charge of the elven pair's security. They were not allowed to leave the room at the same time, a guarantee against flight as I knew neither of them would abandon the other. The clinic must've felt like a prison to them, because it was.

CHAPTER 11

While the rest of the house settled in for the night, anticipating an early rise, I spent the next two hours lifting weights and working the cardio machines, intending to exhaust myself. Only in the depths of hard physical exertion could I forget the constant, agitating thrum of dark elf magic as it coursed through my body, but anxious thoughts remained. The dark forest was a prison for all the dangerous creations the elves had made over the centuries. We'd no idea what dangers we'd face there. Distraction could mean death. Others depended on me, and on this mission there was no margin for error. There were simply too many variables, too many unknowns to anticipate. We'd have to go with our guard raised, alert to any danger that would have to be resolved on the fly.

Eventually I tired of the constant loop of worried thought and showered before climbing into my bed. As I slowly lowered my head into the softness of the pillow, the thoughts continued, magnified by the silence. The vibration of dark magic reappeared, as well. In an effort to distract myself, I sent my mind casting for some other thought to focus on and found myself calling up images of deceased Dennis; not the images of him as he'd appeared to me, but as I imagined his death, his throat torn out and his life draining in crimson pulses. Did he think of his daughter in his last moments?

As my mind played through his possible deaths, a pattern emerged that raised questions about the wounds on his doppelgänger. At his last appearance, his throat had been torn and his torso shredded, as if an animal had gripped his throat while eviscerating him with its claws. Michaela's love for torture was well known, but her methods were more precise. The detective's torso had been a gory mess. A wolf might do that. In his previous appearances, he'd had deep claw marks across his face and bite wounds to his chest. A wolf might do that as well, but not a vampire.

I sat up and glanced about the room, expecting Dennis to appear. There was something about his appearances I wasn't seeing. I was too fraught with guilt, too tired from exertion and lack of sleep. The frustrating pulse of dark elf magic distracted my thoughts, making it difficult to think clearly through the mental cloud of constant agitation. Tired of it all, I tried to push the images and thoughts from my mind so that I could gain at least a little sleep. That was a failure as all those elements came rushing back to me in the evening quiet.

I rose and paced my room like a caged animal. Growling, I lashed out at a lamp and sent it crashing into my dresser before it fell to pieces to the floor. I clutched the sides of my head in both hands, grimacing. For a moment, I considered calling Dr. Baker. He'd already left the retreat, but there might be some sleeping pills in the clinic. I could search for them without bothering him, but there was the medication hangover to consider. For the trip to Elysian, I needed to be alert.

I remembered the silver necklace in a plastic bag in the pocket of my jacket. There was a reprieve there, the kind that might last long enough to allow me to sleep without hindering my ability to operate optimally in the morning.

Glancing at my forearms, I saw the previous marks on my skin had healed entirely. Slowly, I walked to the closet and retrieved the bag from my jacket. The plastic crinkled as I rolled my thumb over the necklace inside. *It's such a little thing,* I thought, staring at the delicate silver chain. Sitting on the edge of the bed, I pulled the necklace from the plastic and let it dangle in front of my eyes before draping it over my left forearm.

I lost track of time. Eventually the smell of singed flesh dissipated and the pain in both arms subsided, leaving clarity behind. The stimulation was too much to allow sleep, but it gave me relief.

By the time the sun rose, the thoughts and agitation were creeping back into my mind. I showered, dressed in jeans and a dark blue shirt with long sleeves, then met Sebastian in his office to finalize our plan for entering Elysian. The map provided by Bernard gave us the location of a hidden gateway, but it didn't guarantee entry. A supplication had to be made. Permission had to be granted, and Liam, the current leader of the Makellos, was not fond of the pack.

"I will do the supplication," I stated.

Sebastian said nothing, while Josh gaped as if the decision were idiotic. "He'll deny you out of hand."

I agreed. "My appeal to his authority will appease him."

"We only have one shot to enter Elysian."

"You think Liam will respond better to you?" I snapped.

Before Josh could answer, Sebastian declared, "Josh won't be going with us."

My brother's expression soured.

"We're already risking the pack's Alpha and Beta," Sebastian explained. "If there's a betrayal, Gavin will need you to launch a rescue mission."

Josh accepted Sebastian's rationale, but he didn't like it.

Sebastian looked to me. "Skylar will perform the supplication."

I faced him squarely. "There is no reason for her to go with us."

"He will demand a price from either of us, a price befitting his disdain. But he doesn't know Sky. He holds no resentment of her. More importantly, she holds no authority to grant him any concession of consequence."

Josh nodded. "He might let her pass for a minor tribute."

I opened my mouth, then bit back a sharp retort. I preferred to try our luck with anyone else, but Josh was right that we only had one shot, and Kelly was counting on us. We had to gain access to Elysian.

Sebastian read my concerns. "If his price is high, I will step in and accept the responsibility for it," he promised.

"She gets us in," I warned Josh, raising a finger to him, "and that's the end of her role. Once there, she's a ghost in our wake."

He nodded unconditionally, but that didn't put my concerns at ease.

A short time later, the twin elves led us to an unremarkable wooded area outside the suburbs. With no trailhead, we made slow progress traipsing through the thicket, weaving our way between mature trees and young saplings as we followed Bernard's directions.

As I walked, I reflexively clenched and released my fists in an effort to expel agitation from the dark elf magic.

"Why do they live separately?" Sky asked, stepping over a fallen rotting tree branch.

Abigail hesitated, considering whether to answer. If she

intended to hide her envy of the Makellos, she failed. "They are different than those of us that populate this world. Most of us are products of a relationship with someone other than an elf. Gideon and I are among the few that are considered 'unchanged' that do not live in Elysian."

"Unchanged?"

Sebastian explained, "They are full elves, from a pure line."

"They're snobs," Gideon said, attempting to soothe his sister's jealousy, "the strongest of our kind, and they do not care to descend from their ivory towers to ever consider associating with the likes of us. A world of only self-professed royalty. They are arrogant, narcissistic jerks that my sister and I would never join no matter how sweet the offers were. They make the vampires seem humble."

My sister and I would never join .... Her envy made me think that she'd never been invited, but Gideon had, and he'd declined the offer rather than be separated from his sibling.

We continued into an increasingly dry, sickly part of the woods where it seemed the rain never touched. Trees and foliage were sparse and thin, with pale brittle leaves and dying branches. The usual clatter of insects and foraging small animals was entirely absent, as if shielded by a void. Even the sounds of our heartbeats and respirations were muted. It was an unnatural silence.

I glanced about, looking for the vague borders of a glamor.

Abigail stopped, bringing the rest of us to a halt. Standing in the center of a small ring of dead flowers, she unfolded the paper given to her by Bernard and read aloud. Whether it was a spell to open a way through the glamor, or simply a formal request, I wasn't sure. Either way, it worked. A narrow doorway opened in the air, just wide enough for us to pass single file. Sebastian went first, followed by Sky and then me. I doubted we would be attacked on the other side, since we could only enter by permission, but it was always best to be prepared.

Stepping into Elysian, I found ten elven soldiers barred our way, the butts of their spears, held in one hand, propped vertically on the lightly wooded hill. Dressed in blue button-down tunics with epaulets on the shoulders, they stood in a uniform line, posture military straight. A gentle breeze tickled the gaudy feather plumes on their ornate galea helmets.

The royal guard, I assumed, suppressing a sardonic smile. Liam was going out of his way to make an impression.

I took in our surroundings at a glance. In contrast to the brittle, dying terrain on the other side of the door, Elysian was a lush green paradise, blooming with fruit and avocado trees, but it was wrong somehow. The flora appeared familiar, but overly bright, like a candy version of itself. The smells were slightly wrong as well, putting my wolf at unease. The greenery extended from the hill as far as the eye could see, peppered with the crystal blue of small scenic lakes.

Tactically, the hilltop was a sound defensible position. Elves always were more style than substance. I assumed the location of the entryway to Elysian was chosen to grant new arrivals a majestic view, but it also put the elves at a disadvantage should they find the need to fend off an invader. Glancing at the elven troopers, I figured we'd have no problem defeating them and then escaping through the doorway before more pressure could be brought to bear. We'd certainly see reinforcements coming—if the situation went sour.

As Abigail emerged from the door and took in the scene, a look of awe came over her, which she was quick to suppress. Gideon arrived behind her, greeting the elven paradise with grim indifference—for her benefit, I assumed. Unlike Abigail, he'd probably been here before.

The soldiers parted as Liam walked through their line, scrutinizing us with a stern expression as if we'd just fouled his precious Eden. His ash-gray linen suit and pear-colored shirt contrasted with the military dress of his guard. He was slightly taller than me, muscular but slender. His hair was gray and his eyes an intense silver.

"Sebastian," he said with tired formality, "what brings you here?"

I glanced at Sky, who appeared nervous in her role, but didn't hesitate.

"He is here on my behalf," she recited from memory. "I am humbly requesting entrance into the dark forest."

He scrutinized her with a chuckle. "You? Who are you, little one?"

She bristled, her anxiety quickly replaced by a fiery indignation. My awareness heightened as I anticipated a snarky response that would likely bring our visit to an abrupt and possibly violent end. Sebastian remained calm, seemingly more confident that she could contain her natural instinct.

She knows what's at stake, I reminded myself, but could she control herself?

After a brief moment, Sky swallowed her pride and declared simply, "I am Skylar Brooks."

"Skylar Brooks," he repeated, testing the sound of her name. His absent gaze shifted to the valley below as he repeated her name several more times, no doubt rifling his memory to determine if she was a person of consequence, if she had something to offer.

A tense ripple passed through her jawline as she ignored the insult and gestured to Sebastian and me. "They will accompany me."

"Perhaps he should go instead of you," Liam said, flicking a glance at Sebastian. "The dark forest is not fit for someone like you."

"Liam, I do believe that would be best," Sebastian agreed.

Judging by Sky's indignant frown, she took his intervention as a personal failure, but he was simply being expedient. The elf had no intention of granting us access without extracting a higher price than Sky could offer.

A triumphant smile crossed Liam's lips. "So *you* will be the one requesting entrance into the dark forest. May I ask why?"

Before he could answer, Sky blurted, "My friend, a human, was bitten by a Tod Schlaf."

Liam accepted the news with a speculative look. No doubt he wondered how such a creature could be taken from his realm. Either one of his precious Makellos was a traitor, smuggling creatures from Elysian to sell on the black market, or an outsider had come and gone without detection. I wondered which bothered him the most.

He turned his attention back to Sebastian, repeating himself with an exaggerated, arrogant emphasis. "Then it is *you* who is actually asking for entrance."

Sebastian answered with a slight nod.

"Excellent." Liam whispered an order to an elf behind him, an unnecessary precaution as he knew full well that Sebastian and I could hear the instruction. Our word wasn't going to be enough for this arrogant bastard. In the human world, formal agreements required meticulously written contracts and notarized signatures. In the supernatural world, word was bond. Even the vampires kept their word, when given, but Sebastian's word wasn't good enough for Liam. He required a formal contract. It was a direct insult. I glanced to Sebastian, noting the tight line of his shoulders, the steely look in his eyes as he glared at Liam.

Once his assistant disappeared behind the line of guards, Liam declared with a pompous superiority, "If I allow entrance, then you must acknowledge you are indebted to me."

Sebastian's lips spread into a thin line. "Of course."

The assistant returned with a scroll, offering it to Sebastian, who made no move to accept it. "We usually use an honor system," he said bitterly. "It is widely known that if you renege, there are severe consequences."

Liam sneered. "The honor system among those that have proven to have very little? How trite. You will not be offended if I choose something a little more official."

I did my best to hide my contempt, not wanting to give him any more satisfaction than necessary. Glancing at Sky, I saw that she understood the insult and was biting her tongue.

Begrudgingly, Sebastian accepted the scroll and read it carefully. "There is no way in hell I'm going to sign this. You do not think we have honor; however, no one I've ever been indebted to would dare ask these things, nor would I of someone else. You want this signed, then take these things out." He gestured to several points on the scroll, then handed it back to Liam.

"You are requesting a favor of me and yet you make demands of what you are willing to do to fulfill the subsequent debt."

Sebastian straightened, taking advantage of his height to glare down at Liam. "What you are requesting is beyond reason." Amber sparks flashed in his eyes as he stepped close to the elf. "I will gain entrance. The only question now is whether it will be over the dead and badly injured bodies of your people or on more amicable terms. I would prefer on good terms. But the choice is up to you."

Liam glared back. He couldn't stop us, not with his toy guard. He'd have to call out half of Elysian to chase away a handful of were-animals, which would be an embarrassment for him. While he weighed his lack of options, I scanned the guard, watching for any slight shift of weight that would indicate the start of an attack.

After a long ponderous moment, Liam conceded, but the

taste of it soured his expression. He scowled as he took back the scroll. "Save your energy for the forest, you will need it." The offending lines promptly vanished as he ran his finger over them, whispering something in elvish. "Better?" he asked, returning the scroll to Sebastian.

After a brief read, he nodded.

Liam gestured and one of the soldiers produced a knife for Sebastian. A broad grin spread across his lips as he met Liam's expectant gaze—enough to remind the elf that he was fully capable of the violence promised—then pricked his finger and signed the contract in his own blood.

Once finished, Liam cautiously accepted the scroll, wary of some unseen betrayal. "You do realize you will have more than just cross words to contend with if you ever default on this."

Sebastian barely nodded at the insult.

"Very well, a guide will be by to escort you." As he walked away, his soldiers fell in behind, forming dual lines as they followed him down the hill.

Sky and I shared a glance, each of us wondering what the terms were that Sebastian had agreed to. He remained inscrutable, his eyes narrowed and hard as the wait tried his patience. It was not a conversation to be had while we were in Elysian; there would be a time later to ask.

While Gideon and Abigail seemed locked in silent communication, their eyes fixed on each other, Sky seemed entranced by the view, and by the vibrant nature of the trees and fauna. As she reached out to touch one of the trees, perhaps to test if it were real, I heard the trotting of horses approaching.

Not horses, I realized, staring down the hill at the approaching small herd guided by a pair of bareback riders, *but close enough*. The riders appeared to be twins, a male and a female, though both appeared effeminate in that elven way. Like Liam, they were clothed straight out of a fashion magazine. The male was dressed in gray chino pants, and a white shirt with a pinstriped tie. His hair was short and stylish and apparently unbothered by the breeze or by gravity. The female wore light gray slacks, and a darker gray sweater. Her long auburn hair was pulled back in a French braid.

They brought their animals to a stop a few feet in front of us, and the female dismounted. She greeted our elves with a warm smile. "Abigail, Gideon."

Abigail mirrored the guide's smile, but Gideon remained aloof, disapproving.

The female guide gestured to the horselike creatures, inviting us to mount for the journey. I wasn't an experienced rider, but the creatures seemed docile enough. The lack of saddles or bridles concerned me. Sky eyed her mount with trepidation.

"I don't know how to ride," she admitted.

"She can ride with me," I said. Curiously, she ignored my offer, instead glancing about for an alternative. I scowled at her, irritated and surprised by the rebuke. If she thought Sebastian or the elves were better riders, then she was welcome to find out.

The male guide offered me a condescending smile. "She will be fine, they take very little skill." He patted one of the creatures' long necks as he spoke to it in elvish. In response, the creature bent its front legs and bowed for Sky. Anxious but willing, she climbed onto the creature's back and gripped its long mane. After another command from the guide, the creature rose back to its feet. Sky's eyes widened as she shifted her weight, tightly clutching the mane until he gently touched her hand.

She nodded, willing herself to relax and release her grip.

The male guide turned to me with a raised eyebrow. Ignoring his unspoken challenge, I mounted my creature easily, firmly taking the mane in my hand and soothing the creature with a gentle pat on the side of its neck. It had been some time since I'd ridden, but the memory came back to me quickly. I drew my legs directly under my hips and turned my toes out so that my calves lightly rested on the creature's side. Testing my control, I shifted my weight and gently squeezed my left calf against the animal. The creature responded as intended, turning left until I faced Sky and released the pressure.

As I trotted toward her, the guide instructed her, "You won't need to steer. She is trained to follow us. If you're not experienced, it's best if you just go along for the ride."

The others competently seated, the guides started off and we fell in behind them. Sky rode behind Abigail. I rode protectively behind Sky, close enough to intervene if she lost her balance.

Long before the forest came into view, I felt the darkness of it like a cold, stifling breeze. It was unmistakable in its contrast to the brightness of Elysian. As we approached the forest's edge, I felt the strong vibration of the elven ward that held its denizens at bay, causing the hair on my arms and neck to rise. A glance to either side revealed the forest extended for miles, leading me to wonder how many dangerous creations had been abandoned there, and what would happen if the magic that imprisoned them suddenly disappeared. Despite the ward's power, a hazy darkness penetrated to our side of the barrier, the faint echo of desperate fingers probing for something.

Just outside the ward, the female guide brought us to a halt, then dismounted. "This is as far as we go." She turned her attention to Abigail, handing her a small scroll. "This will allow you entrance and exit. The words can only be spoken twice, don't lose it or … well"—she smiled politely—"you know what will become of you."

She whispered something to her creature as she stroked it, then abandoned it to join her brother. He reached down a hand and helped her mount behind him.

"My animal will guide you on your return," she promised.

At the brother's command, his creature turned sharply and trotted off, quickly accelerating to a gallop that rivaled the speed of a sports car.

The rest of us dismounted.

"You're with me," Sebastian informed Gideon, who nodded, his gaze transfixed on the gloomy forest. Sebastian turned to me next. "No matter how long I am in there, don't come after me. Okay?"

"I will give you an hour," I stated.

"Ethan," he said firmly, "don't come after me. Understand?"

I stared back at him, refusing to nod. There was no way I could simply walk away and leave Sebastian to whatever horrors lurked in those dark woods. And I wouldn't leave without fulfilling our mission. If I had to ride to the elven city and physically beat every elf there into submission to obtain another key to the ward, I would. But Sebastian was giving me a direct order. To fail his command was a violation of pack law. Reluctantly, my expression grim, I nodded. With luck, I wouldn't need to disobey him, but I would, if necessary. As much as I respected Sebastian's leadership, some commands had to be broken, regardless of the consequences.

Gideon lightly kissed his sister's forehead, then read from the scroll. Unlike his sister, he struggled with the language, but the magic worked. As with the door into Elysian, the earth beneath the barrier seemed to undulate before a narrow vertical tear appeared in the invisible barrier, wide enough for one person.

From the dark gloom on the other side, a fetid breath exhaled through the doorway and washed over me, carrying a whisper that beckoned to me as if I belonged there. My body seemed to betray me as it was inexplicably drawn to that gloom. I wavered, leaned back on my heels, resisting the urge to stride through the door. I glanced to Sebastian and

Sky, expecting to see in them the same struggle, but they seemed at ease.

Gideon and Abigail made their parting while Sebastian prepared to enter the forest. Uncertain what was happening, I said nothing.

Sebastian entered first, wearing a determined look, followed by Gideon. The tear closed behind them, sucking air from around us with such force that we had to take several steps back to escape the pull. Once closed, the tear completely vanished. The force that called to me disappeared with it.

Facing the forest, I stood beside the location of the door and anxiously waited for their return.

The forest wanted me. I knew that, but I didn't know why. Was it the dark elf magic? Was I another elven mistake to be claimed by the forest, to be held in protective custody for the remainder of my life? I squeezed and released my fists in a steady rhythm while I thought, until I remembered that I couldn't afford the distraction. At any moment, Sebastian might face a danger that required him to retreat back to Elysian. I needed to be ready at a moment's notice, should that door open and something dangerous follow him out of the forest.

At some point, I realized Sky was next to me, her breathing shallow and disjointed as she shared my anxiety. I regretted bringing her, putting her in danger. *I should've never agreed for her to accompany us.* But that wasn't the extent of my guilt. *I should've been the one to go into the forest.* Sebastian had made his choice, and I'd had no choice but to accept it.

After what seemed an endless wait, I felt a rush of relief as the earth before us began to vibrate, signaling the ward was about to open. Uncertain what the circumstances of Sebastian's return might be, I tensed in anticipation. But the ward didn't open. Instead, the earth beneath the barrier began to bulge in sporadic ripples. I felt dark fingers reaching for me once more, this time with added urgency as if the forest were exerting every ounce of power available to escape the ward just to reach me. An oppressive pall of gloom engulfed me, attempting to bind me in despair as the power began pulling me toward the forest.

Stunned, I closed my eyes and the rest of the world disappeared, leaving me in a silent void. If the others were holding me back from the forest or carrying me away, I had no sense of anything but my own resistance as I rallied. My entire being was caught up in the fight against the dark power that pulled at me, squeezing oxygen from my lungs as I fought to breathe. Every muscle in my body trembled from the effort.

The power was too much. I couldn't break its hold.

I called to my wolf, only vaguely aware of it somewhere in the distance, fighting furiously in an effort to reach me. I had a sense that the dark elf magic might help me, but I had neither the knowledge nor the skill to use it. My only hope was to escape beyond the reach of the forest. Given the amount of energy it was exerting to penetrate the ward, I doubted its reach extended more than a few feet.

Through the mental fog, I forced my attention to my feet and pressed my heels into the ground. The power of the forest draped over me like a dense, irresistible web as I slowly drew my right foot back, straining with the effort. With each forced step away from the forest, a small portion of my senses returned. The force holding me weakened, but the effort was exhausting, making me more vulnerable. Another step left my leg trembling. I didn't know what had happened to Sky and Abigail, but without their intervention, I didn't have the strength to escape the forest's reach.

With my last step, I felt the firm press of a willow tree against my back. Groaning with the effort, I turned and wrapped my arms around the thick tree trunk and clambered around it to put the tree between me and the forest.

Did it have the strength to rip the tree's roots from the soil? It would have to, to take me.

The forest doubled its effort. The force that pulled me against the tree was shocking, but it was a last gasp. Failing to pry me or the tree loose, the forest finally relented. Its grip on me faded, and I collapsed to the ground in total exhaustion, panting for breath, but the pall of gloom remained, suffocating me. A dark, raspy voice whispered in my mind, beckoning me. I knew that if I stumbled to the forest, it would open the ward and embrace me. If I didn't, it would kill me.

As I struggled for breath, a soft cool hand gently stroked my cheek. I knew Sky's touch, but I couldn't smell her. Forcing my eyes open, I barely saw her outline through a foggy haze before I found myself blind.

"What's the matter?" she pleaded.

I tried once more to change, but my wolf remained suppressed. A cold came over me, despite the sweat that I felt running down my arms and my face. A superior were-animal could force my change, but I knew I wouldn't survive long enough for Sebastian's return.

"I need your help," I gasped, struggling to produce each syllable.

She clasped my face between her palms. "What do you need?"

"Help me. Change."

It was a gamble. Sky hadn't even mastered her own ability to change, and her animal was inferior to mine. It shouldn't work, but thanks to Maya, Sky wasn't a normal were-animal. My life was in her hands, and I was asking the near impossible.

I fumbled at my clothes, but lacked the coordination to do more than brush fingers over fabric. Steady, sure hands arrived to help. Once the last of my clothes were removed, I relaxed against the tree, my limbs weak from lack of oxygen as my lungs barely sucked in air through the gloom.

I felt Sky's warmth descend over me, hovering close, but not close enough. Even I needed contact to force a were-animal's change. With a last, final effort, I leaned—or rather, fell—toward her, resting my head on her shoulder. My fingers slipped around her arm, but my grip was weak. Attempting to draw on her strength, I willed myself to change, but failed. Panic lurched in my body as I took my last breath. Death was imminent.

Skylar's fragile will pushed into my awareness, tentative at first, but quickly strengthening, pushing through the gloom to my wolf. Slowly, painfully, my muscles began to shift. I felt every crack of bone, every tendon stretch to the breaking point. Every strand of hair bursting through my skin was a dagger. The change continued for several unbearable minutes, but at least I could breathe through the pain. The gloom faded, pushed aside by my wolf's magical resistance. When the change finally completed, I lay on my side, panting, trembling, but I was free.

Once again Sky had saved my life.

I turned just enough to rest my head on her lap, enjoying the soothing stroke of her fingers through my fur.

"He's okay," she said quickly, her tone commanding. "He's fine. Stay there. Thank you."

I wondered who she spoke to. I tried to open my eyes, but my body refused to obey. Instead, I tumbled into unconsciousness.

When I awoke, head still in her lap, I had no idea how much time had passed. The exhaustion had lightened some, but I was still panting. After a moment, I was able to open my eyes to see Sky's concerned visage hovering over me. Rolling my eyes toward the forest, I saw Abigail watching me with a cool, calculated regard.

A tear appeared in the ward behind her. I tensed, anticipating the forest would make another attempt on me that I knew would succeed, but then I remembered my wolf form. The forest's magic had no effect on me.

Gideon emerged first, his usual smugness replaced by the shock of someone who had just emerged from a battle. Streaks and blotches of blood and dark ooze covered his pants. He wiped ineffectually at the stains, repulsed by them. As he saw Abigail approach him, he pulled at his shirt to cover the multitude of small cuts that covered his right hand and forearm. Sebastian emerged next, a sealed jar in his hand, his amber eyes afire with a primitive fury as he remained in the grip of his wolf. Deep claw marks ran along his shoulder and back, visible through his torn shirt. I noticed a pair of puncture marks on his arm.

He stood alone, taking slow breaths to calm himself until his wolf finally receded. The tension in his body slackened, but amber sparks in his eyes remained as he finally took in the scene around him. He slowly approached me, wincing at each step.

With some effort, he knelt beside Sky and rested a massive hand on my side. His eyes closed and I felt a wave of calm rush over me.

CHAPTER 12

*a*t some point, I regained consciousness to find my brother hovering over me, but I was no longer in the forest. I felt soft sheets against my bare skin, the edge of a comforter pulled to just under my chest.

"My Jeep's at the retreat," he said, his voice echoing slightly in my ear. "I transported you home after Dr. Baker looked you over."

My throat was dry, my voice hoarse as I asked, "Kelly?"

"I'll come back to check on you," he said, then disappeared.

I thought to rise, then lost consciousness again.

When I woke next, I knew I was in my bed. My body had regained some strength and my mind was alert. Glancing around, I saw Josh across the room, sitting in a wooden chair he'd brought from my dining room. He was leaning forward with his elbows on his knees, watching me intently. Relief washed over him as I sat up and rubbed the fog of exhaustion from my eyes.

"Kelly?" I asked reflexively.

He offered a beleaguered smile. "Weak and tired, but she's fine. It worked."

"She—"

"It was a pretty gruesome procedure, but she has full feeling in her legs. It'll take some rest before she can put weight on them, but Dr. Baker expects a full recovery."

"Good," I said, relieved. We remained quiet for a long moment, staring at each other and waiting for the other to speak. "Why don't you just ask?"

Josh shrugged, a casual gesture belying his growing look of concern. "Why don't you just tell me?"

I glanced at the dresser, hoping to find a glass of water there, only to be disappointed. *At least he tucked me in.* Tossing the comforter aside, I slid out of the bed and walked naked to the bathroom. After quickly downing two glasses of water, I walked back into the bedroom, to the dresser, and found a set of fresh clothes. Turning from the dresser, I noted Josh's amused scowl as he averted his gaze. I tossed the clean clothes onto the bed and began to dress, deliberately saving the underwear and jeans for last.

"Save it for the ladies," he eventually chuckled.

"You shouldn't have carried me," I said, buttoning my jeans.

"Well, I wasn't going to drag you home. Is the magic that hard to control?"

I had to remind myself that the origin of my newfound magic was still a mystery to Josh. He didn't know that I'd almost killed Sky with it, either. "Not when I'm awake. For the most part."

"Is that why the forest tried to take you?"

Fully dressed, I went about making the bed. I couldn't just leave it a mess.

"Ethan," Josh continued, "the forest doesn't just collect magic. It collects the magic of dark things, magic too dangerous to be in the world. If the forest was drawn to this new magic in you, it is more dangerous than we thought."

"You don't say?"

"I was wrong to suggest that you keep it," he said softly. "We need to destroy it."

I quickly fluffed the pillows, set them precisely centered at the head of the bed, then turned to Josh. "Easier said than done. The secret's out now, or nearly out."

His gaze shifted as he searched his memory, then nodded. "Abigail had a front-row seat. That'll come back to haunt us, eventually. Whatever this magic is, we have to get rid of it before she figures out how to take advantage of your situation."

Exhaustion caught up to me in a wave, forcing me to sit rather than lose consciousness. "I'm working on it." As he held my gaze, I knew what he was going to offer. "We can't use the ritual I used on Sky."

His eyes widened as he glanced to his right and left, as if to a waiting crowd that shared his incredulity. "Why not?"

"Because I'll lose it all."

"All," he repeated. A wry grin crossed his lips. "You mean the magic you inherited from our mother, the magic you used to take down my field and then feed me some BS story about how all were-animals can do that?"

I blinked at my brother, wondering when exactly he'd figured it out. "I didn't say *all*."

He gave me a wary look, but refused to take the bait. "The Aufero is your best chance. We'll have to steal it from Marcia."

I shook my head. "*We* aren't taking anything from Marcia."

He slid to the edge of his chair, his expression stern as he jabbed a finger toward me. "You're not doing this without me."

"We both know she's just looking for a chance to strip you of your magic. You can't be a part of this."

I watched his frustration peak to a sharp retort, but he swallowed it and looked away. Anger rippled in his jaw as he slowly acknowledged the risk was too great for him, that my efforts didn't require a sacrifice. Eventually, he managed a begrudging nod.

"You can tell me how to use it," I said.

"You'll need Sky for that, but yeah, I'll look into it and send you what I can." He rose from his chair. "In the meantime, try to rest. Get your strength back before you try to deal with Marcia."

"Put the chair—"

He'd already disappeared. Glancing out the window, I saw him get into his Jeep and drive away. As I watched him, something moving in the bushes across the street caught my eye. I stared at the spot, considered leaving my house to investigate, when a sudden dizziness came over me, as if the world had suddenly lost its equilibrium. I staggered, clutching the frame around the window to steady myself. The feeling lasted only a moment, fading almost as quickly as it had arrived. I shook the cobwebs from my head and glanced out the window again, but saw nothing.

Turning back to the bed, I decided I was too tired to investigate and lay back down supine over the covers. Within seconds, my eyes were closed and I was nearly asleep, when I heard a crashing sound from downstairs, like the smashing of plates or drinking glasses.

Instinctively, I drew the knife from the headboard and rolled off the bed, facing the bedroom door in a fighting stance, but the door was closed. I froze, listening intently for a clue as to whether I was facing multiple intruders, and where they were located, assuming one was in the kitchen. I heard the pounding of a single pair of feet stomping in the living room, accompanied by the creaking of the wood floor.

The footsteps stopped, followed by the cracking and splitting of smashed wood.

I lifted my dining chair and pushed it away behind me, then faced the door. Holding the knife ready, I opened my bedroom door with a snap gesture, just stopping it from slamming into the doorstop. The hall was empty, dark.

A moan rose from downstairs, deep and mournful and crescendoing into a forlorn wail. Another crack of broken wood, followed by the rumble of something heavy being propelled across the floor.

Gripping the knife, I slowly walked down the hall. I glanced into the open guest bedroom, then the open bathroom, before reaching the top of the stairs. The couches below were pushed into the middle of the living room at odd angles and the floor was a wreck of broken end tables and bookshelves. The books that should've been left in heaps were surprisingly missing. I scowled, confused, but then the wailing began again, this time from the dining room.

"Why?" the voice demanded. Dennis's voice.

Another crash that sounded like my oak table being split like firewood.

"Why?" he wailed again. His voice became suddenly guttural as he shouted, "You'll get what's coming to you!"

I walked down the stairs on the balls of my feet to minimize the sound. When I reached the ground floor, I flicked a gaze into the empty kitchen—every dish and drinking glass seemed broken on the floor—then walked deeper into the living room, toward the dining area.

"I know what you did!" Dennis shouted, his voice pitching into unbridled rage.

Stepping around the furniture debris, I quickly shuffled sideways into view of the dining room, knife raised. The table was broken in two and each of the chairs laid smashed over the broken halves of polished oak, but Dennis wasn't there.

"You'll pay!"

The shout came like a rush from the stairs on my left. Pivoting on my right foot, I saw Dennis charging me. He wore the usual blue suit, but this time the bloody wound was on his hip. He charged with empty hands reaching for my throat. Timing my strike, I swept the knife at chest height. The blade should've connected, slicing through fabric and skin. Instead it swept through empty air, landing in my left hand as I transferred the blade and pivoted again, but Dennis was gone.

The couches and bookshelves were in their normal position, as were the unbroken end tables, as if Dennis had never been there. Looking into the dining room, I saw that the table stood normally, undamaged. All six chairs were perfectly positioned around it. I stepped farther into the room to glance in the kitchen; the cupboards were closed and the floor spotless, uncluttered.

Something wasn't right. I glanced back at the table, the chairs.

"You can't kill me twice!" Dennis roared behind me.

I pivoted, driving the blade up into his torso at an angle, but the moment the blade touched him, he disappeared.

"Why!"

The shout came from the kitchen. I pivoted once more, but he was almost on me. Unable to bring the knife to bear quick enough, I punched at his jaw, intending to deflect his momentum with the blow. Once again, he disappeared on impact.

I waited, crouched, my head swiveling in anticipation of another attack. My eyes took in the chairs at the table, all six of them. I pivoted again, then looked back. Six. But one of the chairs was upstairs in my bedroom.

"You'll never know peace," Dennis said from the living room behind me. I swiveled, swinging the knife in an arc, but this time he didn't charge. Instead, he walked toward me in slow, predatory steps. His eyes appeared black and lifeless, like a void. "You'll tell me why before I let you die."

I charged, feinting with the knife, then swinging a kick up toward his head. He disappeared. Almost instantly he reappeared at the base of the stairs, glowering at me with the grim determination of the dead.

"Why?"

Six chairs. I flicked one more glance at the tables around the chair. There were six. Chairs. *This isn't happening,* I realized. Dennis wasn't the undead, and he wasn't a figment of my imagination. He'd been planted there by someone who'd taken the time to learn the layout of my house, the ground floor at least, but there was one detail that had been missed. The unexpected. A chair had been moved from one place to another.

Mind magic. It was the only answer.

"Why?" Dennis growled. His head lowered and his black eyes stared at me from beneath his eyebrows as he tipped his chin toward his chest to glower at me. He shifted his weight from side to side, preparing to attack.

I looked down at the wound on his side, remembering all the variations of wounds I'd seen that more resembled a wolf attack than a vampire attack. And the location and nature of the wounds kept shifting with each appearance, as if the mind witch was only guessing at how he died.

"I didn't kill you," I said, still holding the knife in a fighting stance.

"Liar!"

He charged. I struck again and predictably he disappeared, only to walk back out of the kitchen a moment later to stop and glare at me once more from the bottom of the stairs.

"You can't escape me," he growled.

None of this is real. I forced myself to lower the knife and let it drop to the floor. "Who are you?" I demanded. "If you want to kill me, you'll have to use more than parlor tricks, but I didn't kill Dennis." *I might as well have.*

He roared and charged. I let him come. Instinctively, my body tensed for the impact, but the moment he should've gripped my throat in his pale hands, Dennis disappeared. Realizing I'd held my breath, I released it in a sigh and glanced around for his reappearance, but it never came. After a moment, I realized there were only five chairs at the table.

I strode to the door and walked out onto the porch, scanning the neighborhood. The witch had to have been close, but probably already escaped. I considered whether I had the energy to go out and search the neighboring woods for sight or scent, when I heard a phone ringing upstairs.

The ringtone belonged to my burner phone. It continued to ring as I closed the door and walked up the stairs and found it on the bedroom dresser.

"Caroline," I said stiffly.

"David?" She spoke in a breathless, apologetic tone, but there was a slight edge in her voice that betrayed her. "I'm sorry to bother you."

I swallowed, pitching my voice to sound calm, compassionate. "Anything you need, just tell me."

"I found some of my father's documents that he'd hidden." She paused, presumably for effect. "There's something that looks like a journal of his cases. I can't be sure. He used a code, but I found someone who thinks he can decipher it pretty quickly." Another pause. I held my breath even as I waited for her to continue. "I'm pretty sure it has the name of his last client, the one who killed him." Hard as she tried, she couldn't hide the accusatory tone underlying her practiced enthusiasm. She was good, but now that I knew what I was looking for, the crack in her facade was glaring. I wondered if it was the guilt or the dark elf magic that had put me far enough off my game to miss the obvious. My mind flashed to the dizzy spells, to the black crystal in her pendant.

"When I find him," she continued, "he's going to pay."

I hesitated slightly, then put a hint of anxiety in my voice. "So you're determined to seek revenge, no matter the cost?"

"It's always been about revenge. An eye for an eye. Don't you think that's fair?"

"Of course," I answered quickly. "Perhaps I can help you decipher the code. He probably used a simple character substitution."

She chuckled. "You're a man of many skills, David. Are you a cryptographer as well?"

I hesitated for her benefit, then allowed just a hint of anxiousness in my voice. "If you need me, don't hesitate to call."

"You'll be the first. Talk to you soon," she said heavily, then disconnected the call.

Now I know, I thought, staring at my phone. After a moment, I called Tim and left him a voice mail message on his personal phone: "I'm thinking of inviting our guest to dinner, but I'd like to know more about her first. Maybe you can ask around her neighborhood."

After I killed the call, I retrieved Caroline's number from my phone's caller ID, checked the time, then called my legal assistant on her personal phone. Judging by the clatter in the background, I assumed she was out in a restaurant or bar.

"Hey, boss," she said, barely masking her disappointment.

"Caroline McDuffy," I stated, followed by her phone number, which I repeated.

"Got it."

"She's from Boise, but she's here in Chicago. I need to know where she's staying, where she's spending her time."

Stacy sighed. "So where she's spending her money."

"I'll compensate you, as usual."

"Of course," she said, taken aback. Regret crept into her voice. "I'll get right on it."

I was about to end the call when she said in a rush, "Can I ask you something?"

I winced, massaging my forehead with the fingers of one hand. I didn't have the time or the energy for questions. "Make it quick."

"How do I know if my date is an, uh"—her voice lowered to a conspiratorial whisper—"elf?"

She saw supernaturals behind every corner. I blew out a slow breath before answering, reminding myself that she was an important asset. "Unnatural good looks?"

"On the pretty man scale, he's a twenty. I should probably point out the scale only goes to ten."

"Fair skin?"

"Check."

"Vibrant eyes, probably of an unnatural color?"

She gasped. "He says he's wearing contacts, but who wears violet contacts?"

"Is he an arrogant prick?"

She hesitated. "Am I in danger?"

"Tell him Ethan Charleston sends his regards. You'll be fine." I reached to kill the call, then added, "After he pays the check."

I hung up, stripped, and took a long shower. Letting the water run down the back of my neck, I considered my new reality. I'd gotten Caroline's father killed and she'd come looking for answers, and revenge. Understandable. Did she think she was going to drive me to suicide, or just drive me to make a mistake so that I'd be easier to trap and kill? The latter, I decided. She was already preparing me for the trap. The next call I received would be a request for my help, directing me to somewhere secluded. She expected me to jump at the chance, hoping I'd be able to mislead her, steer her away from discovering my name.

That would be my mistake, according to her plan. She must've known I was her target from the moment I'd met her outside her father's office, when she'd been handing out posters. Word would get out that his daughter was searching for him, stirring up interest in his disappearance. Her very public pursuit of answers guaranteed that eventually the person responsible for her father's disappearance and presumed death would turn up to find out just how much she knew, to assess whether she was a liability. It was a well-thought-out plan, and I'd walked directly into it.

I smiled, splashing my face with hot water. I admired a clever opponent.

What I didn't know was what to do with her. I couldn't have a mind witch stalking me. Could I tell her the truth, point her at Michaela? Caroline was clever and patient, but she was no match for the Mistress of the Northern Seethe. I couldn't send both father and daughter to the same gruesome death. But death was the only way to ensure she'd abandoned her quest for revenge. It was never wise to leave an enemy behind you, but could I kill her?

I finished my shower, changed into loose, comfortable old jeans and a short-sleeved shirt. Almost forgetting, I snapped my iridium bracelet around my wrist, then went downstairs to examine the books on my shelves, pulling one in particular. From what Josh had told me, the chances of finding a reference to mind magic were small, but I had some of the oldest texts from the pack's library. After ordering a pizza, I pushed the cognac-colored ottoman to the couch and sat down to start my research.

By the time the pizza arrived, I'd pulled several more books from the shelves, adding a couple of notepads where I tried to keep track of the various small clues I found, each one leading me down a fruitless rabbit hole. Hours later, the pizza was reduced to nibbled pieces of crust. The bookshelves were nearly empty, contents spread over the couch and the floor. Every notebook I had was scattered among them. I'd been reduced to searching esoteric websites with my laptop, hunting for small kernels of truth hidden beneath mountains of New Age garbage.

I recognized the sound of Sky's Honda Civic moments before it pulled into my driveway. Abigail wasn't the only one who wanted to know how and why the dark forest had tried to take me. If I hadn't been so distracted, I'd have expected Sky. The mess in my living room was only going to lead to more questions. For a moment, I considered not answering the door, but it was obvious I was home. She was on a mission to get answers, and there was no point in putting her off. She'd just reached the porch when I opened the door and stepped aside, gesturing for her to come in.

Walking into the living room, she took a keen interest in the mess of books. She licked her lips as her gaze shifted to the open laptop on the couch, or was she eyeing the pizza box? Using my foot, I cleared a path for her through the various books and notebooks on the floor. As she approached the oversized chair facing the couch, her gaze flicked once more to the open laptop, just before I turned the screen from her view. She sat down, letting her eyes wander over the books and notepads with a practiced casualness.

After a moment, she shook off her curiosity and examined me with an increasingly concerned look.

I guess I look as bad as I feel.

I sat on the couch, facing her.

She stared at me, waiting for me to talk. After the first minute, I realized she was using my tactic of drawing people out with silence. I suppressed a smile and held her gaze. I didn't figure she'd last longer than two minutes. To her credit, she lasted nine. Eventually her look of empathy became a blatant question mark.

"What are you?" she asked.

That wasn't what I'd expected. Rather than talk about the elves and the woods and the things kept inside, she'd cut straight to the heart of the matter. I sank back into the couch, impressed. A lie was the smart play. So far, I'd avoided putting her at risk, but I'd need her help eventually. Once I obtained the Aufero, I'd need her to use it. Most likely I'd have to tell her exactly what she was removing, since I didn't want to lose my mother's magic, as well.

Exhausted, I washed my hands over my face as if I could wipe away the stress. "My grandmother was a dark elf," I said, surprising both of us. "She died eight days ago."

Her gaze shifted while she sorted through the ramifications of my revelation. "Do you have any aunts or uncles?"

Had there been other relatives, we would've shared my grandmother's inheritance. It was an astute question. I shook my head.

"The other day, with me, was an accident, wasn't it?"

I glanced down at my hands to hide my embarrassment. After a moment, I looked up to meet her gaze. "I am not as strong as she was, the wolf part of me controls some of that." I shrugged. "It gets better each day." I leaned back, noting the depth of concern in her frown.

"What happens now?" she asked. "Does Sebastian know?"

"He is the only one that does. *Was* the only one that knew," I said with an uncomfortable smile. *Does she realize the danger I've put her in?*

She pointed to the iridium cuff around my wrist. I'd forgotten it was there, but there was no point in hiding it any longer. "Does it work?" she asked.

"I don't know. I had it on in Elysian and it didn't seem to work."

"We need to get the Aufero."

"I thought about that," I admitted, allowing her to come to her own conclusions, "but I have no idea where it is."

She smiled. "I do. Well, not exactly. I have an idea where it may be." After some rummaging in her purse, accompanied by a fair amount of grumbling, she drew out four torn pieces of plain white paper and laid them out onto the ottoman between us. On the pages were mostly abstract sketches, some more detailed than others. A few I recognized. I leaned over, inspecting them closely while she explained.

"I saw this room that year I was in the in-between."

She was referring to the time I'd killed her. I'd stared directly into her eyes and watched the life drain out of her as I'd strangled her. I shook the memory from my mind and focused on the sketches. Two were drawn in blue ink, but with different thicknesses. Another was drawn in black, and the other in green. "These were done at different times," I observed. "Why?"

The flick of her eyes and the sudden intake of breath told me she considered lying. "I visited it again, recently," she admitted.

I scowled, knowing full well who was behind this reck-lessness. "With Josh, I presume."

She glanced away as she nodded.

Sky was constantly testing boundaries and putting herself —and sometimes others—in danger. After nearly two years with us, I expected more from her, but it dawned on me that I expected too much. No matter how long she'd spent with us, she didn't have the experience of growing up in our world. Up until we'd saved her, she hadn't even known there were other were-animals, let alone other supernatural crea-tures. Her curiosity and recklessness, while frustrating, were understandable, but Josh knew better. "You have indeed become one of his weaknesses," I said, then returned my attention to her sketches.

"Better me than anyone else," she said, piqued. "I will never hurt him, betray him, or point a gun in his face."

It took me a moment to realize she was referring to the time Chris had pointed a gun at Josh in an attempt to get us to surrender Sky. "You say that now," I muttered, choosing not to take the bait.

I placed the laptop on the ottoman and began searching. I

had assumed that Marcia kept the Aufero in one of her magic shops, but the symbols in Sky's drawings opened the door to other possibilities. Based on the public records, I'd believed that Marcia only controlled the two shops that were in her name, but there were other New Age-related shops and businesses in Chicago that might be indirectly under her control.

While I searched, I couldn't help wondering what else Sky and Josh had been up to. Trying to push that out of my mind, I focused on my search, periodically glancing at the sketches. Sky was surprisingly patient while I worked, leading me to keep a cautious eye on her in case she started snooping into things she shouldn't. There were a few of the books and notes that I preferred she not see.

I queued up some pages to print and waited by the printer for the batch to finish. "Are you sleeping with him?" I asked, trying to sound casual while I closely watched her for any hint of a lie.

The question startled her. "With who?"

"You know damn well who," I snapped. "Are you screwing my brother?"

Her lips pressed into a thin line. Her eyes narrowed. "It's *your* brother; maybe you should ask him about his personal life."

I scoffed. "He wouldn't tell me."

"Probably because it isn't any of your business."

She rose and tried to grab the printout from my hand. I snatched it back, glaring at her, but she refused to back down. Her intense gaze fixed on mine.

"Look," she said finally, "we can sit here all day while you speculate about what goes on between me and Josh in the bedroom, but we both need the Aufero. Don't you think we should dedicate our energy to looking for it?" She snapped the pages from my loosened grip and laid them out on the ottoman.

Regretting my outburst, I sat quietly on the couch while she pointed to one of the sketches.

"What is this?"

"It's a protection symbol. Most people have them simply for the aesthetics, but if enchanted correctly, it weakens all magical beings that enter the shop. Marcia would never have a real one where she keeps the Aufero, because it would weaken it and her as well. I've seen them in all of these places, but I am not sure which ones are real. We will have to go to them." If close enough, I could sense whether the symbols were magical.

Sky unclipped a pen from a nearby notepad on the floor and marked off at least a third of the locations.

She's been doing research of her own. I felt a rush of regret in my chest. I'd let the dark elf magic keep me on edge, and too often I'd taken my irritation out on her. She deserved better.

I smiled as I rose from the sofa and offered her my hand, as much to soften the tension between us as to demonstrate a point. She eyed the gesture with confusion, curiosity, and some trepidation. The last time we'd touched, I'd nearly killed her. After a moment, she eased her hand into mine. I gently brought her to her feet and pressed my forehead against hers, surprising her. My lips lightly brushed against hers as we stood there, silently sharing each other's warm breath. Her breath quickened. Her lips parted, but I didn't kiss her. Instead I lingered there, just touching against her softness, then stepped back, still holding her hand, and grinned.

"It's getting easier," I announced.

She rolled her eyes and let out an exasperated breath as she drew back her hand, but her smile remained. "What does it feel like?"

"Chaos. If I'm calm, I can control it better. It's harder with you around." *For many reasons.*

Gazing down at her, I reached out and brushed my

fingers against her forearm, then gently wrapped my fingers around it, enjoying the soft, cool touch of her skin against mine. I felt my shoulders relax. The dread of what had happened in the forest drained from my body as I gazed into her green eyes. "It's a lot better."

After a moment, she gently pulled her arm free and demurely tucked a loose mahogany curl behind her ear. "We should probably get started."

I nodded.

For once I didn't bother to hide my ability to detect magic, which made our search easier. Thanks to Maya, Sky was able to as well. Together, we wandered through each shop, looking for magic in the items there, in the various symbols painted on the walls that were often just for decoration. More importantly, we looked for less obvious sources of magic, such as from hidden rooms or storage spaces. Sharing the search with her, I appreciated the ease of her company, how well we worked together when I didn't have to lie.

Eventually we narrowed the list down to just three possibilities, two of them Marcia's shops. One of those three hid the Aufero, we were both certain.

"We'll wait until they're closed to search those," I said. "We can conduct a thorough search without concern for detection."

She gave me a sideways look. "You're just going to break in?"

"Exactly."

CHAPTER 13

$\mathcal{I}$ tried to rest in anticipation of our late-night prowl. Each time I closed my eyes, I expected the telltale dizziness of another mind attack. I still didn't know what I was going to do with Caroline.

By the time Sky arrived at eleven o'clock, I could barely keep my eyes open. When I opened the door, my eyebrows rose at the sight of her wearing a loose purple t-shirt with the smiling face of a panda bear on the front. Her jeans were reasonable; the obnoxious silver slippers were not.

She frowned, gestured to my faded jeans and wrinkled button-down. "You're going to wear that?"

I rolled my eyes and changed into dark jeans, a black shirt, and dark boots. When I returned to the living room, I was surprised to find she hadn't changed. I'd assumed she'd worn her outfit as a joke.

"We are about to commit larceny," she stated. "If we are caught, who will look like a criminal and who will look like an employee who came back to the store to pick up her forgotten bag?" She winked and tapped a finger to her temple. "You have to think outside of the box."

"I assure you, no one will believe someone would hire you knowing this is your manner of dress."

"Well, I plan to get them to 'see my reality,' while you will be seeing the inside of a precinct."

"So," I said, suppressing a laugh, "let's not get caught."

As usual, she looked anxious in the passenger seat of my BMW as I drove toward the first store on the list. While she gripped the seat with both hands and pumped imaginary brakes, the silence between us allowed my mind to race. Once we found where the Aufero was hidden, retrieving it was risky. There would be magical protection. As long as I detected the traps before they went off, I most likely could break the spells, courtesy of my mother's magic. Should anything go wrong, we'd be on our own. We couldn't be seen as working on the pack's behalf, and I wouldn't risk bringing Josh into the situation.

Once we'd retrieved the Aufero, there was the question of hiding it. Marcia would certainly spend considerable resources to recapture it. Without Josh's knowledge of the Creed's abilities, I wasn't sure how long we could hide the orb from them. It couldn't be hidden at the retreat. Artemis might be of help, but she was also a mercenary. When it came to something as valuable as one of the protected objects, she couldn't be depended upon.

There was the fact that Sky was the rightful Moura charged with protecting the Aufero. We'd kept that secret from Marcia, but once revealed, she'd be unable to make a public claim on the orb. Sky could place it in the pack's protection. She'd be within her rights, but Marcia wouldn't give up so easily. She'd find ways to punish the pack, to punish Josh. She was well aware that he could be used as leverage against me. She'd drum up some bogus charge and haul him in front of the Creed for judgment, and I'd have to give her the Aufero to protect him.

Sky spoke, startling me from my thoughts. "What do you do for the pack?"

I shifted gears, taking advantage of a long stretch of straight road to pick up the pace. "What?"

Pressing back into her seat, she complained, "It's harder to kill us, but not impossible. I am pretty sure going through the windshield is going to hurt like hell and put a dent in our plans."

I smiled as I slowed down to just over the speed of traffic, which seemed to calm her.

"What do you do for the pack?" she asked again. "What is your job besides Beta? Josh manages the pack's club. Sebastian is a day trader and owns real estate, Steven's a student, Winter is an IT consultant. I'm still not sure what Gavin does, and I don't think anyone else is, either. What is your job?"

Gavin is a professional ass. "I'm an attorney."

Her hand covered her mouth as she tried to stifle a laugh. She turned away, then finally let it out. Bemused, I kept my eyes on the road while she enjoyed herself, eventually wiping away tears as she brought herself under control.

"Criminal law for two years," I continued. "Then I switched to corporate."

She nodded, suppressing another wave of laughter, but didn't ask any more questions.

A few minutes later, I took a slow pass in front of the first magic shop. The interior lights in the back of the shop were on, but that was a common security precaution. Confident that the staff had gone home, I parked around the corner.

The neighboring buildings were shops with apartments above. Several of the units were lit, but I didn't find any faces lingering in the windows. Gesturing for Sky to wait by the BMW, I took a walk around the back of the building. Eyeing the edges of the roof for power lines and boxes that would indicate an alarm system, I found none. I didn't feel any magic radiating through the walls, either.

Returning to the car, I retrieved my lockpick set from beneath the driver's seat, then gestured for Sky to walk with me to the front of the shop. The street was quiet. No one was in sight, but I wasn't going to take a chance.

"Stand in front of the door and talk about something," I whispered just loud enough for her enhanced hearing.

Her eyes widened. "Like what?"

"Anything. Just keep talking."

She took a deep breath. "Three of the housewives are from New Jersey, and they hate the other housewife. She's from Florida and is probably hiding a secret past as a high-end stripper slash drug dealer...."

Kneeling behind her, I opened the small leather bag of elegant tools and picked the lock. While practicing criminal law, I'd met an old master thief who'd retired after a bruising stint in jail. She made her living teaching her particular skill set to government spooks and survivalists. And me.

"They got into a catfight in the middle of an art gallery," Sky continued as the door clicked open.

I slipped inside, Sky close behind, and closed the door. "What was that?" I asked, peering out to make sure no one had noticed our entrance.

"Best I could do on short notice." She shrugged and walked into the middle of the store, her eyes scanning the contents of the shelves.

Walking the perimeter of the shop, I noticed a number of magic symbols painted on the walls. While mostly authentic, the symbols seemed haphazardly placed, often in contradictory groups. They were also devoid of magic. A display of charms against the back wall emitted an inconsequential amount of magic, probably from some of the crystals used.

Sky and I wandered until we met in the middle of the shop. Without a word, we agreed the Aufero wasn't there.

After peeking out the front window, we left the shop—locking the door behind us—and made a casual stroll to the BMW. There were just two shops left, both of them directly under Marcia's control.

Next we tried the shop I'd sent Artemis into. Some of the charms there emitted a stronger than expected magic, but there was nothing remotely powerful enough to suggest the presence of the orb.

Only one possibility remained.

Given the late hour, the drive across town to the last shop on our list was brief. We passed the drive in silence, both of us contemplating the sort of magical protections we'd encounter once we found the orb there.

I slowed as the shop came into view, the inside pitch black. After circling the building once, I parked in the dark alley behind it. A quick examination of the exterior revealed that an alarm system was present. I drew a tablet from the backseat and opened the only application installed, a custom piece of software that had cost as much as my BMW. After locating the property in the app's database, the software indicated the alarm was connected directly to the local emergency system, which was a stroke of luck. Were the system connected to a private firm, I'd need to ghost the signal to prevent someone from noticing the broken connection, but the city wasn't that organized. After a few touches to the screen, I closed the tablet and tossed it onto the backseat.

"It's off," I said.

Sky nodded, impressed.

"Do you want me to create a distraction again?" she asked as we approached the front door of the shop.

"I'd prefer you didn't."

At the door, she turned to shield me while I quickly picked the lock and stepped inside. The place reeked of sage. I ushered her inside, closed the door, and turned just as Sky drew a flashlight from her pocket and turned it on, casting a beam of white light across the displays. She scowled when I turned on the shop lights.

I explained, "You draw more attention when you are fumbling around in a shop with flashlights."

She deftly tucked the light back into her pocket. "Seems like you are speaking from experience."

Like the other two shops, the symbols we were looking for were on the walls, along with others for protection, prosperity, wisdom, and more. Unlike the other shops, the symbols here were properly grouped. Also unlike the other shops, several of these symbols possessed strong magic—a notable exception being a protection symbol that would've hampered the Aufero's power had the symbol been real.

Similar to the other shops, there were sections for herbs and essential oils, crystals, homeopathic remedies, music, and books. There was also a large section of magical paraphernalia. Magic was present here, more than in the other shops, but not enough to match what we were looking for.

Large beveled mirrors lined the back wall of the shop on either side of a door, making the space seem more expansive than it was. My attention was drawn to an unusual symbol painted above the door. As I approached, I recognized the smell of blood mixed with henna. I didn't know what the symbol's purpose was, but it radiated strong magic.

Sky paused in midstride, her gaze drawn toward the symbol as well. "It's here."

Standing at the door, I felt stronger magic behind it, the residue of an untold number of spells and rituals practiced by hundreds of witches, their magic so intertwined over time that the individual sources were impossible to trace.

Sky tried the door, found it locked. She jerked at the

handle in frustration, then stepped back and rammed the door with her shoulder—to little effect, but that didn't stop her from trying again. Her usual stubborn determination became fierce as she stepped back and rammed the door several more times. Eventually the door splintered at the frame. The lock broke and the door swung in to reveal a large, open room.

A heavy wooden chair with leather iridium-laced restraints occupied the center of the room, facing a mahogany conference table with five chairs along the far wall. *One for each member of the Creed,* I realized. In the corner near the table was a decorative armoire that radiated powerful magic.

Sky's heart quickened as she fixed her attention on the armoire, as if drawn to it. Through the glass front, I saw three shelves housing talismans and books and a few other objects that required closer inspection.

"Sky," I said, cautioning her as she stepped toward the armoire. As if in response, or perhaps drawing her toward it, a light appeared inside, glowing increasingly stronger as she approached. Shading my eyes and squinting, I could barely make out the origin of the light, a small round orb on the second shelf.

The Aufero.

As she approached the glass, the magic of the orb flooded the room, radiating the combined powers and abilities of every person and creature the orb had ever drained over its lengthy existence. We had no idea how old it was, or how many victims it had left behind, but it had an overarching darkness about it, a signature similar to that of Ethos.

The armoire began to shake in anticipation. When Sky stopped before it, she raised her hand. The glass doors burst open and the orb leapt to her, molding itself to her palm. The orb's power shimmered around her.

I opened my mouth to caution her, but then a force like a

stone fist struck my back, sending me skidding across the room. I managed to turn around just before I struck the wall and collapsed, but I saw her, the frost-haired leader of the Creed, with four witches behind her.

Marcia.

She strode into the room, her attention focused on Sky. At a glance, she was an average height with an average frame, but there was a confidence in her stride, an intensity in her gaze, that spoke of power.

I started to lift myself from the floor when a fresh wave of force flattened me, pinning me down.

"Stay," Marcia commanded, then held out her hand to Sky. "Give it to me."

She clutched the orb to her chest. "No."

Marcia started forward to take it, but the Aufero pulsed as if in warning, giving her pause. *She fears it!* If Sky knew how to use the orb, she could drain Marcia's power with a command.

"Now!" she shouted, unleashing a wave of power meant to send Sky crashing to the floor. The orb unleashed a power of its own, expanding out to bend the attacking energy around her. The floor shook. Glaring back at Marcia, Sky teetered but managed to keep her feet.

"No," she stated, brimming with confidence.

Unable to extricate myself from the floor, I called on my wolf. It was there, just beneath the surface straining to escape, but the magic that pinned me down prevented me from changing. I tried to call on my own magic, but the iridium band on my wrist prevented it.

Marcia's eyes darkened like a gathering midnight cloud as she called upon even stronger magic. For a moment, nothing happened. I wondered if the orb had canceled her spell, but then she spread her arms wide, muttering her commands, and a loud rumble shook the room. The lights flickered and a new force struck me, driving me back and slamming me into the wall, pinning me.

I winced in pain.

Somehow, Sky remained standing. A powerful protective field shimmered around her—not hers, but the Aufero's. The orb shone and pulsed in her hand. It was protecting her, and it was far more powerful than anything Marcia could muster. But there were four other witches in the room, nearly as powerful, and they had yet to join their power to hers.

Growling and grunting, I tried to peel myself from the wall through sheer rage. The force pinning me was unassailable. *Run!* I tried to shout. *Escape!* I feared it was only a matter of time before the other witches joined with Marcia. No matter how powerful the orb, Sky didn't know how to wield it. She was casting spells she knew, relying on the orb's superior magic. Eventually, the witches would overcome her unless she gave up on me and ran.

Leave me behind!

As Marcia's magic assailed Sky's protective field, her brow furrowed in intense concentration. After a moment, the field protecting her blossomed gold and orange sparks, then shattered completely, leaving her exposed and vulnerable. Marcia smiled as the other four witches fanned out behind her, joining their power to hers.

Run!

Sky stood her ground, defiant.

The Creed began a combined chant and my heart sank, anticipating her defeat.

Sky's lips twisted into a wicked smile. With a slight gesture of her hand, she threw the witches back against the wall. Only Marcia managed to keep her feet, working to just barely maintain a protective field around her. Another gesture and Sky picked the witches from the wall, then slammed them back against it, then did it again until they were incapacitated. When the attack ended, she left them pinned to the wall.

Staring Marcia down, Sky commanded, "Let. Him. Go."

"You are way out of your league," Marcia snarled. "If you want to walk out of here with him alive, you will relinquish it to me." She raised a finger and a powerful wave of magic whipped through the room. Sky's eyes widened in surprise as she was thrown back against a wall.

The force continued to buffet the room, knocking the air from my lungs. I struggled to breathe as the assault continued.

Pressing her advantage, Marcia walked toward Sky, her fingers outstretched as if expecting the Aufero to leap from Sky's grasp. As she called on stronger and stronger magic, the orb glowed angrily. Sky screamed at the sheer force that threatened to crush her hand.

Her green eyes turned entirely black.

The room rumbled and shook from her rage, and she threw Marcia back against the wall, but it wasn't enough to stop her. Sky didn't know how to use the orb's inherent power. She couldn't stop Marcia from releasing herself, and already two of the Creed had released themselves from the wall.

Leave me! I screamed in my mind, pleading with my eyes. *Run!*

As a last, desperate gasp, I called upon the dark elf magic. I had no idea what it could do, or how to wield it. I didn't know if it was Marcia's magic or the iridium band that kept it at bay, but the magic didn't answer.

Shaken, Sky raised her protective field just in time to stop a magical force that rolled over the field in shimmering waves.

I wondered if Marcia had intended that attack as a distraction. While Sky focused on sustaining her field, Marcia freed the other two witches with a wave of her hand.

When she glanced at me, I knew what was next. If she couldn't beat Sky into submission, Marcia could use me as leverage. I only hoped Sky had the strength to see through it and endure. No matter what happened to me, the Aufero couldn't fall back into Marcia's hands.

She would blame the pack for our intrusion. As punishment, she'd use the orb to take Josh's magic.

"Give it. To. Me," she demanded of Sky.

When she didn't respond, Marcia waved her hand at the mirrored glass on the wall near the armoire. The glass shattered into jagged shards that hung in the air. Following her gesture, the shards flew straight toward me. Refusing to close my eyes, I watched the swarm of ragged daggers approach. I would defy my death to the very last moment.

The shards stopped suddenly, just inches from my flesh.

"Give it to me," she commanded, straining as she held the shards at bay.

Sky closed her eyes in seeming concentration. If she was trying to cast a spell to help me, it didn't work.

Marcia walked toward me with a twisted, sadistic expression and plucked one of the shards from the air. It was an impressive gesture, considering the concentration required to hold the swarm in suspension.

"I've always been curious how much a were-animal body can endure before it shuts down from shock and dies," she said. "Relinquish it to me."

Sky didn't answer.

Good. Don't. Survive this. No matter what, keep the Aufero.

Marcia's lips twisted into a deviant smile as she plunged the shard into my stomach. I winced but clamped my jaw shut, refusing to give her the satisfaction of even a breathless whimper. She wanted me to put on a show for Sky's benefit. Glancing down, I saw Marcia's hand pressed against the wound. She'd driven the shard in up to her fist, which was soaked in my blood. Only when I shook my head against the pain did I realize the force that held me had relaxed, just enough to let me squirm. She stared into my eyes as I struggled to maintain consciousness, thrilled by my agony.

Once more I fought to break free and failed.

"Oh, stop struggling," she gently chided me. "You'll need your energy."

She waved her fingers and the swarm of shards pulled back—just enough to strike with momentum when she commanded it. It was an unnecessary cruelty. I might survive one or two of the shards, but I doubted I could survive the entire swarm. Even if I survived the initial blow, Marcia would never allow me access to medical help. I doubted I would ever leave the room alive.

"I didn't realize you all had a Moura," she said to me. "That explains quite a bit. Your pack has been quite busy. Do you have any others?"

Go to hell, I thought, but the words only emerged as grunts and gasps for breath.

Apparently I disappointed her. At a flick of her fingers, several shards of glass drove into my torso. Blood filled my mouth. Before I could spit it in her face, another set of shards burrowed into me. I bit my lip, stifling a cry as it seemed my body was nothing but pain and blood. At some point, I fell limp against the force that pinned me, finally unable to resist. I expected the force to crush me instantly, but it only held me in place. When I looked down, I saw over a dozen shards protruding from my body, each dripping my blood.

Grinning with anticipatory delight, Marcia raised her hand to unleash the remaining shards at once.

"Here!" Sky shouted, flicking me a tortured look as she dropped her field.

No! I screamed inside my skull, but still couldn't find the breath to speak.

"You know I can't have it once it is in your possession,"

Marcia snapped. "You need to relinquish it to me. Give up ownership."

"Fine." Sky's shoulders drooped as she glowered at Marcia. "I relinquish the Aufero to you."

Marcia sighed, annoyed as if she were teaching an obstinate child. "*Praeditos*, the Aufero is relinquished to you. Say it."

Don't!

Sky repeated the words, her bitterness echoing in the chamber, but she couldn't bring herself to release the orb. It glowed in her hand with an increasing intensity, pulsing orange and yellow light. She gaped at it, reluctant and awed until she hissed and tossed the orb to Marcia, snatching back singed fingers. The leader of the Creed picked the Aufero from the air and clutched it to her chest. In her grip, the glow quickly faded until the orb seemed a plain gray ball. A moment later, she offered a triumphant smile as the orb pulsed back to life.

"I accept," she whispered, then disappeared along with the other witches.

The force that restrained me disappeared as well. I pressed back into the wall for support as air rushed into my lungs. My chest heaved, each rise and fall sending shocking jabs of pain from the shards embedded in my torso. Sky rushed to me and pulled one of the shards from my abdomen. I grimaced and felt hot blood gush from the wound. Mercifully, she pulled the rest of the shards in quick order, blurring the pain together. I lost consciousness, but only for a moment. When I came to, I was still on my feet. I grunted as she pulled the last shard from my thigh and sent the bloodstained glass skidding across the floor. I frowned at the fresh springs of blood that leaked from me.

"Not safe," I muttered, gathering myself.

I pushed off from the wall and stumbled toward the door. Sky rushed to my side, tried to slip an arm beneath mine, but

I brushed her off. I'd already gotten my ass kicked and cost her the Aufero. The least I could do was walk out on my own.

But I couldn't drive.

I tried to toss her the BMW keys, but my muscles were weak, poorly coordinated. She scooped the keys from the pavement and helped me into the back, then hurried around to the driver's seat. I rolled my eyes and moaned as she gave the gearshift a puzzled look.

Even in my agony, I couldn't help willing her when to shift, mentally chastising her each time she didn't. I groaned with every clunk and grind. The wounds were already healing, but the ride was going to kill me.

"I'll call Dr. Jeremy," she said, a slight tremble in her voice as she tried to fish her phone from her pocket while steering.

"No," I hissed. "My house."

Instead of punishing us, Marcia had let us go. I was sure she was tracking us, waiting for us to call the pack for help or race to the retreat. If we sought help, the pack would be implicated; I'd never be able to claim that I'd acted on my own initiative. Thanks to my failure, I'd put Sky, Josh, and the pack at risk. I'd cost her the Aufero, and I'd gotten my ass kicked by an old witch.

By the time we'd reached the house, most of the bleeding had stopped, but I'd lost a lot of blood. Sky insisted on helping me inside, and I didn't argue.

"We need to work on your driving," I muttered as we climbed the steps toward the door.

"A manual transmission is stupid."

"It's the only way to go." She unlocked the door and helped me into a leather chair in the living room. My eyes traced the trail of my blood back to the door as Sky rummaged in the kitchen cabinets.

"My Civic has an automatic transmission and a cool little camera that keeps me from running into things," she called

back to me. "You would think that BMW would catch on."
She abandoned the kitchen to continue her search in the
bathroom. *Is she searching for a first aid kit?* I chuckled. *You
could just ask.*

She returned with the kit and knelt in front of me, priori-
tizing my wounds. "You sure you don't want me to call Dr.
Jeremy?"

"No."

I grimaced as she helped me pull off my shirt, then my
pants. Pain shot through me like a lightning bolt as she
attempted to probe one of the wounds, feeling for remnants
of glass. "Wait," I gasped, gripping her shoulder. Closing my
eyes, I took a pair of long, calming breaths to prepare myself,
then nodded. "Okay."

With each wound she probed, I held my breath and
absorbed the pain until she moved on to the next. Fortunately, there were no remaining splinters. When she quit
probing and began cleaning my wounds, I gave a sigh of
relief.

"I should have given her the Aufero sooner," she said,
shaking her head in disgust.

"I didn't expect you to choose me over it."

She flinched, then silently carried on with cleaning my
wounds.

I hadn't meant it as a rebuke. She'd made the wrong decision, but I couldn't fault her for saving me. It wasn't the first
time. "I would have given it to her, too," I said, breaking the
uncomfortable silence.

Her shoulders relaxed. "Well, I hope so," she said with a
hint of a smile. "Even you aren't that big of a jerk."

I glanced down at the job she'd done patching my
wounds, then stood. A fresh stab of pain nearly sent me to
the floor. I staggered, caught myself. Sky stood close, her
arms extended to catch me while I took a breath, then
straightened.

"She knows what you are," I said. "She will likely approach you soon."

"What would she want with a Moura?"

"Your connection to the Aufero is stronger than hers is. I am willing to bet she thinks she can use it and you to find the other protected objects. More specifically the Clostra. Believe me, if she ever gets a hold of it, we are done. The first spell she will use is the one to kill us." I glanced at the clock on the wall. "It's getting late, and I'm tired."

"I should at least stay until—"

I gave her a look that said I needed to be alone. She'd already witnessed my failure. She didn't need to witness the overwhelming guilt, as well.

She nodded, gave me back my keys, and left.

If I'd had the strength to destroy every bit of furniture I owned, I would've. As it was, I could only stew in my anger.

CHAPTER 14

*O*nce again I couldn't sleep. My body ached from the lack of it. I'd developed some control over the dark elf magic, but the persistent, driving thrum of it in my body was a slow burn to my sympathetic nervous system. My failure at Marcia's shop didn't help. I hadn't been thinking clearly. If I had, I would've questioned more about the symbol that protected the door to the back room. Most likely the symbol had been an alarm, and I'd just walked Sky right through it into a trap. She'd obtained the Aufero just long enough to surrender her rightful claim on it in order to save me. It had been a foolish and noble gesture.

The dark elf magic was affecting my work, making me distracted and careless. If I didn't find a way to rid myself of it soon, I'd have to consider resigning my position as Beta. I couldn't let my distraction put the pack at risk.

I'd just begun to drift into a shallow, brittle slumber when an alert on my nearby phone sent my heart racing. I leapt out of bed, anticipating an attack, to find only silent darkness. Slowly, I forced myself to relax and sat back down on the edge of the bed.

Dennis is no longer a threat, I reminded myself as I ran my hands down my cheeks. He was an illusion, a manifestation of Caroline's mind magic, but my ravaged nervous system wouldn't recognize sense. I also couldn't be sure that she couldn't manifest her magic in a more dangerous manner. How could I trust anything I saw or even felt? *There is the dizziness,* I reminded myself, the telltale sign that I was about to come under her influence.

Remembering the alert, I slid out of bed, crossed to my dresser, and picked up my phone to see a message from Stacy. I took the phone down to my kitchen, poured a double Scotch, drank half, then opened the attached document. She'd been busy.

The pack's enemies often underestimated us. They focused on our physical prowess and our ability to resist magic while in animal form. The true strength of the pack was our resources. It didn't matter how strong we were if we didn't know what we were facing.

Taking a quick inventory of the pages, I found credit card transactions and cell phone activity reports that included GPS tracking obtained surreptitiously through a game application on Caroline's phone. She probably had no idea the so-called free game was tracking her every move along with her phone and browser activity and selling the data to marketing companies. Stacy had highlighted a hold on Caroline's credit card from a motel on the outskirts of the city. I recognized the address. The rest of the transactions were mostly restaurants and grocery stores, most of them close to the motel. The GPS data also indicated Caroline had made a series of trips to a somewhat secluded location a short distance outside the city. The next page was a search engine satellite view of what appeared to be a shack surrounded by woods.

After finishing my Scotch I poured another, then took it to my leather chair in the living room. I was debating my next move when I woke up with a start to a bright room, lit by sunlight shining through the windows. According to my phone, it was nearly eleven, but I still felt groggy and exhausted, as if I'd never slept.

Rising, I realized the glass of Scotch had spilled in my lap.

After a quick shower and a change of clothes, I decided to investigate Caroline's mystery shack first. Following the GPS coordinates, I turned onto a narrow dirt road that meandered its way through the forest. After fifteen minutes, I found the shack just off a bend in the road. Without the coordinates, I doubt I would've noticed the unassuming structure shrouded by trees and brush. The shack had the appearance of misuse. The wood was old and rotting in places, and a broken window remained in disrepair.

Parking in the bend, I turned the engine off but left the keys in the ignition and the door open. For a moment, I stood there, smelling, listening, and watching first the surrounding forest, then the shack, until I was confident that I was alone.

The front steps groaned and bent beneath my weight. The unlocked door clicked, then creaked open. Using a flashlight from my pocket, I found the shack was little more than a large closet—shelves lining each of the walls—except for the wooden chair in the center of the floor. Attached to the arms and legs were thick metal bindings. Kneeling in front of the chair, I used the handle of the flashlight to lift one of the wrist cuffs to my nose and sniffed. Iron, but no silver. I let the cuff fall to clatter against the chair.

A quick search of the shelves revealed little; an old oil lamp, some old plates and cups, cutlery, a few books, a private investigations magazine. This was Dennis's place, I realized, though it seemed he hadn't used it much for years. Someone had been there recently, however; there were fresh shoe prints in the dust on the floor, and the chair was clean as if recently placed.

I took close-up pictures of the chair and the room itself. Taking a business card from my wallet, I laid the card next to the foot shackles as a reference and took close-up pictures of the lock mechanism from several angles. Once finished, I walked outside, found a fallen bit of brush to scrape my tracks from the dirt, then drove off without turning around. Turning around would've been a quicker path out of the forest, but I couldn't hide the tire tracks. As it was, Caroline would only notice that a vehicle had driven past the shack, an event that probably happened periodically.

An hour later, I parked across the street from her motel and settled in for a long surveillance. The light blue building was a typical L-shape, with two floors of rooms with gaudy pink doors, each facing the narrow parking lot. From my vantage point, there was no chance of Caroline coming or going without my noticing.

Only a half hour later, a second-floor door opened and she emerged wearing a white summer dress with a yellow floral pattern. Her expression was sober, her eyes vacant as if she were deep in thought as she got into a rental car. I noted the make, model, and license plate. Once she'd driven out of sight, I slid out of my BMW to cross the street. On my way up the stairs, I pulled on a pair of disposable gloves from my pocket.

At the door to her unit, I drew my lockpick set, made sure I wasn't observed, then knelt at the door. A moment later, the lock clicked, the door opened, and I stepped inside, closing and locking the door behind me.

Sunlight bled easily through a sheer white curtain, revealing a small, narrow room largely occupied by a double bed neatly draped with a light blue comforter that matched the walls. The furniture was nondescript tan—a small round table at the window, a dresser beneath a flat-screen television bolted into the wall, and a nightstand that held a delicate cream lamp, an alarm clock, and a half-empty bottle of water. The carpet was dark blue, patterned with gold suns.

The drawer of the nightstand contained a small blank notepad and pen, and the obligatory bible. There was nothing beneath the bed, or under the mattress. In the dresser I found socks, underwear, pajamas, and a phone charger. The closet contained a handful of outfits carefully hung on plastic hangers that she must've brought herself, and a suitcase.

Lifting the suitcase to the bed, I could tell by its weight that it was probably empty. I opened it anyway to find a stray pair of socks. Rifling the pockets and folds I discovered a sealed plastic bag of jewelry that stank of silver. Resisting my instinctual urge to cast the bag aside, I brought it to the window and held it up to the light to examine the contents, at least a dozen simple silver chains. Cheap jewelry, but that wasn't the point. Caroline wasn't collecting necklaces to wear. Together with the shack, the chair, and the bindings, the silver completed a grim picture.

Sighing, I put the bag back as I'd found it, then returned the suitcase to the closet. I sat down on the edge of the bed, facing the door, and considered my options, none of them good. Killing Caroline was the practical choice. *She's not a civilian,* I reminded myself. She possessed a dangerous magic and had used it against me. I was within my rights to eliminate the threat. I couldn't spend my life looking over my shoulder, waiting for her to strike again. Her plans were too advanced for her to give up. Revenge was a motivation that only got stronger with time.

Killing her was the simple, strategic choice.

I glanced at the time on the clock. Eventually she'd walk through that door. She'd no reason to expect a predator in her room. Before she knew what was happening, before she could call on her magic for defense, I could break her neck and be done with the problem. There'd be no blood to clean up, which Josh would appreciate. He'd use his magic to get rid of the body and her belongings. He'd scrub any trace of our presence in the room. The car would take slightly more effort to dispose of, but it could be done.

To the hotel manager, it would appear that Caroline left without paying her bill. They would charge her credit card on file and promptly forget she was ever there. Her friends and acquaintances might take more notice. I'd have to send Markos to Idaho to monitor the situation there and alert me if any serious flags were raised over her disappearance.

Josh will want answers, I realized.

I frowned. It would be obvious to him that I'd sought her out, and he wouldn't approve. I could hear his voice in my head, nagging me.

"You made this mess," he said. *"You got her father killed. What did you expect her to do?"*

Until her father had died, she'd known nothing about me or the Midwest Pack. She'd been living her life in Idaho, enjoying her recent acquaintance with her father.

I stared down at my palms.

"She has the right to seek answers," Josh said, scowling.

She wants revenge.

"She has the right to that, too."

So I should just let her kill me?

Josh didn't have an answer, but I could feel the weight of his absent gaze, judging.

I rose, growling, and crossed to the window next to the door. After peeking from the curtains, I opened the door and left.

I returned home to find a manila envelope just peeking from under the doormat on my porch. Carrying it inside, I settled into my leather chair and spilled the contents of Tim's research, Caroline's official record obtained from the Boise police department, onto my lap. No arrests. She'd had her share of traffic violations, including one incident of running a red light and causing a minor accident. Checking the date, I realized she'd been seventeen at the time. Kid stuff. The only entry of note on her record was a restraining order she'd obtained against an ex-boyfriend. That had been six years ago. There'd been some complaints that he'd violated the order, but after a talking-to by the local police he'd decided to behave.

Along with the official report was a typed summary of Tim's unofficial research. From a pair of unaffiliated were-animals in the area, he'd learned that a number of rumors surrounded Caroline's mother, rumors of mysterious powers that she'd used to confuse anyone who attempted to interfere with her life. They were the kind of rumors I'd easily ignore, If I hadn't experienced the mind magic for myself. The mother had died only a few years ago. She'd largely kept to herself. Tim included one picture of her taken from her driver's license. In the photo, she was wearing a silver necklace with a black stone pendant. Caroline's pendant.

Pulling out my phone, I sorted through the pictures I'd taken of the shack, the chair, and the shackles. I reviewed Tim's reports again, looking for something I could use to justify eliminating Caroline, but I couldn't. All I found was a deepening source of guilt weighing on me until I finally threw my phone across the room in frustration.

Later that evening, I was still floundering in guilt and indecision when I heard Sky's Honda Civic rush into my driveway and lurch to a stop. Even before I opened my door, I could smell the chlorine, as if she'd bathed in a swimming pool. She stood on my porch, drenched and anxious. Her pupils were dilated to saucers, the whites of her eyes were irritated red, and her heart raced from adrenalin. My eyes traced the angry crimson marks down her arm to find the Aufero glowing faintly in her palm.

My jaw dropped. *What have you done?*

I stepped aside, scanning the area behind her for danger as she walked past me, then closed the door. She was leaving a wet trail toward the couch when I stopped her.

"Wait until I get you some dry clothes."

She rolled her eyes at me, then defiantly dropped onto the couch, her glare daring me to chastise her.

My gaze was drawn to the Aufero as she set it down beside her. *There will be repercussions, but she did it!* At last, there was a chance to lift my curse, the dark elf magic that made me a fugitive.

For the moment, I brushed aside my admiration of Sky's brave achievement. I'd no doubt Marcia had kept the orb very close. Going after it had been brave and foolish. Had someone helped Sky? If she'd had help, she wouldn't be at my door now. How she'd stolen the orb from beneath Marcia's nose was a mystery.

Marcia underestimated her, I realized, *the way she underestimates all of us.*

Seeing Sky shivering, I chided myself and retrieved a towel for her from the bathroom.

"Is she alive?" I asked.

The towel did little for her as she rubbed the back of her neck and down her chest. Her clothes were soaked through.

She nodded.

"She'll want it back," I warned.

"I want red velvet cake to be part of the food pyramid. We can't always get what we want. She may as well learn it now."

I went upstairs to my bedroom and opened the bottom drawer of my dresser, where I kept the clothing that my guests occasionally left behind. After some searching, I found a pair of jeans and a teal t-shirt that were close to her size and returned to the living room.

She accepted them with a raised eyebrow. "So do you have your own little women's consignment shop back there?"

I shrugged. "People leave things here."

"People, or women?"

Women. "People."

She shook out the t-shirt, noted the plunging neck line, then tossed it at me. "Fine, then you can go back there and get me a guy's t-shirt; they're more comfortable."

I watched the shirt bounce off my chest and then fall to the floor at my feet. The jeans followed. I smirked, crossing my arms over my chest. She had the confident edge of someone who'd just won a fight. "You're the one that's wet; I didn't think you would be so picky."

She glared, waiting expectantly for me to fulfill her order. When I didn't move, she said, "I'm cold."

My gaze shifted to the wet blot on my couch. "You're also wet."

After another brief staring contest, she rose with a sigh and went to the bathroom. A moment later, she emerged with a large bath towel wrapped around her and her wet clothes in her arms.

"Dryer?"

I gestured to the stairs, then followed her up and opened the closet that hid the laundry machines.

"Marcia will not come after you for it," I announced after she'd started the dryer. "Being a Moura will offer some protection, because you all are enigmas. We know there is a bond between you and the Aufero, but she doesn't know how strong. You now possess the power to do what she has done to many other witches. She'll stay away because she doesn't want it done to her."

"First I have to figure out how to use it," she said, her confidence quickly deflating.

I volunteered, raising my hand. She agreed with a reluctant nod, her mind no doubt absorbed with the risks. She didn't want to be responsible for causing me harm should the experiment go south, but the risks were mine. I was ready to accept any risk to be rid of my grandmother's inheritance. We stood quietly next to the rumbling dryer while her doubts played out in her expression. I considered a pep talk, then decided better of it. She was willing, and that was enough.

After a few minutes, she checked her clothes and found them dry. Responding to an expectant look, I returned to the living room. She arrived a moment later, dressed. After acknowledging the wet stain on the couch with an impish smile, she sat on the other end of the couch and placed the orb in her lap.

"It shouldn't be hard," I explained. "The Aufero should do most of the work."

When I reached for the orb to demonstrate, a shimmering protective field sparked to life around it, quickly expanding to engulf Sky. Orange-red light pulsed from the orb. I froze, suddenly aware that the Aufero had a mind of its own, and it saw me as a threat. Slowly, I withdrew my hand and took a cautious step back. After a moment, the pulsing faded and the field slowly dissolved.

I straightened, clearing my throat. "I guess I will walk you through it."

Crossing to my desk, I unlocked the top side-drawer and retrieved a printout Josh had sent me, replacing it with the iridium band. Keeping a wary watch on the orb, I slowly extended the instructions to her.

She glanced at it and bit her lower lip. "Shouldn't Josh be here?"

"You can do it," I promised. "When you read, it must be continual; you can't break the invocations. If you stop, then you must start over. Okay?"

She nodded, but her doubts remained.

I retrieved the candles required for the ritual. Preferring

not to antagonize the orb again, I placed the candles on the ottoman, then pushed it toward her and took my seat in the black-and-white chair.

Following the directions on the paper, she went about placing the candles in the required pattern. To her chagrin, I made a few slight but necessary adjustments; precision was important. Once the candles were in place, I retrieved a knife from its hiding place beneath the ottoman and handed it to Sky.

She frowned at the blade. "Why is it always blood? Why not a strand of my hair, a tear, a flake of dandruff, or something?"

Withholding an amused smile, I leaned toward her and drew her gaze to mine. "You can do this."

She closed her eyes for a moment, gathering her courage, then smoothed out the already flat paper. Skimming over the instructions, she placed the knife next to the candles, then quickly adjusted its position before I could do it for her. Her frustration grew as she adjusted the knife several more times, each slight, until she rose to retrieve her phone and placed it beside her on the couch. Her hand rested on the phone, pushing it against her leg as if she took comfort from its presence, like a security blanket.

"Whatever happens," I cautioned, eyeing the phone, "you can't involve Josh. Understand?"

She answered with a half-hearted nod.

"Promise me you will not involve him."

Anxiety gave way to a flash of anger as she raised her eyes to glare at me. "Your constant protection will form the resentment that will eventually destroy your relationship with him."

I bristled. "I didn't ask for your advice, just your compliance."

She shook her head in disgust.

When I reached out to touch her arm, she reacted reflexively, jumping back into the couch. She struck the frame, causing her to wince and clutch at her elbow. I straightened and pushed away from her, surprised and horrified that I could've frightened her into such an instinctive reaction, just by the mere act of touching her. Blood rushed to my cheeks, coloring my embarrassment.

"There are many things in my control," I said in a restrained voice, "but far more that aren't. I protect Josh because the things that I can't control are the things that could hurt him the most. You may not see the point of what I do, but there is one. I ask that you respect that. Please," I stressed, "don't involve him."

She offered a begrudging nod as she massaged her elbow, then slowly slid off the front edge of the couch and knelt next to the ottoman. Relieved, I took my place next to her.

With the Aufero in one hand, she stretched the other arm across the ottoman, leaving her palm up. My heart raced as I stared at her hand, afraid to touch it. I closed my eyes and took several slow, deep breaths to calm myself, then looked to Sky for approval. She scrutinized me for a moment, perhaps surprised at my deference, then nodded. Slowly, I laid my hand over hers. When she didn't flinch, I weaved my fingers into hers and felt the slight squeeze of her acceptance.

"Please," I whispered, "don't get Josh involved."

She nodded again, seemingly sincere, but I knew if something happened to me, if the ritual went truly wrong, she would call him to save me. If I pressed her, she would admit it, but no amount of arguing would change her mind. I gave her a warm, appreciative smile and she smiled back.

Concentrating, I allowed my own doubts to melt away and shared my strength and confidence with Sky the way only Alphas could.

Visibly bolstered, she began to recite the invocation from the paper. Following along from memory, I slipped back onto my heels, waiting for my part of the ritual. When the time came, I picked up the knife and gently cut a long shallow line across her palm, just enough to draw a faint trickle of blood. Ignoring the sting, she continued the invocation, passing the Aufero to her cut hand, where the orb came into contact with her blood.

At the required moment, I drew the knife across my palm, then placed it over top of the orb.

A hostile wind rushed into the room as if through an opened door, creating a wailing sound as it snuffed out the flames of the candles. The wind whipped about, gathering loose books and candles and other objects and flung them in an increasingly violent storm. Glass shattered. The Aufero expanded until I thought it might burst, casting a stifling magic that descended on us like a smothering shroud. Suddenly the orb collapsed to its original shape, then expanded again, this time releasing a force that sent us tumbling from the ottoman.

Sky crashed into the bookcase, toppling it. I barely managed to drape my body over hers, absorbing the weighty impact on my back with a grunt as books spilled over us. Resisting the wind, I threw off the bookcase, but continued to shield her body with mine, absorbing the impact of flying objects until the wind finally died. The magic retreated, and an eerie calm descended over the room.

Expecting the Aufero to react with a new, more powerful burst of magic, we remained entwined on the floor, gazing into each other's eyes. For a moment, I was lost there, entranced by the warmth of her body against mine. Instinctively, I bent to her neck and lightly brushed my lips against her skin. Her head turned almost imperceptibly, inviting my touch, and I felt a rush of anticipation fill my body. She relaxed against me, her heart calming faster than mine as we listened to each other's beats.

"Are you okay?" I finally whispered.

Slowly, reluctantly, she nodded.

Swallowing my desire, I lifted from her, pushing aside the books and debris that spilled from my backside. Once standing, I helped her to her feet. The Aufero remained on the ottoman, its orange-red glow stifled now, replaced by a dark fog within the orb. It remained active, vibrating and throbbing until it expanded once more. Anticipating another burst of magic, I positioned myself protectively in front of Sky, but then the orb snapped back to its normal size. A battle seemed to continue inside of it as it alternated between bright and subdued colors, until it finally settled on a dull burnt orange and became suddenly still.

Had it worked?

I froze, tuning into my body. The disconcerting thrum of the dark elf magic was gone. For the first time since my grandmother had died, I felt like myself. Suddenly panicking, I reached for my mother's magic and found it. Panic gave way to relief.

"How do you feel?" Sky asked, her gaze still fixed on the orb.

"Fine," I said, surprised.

The orb, it seemed, had permanently changed, as if marred by the magic it had absorbed from me. Wary of it, I picked up the scattered candles and returned them to the kitchen cabinet. My movements were sluggish; I felt drained but relieved. We set about cleaning up the living room, avoiding each other's gazes while silently acknowledging the tension between us. By the time she finally broke the silence, the tension had become unbearable.

"If your grandmother was able to hide," she said, "I'm sure there are others. We can use the Aufero to convince the elves that they no longer need to 'contain' the dark elves, but instead remove their magic."

I offered her a comforting smile. Dark elves possessed a dangerous, deadly power that none of the factions could tolerate. It would always be easier to kill power than to tame it.

"I'm serious," she said.

"I know. You want to save the world, but realistically, you can't," I gently admonished her. At her core, she remained stubbornly altruistic, untainted by the moral flexibility that pervaded our world. Better to serve a cause than an ideal, I felt, but I admired her conviction. She was not easily swayed from her moral center.

"No, not the world," she said defensively, "just people given a death sentence for being born into something they can't help. Maybe we could work out something with Mason and save the lives of these people."

She carried on her argument for some time before I interrupted. "Letting everyone know you have the Aufero and what you are capable of doing with it isn't a good idea. You are part of this pack; just by association people will be reluctant to trust you because they will not believe your motives are altruistic. They will assume that you have ulterior motives."

"Then you all need to do better about improving your public image. Doesn't it bother you that people have so little trust in you all?" Her eyes widened, as if she'd only just realized she was one of us. "We need to do more about our image. I don't like people fearing us."

"Perhaps you're right," I said sardonically, my irritation rising. "We should work harder at making people see us as docile and ineffectual, deny what dwells in us, and work on people seeing us as soft and cuddly pushovers. Easily subjugated by anyone who would choose to dominate us. Sounds like a brilliant plan."

Her hands went to her hips, complimenting her scowl. "I realize the importance of a strong pack; there isn't a need for you to be such a jackass. But what's wrong with helping others? I can assure you that possessing the ability to restrict those that have the ability to kill with just touch will work in our favor. I think Mason would appreciate that, and if he can't, then whoever is chosen next might."

"You mean Gideon." I smirked. "Contrary to what you choose to believe, we are not monsters. Less than a century ago, others felt they needed to contain us, so we are more understanding of the situation. The three times that we abided by the agreement were unavoidable situations and we didn't find any joy in doing so." The memory of the last incident rose to sear my thoughts, reminding me that I'd nearly been a victim of the same cruelty, had it not been for Sky and the Aufero.

Perhaps I shouldn't be so quick to dismiss her ideals.

As I took a seat next to her, she shifted a few inches from me. "Mason is unnecessarily difficult," I continued, softening my voice. "He will not trust such an altruistic gesture because it is easier to believe we are incapable of such acts. When Gideon is in power, then we will visit this again."

I couldn't blame her for distrusting my sincerity, but I was too tired to argue further. Exhaustion was quickly overtaking me. For the first time in over a week, there was a chance I might actually sleep.

"It's getting late," I said. "You should go home, get some rest."

She frowned at the clock as if I'd just sent her to bed. "Of course, I can't continue to live this party lifestyle." She settled herself deeper into the couch, like an anchor. "Tell me about the fifth object," she insisted.

I stiffened, surprised by the sudden shift in topic. "It's late," I said dismissively. "We will talk about it tomorrow."

"Promise?"

I sighed, rubbing exhaustion from my forehead before answering. "If possible, we will talk and I will answer whatever question you have to the best of my ability. No more secrets."

She rose from the couch with a skeptical look. "I expect more than answers 'to the best of your ability'; I expect the truth and real answers." Eyeing me sternly, she gathered her purse and the Aufero, and then walked out the front door. Before I could close it behind her, she stopped and turned at the bottom of the porch, dangling my spare keys from her finger.

"I'll be back tomorrow at nine." She grinned. "I'll let myself in if you're not awake. Is this one for the office? Oh, let's not bother with such trivial things. I will just snoop around until you get up. Okay?"

I barely stifled a laugh. First she'd beaten Marcia, then she'd taken my keys right from under my nose. She was becoming formidable. A smile cracked my lips when I felt my wolf suddenly rush to the surface, warning me.

Danger.

Peering into the shadows across the street, I caught a hint of movement. Chains clanked as something approached. Six doglike beasts stepped into the street, revealed by the light of the half-moon reflecting from the pavement. The beasts growled, spilling drool from their lips and baring rows of daggerlike teeth. Only the thick, clinking chains around their necks kept them from charging. At the end of the chains, a tall, thick man in a dark blue duster effortlessly steered them, three chains clutched in each hand. A rifle was strung across his back, and I noticed the protruding pommel of a sword beneath his duster.

Samuel.

"Skylar," I hissed, my eyes fixed on the oncoming threat, "come here."

The chains groaned as the dogs lurched toward her, their jaws snapping, but Samuel held them to a steady, driving advance. She hesitated, her eyes straining to her left as if to drive her head around to face the threat, but she was terrified, frozen as if by a spell.

272

"Skylar, come here," I commanded.

She remained frozen.

The elven hounds strained against their chains. They were magical creatures, mutated for war. Six of them were more than a match for me, but I could draw their attention, buy some time for Sky to escape. Ready for a fight, I stepped out onto the porch. Before I could unleash my wolf, the Aufero glowed in her hand. Suddenly freed from her fear, she clutched the orb to her chest and charged up the steps. I pulled her up, stepping aside to let her run into the house, then barred the doorway.

"Samuel," I growled.

He pulled at the clinking chains, stopping the hounds just a few feet from my porch. He fixed his attention on Sky behind me, and his lips twisted into a cool and mirthless smile.

"Can you read the Clostra?" he asked her.

How the hell did he find out about that?

When Sky didn't answer, he urged his beasts closer, allowing them to lunge and jump against their restraints until he whispered a command that calmed them.

My wolf's howl echoed in my skull as it demanded to be set loose. "What are you doing here?" I demanded.

"Give me the books," he said almost casually.

"You know that will never happen."

"Of course it will," he promised, then disappeared, taking the chains with him.

The hounds charged.

Targeting the largest of them, I leapt from the porch. If I could face down the leader, the rest of the pack might scatter, but he was an experienced fighter, his neck and face marred by scars. The leader pulled up short, growling and snapping and baring its teeth as we squared off. As we half circled each other, looking for an advantage, the other hounds barked and gnashed their teeth, waiting for blood.

Surrendering to the primitive ferocity of my wolf, I slammed into the leader just before it leapt, driving it back. Its jaws clamped on to my left arm, its teeth piercing my flesh. Ignoring the pain, I hammered my right fist into the hound's ribs, blow after blow. The unusually dense bone refused to break, but the rain of blows loosened the hound's grip. Pulling my arm free, I slipped around the hound, wrapped my arm around its neck, gripped its jaw, and twisted. Bone snapped. The body went slack and I released it, allowing the hound to collapse to the ground in a heap.

Another hound leapt, its teeth reaching for my throat. Turning, I struck the animal in the side, sending it sprawling across the grass.

Sky cried out from inside the house. Glancing around, I realized with panic that two of the hounds were scrambling in the doorway. Two other hounds were already inside. Howling my rage, I charged up the steps, took one of the hounds two-handed by the scruff, and hurled it toward the driveway. The other hound turned, snapping its teeth at my hands until I kicked in its skull with my boot.

Inside, Sky was on the floor of the entryway, a hound clamped on to her leg. Her face was scrunched in violent rage as she drove her elbow into its head, forcing it to release her. Before it could lunge, she raised the glowing Aufero. Magic hurled the animal into the wall next to me.

Believing herself safe, she looked to me with a shocked, relieved expression, unaware of the hound crouching behind her. Leaping over her, I slammed into the hound as it pounced, driving it back into the wall, then snapped its neck.

I heard Sky's gasp as two of the hounds I'd left outside came into the house. The hound Sky had knocked from her leg rallied. Together the three remaining hounds growled and snarled as they encircled us. The orb glowed a dirty orange in her hand as she held it out at them in warning, but they remained determined. Crouching, wary of every movement, I slowly backed up to Sky. The moment she felt me against her, a strong protective field formed around us. Deprived of their prey, the hounds flung themselves against the field with ferocious abandon. It wavered beneath the weight of their rabid assault but held.

My relief quickly faded as I realized something was wrong with the magic. The field was dull gray in color, like a fog. Within it, the air was growing increasingly thin, as if the field was drawing out the oxygen. Already we were panting.

Soon, Sky would have to lower the field and we'd be forced to deal with the hounds. If necessary, I could occupy two of them, but that would still leave one for her to deal with. The orb might help her escape, but in a direct fight she was no match for an elven hound; few were. I scanned the entryway, looking for a path to escape.

Amid the snarling growls and barks of the hounds, a whimpering emerged. Their attacks seemed increasingly weak, as if each strike against the field weakened them. The animals refused to relent. Even after one of the hounds collapsed, apparently dead, the assault continued. A second hound quickly fell, leaving just one more, but my muscles were weak from oxygen deprivation.

Sky's gaze was fixed on the hound. Her chest heaved, her lungs straining for oxygen. She was close to losing consciousness. She needed to lower the field and let me distract the hound. I could put up enough of a fight for her to escape. I tried to call her name to get her attention but failed to create more than a squeak.

The last hound finally whimpered and collapsed.

The field disappeared and oxygen rushed into our lungs. For a moment, we sat there catching our breath, but we weren't safe. Samuel would come back. We were in no condition to take on a witch of his power.

Grabbing Sky's hand, I led her outside toward the garage. When I saw the door had been torn open, I knew Samuel had disabled all five of the vehicles inside. The tires of my dark green Hummer were blown out. The same was true of my SUV, Mercedes-Benz S Class, and Jaguar XJ. I felt a rush of pure hatred as I saw my newest addition to the collection, a red 1967 Ferrari GTB, sitting on its rims. No doubt the engines had been rendered inoperable, as well.

Cursing under my breath, I pulled Sky after me to the backyard and through a narrow gap in the thicket there. With my free hand in front of me, I crashed through the overgrown brush until we entered the small clearing where I kept a Jeep Rubicon in case of emergencies. Finding the key fob underneath the front bumper, I unlocked the doors and gestured for Sky to get in.

She obeyed without question.

"Do you have your phone?" I asked, starting the engine.

"Not with me. I left it in my car."

I reached across her and retrieved a flip phone from the glove box, then dialed the first number on the speed dial. Josh answered immediately, his voice tense.

"What's wrong?" he asked, recognizing my emergency number.

"Samuel's in town. He has the third book and wants the other two." He unleashed a stream of obscenities. "You need to get out of there. Go to the cabin."

"Okay."

Through the phone, I heard a loud blast, followed by a crack and then something heavy hitting the floor.

"Josh!" I shouted.

I heard grunting, glass shattering, and then the line went dead. When I tried his number again, it went straight to voice mail. I sped as fast as I could to his house, carelessly weaving through traffic while Sky glanced anxiously behind us, as if the hounds were going to appear on our tail at any moment.

As Josh's house came into view, I felt the air forced from

my lungs. For a moment, I couldn't breathe. The front door was open, hanging on a single hinge. I brought the Jeep to a sudden, screeching halt in the driveway, then leapt from the vehicle. Running inside, I discovered broken furniture and glass, but no bodies. Josh was gone, leaving behind the distinct feeling of his magic, freshly used. Samuel's magic was there, as well.

Had Samuel taken him, or had he disposed of my brother's body with the same ease Josh had practiced dozens of times for the pack? Frantically, I kicked through the debris for proof of life or death. Dread washed over me as I uncovered first a splatter of blood, then a nearby knife, wet blood dulling its sheen.

Sky gasped.

I picked up the knife and sniffed the blood. "It isn't his," I said, relieved.

"But this is," she whispered.

Following her gesture, I found a trail of blood that led to the bedroom. I ran down the hall and found the room in violent disarray. The bed had been turned and the mattress thrown from it. The dresser was half embedded in a wall, and every one of the windows had been blown out.

The fight had started in the living room. Josh had been wounded and made a last stand here. Tearing through the debris, I assured myself that there was no final pool of blood, no splatter on the walls from a mortal wound. He'd been taken or fled, but Samuel's magic in the room was dominant. The chances Josh had escaped were low.

Even as I ran back to the Jeep, I knew I wouldn't find my brother at the cabin, but I had to try. Sky jumped into the passenger seat just as I put the Jeep into reverse and sped back onto the road.

The cabin was a rural farmhouse that Josh and I maintained as a personal retreat of last resort. Its existence was a secret, even from the pack. My last hope was crushed as I turned into the empty driveway. The house was dark. Had Josh taken refuge inside and feared pursuit, there would be a subtle red LED light blinking in the corner of the front window.

I had to be sure.

After retrieving a flashlight from the glove compartment, I tested the front door, hoping it was locked. It swung open. The echo of Samuel's magic washed over me, along with the scent of his hounds. Stepping inside, I found everything was in place. I realized with dread that Samuel hadn't come to the house in pursuit of Josh. Samuel had come to make a point. *I know your secrets.*

Dreading what came next, I walked into the kitchen and found his note on the counter. Reading it, I cursed and growled and swore vengeance if he harmed my brother. If necessary, I'd abandon Sky and the pack and everything I'd built to spend my life hunting him down. At least, for the moment, I knew Josh was alive; Samuel wanted the Clostra.

Sky's family had said they'd been working with a witch, and I'd been foolish not to investigate who. I'd never have guessed it would be Samuel.

She followed me back to the Jeep, watching me closely. She appeared shaken, as if she'd never believed Josh could be beaten.

Wherever Samuel held Josh, it was close. Magical transportation had a limited range, and I doubted Samuel would've taken the risk of trying to stuff my brother into a car. Besides, Samuel wasn't going to leave the area until he obtained what he wanted.

He was smart enough to know I'd comb the city looking for him. I doubted he'd stash Josh in one of the properties he'd been known to use previously, but the obvious couldn't be overlooked. One by one, I sped to the houses and ransacked them, looking for hidden rooms and anything Josh might've left behind to indicate he'd been there.

All I found was dust.

When the last house failed to yield even a clue, I tore it apart in a fit of frustration. Sky kept her distance, watching wide-eyed until the core of my rage was spent and I'd run out of furniture to destroy. The sick feeling in my gut remained.

"Ethan," she said softly.

"He's gone," I whispered, unable to meet her gaze, then walked out of the house.

En route back to the retreat, I called Sebastian and filled him in. When I walked in the front door, he was in the entryway, waiting with Marko, Gavin, Winter, and a few other members of the pack.

"It was definitely Samuel?" Sebastian asked.

I nodded, handing him the ransom note.

His jaw clenched as he read. "He thinks we are stupid enough to drop the books off at some disclosed location and trust that he will release Josh. How arrogant."

"I don't know how he knew we had the books," I said, pacing in an attempt to control my rage. Time mattered. Throwing another tantrum would only waste time Josh didn't have. "I am sure Samuel thought Josh had them in his possession. The house was trashed." I knew exactly what was going through Sebastian's mind as he watched me pace. If the spells against were-animals were used, we could be wiped out. We didn't know why Samuel wanted the Clostra, but there was no chance Sebastian would allow the books to leave our hands.

He also knew I wouldn't abandon my brother.

We could give up the books, then hunt Samuel down once Josh was returned. Every one of the packs could be called upon to help. Sebastian would resist, but he could be brought to reason. If not, I'd act on my own initiative. *I could retrieve the books before any damage was done. Ask for forgiveness later.*

"Ethan," Sebastian said, his voice deliberately soothing,

but there was a tension there, a subtle warning. "We cannot give him the books for Josh. I can't let that happen."

I blanched, turning my anger on him, then returned to pacing. *I need to be calm.* Sebastian was just as worried as I was. He wouldn't abandon Josh. He wasn't going to risk the pack, either, but I would. I'd risk everything to get my brother back. I'd steal the Clostra if I had to, or challenge Sebastian for the pack's leadership.

I felt his anger rising in the room, meeting mine. Before I could confront him, Winter stepped between us, an unusually casual gesture calculated to cut the tension rather than inflate it. Sky joined her, her expression anxious but defiant.

"I need Josh back," I growled, pacing.

Sebastian nodded. "I know."

"Samuel has elven hounds with him."

Sky suggested, "Maybe we can track the animals. Their scent should still be in Ethan's house. It is quite strong and very distinctive."

"We can," Sebastian acknowledged, "but that will take time; even with our best hunters that could take days. We may not have days. Samuel isn't known for his patience."

Winter spoke for the first time. "There is no way he's in town and Marcia isn't aware of it. She makes it her business to know where he is. Power like that can't go undetected very long. They can find him."

"Are you sure she will know?" he challenged. "Our surveillance lost him three months ago."

Winter remained confident. "If anyone will know of his whereabouts, it's her."

Marcia will never help us!

"I'll arrange a meeting," Sebastian said, his gaze settling on me for a moment, then started toward his office.

We're wasting time!

Sky called after him. "When you call her, tell her that if she helps us find Josh, she can have the Aufero."

I stopped, taken aback. Sebastian was surprised as well. His wary gaze shifted from Sky to me as he debated whether to ask how and when we'd obtained the orb. My eyes remained locked on her, my mouth agape. The Aufero was her birthright, a magical object of immense power that creatures in our world would kill and die for. Yet she seemed unreserved in her offer, eager even. With a single act of extreme selflessness, she was giving Josh a chance.

"Sky," Sebastian said carefully, "are you sure?"

She didn't hesitate. "Positive, but I want to meet with her, too. I have some conditions."

CHAPTER 15

I continued my pacing in Sebastian's office.

"Is there anything I need to know about the Aufero?" he asked, his phone in hand.

He wanted to know if we'd killed anyone Marcia cared about. I shook my head. "Sky retrieved it on her own." His eyes widened in surprise as I continued, "There's no liability for the pack. Marcia will try to blame us, but she is now aware that Sky is a Moura. She can't deny her right to the orb."

He nodded and made the call. To say that Marcia was furious was an understatement. After several minutes of accusations and threats, he made our position clear; we recognized only the Moura's right to possess the Aufero. Marcia had no inherent right to it, but if she was interested in obtaining the Aufero legitimately, the Moura was willing to trade. She agreed to meet us, but under specific and insulting conditions. Under the pressure of time, we had no choice but to agree.

A short time later, Sebastian, Sky, Winter, and I approached a windowless dark van in a shopping mall parking lot. I recognized the driver and his passenger, who had accompanied Bernard on his visit to the retreat. Once locked in the van, we were blind and trapped. Only Sky seemed comfortable with the situation.

Once the van was underway, I started the timer on my phone. Winter and I both made digital notes of the stops and turns and time taken between actions, until the van finally came to rest ten minutes later. After the meeting, we'd compare notes and attempt to plot Marcia's secret location.

The van door opened and we emerged into a windowless garage. From there, we were led down a dark hallway, through an empty room toward an open door. Sebastian crossed the threshold first. Even before he gasped, I'd felt the powerful magic emanating from the room. As I entered behind him, I felt the weight of the oppressive magic engulf me, forcing my wolf into retreat. Glancing around the room, I saw the source of the magic, dozens of powerful runes painted onto the walls. The stench of henna, tannin, and metal hung in the stale air.

All five members of the Creed were present, seated at a long banquet table lit by muted gas lamps on the wall behind them. Marcia sat in the middle, glowering from her ornate, rune-carved wooden chair that was raised slightly higher than the others in a gross display of authority. Several servants were in the room as well, Bernard among them. At a nod from one of the Creed—a dark-haired Korean woman— Bernard walked to the heavy metal door, closed it, and locked it.

Marcia waved toward the rune-covered wall. "You will not be able to change, we've assured that. Perhaps that will ensure our safety and prevent us from being accosted by animals that do not respond to our magic."

Sebastian maintained a calm demeanor, but I recognized the hard set of his jaw, the thick cords of muscle in his neck. He didn't like being cut off from his animal any more than I did. Winter chafed as well, while Sky was unsurprisingly calm; she'd spent a great deal of her life trying to hide from her wolf.

Marcia extended her hand toward Sky. "You promised me the Aufero if I met with you."

Sebastian answered the childish ploy with an exaggerated sigh. "You said that you wanted the Aufero in exchange for meeting with us. I applaud the confidence you have in your presence." He made an overt gesture toward the runes. "However, I made it clear that it is yours if you help us. Are we going to have a discussion, or should we leave?"

Sky drew the orb from her pocket, displaying it in her open palm. Greed flashed in Marcia's eyes, but she remained still, posturing. The lustful drum of her heart betrayed her. Like all witches, she craved power above all else. After a moment, she tore her gaze from the orb and clasped her hands in front of her.

When she spoke, her tone was rich with contempt and scorn. "What can we do for you?"

"I need your help," Sebastian said.

"I figured that much. At some point, do you plan to offer specifics?"

A hint of a smile creased his lips. "Samuel is in town."

I watched the Creed closely, gauging their reactions. None of them were surprised or even concerned. Odd, considering the resources they spent attempting to monitor him, as we did.

"Yes, we are aware of this," she admitted with an unexpected smirk. "I am sure when he has acquired whatever he came to town to retrieve, he will leave as quietly as he arrived."

Does she know that he has my brother? I tensed, clenching and releasing my fists to calm myself.

"He has Josh and is threatening to kill him."

Marcia eased back into her chair, her expression smug. "Well, that hardly seems any concern of ours."

"He is a witch. It is your concern. Do you not have a duty to protect your own?"

"Josh is no more a witch than you all are Homo sapiens. The world sees one face in the daylight, but when the moon is full, Mercury rises, or the world is eclipsed, your true being is exposed. He is not one of us. When I was being brutalized by *that*"—she glanced scornfully at Sky—"where was Josh to muzzle the rabid dog?"

Sky licked her lips, trying to let the insult slide. She seemed oblivious to the faint glow that arose from the orb in her hand, but the buildup of magic there wasn't lost on the Creed. They rose from their chairs in alarm just as the banquet table slid into their stomachs, forcibly pressing them against the wall.

Sebastian and Winter turned agape to Sky, who stared at the glowing orb in equal surprise.

At a gesture from the Creed, the table flew across the room toward us. We just ducked beneath it, letting it clatter to the floor at the back of the room.

Marcia's cheeks flushed as she roared, "That is unacceptable! You come here for favors and you allow one of your were-animals who is able to control magic to come here. Now you see what happens when an animal is given gifts that belong to those that have a civil nature."

"I apologize," Sky stammered, genuinely taken aback. "That was unintentional. Please do not let my poor manners be a death sentence for Josh. I am sorry." She lowered her head in supplication, but I saw a slight smile tug at the corner of her lips.

Another time and place, I would've enjoyed her display of power, but there was too much at stake.

Marcia remained on her feet, fuming, while Bernard hurriedly picked up her chair and placed it behind her. The rest of the Creed picked up their chairs as well. After a long, violent glare at Sky, Marcia sat with regal finality as she declared, "This meeting is over."

Bernard approached Sebastian, gesturing toward the door, but he remained firmly planted, as did I.

"Samuel has the Clostra," he announced.

There it is, I thought, finally catching a hint of surprise and fear in Marcia's expression. She didn't know as much as she thought she did.

"That isn't an issue we care about," she announced disingenuously. "According to my knowledge, the spells in that book don't affect us."

I stepped forward. "That is where you are wrong. We have it on full authority that the book has spells that will strip magic from all that hold it. You do not believe that with the books in his possession he will fail to seek to control you all as well. You want him dead as much as we do."

Her expression hardened. "We will stand against him if needed. His grievance isn't with us, but the existence of your kind." *Is that his plan?* "I assume you have the other two books. Once he has them, I am confident we will not hear from him. So tell me, why should I help you?"

Sky stepped forward, raising the Aufero in her palm. The Creed tensed, wary. "You want the Aufero," she said. "It's yours if you help."

Now it was Marcia's turn to offer a hint of a smile as she clasped her hands in her lap. She remained quiet for several uncomfortable minutes, relishing our impatience. Aware that she was gauging whether she could demand more from us, I did my best to hide my anxiety, but the clock was ticking. Josh's safety was at stake. An undeniable rage slowly built in me like a volcano, the pressure building toward a violent explosion when Sky spoke.

"It is a difficult decision," she announced, "but one you need to make quickly."

"Let us discuss this for a moment."

The Creed chanted in unison, casting a dampening field around us. The effect was an enforced deafness. I tried to read their lips, but they were too animated, talking too quickly. After a lively debate, the dampening field collapsed, bringing a welcome onrush of sound.

"Okay," Marcia announced. "We will help."

Sebastian was about to accept the offer when Sky declared, "First, you will help us find Josh. As you stated, he isn't one of you, therefore he can no longer be governed by your laws. You are not allowed to sanction him under any circumstances. He now belongs solely to the pack."

I remained stoic, resisting the urge to look at Sky. Buying Josh protection from Marcia's jealousy was a reasonable request, given what Sky was giving up—as long as she didn't push too far.

"No," Marcia snapped. "That is not acceptable. In the event Josh requires discipline, I doubt that the pack will ever do it justly. He is coddled because he is the brother of the Beta and you all need him."

"Well, I worry about the fact that you conveniently and often punish those whose powers mirror if not exceed yours. I am not confident that he would not be punished far too severely for a minor infraction."

Marcia bristled at the rebuke. "No."

"Fine," Sky conceded. "All possible sanctions must be agreed upon by you and Sebastian."

"He and I would never come to an agreement. You are wasting our time with your unreasonable request."

I felt a rising tide of panic. Sky was going too far. Marcia was on the verge of backing out of the deal.

"Then all sanctions will be handled by you, Sebastian, and an agreed-upon third party," Sky countered.

Marcia's eyes narrowed. After a moment's hesitation, she accepted the terms with a half nod, but Sky wasn't finished.

"And you have to help us find Samuel and retrieve Josh. If

he isn't retrieved safe and unharmed, then the agreement is void."

Marcia scoffed. "We can't guarantee that he is unharmed. That isn't in our control."

"He's been gone for two hours now. The longer he is gone, the greater the chance that he will be harmed or even killed. If I were you, I would agree, climb down off your high horse, and go find Josh to make sure this deal isn't voided."

Marcia glared at Sky with a stony gaze. Gasps and murmurs erupted from the servants and some of the Creed, until Marcia brought them to a sudden end with a raised hand. "We will need a minute of discussion."

The dampening field was cast once more, but the conference was brief.

"Agreed," she announced with a sober expression. "However, a restriction will be placed on the Aufero. The Aufero is drawn to you, therefore it will continue to seek your ownership as long as you are near it. You must agree to stay away from it and allow us to place a restraint that will force it to return to us even if it must be over your dead body."

My jaw clenched along with my fists. Sky had pushed too far. She'd gotten a good deal for Josh—more than I'd thought to ask for—but now she was going to have to pay an even higher price. I glanced at Sebastian, wondering if he would accept such a condition. He was calm, reflective. I knew there was an anger in there, but he wouldn't give the Creed the satisfaction.

"Restriction?" Sky asked.

"A curse that will not only sever the tie, but if you are ever in possession of it, will return it to me."

Winter's disgust was naked. "But not without killing her first."

Marcia smiled.

Sky took in the news with a calming exhale. "Okay."

"Very well." Marcia turned her gaze to Sebastian. "My

final condition—I want Samuel. You are not allowed to kill him; preferably, I would like him unharmed."

Finally I saw the anger flash in Sebastian's eyes. My own fury was barely contained. Marcia didn't care about Samuel. If anything, she considered him a rival. On any other occasion, she would welcome the news of his demise. Protecting him was just a means to punish us, to twist the screw deeper by denying us our revenge, but the pack wouldn't be denied. We would get it eventually, against Samuel *and* Marcia.

After some discussion, Sebastian and Winter were returned to the pack's SUV in the mall parking lot. They would gather as much of the pack as they could while Sky and I led Marcia and her witches to Josh's house.

I gestured to the knife on the floor. "That's Samuel's blood, and that ..." My brother's name choked in my throat. I cursed myself, refusing to put my worry on display for the witches. "That is Josh's."

"I am aware," Marcia said.

Samuel would expect us to track my brother. Very likely, he would've arranged a trap. Tracking Samuel made more sense. "Although Josh is our priority," I said, "if we find Samuel, I am confident Josh will be near."

Squatting over the knife, she drew a pouch from her belt and sprinkled tannin on the blood there, followed by a dull white powder. Her fingers flickered over the blade as she whispered her invocation. In response, a golden smoke rose from the blood to form a cloud just above the knife. Within the cloud, an image appeared of a house. A few more words from Marcia and the image zoomed in. Just before we could read the address, the image quickly dissolved into a dissipating cloud of smoke.

Marcia cursed under her breath, but there was a crafty smile on her lips. I recognized some of the words as she performed the spell once more, but there were variations from the first attempt. The smoke rose. The cloud formed, but the image quickly burst in a display of sparks and flashes. Samuel was blocking the tracking spell, and he was doing a damn good job of it. *If she can't locate them, Josh is lost,* I realized with a desperate hope, but Marcia appeared confident, amused even.

"His skills have improved." She smiled.

Responding to her gesture, the other witches clasped hands around the knife. They joined their chant, casting the spell with their combined abilities. Once more, the cloud appeared, shimmering in alternating colors until it finally turned gold and the image of the house returned, crystal clear. Marcia zoomed in to get the address, then shifted the image to reveal a map of the house's location. They were in a rural area, far from any of Samuel's known properties.

I made the call to Sebastian, giving him the address.

We arrived with the witches, transporting in after the pack had arrived. Twenty-five were-animals, half in animal form in anticipation of magic, surrounded the farmhouse, assuring that Samuel could not physically escape. If he tried, the farm fields around the house were nothing but dry and barren soil. His most likely path of escape was magical transportation. For that, he'd have to lower the protective field that surrounded the house—the strongest field I'd ever encountered.

I'd never felt more uncertain than while I waited, pacing next to Sebastian, while Marcia worked her magic on the field. Samuel knew we were there. Because of his field, we couldn't overwhelm him with surprise. If he wanted to kill Josh, he had plenty of opportunities. I could only hope he had enough sense to realize that harming my brother was a death sentence and gained him nothing.

I found myself putting tremendous faith in Samuel's reputation as a rational man. As I paced, I felt my burner phone vibrate in my pocket. Caroline. I declined the call and pushed the phone back into my pocket.

As Marcia worked her magic, rolling waves of black and gold shimmered against the translucent barrier, but it didn't break. Her expression was taut as she gestured to the rest of the Creed to join her.

Should've used your combined power in the first place. I snorted derision. It was just like Marcia to showboat.

The Creed joined hands, facing the house, and began their chant. Black and gold shimmered once more, this time in a violent pitched battle. For a moment, it seemed their combined strength would fail, but then the field buckled and collapsed.

Sebastian gave the signal and we approached the house, a slow strangling noose. With any luck, Samuel would see the futility of a fight and surrender, but I didn't believe in luck. He was too powerful and too motivated to give up so easily. As we steadily closed the gap, my eyes flicked along the house in anticipation, cycling through the door and each of the windows. We were ten feet from the house when I began to wonder, *Is it possible that this is a ruse, that Josh isn't here? Were we walking into a trap?*

A powerful wave of force burst from the house, knocking all of us onto our backs. It took the air from my lungs, as well. Along with the rest, I clambered back to my feet as I caught my breath.

Anticipating the next attack, Marcia and the witches quickly spread out, erecting a protective field in front of us just before another wave of power burst from the house. It struck the field in a savage eruption of sparks. The field bowed and dented at places, but it held.

The front door of the house creaked open and Samuel casually walked out onto the porch wearing canvas pants, boots, and a wrinkled t-shirt. "Marcia, this isn't your fight. I urge you to not make it yours."

She stiffened. "Samuel, release him."

"Of course. When I have the books, you can have the witch. I can see why you were so distraught over losing him to Sebastian. But you should find comfort in the fact that he will never take your position in the Creed, although with more practice he will make your little dog and pony show look like mage magic."

Josh is still alive!

He brought down the Creed's field with a simple gesture. Six elven hounds rushed from the door and leapt off the porch. One of them clamped its jaws on to Marcia's arm. She screamed, flailing at the hound with her fist until Gavin's panther sank his teeth into its flank. The hound yelped, releasing her to defend itself, but Gavin ripped out its throat. Before the body collapsed into the dirt, he was charging another hound until Winter decapitated it with a swing of her katana.

The Creed rallied behind Marcia, making a V formation with her at the lead. She glared at Samuel, blood dripping from her wound, as the Creed advanced in lockstep. He stepped off the porch to confront them, giving Sebastian and me the chance to run past him into the house.

Wary of a trap, I pushed past Sebastian to be the first one through the door. Once inside, we split up, going from room to room and calling Josh's name. At the end of the hall, I found him bound to a bed, struggling against his restraints with a rag crammed into his mouth and an iridium band around his arm. I froze at the sight of him. A large bruise swelled on his cheek, and his shirt was stained with blood seeping from a slash across his chest. A number of cuts on his hands indicated that Samuel had attempted to perform some magic on Josh—numerous times.

Seeing me, Josh let out a raging muted scream.

Frantic to release him, I pulled at the ropes, but the knots were complicated. Thankfully Sebastian arrived with a knife and cut Josh loose. The moment he was free, he was tugging and biting at the iridium band, but that would have to wait. A dozen were-animals swarmed into the house as I pulled him from the room. They quickly cleared a path, eyeing Josh's wounds with relief and rage.

We emerged from the house to find Samuel surrounded by the Creed, his arms bound to his chest by a ring of magical force that embraced his torso. An iridium brace was clamped to his leg.

Marcia glanced distastefully at the were-animals gathering around her as she told him, "This was one of the more distasteful dealings I will have to live with. I doubt you will ever understand my position, and I realize that. I don't want to hurt you, but you will have to let this go. I need more than your word. We will need to perform a *pacem fœderis mei* to ensure that you won't retaliate against us. We need a binding of peace."

Snarling in contempt, he struggled against the magic that bound him. Josh struggled as well, obsessed with the binding on his arm that neutered his magic. The skin around his band was red and bleeding as he bit and pulled at it like a trapped wild animal. I swatted his hand away from it, then turned back to Samuel and the Creed as Marcia raised a knife against the skin of his throat, drawing small rivulets of blood. For a moment, I hoped she'd kill him.

"Do you really want it to end like this?" she asked Samuel. "Defeated by Sebastian and his pack because of your tenets? Agree to the *pacem fœderis mei* or we say our farewells now. Understand, I do not want you dead." Her tone softened, almost pleading as she continued, "I needed to do this for reasons you will one day understand. It is not personal. Do not make it so."

He glared down at her as she slowly withdrew the knife just enough that it was no longer touching his skin, but red glistened on the blade. "Will you agree?"

His jaw twitched before he answered with a bitter, reluctant, "Yes."

At Marcia's direction, the witches cautiously removed the iridium brace from his leg before releasing the power that had bound his arms to his chest. I tensed. If he fled, released from their hold, I would consider myself free to chase him down and kill him. Surprisingly, Samuel remained still, seemingly accepting his fate. The witches began their brief incantation. Once complete, Marcia pressed her knife across the palm of his hand, drawing blood. His gaze turned to Sky as he spoke his part of the spell. Once complete, he gave her the slightest smile, as if they shared some unspoken bond.

As the Creed walked away from him, he told them, "May you receive the true peace that you all deserve."

Marcia turned and snapped, "If we find it, at least it will not be at your hands. Now that we are bound in peace, you can't hurt us."

He nodded to Sky, then disappeared.

Sebastian gave directions to the others while I guided Josh to one of the pack's SUVs. I eased him into the backseat, then slid in with him while Sky scooted in on the opposite side, eyeing his wounds with a concerned look. Winter took the passenger seat while Sebastian wasted no time putting the car in motion.

The rest of the pack vehicles fell in behind us.

Until we reached the safety of the retreat, our fight wasn't over. Samuel's agreement to not retaliate applied to the witches, not to us.

Once we were underway, Josh returned to worrying at the iridium band.

"Does it hurt?" Sky asked.

He shook his head. "I just don't like it on."

I gripped his arm, trying to calm him, but he yanked himself free. "Josh, stop." He was going to hurt himself. "Sebastian, will you pull over?"

He brought the SUV to a stop on the side of the road before glancing over his shoulder at Josh biting and pulling at the band as if his life depended upon it. By the time I emerged from the vehicle and reached the wayback, Sebastian had popped it open. I caught a worried look from Sky over the seat, then found the box of tools and brought it with me back to Josh.

"Hold still," I said, reaching for the band with a vise-grip. Ignoring me, he continued biting and tugging. "Josh!" I pushed him back into the seat with my arm, then clamped on to the band. After some squeezing and twisting, it finally broke.

Josh tore it from his arm and threw it to the floor. His relief palpable, he leaned back into the seat, rubbing at his raw skin as he caught his breath. Sky and I exchanged anxious looks as Sebastian got us back onto the road.

CHAPTER 16

*E*n route to the retreat, I kept a watchful gaze over Josh. The wound on his chest was mostly shallow, presumably made by the bloody knife found at his home. Since he didn't share the enhanced healing ability of the rest of us, I assumed Dr. Baker would order a round of antibiotics as a precaution. He'd be waiting in the clinic when we arrived.

I was more concerned with my brother's state of mind. Josh's magical power was a point of pride. He placed great confidence in his abilities. For the first time, he'd been denied that power. Worse, he'd been bound and gagged and made completely helpless, something I'd hoped he'd never have to experience. When I'd brought him into the pack, I'd sworn to protect him.

This was my failure.

Josh remained withdrawn during the drive, refusing to meet my gaze. I recognized his angry, forlorn expression. *We're all vulnerable,* I wanted to tell him, but he needed to face his mortality alone.

When we returned to the retreat, he motioned for me to follow him into a side room. "How did you do it?" he demanded, bracing for the answer. His voice was sharp, accusatory. "How did you get Marcia to help?"

I told him everything. As I spoke, Sky slipped into the room, hesitating by the door and watching us with a worried expression. When I finished, he attempted to rub away the growing frustration from his face. His cheeks only grew redder, his brow tighter.

"We have to go back to the Creed's house," I said softly.

Josh's scowl deepened as he straightened and defiantly folded his arms across his chest. For him, it was bad enough that we'd had to bargain with the Creed to save him, he didn't want to give Marcia the chance to gloat. We held each other's gaze for a long moment, holding a silent debate, but the result was inevitable. We had no choice but to follow through with our agreement, no matter how distasteful.

"Perhaps it's better if you stay," I said gently.

Josh swallowed an angry retort, then turned away as I gestured for Sky to follow me from the room.

"I know you didn't have a lot of choices," Josh said, his voice suddenly tired. "I hate that I am the cause of this."

Sky asked him, "If the situation were reversed, what would you have done?"

His lips pressed into a thin line as he shook his head, but she knew the real answer. So did I.

Rather than follow the agreed-upon protocol to arrange for another windowless van to deliver us to Marcia's secret location, I used the information from our previous visit to locate the house in a quiet, middle-class suburb. Bernard emerged from the house to greet us with an annoyed scowl.

Message delivered.

Without fanfare, he and his bodyguards escorted Sky and me to the back of the house to a concrete-framed door that opened into the hillside. He led us inside to an unfurnished anteroom with a single steel door at the other end. Several cameras were attached to the ceiling, allowing a full view of the entire chamber.

Nowhere to hide here.

"You will be called at the appropriate time," Bernard said, then led his bodyguards back the way we'd come. The door closed with a loud, heavy clank, leaving us in nearly total darkness as the chamber lights dimmed. The click of the door locking confirmed that we were temporarily Marcia's prisoners. No doubt, she would take her time to get to us.

Sky paced, adjusting the bag that hung from her shoulder while throwing increasingly anxious glances to the inner door and the cameras. Keeping my mind distracted from our containment, I imagined how far the bunker extended into the hillside. How many levels were there? If the pack ever found itself in a war with the Creed, what inherent vulnerabilities could the bunker have that we would be able to take advantage of? Like any bunker, they would need to intake oxygen and vent carbon dioxide, which meant exposed vents on the surface, somewhere nearby. By plugging the vents or using them to circulate tear gas, we could flush the inhabitants out.

Watching Sky pace, I picked up the accelerated beat of her heart, heard the shallowness of her breath.

"Are you afraid?" I asked.

She turned sharply, surprised by the break in silence. "No," she lied.

You have the Aufero in your bag. I wasn't sure she realized she could easily draw upon the orb's magic to break down either of the doors. The orb might even be capable of destroying the entire bunker, if she knew how to use it. Worried that she might try, I opted not to remind her.

Frowning at the camera above the inner door, she wrapped her arms around her chest and began slowly

298

rocking from heel to toe. After a moment, her heart slowed somewhat. Her breathing eased.

She was braver than she realized. It came out in times of great stress, when she made the kind of selfless decisions that saved lives—like mine, and Josh's. To save him, she'd offered up unprecedented power in giving up the Aufero; she'd done so without a second thought. Securing the Creed's assistance to save him had been crucial. Considering the level of power we'd encountered at Samuel's home, I doubted we would've ever retrieved my brother without their help. I would've been forced to challenge Sebastian in order to trade the Clostra for my brother.

Sky's sacrifice was all the more remarkable in that she gained no advantage from the trade. Truly selfless acts were rare in our world.

After a few minutes, the anxiety caught up with her once more. She began to pace more furiously than before. I could smell her fear. She was on track to a full claustrophobic breakdown. Once I realized she wasn't going to be able to calm herself, I stepped closer, trying to extend my calm to her.

"Are you okay?" I whispered.

She flinched in surprise, then nodded.

"If you want to leave, we will." The consequences would be severe, but I couldn't ask her to surrender the Aufero for me, or Josh.

She backed away from me and returned to pacing, but she was calmer. I'd given her a choice. She was no longer power-less, trapped in a dark room waiting for someone else to release her. While she considered the possibility, I made another survey of the cameras, then the walls, looking for any hint of a concealed door. Even with my enhanced vision, it was difficult in the dark without giving away my intentions to whoever was watching us through the cameras.

"I can't leave," she said, gathering her bravado.

Relieved, I took in a deep breath and slowly released it.

Our wait continued. Marcia was in rare form. I checked my phone for the time, noting the lack of signal. No doubt that was intentional.

Sky managed to maintain her calm for another fifteen minutes before her agitation began to rise. Before she could start pacing, I stepped forward and gently placed my hands on her hips. She jolted, surprised, but didn't resist as I pulled her against me so that she could feel my heart beating, enticing hers to match mine as I exuded calm. Tension eased from her as our hearts began to beat in sync, but it didn't last. I was grateful when the inner door opened and Bernard appeared, waving us to join him.

"Ms. Brooks," he said, "please follow me back."

If you intend to take Sky alone, you have another thing coming to you.

I followed her closely, giving him a warning look. As we walked down a long, narrow hall that gently sloped downward, I counted my footsteps, estimated the angle of descent, drawing a map in my mind. At the end of the hall, Bernard opened another steel door. The strong scent of salt, sulfur, and blood spilled into the hall. There was another scent there as well, something I couldn't place.

Passing through the doorway, we were greeted by a low chant. In a long room dimly lit by candles, six figures obscured by hooded robes stood in a line behind a tall table, facing us. The Creed, I assumed, joined by a mysterious sixth figure. The robes and hoods made identifying the figures a challenge, but I was confident that Marcia was at the center. A cauldron rested before her on the table, next to what appeared to be a dead lizard splayed on its back with its belly cut open.

"You are not welcomed," she snapped.

I smiled, baring my teeth. "Then I will remain here unwelcomed."

Taking his cue from her tone, Bernard approached, reaching for my elbow.

"I wouldn't," I growled.

Marcia waved him off, then turned her attention to Sky. "Come closer."

Reflexively, she backed away from the command, bumping into me. I placed my hands on her hips, gently reassuring her that she wasn't alone.

"Now," Marcia commanded.

Sky took a tentative step forward. In response, the chanting grew louder, more insistent. Marcia added her voice to the rest as she flicked a powder into the cauldron, triggering a burst of fire from within. As the ritual continued, I logged every detail in my mind to report to Josh. The more he could decipher regarding the magic used, the more likely he could find a way to counter it. The motions of the witches gave away their identity, all except for the figure on the left end, the mystery witch. With the end of each verse of the chant, the figure waved a hand over the lizard, then gestured toward Sky.

I didn't recognize the type of lizard on the table. Its coloring wasn't dependable, but the patterns on its scales were unique.

At one point, a circle of salt and sulfur was laid around it. Several materials were added to the cauldron, each at the crest of a rising chant. The last material was granular, and a bright green.

The intensity of the chant seemed to be escalating to an apocalyptic finale.

Marcia cast off her hood, then thrust her hands into the lizard's belly. When she looked up at Sky, her expression was hardened, her eyes jet black. "Come to me."

Sky pressed into me.

"Do you want to leave?" I asked, my voice so soft only her enhanced hearing could pick it out.

She faintly shook her head, but I could smell the fear pouring off of her.

"Skylar," Marcia snapped, "come closer and give me the Aufero."

She swallowed, then slipped the bag off her shoulder and drew out the orb in the palm of her hand. Excitement flashed in Marcia's eyes as she accepted the Aufero in one bloodied hand, then drew out a knife in the other.

"Show me your hand."

Sky did so. A ripple of pain shook her shoulders as the knife sliced her palm deeper than necessary. Marcia placed the knife on the table, then took Sky's bleeding palm and held it over the cauldron, letting the blood drip into the mixture. Once satisfied, Marcia tossed a handkerchief to Sky, who quickly wrapped her hand with it.

As the chanting continued, I noticed a change in Sky's heartbeat. Her hand went instinctively toward her chest and her head craned as if she were going to vomit.

Marcia smiled. "Step back."

Sky quickly backed all the way to the wall next to me before she seemed to recover.

The chanting suddenly ceased. The mystery figure completed the ritual with a final wave of a hand, then stepped back from the others and disappeared through a side door I hadn't previously noticed. The figure moved with a peculiar gait, as if disfigured—or not familiar with the human form.

"See," Marcia gloated, "I gave you a fail-safe. Now you will know when you are too close. It is up to you whether or not you want to preserve your life."

"You are more considerate than I have given you credit for," Sky said demurely. "Thank you."

On our way out through the darkened corridors, I could hear the erratic beat of Sky's heart, the subtle effect of the curse placed on her. Upon exiting the bunker, she glanced about as if nervous or on edge, and her lips were bent into an unhappy frown. She appeared jittery, anxious, all the things that I'd felt under the influence of the dark elf magic.

During the drive back to her house, she remained quiet within herself while she unceasingly shifted in the passenger seat, unable to find comfort.

After parking in her driveway, I asked, "How do you feel?"

"Fine," she lied.

She hesitated as if to say more, then sighed, shook her head, and climbed out of the BMW. When I stepped out after her, she gave me a puzzled look, as if she'd rather be alone to stew in her misery. As much as I wanted to allow her the privacy she needed, nothing good would come of leaving her alone. Catching up to her, I took her hand and turned her from the front door. She gave me an annoyed, questioning look as I drew her around the house to the coppice at the edge of her backyard. Within the protection of the dense bosk, I began to remove my clothes.

"We should go for a run," I said. "You'll feel better." Her wolf's resistance to magic would provide a temporary buffer to the effects of the curse.

I began to strip, expecting her to do the same. After unabashedly shedding my pants and underwear, I looked up to find her frozen, wearing a shocked expression. She pointedly stared at my chest, embarrassed by my nudity until she couldn't help herself. Her eyes drifted down to linger on my abdomen, where she forcibly resisted the pull of her curiosity. Another time I might enjoy attention, but I was more concerned with her state of being. When I approached to help her undress, her focus shifted to the ground at her feet. Never comfortable with nudity, she seemed less confident than usual.

The sooner I get that curse removed, the better.

Gently lifting her chin, I met her silent plea with a reassuring smile, then lightly tugged at the bottom of her shirt.

Slowly, she raised her hands over her head and allowed me to lift the shirt from her. I lowered it to the grass by her feet, then knelt and carefully unbuttoned her pants. An unexpected rush of desire flushed my body, but I brushed it aside. I wrapped my palms around her calves and looked up to find her glittering green eyes staring down at me. I waited patiently until she placed a steadying hand on my shoulder and drew first one leg up, then the other, as I eased the pants to a crumpled bundle at her feet.

Rising, still holding her gaze, I slid my hands up the cool skin of her back and gently unclasped her bra. She shrugged it off and I let it fall between us onto her pants.

When I reached out to help her transform into her wolf, she lightly pushed me back.

"Go ahead," she urged me. "I'll catch up."

Reluctantly, I backed away a few steps. I welcomed the cool, soothing change to my wolf and padded into the brush, but I remained close. She'd not yet mastered the change—for her it was often a long and torturous process. I could ease that for her, but not unless she wanted me to help. Nosing through the brush, I found a nearby patch of grass to relax on, sniffed the air to be sure I had her scent among the pungent odors of grass and pine, then waited.

After only a few minutes, I noted the telltale shift in her scent. A moment later, a beautiful gray wolf with pale gray eyes emerged from the bosk, shook off her worries, then ran past me with a playful look.

I chased after her, nipping at her heels as we raced through grass and brush. We were at the height of our play when a mood suddenly came over her. She turned and darted away from me in earnest. I started after her, but quickly thought better of it. She wanted time with her wolf alone. Recognizing her need, I let out a slight whimper as I glanced at the surrounding brush, wondering how to bide my time. From somewhere nearby I heard the rapid beating of her paws on the ground as she raced, turned, and raced some more. She was reveling in her animal form, temporarily liberated from the oppression of Marcia's curse.

I distracted myself with the faint scent of a small animal that had passed through the area, but I didn't feel like hunting. Instead I practiced my tracking skills, embracing the heightened sense of smell of my wolf, but my mind remained attuned to Sky's scent, always making sure that I was near her in case she needed me.

Eventually the sound of her play ceased. Her scent lingered in a single area, and I went looking for her. I found her soundly asleep in a sheltered patch of soft grass. Careful not to wake her, I lay on my stomach in front of her, rested my chin on my extended paws, and took comfort from the easy, steady rhythm of her breath.

An hour passed, maybe more. If I could've left her in such a happy slumber, I would have, but dawn wasn't far off. This copse was large, but not expansive. In the daylight, a large gray wolf would be noticed. Neighbors would likely call the police, or worse, bring out their rifles to investigate.

I should've taken her to the retreat.

I waited a short while longer, then gently nuzzled her neck. When she didn't wake, I lay my body over hers and playfully licked her face. She woke with a mild yelp and a start, turning back to me with an indignant look. If only I could've laughed while she wiped a paw over her face.

When she was through, I trotted in the direction of her house, then turned back to make sure she followed. She did, but at a reluctant pace. As long as she came, the pace didn't matter. I continued on to where I'd left my clothes, changed from my wolf, and dressed. I carried her clothes with me to the side of the house and waited patiently. A moment later, her gray face peeked from the bosk and glanced about before she slowly trotted to the house.

She stopped in front of me, staring expectantly. I playfully

305

ignored the unspoken request for privacy. After a moment, she sat and glanced away as if she had all the time in the world to wait me out. Suppressing a laugh, I rolled my eyes, placed her clothes on the grass, then walked around the house to wait next to my car; I'd prefer to watch over her, but I assumed she'd want me gone.

I expected a long wait, but after only a few minutes, she emerged from behind the house, dressed and visibly relaxed.

"Do you feel better?" I asked.

She nodded, frowned at the BMW. She started toward the door, watching me with a hopeful expression. Pleasantly surprised, I followed her, noting her palpable relief.

Once inside, she announced, "I need a shower."

I lowered myself onto the couch and draped my arms across the back. "I'll be right here when you get back."

After a faint smile, she disappeared into the bathroom. A moment later, I heard the shower. Assuming she would be a while, I decided to take a shower as well. There was another full bath in the guest room. Opening the door, I received a stark reminder that Steven had claimed the room for his own. The bedding was the most obvious, with the posters a close second. The room was surprisingly clean of clutter, but I assumed that was Sky's doing.

My jaw twitched as I felt a surge of anger. Both of them claimed that their relationship was a familial one. They denied a romantic interest, which I didn't understand. If they weren't together, why was Steven living in her home? It was inappropriate. I'd made my opinion known, but neither of them seemed to care.

The only reason I hadn't caught his scent in the rest of the house was because he'd been with the Southern Pack for the last few weeks helping his mother Joan reorganize after Ethos had nearly destroyed it.

After a quick shower and a change of clothes, I stepped back into the hall to find Sky was still in the bathroom.

Listening at the door, I could only just distinguish her ragged breath from the tumult of water.

I placed my hand on the door handle, but hesitated. Frowning, I decided to give her the space she required. After all, she wanted me in the house. She'd come out when she was ready. In the meantime, I determined to make myself useful. In the kitchen, I found what I needed and set about preparing an early breakfast. By the time she finally emerged from the bathroom, dressed, I had a warm plate of waffles and bacon ready for her. The eggs were nearly done.

She gave my clothes a suspicious look that shifted to my damp hair.

"I used Steven's shower," I explained.

"Steven doesn't have a shower, that's the guest bathroom."

"Of course," I said with a wry smile.

"And the clothes?"

"I always keep some in my car. Don't you?" Looking her over, I noticed she'd changed into a gray tank top and matching pants.

"What?" she asked, following my gaze.

"Cute outfit." I shrugged. "Maybe for your birthday you can get some grown-up pajamas."

Giving me a playful scowl, she snatched some bacon from the plate and slid onto a barstool at the counter.

After we ate, she asked, "What happens next?"

"We find someone to remove the curse. But it will not be anyone here. Marcia commands too much loyalty around here."

"Then what?"

"I don't know. Right now there aren't many options. We have friends in the east that may be able to help, but honestly, finding someone to remove a curse is going to be a task. It's such an archaic practice, the younger ones only know how to do it in theory."

"Your friends in the east, are they experienced witches that can do it?"

"They aren't witches at all. They're fae."

She frowned, skeptical. "How are they going to be able to help?"

"Most fae can do spells. Like witches, there needs to be a certain skill level. I've never needed them for anything of this nature," I admitted.

I watched as she fought a yawn, then lost.

"You need to sleep," I said. "You're running on fumes."

"I'm fine."

I edged closer to her, noting the lines of exhaustion in her face, the way her shoulders drooped and she seemed to have to fight to keep her eyes open. "What?" I grinned. "You think you are going to turn into a troll or fall into a deep sleep that can only be broken by a prince's kiss if you go to sleep?"

A sideways look accompanied her half-smile. "Yep, and where the heck are we going to find a prince this time of night?"

"Go to sleep, Sky, you've had a long day. Things will look a lot better tomorrow after you've rested."

She nodded, but still insisted on helping me clean up from our meal. By the time we finished, her eyes were only half open. Smiling, I bent down and kissed her lightly on the cheek. I felt the warm softness of her skin press into my lips as she turned toward me. Her lips gently brushed mine before she kissed me. Her fingers reached into my hair and pulled me toward her as she pressed her body into mine.

The warmth of her need was intoxicating.

My own kisses growing in urgency, I pressed her back into the counter. Our passion quickly ignited into a mutual, feral need as we pressed against each other as if we could merge into one. Our lips desperately roved over each other in a blind, primal passion. She pushed my hand just under her shirt and my fingers slid up along her skin, roaming and kneading.

Unable to contain my desire further, I bent and lifted her legs around my waist. Her heels dug into my back as I carried her to her room and fell to the bed with her in my arms, our lips pressed together. Reluctantly, I broke our embrace just long enough to pull off my shirt, then my pants. My lips roamed as I undressed her, leaving just her underwear.

Taking a moment to cool my desire, I sat back and took in the beauty of her curves before I lay my body against her and kissed her once more. Her arms embraced me, her fingers drawing electricity up the back of my neck, over my scalp. She clutched my hair and pulled me close as we tried to consume each other.

Our passions laid bare, I knew that I'd wanted her from the beginning.

Reluctantly, she released her grip as my lips slid down her neck, over her breasts, and down to her stomach. My fingers caressed and kneaded her as I slid lower, brushing my lips against her underwear, moving to her inner thighs. Her body squirmed and undulated beneath my lips until I rose once more to kiss her mouth.

Trembling with excitement, I slipped off her panties and eased myself between her thighs. My fingers stretched over her smooth, hot skin. My lips followed. Her legs opened and I accepted the invitation, pressing gently into her. She gasped, clutching at the sheets as I gently rocked into her.

Realization dawned that I was her first.

I paused in surprise, suddenly confronted with the jealousy of my prior accusations. I'd been wrong about her relationship with Steven. Guilt settled in, but not enough to replace my desire. I wondered why she'd waited. Why now? There was a time I'd have ignored such questions and given in to lust, but I couldn't ignore my unusual concern for what would follow. She was vulnerable.

I'm not the one, I realized. *Not now. Not just as a means of distraction.*

Realizing I'd stopped, she opened her eyes, turning to me with a searching look. Somewhere in that urgency was a command, and a permission. *Nothing else matters right now,* her eyes said, but that was just an illusion. For the moment, she wanted comfort. She wanted to lose herself in passion, but she needed more.

I'd only just earned her trust, yet the morning would see new barriers between us. She'd regret her decision because it had been made for the wrong reasons. Would we recover from such awkwardness?

Slowly, I bent toward her and kissed her one final time. My lips lingered over the curve of her neck as I gathered my will before I gently pulled away. Ignoring her bewildered, angry expression, I slid next to her and cradled her against me.

"You should get some sleep," I said.

I could feel the questions in her body, could hear the accusations of her thoughts. As anger took over, she tried to push away, but I held her close until the anger finally burnt itself out and she relaxed against me. I swallowed, concentrating to resist the desire that still coursed through my body. I longed to slide my hands over her breasts, to once more explore every inch of her body.

Feeling me against her, her head turned slightly toward me—a question.

"I will wake you in an hour," I whispered. "If you don't wake up, I'll go look for that prince for you." I chuckled to lighten the mood, but it didn't help.

Eventually she drifted off to a peaceful slumber. An hour later, I slipped out of bed and went home to take another shower. Once I'd finally calmed myself, I called Joan, the Alpha of the Southern Pack.

"What can I do for you?" she asked.

"Steven's been there for a few weeks. Do you still need him?"

"He's been helpful, but no. Do you want me to send him back to the Midwest Pack?"

"Yes."

She hesitated for a moment. "Is this for the pack, or for Sky?"

"Both," I admitted.

CHAPTER 17

A few hours later, I walked into my brother's house without knocking, coffee in hand. From his leopard-patterned chair, he gave me a mildly rebuking scowl. He appeared haggard, a bandage wrapped around his arm where he'd injured himself attempting to remove the iridium band.

Seeing the bandage triggered a rise of anger, reminding me of a debt still to be paid. For the moment, I'd allow Samuel to look over his shoulder. Eventually he'd let down his guard. At a time of my choosing, I'd let him know exactly what I felt about him taking my brother hostage.

I handed Josh his coffee and sat across from him on the couch. "Can you break Marcia's curse?" I asked. His expression remained blank as he sipped at the coffee, his eyes glazed and distant as if he were reliving his captivity, or his defeat. "Josh."

"What?" He jerked, forced back into the present. "Ethan, I think I need some time alone."

"No."

Irritation flashed in his eyes. His nose crinkled, but then he snorted in exasperated amusement. "You know, you can be a real pain in the butt sometimes."

I leaned toward him, holding his gaze for a moment. If I could take back what he'd experienced at Samuel's hands, I would, but there was still a lesson there for both of us.

Josh frowned at his coffee. "I knew Sky's family was working with a witch. I'd no idea it was Samuel."

"I didn't know either. We got beat. Better not to dwell on it."

"Well," he sighed, "give me a few minutes to wake up and I'll see about finding him."

"Forget about Samuel for now."

"He still wants the rest of the Clostra," Josh insisted. "He's not through with us. I'm not going to sit back and wait for him to break down my door again."

"He knows you don't have it. Now that he's shown his hand, he'll assume we're protecting the books at the retreat. Even if he could break your protective field there, he won't attack a house full of were-animals."

"He's desperate," Josh cautioned.

"What does he want with the Clostra?"

Josh shook his head. "Whatever it is, his fervor borders on the fanatical. The spells in those books are too powerful to let fall into his hands."

"He'll never have them," I swore.

Josh relaxed into his chair.

"Back to my original question," I said. "Can you remove the curse?"

"Describe the spell. Don't leave out any of the details."

While I did, he brought a foot up to the edge of the chair, drawing his knee close to his chest, and chewed his nails. I finished by describing my plan to enlist the aid of Austin and Orchid.

"Have you called them yet?"

"I wanted to check with you first."

Josh nodded. "I don't know if I can do it myself, but I have some ideas to try before we take a trip to New York. I won't need the pack's library," he explained, answering my unspoken question. "I have what I need here."

"Good." I smiled, noting a number of the pack's oldest books on his shelf. "Let's get started."

He shook his head. "First I'm going to cast a *terrorem* on you."

I scowled, deeply offended. Alarm spells allowed the target to call for help by speaking a key word or phrase; they were for the weak and helpless, for victims. "I don't need a *terrorem*," I growled. "Just keep your phone handy."

He folded his arms over his chest, staring at me as if chastising a willful child. "If you insist on going through with this reckless plan of yours, you're going to have a fail-safe. I'm not taking no for an answer."

Reading his resolve, I begrudgingly agreed.

After the spell was cast, we spent the rest of the morning poring through books and making notes. I made a trip to our favorite sandwich shop, and we continued through the afternoon and into the evening. By the time Josh began putting our notes to practical use, we'd both accumulated a sense of hope that slowly disintegrated as one idea failed after another. After our fourth failure, we took a break to clear our heads.

"Another set of eyes would be useful," Josh suggested. "Sky could help."

I scowled. "I forbid it."

He shook his head at me but kept his rebuke to himself.

"She's not in a good place," I explained. "Until we're out of ideas, let's leave her out of this."

"Fine," he sighed.

My phone vibrated in my pocket. Drawing it out, I saw Caroline's number and declined the call. *Not now.* I growled, drawing a questioning look from Josh.

"It's nothing," I snapped.

"Right. I'm only your brother." He gestured for emphasis.

"Why tell me anything?"

I found myself staring down at my shoes, my expression a tight grimace. I could put Caroline off for a little while, until she got impatient and forced the issue. When the time came, I had a plan, but there were risks. If her passions got the better of her nature, or if I misjudged her, I likely wasn't going to walk away from her scheme. Josh's help would improve my odds considerably, but I'd be putting him at risk as well.

I need him.

Did he have the restraint my plan required? Once he knew what I intended, he was going to be furious. *Better to let him vent that anger now*, I decided. Once he'd vented and calmed, he might listen to reason. My decision made, I leaned back into the couch with a sigh, draped an arm over the back, and described Caroline's mind magic attacks. By the time I finished, his cheeks were bright red. As predicted, he didn't lose his temper completely until I gave him the details of my plan.

"That's absurd!" he shouted, jumping to his feet and pacing angrily in front of me. "You can't do it! I won't let you!"

"There's no other way."

He jabbed a finger at me. "You don't get to put yourself in that kind of danger and then ask me to just sit back and watch."

"What's the alternative?" I demanded.

He swallowed, glaring harder. "I generally don't like your plans," he confessed, "but you've always been practical—annoyingly so. But this plan of yours … you're putting yourself at tremendous risk, Ethan. For what?" He stopped pacing to face me squarely. "You've never hesitated to eliminate a threat. Why is this threat any different?"

"If it wasn't for me, she wouldn't be a threat."

He swept a hand between us. "You do moral ambiguity

better than anyone. Don't stop now. Deal with her, and bury that guilt in the same place you always do."

It was an unfair accusation from someone who'd never had to make the kind of choices that kept him awake at night. I rose to tower over him, glowering down.

Josh continued, undeterred. "Eliminate. The threat. Save the moral redemption for next time. If you're wrong, you'll be helpless. She could kill you and there's nothing I'll be able to do to stop her. Are you really going to ask me to just let that happen?"

"This is the way it has to be."

Still staring up into my eyes, he slowly shook his head. "You picked a hell of a time to grow a conscience." He turned and snatched his wallet from the kitchen counter.

"Where are you going?" I demanded.

"More coffee. It's going to be a late night."

"I'll go with …" I started, but then he disappeared.

An hour later I was hunched over a book at Josh's dining table when he reappeared with coffee and bagels.

"That took a while," I grumbled.

"Traffic," he said as he pulled out a chair and sat. "Let's get back to work. I've got a couple more ideas to try, but we need to do a little research first."

The next morning, we were still at work when I received a text message from Sky.

"Are you making progress?"

"Yes," I lied.

"Like?"

"I will let you know later." I tried to set down my phone, but her reply was nearly immediate.

"Do you think Logan can help?"

"Don't go to Logan!" I shouted at my phone, then texted the same.

Josh scowled. "The Tre'ase?" He shook his head. "She doesn't do idle well."

"I'm going to make the reservations for New York," I announced. "If we can't come up with a solution today, we're putting her on a plane tomorrow, before she does something rash."

A short time later, I called her with the information about our flight, but she didn't answer.

"You try," I told Josh. Sky had a habit of ignoring me when she was irritated.

She didn't answer for him, either. I tried once more. When she didn't pick up, I began to panic. Fearing she was at Logan's, I opened the tracking application on my phone, counting the seconds until the map rendered and a small blinking blue dot showed me her phone's location. I blinked, zoomed in on the address to be certain.

"She's at Quell's," I growled, then slammed my fist on the table, hard enough for Josh's empty cup to teeter and fall over.

"How do you know?" he demanded, skeptical.

I took a moment to inhale and release a sharp breath. Realizing we were on the other side of town from the vampire's home, I called Steven. He picked up immediately.

"Get Sky and tell her she has a flight to New York tomorrow afternoon."

"I'm almost to her house now."

"She's not there. She's with Quell," I added, making my disgust plain. There was an audible gasp on the other end of the call. "If he's harmed her," I added, "kill him." I hung up and tossed my phone onto the wooden table.

Josh shook his head at Sky, sharing my disappointment.

"She's the only were-animal with a pet vampire," I exclaimed.

He sighed as he sat back in his chair. "I don't agree with her, but she's doing what she thinks is right." He ignored my scoff, continuing, "She's putting herself in danger to help someone whom she thinks deserves it." He blinked at my darkening face as my anger boiled. "Please, don't punch a hole in my wall."

He turned an open book toward me, tapped a page, and pushed the book in my direction.

Grumbling, I pulled it close enough to read and got back to work.

We spent the next hour checking our phones while we continued our research. When Steven finally called, I snatched the phone from the table.

"She's home safe," he said immediately, but there was an edge to his voice, a hardness he rarely associated with Sky. "I'll stay with her until the flight tomorrow."

"Quell?" I asked.

"I made the pack's position clear," he said, his voice devoid of emotion. "If you want, I can kill him while she's away. No problem."

"I'll get back to you."

On our way to the airport the next day, Sky seemed withdrawn, angry. Even Josh's usual jovial nature failed to illicit a smile. I knew that she suffered from the residual effects of the curse, and that Steven's warning to Quell had irritated her. There was also a good chance my leaving her in the middle of the night played some part in her smoldering silence.

Either way, I found it best to leave her be. Josh did the same.

O'Dowd was waiting for us next to his Gulfstream jet. Once we were in the air, I messaged Orchid to confirm our meeting the next day at noon.

A few hours later, we checked into our hotel in New York. I'd arranged separate rooms for each of us, though I wondered if I should keep a closer eye on Sky. Given what had transpired between us, I suspected distance was more appropriate.

After settling into my room, I took a long walk to one of my favorite restaurants. As I walked through the door I was greeted by a welcome, familiar scent of delicately spiced meat cooked to perfection. Once seated, I texted Josh to let him know where I was in case he wanted to join me. I was just about to dig into my steak cheeseburger when I noticed Sky dawdling outside the front windows.

Is she stalking me? I wondered, surprised.

She seemed to be eyeing the decor rather than the patrons, but the likelihood that she could wander twenty-five blocks and randomly pick this nondescript restaurant was staggering.

Deciding to explore farther, she walked through the door. A smiling hostess immediately led her to a booth very close to mine.

"I'll bring you some bread," she stated, then walked toward the kitchen.

Just as Sky started to slide into the booth, she caught my eye. We stared at each other, both bewildered and somewhat skeptical to have randomly encountered each other so far from the hotel. For a moment, I considered she might prefer to be alone, but civility caught up to me. I gestured for her to join me, prepared to be rebuffed.

After a surprisingly brief internal debate, she agreed, fixing her ravenous eyes on my cheeseburger as she sat across from me. Reluctantly, I slid my plate toward her. She ate greedily until her hunger was eventually sated enough to talk.

"Did you track me here?" I asked.

"No." Her eyes widened in genuine surprise. "I didn't

track you. I tracked down a very good burger and some mediocre fries." She took another large bite from the burger and chewed, watching me.

I smirked. "You passed at least six other places that served burgers. Why this place?"

She shrugged. "The same reason you did. I could smell it from the street."

Either we'd been brought together by a conspicuous coincidence or she'd improved her skill at lying. I leaned forward and gently wiped a dab of ketchup from the corner of her mouth. "It is one of my favorite places to eat when I am here."

She seemed to consider scolding me as she made a show of dabbing her lips with her napkin. Following my gaze, she smiled at the nearly devoured burger.

"I guess I was hungrier than I thought," she said.

The waitress arrived with her bread. I ordered another burger, rare. To my surprise, Sky ordered a salad and chicken wings.

"Salad?" I scoffed.

"I like salad," she said defensively.

"No, you cling to the idea that you like salad because it makes you feel 'typical.' Like the average human having an average meal. You do not like salad any more than I do." I gestured to her now-empty plate. "You didn't answer my question. How did you end up here?"

I knew by the way she considered her answer that she hadn't lied. The coincidence seemed to intrigue her as much as it did me. By the time our food arrived, she hadn't answered. Our conversation devolved into small talk while we ate. Following the urges of her wolf, she devoured her wings while taking only token stabs at her salad. Did she notice?

"Why did you leave me in the middle of the night?" she asked, surprising me.

"It wasn't the middle of the night," I deflected. "We didn't go to bed until morning."

Her lips thinned as she gave me a sideways glance. "Okay, I'll play your little game. Why did you leave in the middle of the morning like a tacky jerk?"

I took a sip of wine to steady myself. "Does it matter?"

"If it didn't, I wouldn't have asked."

I leaned toward her, curious. "What creative reason have you drafted?" Given the importance of the trip, this was hardly a time to explore our personal relationship.

She considered for a moment, giving the impression that she only now formulated an answer, but I knew better. "I think you are complicated and I will never understand why you do half of the things you do."

"I didn't want to be there when Steven arrived," I lied, my tone softer than before. I didn't want a scene or an argument. I didn't want to make her any angrier than she was. "You were really nervous with me. Why?"

Did you really want me, or just temporary comfort?

It was her turn to lie as she reacted with indignant surprise. "I wasn't nervous."

"Women are a lot of things with me in the bedroom," I said, "but never nervous."

"It's probably because your modesty and humility put them at ease," she snarked.

I was going to suggest we drop the subject when I noticed Josh walk into the restaurant. Relieved, I didn't hesitate to wave him over.

"I guess he tracked you, too," Sky muttered into her drink.

"Right after I texted him the location," I said.

Greeting us with a smile, Josh slid into the booth next to her. It took him all of five seconds to steal fries from my plate, to my chagrin. Not that I cared about the fries, it was the principle that mattered.

Frowning, he gestured to my burger. "Rare?"

"Of course."

His interest lost, Josh turned his attention to scanning the restaurant for someone to take his order. "There's a club down the street," he said to Sky. "We have to check it out."

"Our meeting is at noon," I reminded him.

"Yeah." He made a show of checking the time on his phone. "Fifteen hours from now."

"I don't need you hungover," I said, realizing my mistake too late. Judging by the childish grin on my brother's face, he was going to go out of his way to prove he could function just fine while hungover.

He draped his arm behind Sky. "Can I coax you into a naughty night of fun that is only going to piss off my brother?"

She nodded, then took a sudden intense interest in the restaurant's bland decor, anything to avoid my scowl.

"There we go." Josh beamed triumphantly at me as he patted Sky's shoulder.

Josh hit the bar like a tidal wave, drawing Sky behind him as he announced his presence to everyone around him. As the manager of the pack's club, he'd developed a hypersocial club mode that served him well. I'd gotten so used to it that I'd forgotten the persona was more than just his professional skin. Among the booze and the bass beat and the women, he was in his element. Sky was just along for the ride, but she was enjoying herself as he made a point to introduce her to his new friends, whom he met at a dizzying pace.

I found myself a seat at the end of the bar that afforded me a view of the main entrance and the dance floor. The bartender appeared a moment later.

"Scotch, neat."

The club was popular among supernaturals. Like all such clubs, it was informally recognized as neutral ground.

322

Vampires, were-animals, fae, and witches all mingled, their historical enmities set aside for the night.

As Josh escorted two attractive young women—both witches, I was certain—to the dance floor, I understood why he wanted to be there. Even with the club, his interactions with other witches in Chicago were limited. Marcia's displeasure with him was well known. Witches feared her ire. Those who didn't feared his relationship to the pack.

Sky remained on the edge of the dance floor, swaying gently to the music. Her attention seemed fixed on the band; particularly the guitar player. The club was a morass of magic, radiating from dozens of figures, but I'd passed the stage when we'd first entered. He was a mage, a type of witch with minimal abilities largely limited to mediocre defensive magic.

He'd noticed Sky as well, was smiling, charming her from behind his guitar.

I nearly downed my Scotch, reminding myself at the last moment to sip. This night was a one-drink maximum. Josh was going to be a handful in the morning, as if I didn't have enough reason to stay sober.

Sky accepted an invitation to dance from a human, thin and tall as a wafer, but he had a disarming charm. A low growl rumbled in my chest as she followed him to the center of the dance floor, but the mage guitarist remained her priority.

An auburn-haired vampire wearing a glittering skintight top slipped into the seat next to me with a sly smile on her lips and pupils that blotted out the color in her eyes.

"Buy me a drink?" she suggested.

"If you're looking for an interspecies cuddle, try the kennel," I said casually. "I'm not interested."

She gestured with one finger, then slid off the stool and walked away while I returned my attention to the dance floor. I quickly picked out Sky, then Josh.

Eventually I caught her eye and waved for her to join me. She frowned, gave a slight shake of her head, and continued dancing.

Out of the corner of my eye, I noticed a woman approaching me with a feline grace. As I turned, the blond were-animal slid into the seat next to me, wearing a low-cut sleeveless ruched shirt, skintight jeans, and an impish smile. It occurred to me that I'd be facing a revolving door of flirtations if I chased her away.

I smiled, exchanged pleasantries. Her name was Sara. Over her bare shoulder I noticed Sky throwing glances and seemingly going out of her way to appear to be having fun.

For a few minutes, I became lost in conversation. When I glanced to Sky again, I noticed Josh next to her, wearing a concerned look as she covered her stomach, her expression pained.

Forgetting Sara, I rose and rounded the bar, aggressively pushing my way to Sky's side.

"Are you okay?" Josh asked, shouting over the music as I joined them.

Dazed, she glanced around the club as if searching for something.

I bent to her ear and called her name.

"I think I had too much to drink," she answered, shaking her head.

She'd had two drinks that I'd noticed. Given the pace she drank at, she'd had three at most, not enough to get her drunk considering the amount of food she'd eaten at dinner.

I took her hand, explained to Josh, "We are going back to the hotel. You can stay, but remember—"

"We have a meeting at twelve," Josh finished, rolling his eyes. "No, I'm going with you."

I glanced at Josh's new acquaintances, who were calling to him to stay. *He needs this.* "No, you stay. I'm fine," I promised.

He frowned at my hand clasped around hers, as if stung, then nodded.

His reaction surprised me. *That's the alcohol talking.*

I led Sky outside, hoping the fresh cool air might help her rally. Turning to her, I cradled her face in my palms so I could examine her eyes. Her pupils were only mildly dilated.

"You're not drunk," I said. *Or drugged.*

"No," she agreed. Something was still affecting her, making it hard for her to concentrate.

"Then what happened in there?"

She debated whether to answer, then sheepishly admitted, "I heard voices."

I frowned, doubtful. "Voices?"

"I heard someone say we are all monsters that don't deserve to exist," she explained in a tone that suggested she understood the absurdity of her story. She wasn't lying.

My mind shifted to the mage who had taken such an interest in her. "Stay here."

Stepping back into the club, I nearly bumped into Josh on his way out. I quickly filled him in. We approached the stage first, observing the mage. He appeared oblivious to our attention, fully absorbed in the song he was playing. Josh shook his head at me and we split up, combing the club for anyone suspicious. In a room full of drunk supernaturals, who wasn't? Someone in the club had used magic to communicate with Sky. Was it mind magic? Was someone trying to warn her, or chase her away?

After a few minutes, I slipped out the main door while Josh continued his search. Sky appeared relieved to see me.

"I didn't hear anything or see anything suspicious," I explained. "Josh and I checked out the mage, it couldn't be him. In fact, there isn't anyone in there strong enough to do anything remotely like that. Maybe there was a witch in there screwing with you."

"Maybe the fatigue and the alcohol are getting to me," she

admitted with a nervous chuckle.

I was looking for a cab when she started to walk in the direction of the hotel. Deciding the walk might help clear her mind, I caught up to her, quietly observing her as she seemed to fall deeper and deeper into her thoughts.

"How far is the hotel?" she eventually asked.

"About sixteen more blocks."

"Really?"

"Yeah, you walked quite far to find me." I stopped her, then reached out to hail a cab.

"I walked that far to find a steakburger?" she asked as I opened the door for her.

I smiled, guiding her into the backseat.

She remained quiet, pensive, as we stepped out of the elevator onto our floor of the hotel. At the door to my room, she intended to continue on to her own room when I took her hand and pulled her close to me. Staring into her green eyes, I searched for some sign that she was okay. Misjudging my intention, she pushed against me, her lips pressing into mine in a sudden burst of passion. For a moment, I lost myself in the taste of her lips.

"You should stay here tonight," I whispered, surprising myself. A faint voice screamed a warning in the back of my skull, obscured by our mutual desire that seemed only to have intensified from the previous night. The heat of her breath caressed my lips as I stroked the curve of her neck. The longer she hesitated, the louder the voice in my skull became, warning me to not make the mistake I'd already run from.

Gathering myself, I kissed her lightly on the cheek, then whispered, "If you have to think this long about it, you should say no."

I turned, opened the door to my room, and left her in the

hall. Just inside the door, I hesitated, listening. A foolish part of me waited for her soft knock. If it came, I knew I couldn't stop myself from answering it. When I finally heard her footsteps continue down the hall, I leaned back against the neighboring wall and let out a long sigh of relief.

As I emptied my pockets on the counter, I found Sara's phone number on a torn piece of paper. She'd tucked the note in my pocket when I wasn't looking. The debate went on for some time. The smart choice was to go to bed, but I wasn't in the mood for the smart choice. If I wasn't careful, I'd end up knocking on Sky's door. At least, that's what I told myself as I called the number.

The next morning, I invited Sara to join me for breakfast in the hotel restaurant. Since she had only her evening wear, I loaned her one of my button-down shirts. Over steak, eggs, and pancakes, she probed me about the liaison in Indianapolis. The Midwest Pack was too large to control centrally. Sebastian assigned liaisons to manage pack affairs in some of the cities outside of Chicago. Anytime a were-animal wanted to move from one pack territory to another, even a new territory within the same pack, there was a hierarchy to follow.

While I answered her questions, I noticed Sky walk into the restaurant. She smiled and started toward the table, then froze when she saw Sara. Her lips bent into an accusatory frown before she stiffened, turned, and walked out of the restaurant.

"Something wrong?" Sara asked, turning in time to see Sky disappear into the hall.

"It's complicated." I slipped enough cash onto the table to cover the bill, followed by the keycard to my room so that she could retrieve her belongings, then left the table to follow Sky.

Tracking her scent, I followed her out of the hotel to a small café a block away. I found her at a table, brooding over a large pancake breakfast, with French toast, eggs, and bacon. She pushed a forkful of pancake into her mouth, reluctantly chewing as I dropped into the chair across from her. Scowling, she bent her head to her meal and tried to ignore me.

I waited, watching.

"What?" she demanded, glaring from beneath her eyebrows, then returned her attention to her fork as she cut another section of pancake.

"Her name is Sara," I explained. "She lives here—"

"Good. Now you can refer to her by name instead of 'what's her name that I screwed in New York.'"

I sighed. "She is considering moving to Indianapolis to be closer to family and wanted some information about the liaison, but I don't think she really liked my opinion. I only know her by reputation and she seems like a wild card. She will not fare well under his direction."

Only slightly mollified, Sky continued glaring between bites. Her appetite lacked fervor. Watching her, I began to wonder if she continued to eat just to avoid conversation. Thankfully, neither of us wanted to talk about last night. Hoping to shift her mood, I changed the topic.

"Do you think about it?" I asked, using an open question to draw her interest.

She scowled. "About what?"

"Do you think about what Logan told us about spirit shades?"

She considered for a moment, debating whether she'd allow me to redirect the conversation. "All the time," she decided. "Maya could be a Faerie. Wouldn't it make sense? Elves and witches can bring a vampire back from reversion, but to the best of my knowledge, they can't manipulate magic. I am assuming Faeries can." An idea occurred to her. "Can demons feed vampires?"

I wasn't sure there was a difference, whatever Maya's origin. "Not to my knowledge."

"And elves?"

I nodded.

She pushed her plate aside. "I can read the Clostra. Josh can't nor can you. You are—*were* holding the magic of an elf and can't read it. Josh is a witch and can't read it...."

"So can Senna," I added.

"Yes, but we don't know what she is. We just know that she isn't really related to me. This means she probably isn't a witch."

A puzzle for another time. "We'll deal with that later. We need to remove the curse so that you can get the Aufero back."

She nodded. "The Tre'ase that created Maya, I really want to know who it is. After all, my survival is based on his. If he dies, so does Maya and so do I."

I agreed. Unfortunately, there was only one way I knew to identify the specific Tre'ase, and it was going to cost us. The thought left a bitter taste in my mouth. "When we get back, we should pay Logan another visit."

I rose to leave, then hesitated. "Skylar," I said, drawing her from her reverie. "Don't make things awkward between us. Okay?"

Her nose scrunched as if she'd just caught a noxious odor. Her lips parted, but then she abandoned her snark for a simple nod and returned to her reverie.

"Go ahead Sky, ask," Josh said from the backseat of our rental car as I drove us into Brooklyn.

"I just don't get it," she said from her seat beside him. "Fae magic is vastly different from the witches'. How will they be able to help? What are they going to do, will the curse away?"

He happily explained. "Yes, the majority of fae magic is

limited, but just like we have levels, so do they. There are some that are quite strong, and their minor spells are not very trivial at all."

"But it's not the same. You told me that elven, fae, and witch magic worked differently, like being on a different frequency. How will a fae be able to remove a curse made by a witch?"

"Just think of it like opening a door. Using a key is ideal, which would be equivalent to a witch removing it, but a sledgehammer or locksmith tools will do the trick." He grinned. "Let's just say that if these fae can help us, it will be like taking a big axe to the door."

Austin answered the door, sporting a full brown beard that contrasted with his bald head. Long red sleeves continued from beneath his short-sleeved green Kermit the Frog t-shirt, and he'd taken to wearing black square-rimmed glasses that distracted from his pale golden eyes. It had been a while since we'd seen him last, but his affection for us hadn't changed. The feeling was mutual. In the doorway, we exchanged hugs, slaps on the back, and loud exclamations about how long it had been.

Sky watched our collegial display with pleasant surprise. Austin and Orchid were unlike any fae she'd encountered, or likely ever would. They were entirely original.

"Austin," I continued the pleasantries. "Thank you for meeting with us."

"Orchid, they're here!" he shouted over his shoulder as he directed us into their living room.

The decor of the brownstone reflected the differing personalities of its occupants. On two redbrick walls hung metal sculptures, while modern abstract paintings stood out against cream-colored plaster. A delicate, mother-of-pearl fabric couch was accompanied by a coffee table built from a shaped piece of charred wood framed in brass.

Orchid appeared, grinning and squealing as she jumped into my arms and kissed me directly on the lips, a formality I'd have preferred to avoid, but she caught me by surprise. With no other choice, I returned the kiss. When she finally withdrew, the taste of menthol lingered on my lips. She turned to Josh, who accepted her kiss readily. I turned to Sky, wondering if she'd be spared, but that wasn't the case. At least I could enjoy the utter look of surprise as Orchid hugged Sky tightly and kissed her.

Like all fae, Orchid possessed the ability to compel truth with a kiss. In exchange for the use of her gifts, she required full and unvarnished truth from her customers. She made no exception for old friends or trusted companions. As a practitioner of tactical lies, I appreciated the expedience of her requirement, though I didn't like it.

As she withdrew from Sky, I saw her cheeks flushed. Josh hadn't warned her, I realized. I smiled, wondering what must be going through her mind.

In contrast to Austin's pop culture style, Orchid wore a muted plaid shirt that blended shades of yellow, gold, and beige. Strands of black hair streaked with sapphire protruded from the edges of her ivory slouch beanie. Her pale eyes were the same color as Austin's.

"Come in, have a seat," she declared, pulling Josh and me farther into the living room.

She guided us to the couch, where Sky joined us, then disappeared into the kitchen. A moment later, she returned with a bottle of water, a glass jar of milk, and a plate of five homemade marijuana cookies, which was also expected.

"Have one," Austin said, lifting the plate to Sky. "That's all you'll need."

She wrinkled her nose at the contents of the plate. Out of

politeness, she reached out to the smallest cookie until I gently clasped her hand.

"Thank you for the offer." I said politely, "Unfortunately this trip is strictly business."

Austin smiled graciously and set the plate on the coffee table in case we changed our mind. He sat across from us in a brass-framed wooden chair, the companion piece to his coffee table, while Josh bent over to reach the plate. Seeing my disapproval, he sighed and wrapped three of the cookies in a napkin that disappeared into his pocket.

As she read our expressions one by one, Orchid's smile thinned. "So, Marcia must really be causing trouble," she said as she slipped into Austin's lap, resting her head against his neck.

"What isn't she doing?" Josh said.

She glanced from him to me. "Ethan, what brings you to us?"

The pull of her magic, driving me to answer her with every unvarnished detail, nearly overwhelmed me. "We discussed what I needed on the phone," I stressed. There was no need to repeat the information.

"Ethan," she sighed, "I am stronger than I was as a teenager; you aren't going to be able to resist it. Just relax and talk to me."

"We discussed it," I repeated, resisting the slow strangulation of my throat as the words she wanted accumulated there. "On the phone."

Frowning, she turned to Sky. "Can you tell me what happened?"

"I would prefer to handle everything," I insisted.

"Of course you would. Ethan, I understand your need for discretion in many things, but I need as much information as possible." She grinned. "You are going to hurt yourself trying to deny me my answers. I can't do that to you. Skylar, please answer my question."

I sighed, stifling my irritation as she launched into her story, beginning with our attempt to steal the Aufero from the magic shop. I found myself holding my breath, hoping she would leave out certain details that would lead Orchid to pry into my family background, but she was a skilled interrogator. She chuckled when Sky related how she'd stolen the orb back from Marcia, nearly drowning the witch in her own swimming pool before Quell intervened.

My eyes widened in surprise. She'd never told me. By preventing Sky from killing, he'd spared her a lifetime of regret, but I wondered why.

I tensed as she began to describe performing the ritual in my home. Orchid interrupted, asked her usual pointed questions. Her eyebrows rose in surprise as Sky revealed that my grandmother had been a dark elf, that I'd inherited her magic, and that we'd used the Aufero to remove the magic from me. Orchid accepted the news as if absorbing an exciting bedtime story, while Josh grew increasingly frustrated, shooting me angry glances.

At her urging, Sky continued, describing the ritual the Creed used to curse her. Here, Orchid asked a number of questions, ferreting out even the smallest details. She took particular notice of the words used, the description of the animal, and the mysterious witch who had participated in the ritual.

Austin shared his partner's intrigue.

Once Sky finished, the room was quiet for a long moment as the fae absorbed the information, silently communicating while revealing nothing in their expressions.

Eventually, Austin asked, "Will we be the first to try to remove the curse?"

Josh answered. "The moment I bring up Marcia's name, most witches refuse to be involved. Even those that I know despise her will not do anything to provoke her wrath. And the rest don't like to mess with curses, it is too dangerous."

The fae exchanged another inscrutable look.

"We will not be able to remove the curse," Austin announced, "but we can weaken it. Josh and Ethan, we will need you for it."

I nodded readily, as did Josh.

Sky glanced between us, then asked Austin, "How do you plan to do this and why do you need them?"

Orchid smiled at her. "I like you. We will dilute it. I will find which of my animals is your compatible and transfer it through them and then transfer it back. It will need to be done quickly, because I don't want to kill them."

Sky's expression tightened, her concern unswayed.

In response, Orchid sang a single, melodious note, slowly rising in crescendo from bass to near falsetto. At its apex, the note suddenly ceased. A wave of sound lingering in the air became a ripple of gentle magic that filled the room with its sustained vibration. A moment later, a number of snakes appeared, twenty-four in all, slithering their way toward us from beneath the furniture and around the corners. Sky tensed, raising her shoes as snakes passed beneath her.

As the serpents gathered at our feet, Josh and I shared our calm with Sky, but the display was unusual. Orchid worked with a number of animals, but I'd never witnessed her using so many serpents at once.

The fae reached down and each picked up one snake, staring into its eyes for a few seconds before releasing it back onto the floor.

I could feel them slithering around my legs, over my feet. Sky gritted her teeth as she tried not to squirm. The mass of serpents slithered among the three of us. Slowly, three separated from the rest, each sliding its way to the feet of its chosen person.

A black snake with odd patterns draped over my shoes, flicking its tongue over the laces, while Josh's compatible coiled around his ankle, rubbing its head against his sock.

334

The serpent that chose Sky wrapped its silver-and-rose body up her ankle and around the first half of her thigh. She blinked down at it, forcibly calming her breath.

At Orchid's signal, a low throaty bass sound, the snakes reared back and sunk their teeth into our legs. Each one of us hissed at the unexpected pain as our compatibles forcibly sucked blood. I glared at Orchid. I'd never known her to use blood and I didn't appreciate the lack of information.

Sky gasped from the pain and cursed under her breath.

Orchid remained surprisingly indifferent.

When Sky gasped once more, I'd had enough. Wrapping my fingers around the now-bloated black snake, I tugged at it. When it refused to let go, I forcibly pried its jaws open and dislodged its teeth from my flesh.

"Ethan," Orchid whispered a sharp warning as I held the snake at arm's length, "let go of Franky."

I happily dropped the snake to the floor. When it reared up and hissed angrily at me, I dared it to strike. After a brief standoff, it slithered away to join the mass of snakes beneath Austin's chair.

I glanced at Sky, who seemed to have abandoned her fear. Josh remained engrossed in the ritual. While their compatibles continued to feed, Orchid played with the other snakes, snuggling and kissing them as if they were pets.

Once Josh's compatible was satiated, it withdrew, joining the others. Sky's compatible opted to climb up the couch and wrap itself around her arm, gently nuzzling her shoulder. I tensed anxiously, but she accepted the creature's apparent affection with an enamored smile.

"Very well," Orchid announced. "I will need a couple of hours to get the others. I suspect I will only need two more fae."

She ignored my scowl as we rose and walked toward the entryway. Each of us received one more kiss to remove the truth spell, while Austin gently unwrapped the serpent from

Sky's arm. He favored her with a hug, something he rarely offered to strangers, then opened the door for us to leave.

After climbing into the BMW, I slammed the door.

"Relax," Josh said, stoking my anger.

Sky glanced out the window, either lost in thought or doing her best impression of not giving a crap over yet another example of my brother starting a pointless argument.

"Did you know she was going to use blood?" I demanded.

"News to me," he admitted, "but strong magic often requires a powerful catalyst like blood. If you want to talk about someone leaving out important information ..." he said with a dark look as he let the thought trail off.

"You didn't need to know about the dark elf magic," I growled, turning the car into traffic.

"That's very parental of you."

"If I'd told you," I said carefully, "your life would've been in danger."

"That's not the point, Ethan."

"Could you have done anything about it?" I demanded, throwing him an impatient glance before turning toward the bridge.

Josh thought for a moment. "No," he begrudgingly admitted, holding on to some of his anger for the sake of obstinacy.

The rest of the drive back to the hotel was tense, but quiet. Thankfully, we had separate rooms.

Two hours later, I felt the increased presence of magic as we returned to the brownstone. Aside from Austin and Orchid, we were joined by two other fae, who watched our entrance with nervous anticipation. At Austin's direction, we joined them standing around a wooden table that had been placed in the living room.

Orchid's gaze was fixed on the center of the table, lost in deep concentration. After a long moment, she acknowledged us for the first time, offering a confident smile. After steadily glancing around the table, she placed a large black stone at the center, surrounding it with sprinkles of powders and salts. Satisfied, she lifted the three compatible serpents from earlier and placed them on the table to slither over and around the stone.

"Are you ready?" she asked, glancing between Josh, Sky, and me. After we nodded, she gently lifted each of the compatibles and handed them to us. I scowled at mine. Perhaps expressing its own displeasure, it reared up and hissed just before sinking its fangs deep into my arm. Grimacing, I endured the sharp pain—sharper than before— as it gorged on my blood. Sky and Josh seemed at relative peace with their compatibles. I offered mine a faint, appreciative smile and the pain seemed to ease, but only slightly.

Once bloated, the snakes withdrew their fangs and retreated to take positions around the stone. Orchid placed a small pale stone in front of each compatible, then sprinkled powder around them.

The fae chanted in unison while she drew out a ceremonial blade from a scabbard at her hip and pierced the skin of my compatible, just enough to draw blood that she then dribbled onto the circle of powder. Blood and powder combined to form a foam that expanded to cover the small stone at the center of the circle.

While Orchid worked, Austin and one of the others did the same with the other compatibles.

Once complete, the chant grew faster, more urgent. The calming magic that had previously filled the room grew chill, raising the hairs on my arms. As the temperature in the room dropped, I saw the steam of our breath converging over the table.

The pale eyes of the fae were almost entirely white.

In answer to Orchid's spell, a fiery force burst from the center stone, buffeting us. Every nerve ending in my body ignited in pain. I buckled, clutching at the table, but managed to hold on, gritting my teeth against the pain. After a moment, the pain subsided as the force contracted back into the stone. I had just enough time to see Josh and Sky recovering before the force pulsed outward once more in a torturous ebb and flow of agony.

The fae continued their chant with added urgency, while Josh began a rapid chant of his own. Sky and I could only concentrate, resisting the pulse through sheer will. The pain proved to be too much. Josh was the first to buckle, falling to one knee. Despite his grimace, his chants continued as he moved from one counterspell to another. Orchid's pale eyes rolled back into her head just before she collapsed sideways and fell writing on the floor. Austin immediately collapsed next to her, followed by the other fae. Within their circles, the compatibles writhed as well.

Sky and I held on to the table with a white-knuckled grip, but Josh had yet to find an effective counter, and we had no chance against the magic without the fae. Straining against the magic, I reached out and swept salt and powder from the table, then smashed each of the stones with a closed fist. Brittle from the magic, they shattered easily, but the pieces continued to glow.

Suddenly the compatibles ceased moving. The fae stopped as well. The magic force ceased and the glow emanating from the chunks of rocks faded until they returned to their natural color.

I collapsed to my knees from the shock of relief, then quickly pulled myself back up. Josh did the same, while Sky stumbled to Orchid and knelt beside her, checking for a pulse. Josh and I staggered around the table to help.

Even before Sky started CPR, I knew that Orchid was dead. A quick check revealed Austin and the others had stopped breathing as well, but Sky refused to give up, giving rescue breaths between series of chest compressions.

"Come on!" she growled, working.

Her determination jolted Josh and me into action. While he worked on Austin, I alternated between the other fae, but there was no chance. After several minutes, Sky finally conceded. They were all dead. Staring at the lifeless bodies of my friends, I wondered if I could ever take enough vengeance on Marcia.

Knowing we'd attempt to lift the curse, she'd made sure that anyone who tried to cancel her magic suffered the same fate that would befall Sky if she came too close to the Aufero. Of that, Marcia hadn't bothered to warn us. She'd wanted us to try and suffer the loss of someone we trusted, someone who dared challenge her power. Her cruelty was limitless.

Already the smell of death rose from the bodies.

"Josh," I said. He looked up from his place next to Austin, his expression somber, wounded. I continued softly, "Leave the bodies as is, but you will need to remove all evidence that we were here."

His desperate gaze flicked over the bodies.

"Josh! Get it together."

His head snapped toward me, his eyes flashing anger for a moment, but then common sense returned. Someone would've heard the commotion and called the police. If not, the bodies of our friends would be found sooner rather than later. Eventually, four dead bodies were going to attract a police investigation.

There would be time to grieve. For the moment, we had to be practical.

His expression somber, Josh muttered his chant as he waved his hands around the room, illuminating with glittering blue light anything that revealed our presence in the brownstone. With another spell, those traces quickly disappeared.

CHAPTER 18

Persistent rain pummeled the windshield of the rental car as I drove us back into the city. In the passenger seat, Josh looked like a ghost of himself as he stared out his window and chewed his nails, while Sky fidgeted her anxiety behind him. I needed to think but couldn't focus beyond my hatred of Marcia.

My fault.

I wondered how many more people I was going to get killed. I glanced at my fingers wrapped around the steering wheel, but couldn't shake the vision of Austin's and Orchid's bodies that had been seared into my brain.

Arriving at the hotel, we escorted Sky to her room before I gestured for Josh to follow me into mine. Once inside, he began to pace.

"She blames herself," he said, meaning Sky.

"It's not her fault."

He stopped, suddenly defensive. "So it's mine?"

I opened the minibar, picked out a handful of shot bottles, and retrieved clear plastic cups from the bathroom. "That's not what I said."

His frown deepened as he returned to pacing. "If I hadn't

let Samuel take me in the first place, she'd never have had to make a deal with Marcia."

I poured two whiskeys and handed the cup to Josh, then poured my Scotch, only to down it in one gulp, leaving me wondering why I'd bothered with the cup.

Get your mind clear!

He sipped as he worried a path into the carpet.

"We need to get out of here and regroup," I said.

He nodded. "The pack should buy Sky's house. We need to get her out of Chicago as quickly as possible, preferably somewhere far away. Texas, maybe."

"You're overreacting."

He turned on me, his anger bolting to the surface. "You don't get it! Marcia can kill Sky anytime she wants, just by getting close to her. She's toying with us." He nodded to himself. "She won't hesitate to kill Sky just to punish us more. And she'll have the perfect alibi. She can always claim that she had no idea Sky was anywhere near her."

I stared down into my empty plastic cup for a moment, then threw it at the wall across the room, only to watch it merely flutter a few feet then tumble lightly to the floor.

"There has to be another way to break the curse," I said.

"And risk killing someone else we care about?" He started to pace again, then suddenly stopped. His back straightened. He turned toward me with a glint of hope. "The Clostra."

"What about it?" I growled.

"The books are full of remedies to magic. There are spells to eradicate us, spells to eradicate magic altogether. There must be a spell—"

"To break curses," I finished for him.

"I'm pretty sure I've found part of it, I just didn't realize what I was looking at." His hope quickly deflated. "We'll never get the third book from Samuel."

I brought out my phone to change our flight. The sooner we got back, the sooner we could hunt down Samuel.

Finding him wasn't going to be easy. "Everyone has a price," I said.

"We can't just give him the books, not without knowing what he wants from them."

"No. We'll find another price."

After a short conversation with the airline, I'd changed our flight to eight in the morning, then texted Sky with our new itinerary. Once finished, I met Josh's gaze.

"Pizza," he said, reading my mind. "I'll get Sky."

"Let her be. We've got a lot to talk about, and I don't want to get her hopes up. She's been through enough today. What are you doing?" I asked as he brought out the napkin-wrapped pot cookies from his pocket.

He stared back at me. "You really have to ask?" He extended one of the cookies to me, but I declined. "All the more for me, then."

By the time our pizza arrived at the restaurant table, the pot cookies had obviously done their job. Josh gobbled his first two slices while I stared at mine, the images of dead friends killing my appetite. Watching him eat made me wish I'd taken one of the cookies after all. Since the restaurant didn't serve liquor, I ordered an IPA.

Josh seemed happy to have the pie to himself while I watched. Between bites, we debated how and where we'd find Samuel and what he'd want in exchange for helping us. We were just making progress when Sky wandered into the restaurant, apparently drawn by the contents of the dessert case.

I frowned, annoyed at the interruption as our discussion came to an abrupt end.

"She couldn't have just found us by accident," Josh said. "We're ten blocks from the hotel."

"No. She found me last night as well."

We watched as she licked her lips at a piece of red velvet cake on the counter, then walked to a table near the front window before she noticed us staring. Her expression hardened. She seemed about to walk out when Josh gestured for her to join us.

She glanced at the door once more, then reluctantly ambled over to our table.

"Have a seat," he encouraged her, then bit into another slice.

As she dropped into a chair, she took in the untouched slice on my plate, the glass of beer I lifted to my lips. She turned her attention to Josh, but couldn't help throwing me sideways glances. It occurred to me that she felt abandoned because we hadn't invited her to join us. I didn't have time for niceties.

I took a long pull of beer, trying to swallow my irritation.

Josh asked her between bites, "Did you get our messages?"

She glanced at her phone, surprised to find my messages about the flight.

Josh gestured an invitation to the pizza. Sky helped herself, reluctantly at first, but after the first bite she regained her enthusiasm. He helped put her at ease by rambling into an inane conversation that allowed them both to forget, for the moment, what we'd experienced earlier. I understood his intentions. I also understood the role the pot cookies played.

I didn't need that kind of distraction. I needed to figure out the angles and come up with a plan to break Marcia's curse that wouldn't get anyone else killed.

With another long pull, I finished my beer and rose to my feet. I put some cash on the table, setting my empty glass on top of it, dropped my crumpled napkin onto my partially eaten slice, then slid out of the booth.

Josh called after me, "Are you going back to the hotel?"

"I just need to get out of here," I said, glancing between him and Sky, then walked away.

"You know how he is," I heard Josh whisper. "Don't take it personally."

Absorbed in my irritation, I ignored the rain beating down on me. After a few blocks, I calmed enough to feel embarrassed. Leaving Sky at the hotel had been callous. I'd let my tactical mind get the better of me, forgetting that she'd been through a traumatic ordeal. For Josh and me to go out to dinner and leave her behind was unforgivably inconsiderate. No wonder she'd seemed angry when we'd invited her to join us.

I'd witnessed and delivered so much violence in my life that I'd become largely immune to it. Looking around at the pedestrians on the street, I wondered how many of them could witness the deaths of their friends, of four people murdered in a horrible fashion, and then go to dinner. What Sky had endured this night would've left those people curled into fetal positions in the gutters.

I stopped on the sidewalk and shook my head. Any other night, I'd take the lesson of my mistake and let the consequences fade with time, but tonight wasn't like most nights. Sky deserved better.

I walked back to the restaurant. By the time I arrived, Josh and Sky were gone. I texted both of them, but the only response came from Josh.

"I found a place that serves late-night pie!" he declared.

"Is Sky with you?" I texted.

"Went for a walk. You were a real ass, btw."

I sighed, pocketed my phone, then walked back to the hotel. Eventually, she'd return. Considering how rarely I gave out apologies, I could use the time to formulate one.

. . .

She walked into the lobby two hours later, looking unnerved and soaking wet from the rain. Rising from my chair to meet her, I was greeted with a dismissive look as she walked past me to the elevator. Once inside, she jabbed a button repeatedly, trying to close the doors before I could join her, but the elevator was too slow to respond. Accepting my presence with an exaggerated sigh, she tried to ignore me as we rode to her floor. Something was off about her. She was angry, resentful, but her rapidly beating heart betrayed more; she was frightened.

When the elevator opened, we stepped out. I followed her to her door and slipped past her inside once she'd unlocked it. Determined to ignore me, she walked into the bathroom, picked a towel from the rack, slipped off her shirt, and went about drying herself with a surprising lack of modesty. Scrutinizing her from the doorway, I wondered what had happened during her walk that could explain her surprising shift in mood.

Rubbing her hair with the towel, she walked past me into the main room and finally lost her patience. Stopping at the end of the bed, she turned and demanded, "What do you want?"

I remained still, observing the subtle shifts in her expression, the way her body betrayed the fear behind her mask of anger. "Occasionally," I said softly, "I can be a little rude. Today I was. I'm sorry."

She turned away, unable to hold my gaze.

"I went back to the restaurant," I explained, slowly walking toward her, "but you weren't there. Where were you?"

She shrugged. "I went for a walk."

Too casual, I thought. *Too dismissive.* My eyes narrowed. Intuitively she lowered her towel to cover herself, as if suddenly afraid to be seen.

"Did you enjoy your walk?" I asked.

She found something on the carpet to stare at, then nodded.

"Thirteen," I said.

"What?"

"When you are not giving me the full truth, your respiration drops from fifteen to thirteen times a minute. You blink six times instead of your usual eight times, and your heart rate jumps to between sixty-nine and seventy-seven instead of sixty-four. Shall we try this again? Where were you?"

She bit her lower lip and said nothing. While she was searching for a way out of the conversation, I slid my hand into hers. "I hate when you lie to me."

"And I celebrate with a dance-off each time you do it to me," she snapped.

"I don't enjoy keeping things from you. Often it is to protect you when I hold back information from you."

Turning her head aside, she brushed her chin against her shoulder. "I don't want to tell you."

I nodded, releasing her hand. "Our flight is at eight. I will meet you in the lobby at nine."

As I walked to the door, she asked with a suspicious tone, "What is the Vitae?"

I froze, too surprised to show indifference. A moment's hesitation had just betrayed my greatest secret. Very few people knew about the fifth protected object. Sky hadn't just gone for a walk, hadn't just talked herself into a strange mood. She'd talked to someone who knew more than they should, someone with an agenda.

Was this also part of Marcia's plan? If she knew about the Vitae, Josh was in grave danger.

Glowering, I turned to Sky and slowly stalked toward her. "What do you know about it?" I demanded.

Bravado wilted to fear as she backed away from me. "It's the fifth protected object that you and Sebastian want to pretend doesn't exist."

"Did you discover this on your *walk?*" I asked as she backed into the corner of the bed and stepped around it.

"I met with Samuel today," she blurted, challenging me as I towered over her.

"What?" Shocked, I stumbled back a step. "And?"

She shrugged, as if their conversation had somehow been innocent. "We discussed the protected objects. He says that the Clostra is rumored to have spells that will not just kill us, but that can dissolve the symbiotic relationship between us and our animal halves," she added in a rush of breathy excitement.

The thought of being separated from my animal half was akin to losing all of my limbs and being left a useless cripple, yet she seemed genuinely hopeful at the prospect. I backed away from her, horrified as she continued.

"A spell to remove magic from the world. We wouldn't change anymore. He thinks it can make us all whole, normal. I wouldn't have to worry about protecting the Aufero, because without magic, there wouldn't be a need for it to exist. We would be normal."

She'd grown up thinking her wolf was a monster, the result of a curse. Despite her seeming progress, two years with the pack had done nearly nothing to change her mind. Samuel had seen her weakness and known just how to exploit it.

"And you believe him?" I said.

"Yes," she answered in a rush. "He could have been dishonest about a lot of things, but he wasn't. He doesn't think that magic should exist in any form, and I think I agree with him. Think about it. If we can do a spell that rids this world of magic, that makes us all normal, then this … this world of dominance, curses, bad magic, and manipulation ends. It would just be an ordinary life that I think we all deserve."

I choked back my anger. This wasn't the time, or place.

Samuel was nearby. I took a moment to calm myself before asking in a deliberately neutral voice, "Where did you meet him?"

"Well, he kind of grabbed me off the street."

I should've never left her with Josh. "Did he drop you off at the hotel?"

"No, I walked."

"Do you have a way to contact him?"

She nodded.

"A phone number or an address?"

"A number."

"Is he still here in the city?"

She shrugged. "I don't know."

"You should call him," I advised. "Let him answer whatever questions you have, and when you're done listening to his spiel, you pick whose side you want to be on."

"There isn't a side to choose. I am trying to help," she insisted. "He's not our enemy."

"You don't have to be enemies to be on opposite sides of an issue. He wants to rid the world of were-animals and magic, and the way I see it, that seems to be where you stand, too." I scowled, weighted by my disappointment. "I guess I was right about you all along. We shouldn't trust you."

Frustration screwed up her expression until she blurted, "Now you know how I feel about you and this pack."

"Whether you believe it or not, I have never enjoyed keeping things from you, or from anyone."

"I think you and Sebastian go to great lengths to keep this pack safe. You act as gatekeepers of information that I think people should know, and because of that I don't—no, I *can't* —trust you. I get it: I spilled my guts to a fae and gave in to their magic while you held strong. I am weak. Yay for you ... you were right. I hope you enjoy whatever prize you win for being correct."

"I don't think you're weak," I said softly.

"Whatever you think, it's a hindrance. You think things are easy for me? Three years ago I had a boring life that I kind of enjoyed. Now I am part of a pack I can't fully trust because of all the secrets. I am a Moura Encantada without the object I am supposed to be protecting. I host a spirit shade that I'm afraid may be Faerie, that I may not be able to control. I watched four people die today because of me. You think I am okay with it? Well, I am not. I'm tired, frustrated, and scared."

She was honest, at least. Perhaps I'd overestimated her, put too much on her. I'd agreed to bring her into the pack to protect her. I'd come to regret that, but for the wrong reason. She wasn't ready. She might've never been ready. The rest of us joined the pack with our eyes open; we wanted the life of the pack. For Sky, it was a necessity, a choice between the danger she knew and the danger that crept out of the shadows.

I slowly wrapped my arms around her and hugged her to my chest, gently stroking her hair. "The Vitae has nothing to do with you," I whispered. "I swear it does not. The less people know about it, the better. Will you please trust me on this?" When she didn't answer, I pulled back to look in her eyes. "Please trust me."

Seeing the sincerity in my eyes, she frowned, nodded.

I couldn't ask for more than her tacit trust without revealing more of my secret, something I'd spent my life protecting. Backing away from her, I sighed and turned toward the door. Opening it felt like walking away from something I cared about, something I couldn't retrieve once I'd left it behind. With one foot over the threshold, I hesitated, then turned back.

Taking her hand, I led her to the edge of the bed. "Have a seat."

She watched as I paced in front of her, running my fingers through my hair and taking deep breaths. Was I

349

making a mistake? I didn't tell secrets. I kept them locked away, but I didn't want to hold back from Sky. Either I opened up to her now, or there would forever be a separation between us. After a moment, I made my decision and settled onto the bed next to her.

"Children always bear the sins of their parents," I started, then took another deep breath before continuing, "My mother was very similar to Josh: very powerful and very tenacious, which gained her quite a few enemies and provoked the Creed too many times. She performed a forbidden spell to help a friend and it was discovered. The punishment was death—but not hers. They wanted her to live with the consequences of her mistake, so she had to choose one of her children."

Sky blinked. "Did she perform a *rever tempore?*"

The *rever tempore* was a powerful spell that altered time. I gave her a sideways look, but decided not to ask where she'd heard of the dangerous spell. She hadn't learned that from Samuel. Sky was always full of surprises.

I stared at my hands, unable to admit the truth.

Sky waited patiently, blinking back tears as her eyes implored me to continue.

Too late to stop now, I realized. "She chose Josh," I admitted.

"Josh?"

"Never underestimate their cruelty when defied. Josh's eighteenth birthday, he was supposed to die."

"But he's still alive," she said, bewildered.

"Yes, but not without great effort on our part. You want to know where the Vitae is?" I sighed. "It's on Josh. Well, part of it is on him." I drew out my wallet and found the folded picture of a small, metal, helix-shaped object. "This is it."

I watched the confusion on her face as she took in the picture, and then I smiled. "There is a quarter-sized mark just above the top of one thigh that he believes is a birthmark. The metal is in the ink."

350

"What about the Moura?" Sky asked, one of probably dozens of questions. "What became of her?"

"She's fine," I assured her.

The corners of her eyes crinkled as she studied me. "It's Claudia, isn't it?"

I nodded, gutted by another secret revealed.

"And Josh has no idea?"

"None." *And he never will.*

She didn't understand. "Why wouldn't you tell him?"

"Do you think that is something he really needs to know?"

"Yes," she answered immediately. "I would want to know."

"When you found out about the specifics behind your birth, do you remember how you reacted?"

"But this is different," she pleaded.

"How? He will have to deal with the fact that, when my mother had to sacrifice a life, she chose me over him. I don't want him to know that. To live with that."

"She chose you to live because of the age difference. You all were given six extra years to remove the curse."

It was a practical decision, but that wasn't the point. "I know, and I am sure he would understand, but I can't imagine knowing something like that would not mess with him. I don't see why he needs to know. And you can't tell him." I turned toward her, taking her hands into mine. "Promise me you won't tell him."

She frowned, her expression empathetic but resolute. "I can't do that."

Regretting my decision, I let go of her hands and rose to anxiously pace the room. "Do you remember how easily we destroyed the Gem of Levage?"

She nodded.

"The Vitae is the only thing that is keeping Josh alive. That spell book has the ability to contain such objects, a spell that even a mediocre witch can perform. Do you think that is something he needs to know?" *Isn't it bad enough that we will spend the rest of our lives wondering if the Tre'ase that made her spirit shade is about to die?*

She held her breath for a moment before answering. "I will not tell him, but you should."

Awash with relief, I knelt and kissed her on the cheek. "Thank you," I whispered.

CHAPTER 19

$\mathscr{N}$one of us slept. By the time we returned to Chicago the next morning, we were all exhausted. I went home for a shower and a chance to reflect. A few hours later, I met with Josh at the retreat to debrief Sebastian. Once in his office, I described everything that had transpired, from the deaths of Austin and Orchid to Sky's encounter with Samuel.

Sebastian's lips pressed into a thin line as he absorbed the information. "She nearly betrayed the pack."

Josh explained in a rush, "She wasn't in her right state of mind."

Sebastian ignored the outburst, coolly waiting for my assessment.

"She doesn't trust us," I said matter-of-factly. "Samuel exploited that weakness, but she admitted their interaction before he could gain an advantage from her. No damage was done."

Sebastian rubbed the stress from his face. "Perhaps you were right, Ethan. She isn't ready to be part of this pack, but she is one of us. As such, she is subject to our rules. And our punishments."

"She is guilty of listening to poison," I said carefully.

"Is she a risk?"

"She's still adjusting to our way of life," Josh insisted, glancing to me for support. "She just needs more time."

"Agreed," I said. "But she may never fully adjust. Once the Aufero is returned to her, we should minimize her role, use her abilities only when necessary. In the meantime, she understands that Samuel is trying to undermine us. I will keep an eye on her, but I don't think she is a threat."

Sebastian leaned back in his chair, drawing his fingers together in a pyramid at his chest. "Will she listen to you?"

I wasn't sure. "Steven has returned," I said after unclenching my jaw. "She trusts Winter, as well. I will talk to them about keeping her out of trouble."

"It might be safer to move her from the area, but I'd prefer not to." As the Alpha of the most powerful pack in the country, it was a point of pride for Sebastian to take on reclamation projects like Gavin. Handling other packs' problems was symbolic of our power. Sending Sky to another pack would give the impression of weakness.

Josh said, "There is one more option to get rid of Marcia's curse." Ignoring my glare, he quickly explained his idea about using the Clostra.

"Assuming there is such a spell," Sebastian said carefully, "it would remove all curses." The weight of unforeseen consequences weighed on him.

"Yes," Josh admitted.

"Can we justify such a broad act to protect one of our own?"

"Marcia has long used curses as a means to punish her rivals," I said, a bitter edge to my voice. "Freeing her victims from their constraints would be a fitting punishment. Considering the emphasis she has placed on weaponizing curses as a means of maintaining power, it would be a direct blow to her power structure."

It would be revenge.

"The ramifications extend beyond Marcia," Sebastian reminded me. "To execute the spell, we would need to make a deal with Samuel." His gaze fixed on me as I struggled to contain my anger at the mere mention of his name. "We obviously can't give him the access he desires to the Clostra. Is there something else he'd take in payment?"

Before I could answer, a tentative knock at the door disrupted me. Scowling, I opened it to find Sky's determined green eyes staring up at me. Her hands were clenched into fists at her side and her heart was beating rapidly.

"I went to see Logan," she blurted.

An abiding disappointment compressed against my chest, nearly collapsing my lungs. I should've been surprised, appalled, angry. In retrospect, Sky going to Logan seemed so inevitable that I almost blamed myself for not intervening. But she was an adult. She made her own decisions, and I was done protecting her from the consequences. Her mistakes were piling up, leaving us exhausted.

Josh accepted the news with a pained disappointment, as his defense of her had just been nullified. With a tired gesture, Sebastian invited her to enter and take a seat. She seemed to wilt under his heavy stare.

"I wanted to see if Logan could remove the curse," she said.

"Did you go alone?" Sebastian asked.

Sky nodded.

I folded my arms over my chest. "What was his price?"

After letting out a ragged breath, she explained. "He has a weird fascination with Chris." Her eyes flicked to me, but I gave her no reaction to gauge. "He wants to have her as some kind of companion."

"*Servus Vinculum?*" Josh asked. Seeing my confusion, he explained, "A magical binding that replicates the relationship

355

between a vampire and its creator. It can only be used to bind a vampire to a human. Logan would know that."

I sneered, "What did he want from you?"

She sighed, choosing a spot on the wall to focus her attention as she continued, "He gave me a drug to incapacitate her. I was supposed to bring her to him so that he could cast the spell. Once she was bound to me," she wet her lips, swallowed, "I could order her to serve him."

"You said 'no,'" I assumed.

"I tried to go through with it," she admitted. "I was desperate. This curse, it's like being in someone else's skin." She ran her hands down her thighs as she took in a deep breath. "I went to Chris's house and drugged her, but then I couldn't do it. I just couldn't."

My mouth fell open. I shut it before she could notice, but I had a difficult time suppressing my surprise. She wasn't lying. She had the genuine demeanor of someone who had come close to doing the unforgivable and changed her mind. That she could drug Chris was a shock. That she'd even considered it was more so. As she had with Marcia, Sky had once again brought herself to the brink of self-destruction. This time, she'd saved herself, but she was teetering, looking to implode. Was she determined to live a life weighed by regret?

If the news surprised Sebastian, he chose to remain stoic. "Did you make a formal agreement to do this?"

"No," she said, emphatically shaking her head. "It was an implied agreement."

"One that you did not fulfill," I clarified.

Josh, Sebastian, and I exchanged long glances while Sky gaped between us.

"Did you hear what I did?" she demanded. She'd expected —needed—a rebuke. I'd come to realize her self-recriminations were more valuable.

"Yes," Sebastian answered. "You went over it in great detail. Do you have more to add?"

She bristled.

"Can Samuel be reasoned with?" he asked, changing the subject.

She turned to me with a hardened glare, as if I'd betrayed a confidence. My loyalty to her was important, but her encounter with Samuel was directly relevant to the pack. When it came to the pack's security, there were no secrets.

"In which way?" she asked Sebastian. "He doesn't seem like a psychopath, if that is what you are asking. Just an extremist with an agenda. He doesn't think we should exist because we are monsters, and he thinks I am naïve enough to help him and fall for his rhetoric. Besides that …." Her voice trailed off, and she gave a shrug.

"Call him," Sebastian said.

"Now?"

"No, six days from now," he snapped. "Of course now. We need the third book—"

"He's not going to give it to you."

"Then I would like to hear that from him," Sebastian stated, leaving no more room for argument. He slowly began to pace in front of his desk as he explained, "Josh believes that there has to be a spell in the Clostra that can remove all curses."

"We don't have many choices," Josh admitted.

"I need to talk to him."

Sky pulled out her phone, dialed the number, and handed it to Sebastian.

Samuel's raspy voice sounded pleased, almost victorious. "Skylar."

"No, it's Sebastian."

Silence. When Samuel finally spoke, his voice was harder, intractable. "I am not giving you the other book. And it is not for sale, either."

357

Sebastian chuckled, a rare expression that barely concealed a rising ire. "I am quite comfortable with you having the third book. But I need to borrow it."

Another pause, but Samuel was intrigued. "Borrow for a borrow."

"No. I don't agree with your cause. Frankly, it's a fatuous agenda. You will waste your life trying to end this world. It will not happen, but if you want to go on with your lost cause, have at it. You will never succeed, because in order for that to happen, you will need the other two, and you get those over my dead body. I have no concerns with that. Stronger and better than you have tried to best me and failed. But let me humor you. This magicless utopia that you dream of doesn't have an iota of a chance of success without allies."

"I have no desire to be allies with beasts that present themselves as human."

A hint of anger rippled through Sebastian's jaw. "The feeling is mutual; I don't want you as an ally, either. However, I know a lot of really angry witches that have had their magic stripped from them by Marcia using the Aufero. You loan me the book and I can guarantee that their magic will be returned to them." Sebastian paused. "I assure you their allegiance will no longer be to the Creed and Marcia, and they would be willing to align themselves with anyone who is against her. Don't you think?"

"I don't need alliances," Samuel said carefully—too carefully. "I do fine alone."

"Yeah, I saw how fine you did back at your little hideaway. Marcia and the Creed pretty much handed your ass to you and then made you thank them for the pleasure of doing so by forcing you into an agreement that restricts you from ever retaliating. What I saw wasn't 'fine' by a long shot."

Samuel didn't answer, but I could just make out his breathing on the other end.

"Samuel," Sebastian said after a long pause. He repeated the name twice more, before Samuel answered.

"Yes," he said, with a tone that suggested he might regret his decision. "I'll send you an address."

"No. The books are safe here. I'll not remove them from the property. You have my guarantee of safe passage." After a short pause, he added, "You'll leave with everything you bring with you."

"I'll be there in two hours," he stated and ended the call.

Sebastian and I exchanged glances. The witch's base of operations was much closer than we'd expected; he'd practically camped in our backyard.

I passed the time in the pack's gym, working out my frustrations. After an intense sparring session that sent Marko to Dr. Baker's clinic with a displaced shoulder, I turned my attention to the free weights. By the time Sky found me, I was slick with sweat, working a heavy punching bag.

"You aren't imagining that bag is me, are you?" she asked.

I paused, catching the bag with both hands to stop it from swaying. "Why would I?" Not waiting for an answer, I landed a quick combination of punches, finishing with a kick that nearly knocked the bag off its chain. "How was she when you left her?" I asked, steadying the bag once more.

Sky shrugged. "She was Chris."

"I don't know what that means."

"She's a broken, dysfunctional person. And not in a hyperbolic way, but truly. She wasn't angry—she just wanted to know who the job was for and made a snide comment about me not completing it. Even though my job was to kidnap her."

I chuckled. "That sounds like her."

She frowned, folding her arms over her chest. I recognized the weight of guilt in her eyes as she turned inward. She would reflect a lot on her recent choices, probably for years. As long as she had regret to remind her, there was a chance she'd learn.

I walked to her, watching the dance of her thoughts in her eyes. Empathizing with her internal conflict, I gently brushed my fingers along her cheek, then kissed her gently, intending the gesture as comfort, but it brought to mind our encounter in the hotel.

Her body stiffened. Her lips froze, refusing to reply. Fresh anger beat in her chest as she whispered, "You said back at the restaurant that we shouldn't let things between us get awkward."

"This is awkward?" I asked, taking a step back. Her body seemed poised to fight, but the color of attraction tinged her cheeks. Her feet remained planted, pointed toward me as if flight were unthinkable. "You don't think it's awkward," I teased.

"No. But I think it is the king of bad ideas."

I smiled at her discomfort. "Maybe you're right." Just for fun, I lifted my shirt over my head and tossed it aside before walking back to the bag. Timing the rhythm of her heart, I asked, "How many times did you get sick tonight?"

Her answer was immediate, defensive. "I didn't," she claimed, but her heart betrayed her.

"Seventy-seven," I said with an amused half-smile.

Her fists clenched at her side and she strode out of the gym, mumbling, "That's a stupid skill to have."

After another half hour with the bag, I toweled off, picked up my shirt, and glanced at my burner phone; two missed calls from Caroline, but no voice mail. Ignoring her, I walked upstairs to my room for a shower. As I walked in the door, my phone vibrated.

A text message from Caroline. "I believe I've found the killer. I need your help to be sure. Did I scare you off? Are you avoiding me??"

Scowling, I tossed the phone onto my bed and stripped.

Steaming hot water washed away the sweat and soothed sore muscles, but did nothing for my anxiety.

She's getting desperate.

Standing beneath the showerhead, I felt the water massage my scalp and run down my face while my mind rooted for the means to delay her a little longer, just until the Aufero was returned and Samuel was dealt with. By the time I watched the last of the water run down the drain, I still didn't have an answer.

Once dressed in a fresh shirt and jeans, I checked the time. Samuel would be arriving soon. Josh and Sky were probably already in the library with the Clostra. On my way to join them, I found Sebastian waiting for me in the hall with a determined look.

"Did Samuel back out?" I growled.

"On the contrary, he is on his way. Ethan"—his amber eyes settled steadily on mine—"I think it would be best if you weren't here when he arrives."

I stiffened, holding his gaze and waiting for him to continue.

"Given that Samuel captured and bound your brother, I'm not sure you'll be able to restrain yourself from killing him."

My lips smacked in disgust. "He'll be safe until we get what we want."

"It was one of Samuel's conditions," he said with a flat tone meant to minimize my outrage.

I turned, looking for something to break. Failing that, I turned back to Sebastian with an incredulous look.

"Samuel will pay," he promised, "but not until we lift the curse and retrieve the Aufero. Once those goals are achieved, I'll help you."

My fists clenched as I paced the hall like a caged animal, anger rising to a flash boil. Unable to contain it, I turned and punched my fist into a wall. Pulling back bloodied knuckles, I took a slow, calming breath.

"I'll be there when we take the Aufero," I insisted.

Sebastian nodded, a smooth subtle gesture. He waited, holding my gaze for a long moment until I finally turned and walked away.

They're safe, I reminded myself as I weaved my BMW through highway traffic. If Samuel tried anything at the retreat, surrounded by were-animals, it would be suicide. Venting my anger through raw horsepower, I wondered if I could've restrained myself in his presence. As much as I hated to admit, it was probably better that I wasn't present when he'd arrived at the retreat.

I wonder how Josh will handle working so closely with Samuel? Probably fine, I admitted. My brother didn't have a were-animal's temper.

Eventually, I found myself parked across the street from Caroline's hotel. Her rental car was in the parking lot, and I didn't have to wait long before she emerged from her door, looking disheveled. After lighting a cigarette, she began pacing the landing with her free arm wrapped around her torso.

Her black stone pendant hung noticeably from her neck.

Watching her slight frame, I realized how much her plan required my cooperation. If I continued to ignore her, she would try her mind magic, but I already knew her limits. Her powers were limited to trickery. Whether the dizziness that preceded the effect of her magic was an inherent weakness in the magic itself or a reflection of her inexperience, it was warning enough. She couldn't fool me, and she couldn't physically hurt me.

Until now, I'd humored her, played her game, but I didn't have to. If I chose to ignore her, she would at most be an inconvenience. I'd fooled myself into thinking I could give her closure and at the same time expunge my guilt, but there were greater threats to worry about. It was time I put my focus back on being the pack's Beta.

A dizziness washed over me.

I'd lost sight of her, drifted off in thought like a fool. Turning, I saw her striding toward me across the parking lot, naked vengeance burning in her glare. She flicked her cigarette to the concrete. Her black stone pendant glowed.

Cursing, I pushed the BMW into traffic and raced, weaving between cars to put as much distance as possible between Caroline and me. Her magic wasn't limited to line of sight, but I was sure it was limited in range. Glancing over my shoulder, I saw both her and the hotel were already out of sight. I slowed some, just enough to avoid an accident.

There would be a final confrontation after all, but on my terms.

I changed lanes and took a winding, twisting route home. Once there, I locked the front door and dropped into my leather chair in the living room. On a whim, I took off my shirt, dropped it onto the carpet next to the chair.

In my lap, I found four black towels. As if such a sight were ordinary, I wrapped one each around my ankles, then my wrists. Gripping the ends of the chair arms, I stared at the blank television as if waiting for it to turn on of its own accord.

I don't have a television.

The thought was a whisper in the back of my mind, as if partially buried there. Confused, I tried to rise from the chair, but the towels held me to it. Pulling on them, I heard the light clatter of chains.

I felt another brief rush of dizziness. The towels became iron shackles, the leather chair became wooden. The carpet beneath my feet became old, moldy slats of pine.

You're in the shack, I realized, and the remnants of the illusion vanished.

Caroline glowered over me, her eyes black and her lips

curled into a sneer that was almost inhuman. In one palm she held an open plastic bag. The fingers of her other hand stirred the contents, a viper's nest of thin silver necklaces. I'd underestimated her abilities. She'd tricked my mind into believing I'd escaped while she'd brought me here, entirely oblivious to my fate. I almost laughed at the absurdity of it.

I watched as she raised a delicate necklace from the bag and draped it over my shoulder, igniting a searing pain. I growled from behind gritted teeth, refusing to cry out and give her the satisfaction.

Then I remembered my plan. Would it work? Had my underestimation of her abilities doomed me?

She draped two more necklaces next to the first. This time I screamed, venting pure agony for her consumption. After a moment, the pain suddenly eased. I opened my eyes to find a macabre look of satisfaction on Caroline's face, but when she glanced at the burned flesh of my shoulder, I saw a twinge of revulsion.

"What do you want?" I asked, my chest heaving as I caught my breath.

"Tell me why," she demanded.

Stick to the plan. Steeling myself for another wave of pain, I looked her in the eyes and said, "No."

Furious, she lifted a handful of chains and pressed them against my bare chest. The sudden shock of unbearable pain blinded me for a moment. I turned my head, trying to escape the stench of my own burning flesh.

The pain suddenly eased as Caroline jerked her hand away. Fear contorted her face, mixing with her anger like oil and water. Taking in the burned wreck of my chest, she turned away.

Call Josh.

Once I'd spoken the key phrase, Josh's alarm spell would alert him. He'd instantly transport to my location. But the spell had a limited range. I was supposed to warn him when the time approached.

Watching Caroline gather herself, I knew that she was close enough that she might listen.

"I didn't kill your father," I said between ragged breaths.

"Liar."

She turned back to me with a fresh determination and draped a cluster of necklaces over my other shoulder. Once more for her benefit, I screamed.

That she struggled with her actions, that her underlying morals challenged her rage, guaranteed nothing. I'd brought her to this moment. I'd put her in a position to challenge everything she believed about herself.

Tears ran from my eyes, mixing with snot and spit as I tried to maintain consciousness. In my mind, I saw an image of myself sitting naked on the edge of my bed, draping a single silver necklace over my arm as I bore the pain without resistance, as if my mind were separate from the agony.

Endure.

The pain eased just enough to become bearable. I was distantly aware of the silver on my flesh. I still felt the burning, the searing. I still smelled the charred flesh, but from a distance.

Eventually, Caroline withdrew the silver. I leaned back against the wood frame of the chair while I caught my breath. Tears streaked her cheeks. There was a horror there, a painful regret, but not enough to break the grim resolve of her rage. Suddenly mindful of her vulnerability, she angrily swiped away the tears.

She's not broken yet.

"Where's his body?" she demanded in a quavering, guttural growl.

"More. Silver."

Her expression twisted into one of inhuman fury. She

splashed the contents of the bag, dozens of necklaces, over my chest, then followed up with her hands, gathering and pressing as much of the silver against my bare skin as she could manage.

Even from a distance, the pain was unbearable. In that moment, I gave her my screams, my suffering. In the furnace of agony, I burned my anger and anxiety and guilt until nothing remained but a sense of my unburdened self, waiting in the wings for the pain to stop.

Eventually, my body gave up. My vision went to white, then black.

I woke up to a slap across my face, but the pain in my chest was an echo of what I'd experienced before I blacked out. My chest heaved as I struggled to breathe.

Observing the damage she'd done, Caroline screamed her frustration as she repeatedly smashed a shelf with her hands until it splintered. Regaining control of herself, she held one hand just below her nose, nearly covering her mouth as she resisted sobbing.

"You could've made this so much easier," she said, unable to meet my gaze.

"Anger makes things simple," I whispered. "Some decisions shouldn't be that easy."

"Just. Tell me. Why," she insisted.

Now she's ready. "I hired your father to do a job he wasn't qualified for. He got into trouble. It was a mistake."

"*You* killed him," she swore.

"I am to blame."

"No, you!"

I shook my head.

"Then who?" she demanded. When I refused to answer, she sniffed, summoning courage. "Don't make me hurt you more."

I knew by the loathing in her voice that she'd reached her limit for torture. Now came the real danger. I spat blood onto the wood floor. "You'll only get yourself killed."

"Tell me and I'll let you go," she promised with a merciful tone, but her heart rate accelerated.

"You're lying." When she didn't react, I continued, "After what you've done here, you'd be foolish to let me go."

"Are you going to come looking for me?"

I stared at her until she met my gaze. "There's only one way to find out."

She nodded faintly. There was a slight tremor in her movement as she walked behind me and picked up something heavy from a shelf.

I considered calling Josh. Instead I leaned forward and tilted the chair, allowing me to pivot around to face her. The chair clunked level as I came face-to-face with the barrel of a pistol pointed at my forehead. Caroline blinked from behind the sight.

If Josh were in range of the alarm spell, three small words quickly muttered under my breath would bring him to my rescue. Those same words would make everything I'd just endured meaningless.

With an even, calm tone, I said, "Is this what you want?"

"I don't have a choice." Tears ran down her cheeks.

I stared into the dark barrel. Silver bullets were rare and expensive. She'd just tortured me with a bag of cheap silver necklaces. Had she put her savings into the coup de grace?

"It's a fair trade," I said with a tone of finality.

Her nose wrinkled in confusion. "What?"

"I sent your father into danger. In exchange, you tortured me." Her lips thinned, pressed together as if the word were distasteful. "End this now and I've no reason to hunt you."

She shook her head, disbelieving.

The temptation to call Josh grew stronger. "I give you my word," I said, "I'll leave you in peace."

"If you tell me everything, every detail, I'll consider it."

Even if her heart hadn't betrayed her, I knew by the quiver of the barrel that she had every intention of shooting me. I sighed. "If I told you who killed your father, you'd be just as dead. In our world, there are enemies you can't defeat. I don't want your death on my conscience as well."

She wrapped her free hand around the other, trying to stabilize her aim, but the tremor only exaggerated. Staring up the sight of the barrel, I saw her squint.

"Then I guess this is it," she said.

Josh's alarm phrase was on my lips when I decided to gamble. "Pull the trigger," I said calmly.

We stared over the barrel at each other for what seemed like minutes while she tried to muster the final courage. Water welled in her eyes. She lifted her hand to wipe away the tears, then once more squinted down the barrel. Her finger twitched on the trigger.

"Have you ever killed anyone?" I asked.

She answered with a slight shake of her head.

"Most people think the hard part is pulling the trigger, but that's not the moment that sticks with you. It's the sound of the bullet smashing through bone and then brain. It's the blood and the bits of flesh and tissue that end up on the wall. Most people can't live with it. Can you?"

Her thumping heart suddenly calmed. She answered with a nearly inaudible whisper, "No."

"Nine-one-one," I said.

She hesitated, giving me a puzzled look.

The gentle breeze of Josh's magic rushed into the room. The wall to my left split down the middle and sheared away in two pieces that tumbled like crumpled paper. Josh stood just outside, his eyes solid black. He gestured to Caroline and a force struck the pistol from her hand, threw her against the wall, and pinned her there. Shelves buckled and collapsed behind her.

He took in the bloody wreck of my chest, the silver necklaces that had fallen into my lap and onto the floor around the chair. His face twisted in rage.

"No!" I shouted. He stared back at me with disbelief. "The pendant."

With a gesture, Caroline's pendant snapped loose from her chain and flew to Josh. She was too shocked to object, or struggling to breathe.

The shackles on my wrists and ankles simultaneously burst open, pins and hinges clattering onto the wood floor. I rose, letting the silver in my lap fall to the floor.

"Let her go. Josh," I said when he ignored me. I gestured to the pendant in his hand. "She's harmless now."

His lips bent into a frown, but he released her. She gasped for breath. I faced her, waiting until she collected herself. When she met my gaze, I saw resignation—and relief.

"Get it over with," she muttered.

"You can go."

Josh glared at me while Caroline thought I was toying with her.

"I told you the truth. I didn't kill your father, but I negligently sent him to his death. The creature that killed him is my enemy, but she's too powerful for you. She will always be too powerful. I will never give you her name, but I can promise you that when I kill her—I *will* kill her—I will let you know that it's done. Until then, go back to your life."

She stared at the blood on her hands.

"You didn't do anything that hasn't been done to me before," I said.

"I almost—"

"You didn't. In the end, that's all that matters. Go back to Boise and find happiness. I didn't know your father, but it's a fair guess he'd want that for you."

She took one reluctant step toward the open wall, then glanced between us.

"Give her the pendant," I said.

"No," Josh snapped, aghast.

I shot him a hard look. I'd gone through too much in that

shack to have him destroy my efforts now, despite his good intentions. Taking her power would only give rise to lingering resentment.

Scowling back at me, he tossed the pendant to her. His magic stirred around us, preparing to strike at the slightest hint of mind magic. Caroline clutched the pendant to her chest, glanced once more between us, then hurried out of the shack to her waiting car. She wasted no time driving off.

"You've lost your mind," Josh said.

I took a deep, soothing breath. The wounds on my chest were already healing, the pain now tolerable. For the first time in a while, I felt like myself again.

"Samuel's still at the retreat with Sky," he said.

I nodded. "Take me home first."

He touched my arm and transported us.

I cleaned and bandaged my wounds, then picked a thick dark colored t-shirt to hide any blood that seeped through the bandages. By the time I returned to the retreat, the sun had just dipped below the horizon. In anticipation of our mission to retrieve the Aufero, the driveway was overflowing with cars. Sebastian had called in reinforcements.

"Sebastian said to send you in," Gavin said as I walked through the front door, nodding toward the office.

Inside, I was surprised to find Samuel sitting comfortably in a chair next to Josh. My jaw clenched, but the overwhelming desire to squeeze the life from his throat was gone. Revenge was inevitable, but it could wait. At a gesture from Sebastian, I closed the door and stood waiting for an explanation while Samuel ignored my glare.

Sebastian broke the tension first, watching my reaction closely as he informed me, "Samuel has offered to help us retrieve the Aufero."

My stare shifted to Josh. His eyes flicked to my chest, looking for bloodstains. "The spell was successful?" I asked.

"The casting was successful," he answered, choosing his words carefully.

"What does that mean?"

"We won't know for sure until Sky gets close enough to the Aufero to trigger the curse," he admitted.

I turned to Sebastian. "She can't go with us."

"The orb will only respond to her."

Josh added, "I'll be by her side. The moment she experiences anything, I'll transport her out."

Frustrated, I snarled at Samuel, "What good are you? That spell of Marcia's won't let you do anything to harm the Creed."

"I can't harm her or the Creed," he agreed, "but I can still hit them where it hurts. The peace spell won't stop me from using defensive magic."

"He can't be trusted," I announced without taking my eyes from him.

"You think you can take on the Creed all by yourselves? Be my guest."

Josh interrupted. "We need his magic."

The Creed's magic was useless against us in animal form, but Josh would be there. Sky would have to stay in human form in order to handle the orb. They were putting themselves at great risk.

I growled, but nodded. I'd keep a close eye on Samuel. Attacking the Creed wasn't going to bring him any closer to obtaining the Clostra. Was he simply trying to gain our goodwill?

Gavin and Winter arrived and we spent the next hour going over the plan.

. . .

I padded in wolf form toward the magic shop, walking just ahead of Sky, my head low as I sniffed for threats. Behind her walked Josh and Samuel, side by side. As we approached the door, I felt Josh's magic pass over me. The lock clicked and the door flung open, rattling against the inside wall. There was no point in subtlety. Marcia would be expecting us. She would be prepared for a fight, and we'd just announced ourselves.

My lips spread into a wolfish grin.

Padding between shelves of crystals and New Age music, I saw the door behind the counter had been repaired, the frame replaced, and a stronger lock installed. Josh spoke a brief incantation and the lock shattered into pieces. The door flung open with a dull thud.

Inside, the Creed's sanctuary appeared unchanged from my previous visit. The long table with chairs stood next to the far wall. The windowed armoire that held the Aufero stood in the corner, its doors secured by a pair of metal locks.

We stopped just inside the room and I looked to Sky, anxious for any sign of physical distress. She swallowed and walked four steps toward the armoire, then stopped, testing the curse. Other than the pounding of her heart in her chest, there was no sign of magical attack. After a moment, she took a few more steps and stopped again.

Still nothing. Her shoulders noticeably dipped as it became apparent that the curse had been lifted. As she walked forward in earnest, an orange-black glow appeared within the armoire as the Aufero sensed her presence. With increased proximity, the glow brightened and began to pulse. The armoire began to rock and vibrate. When Sky was just a few feet away, the glass doors shattered as the orb burst through, flying straight to her. She gasped as she caught it at her chest, then quickly stored it in her bag.

As we emerged into the narrow alley behind the shop, I

wondered if we'd caught Marcia by surprise after all. Sebastian's SUV waited, but the engine was off and he wasn't in sight. Sniffing the air, I sensed a sudden atmospheric shift just before we were struck by a blistering wind. A fierce rain followed, pelting us and cutting our visibility. Thunder rumbled in our ears as a bolt of lightning struck Samuel, driving him back against the wall.

I glanced to Josh and Sky, but they were untouched. The whites of Josh's eyes faded to black as he called on his magic.

A clatter of armor rose in the alley as Liam marched from the west at the head of his royal guard, spears raised. Marcia had been busier than we'd suspected. I wondered what an alliance with the Makellos, the elven elite, had cost her.

I charged directly at Liam. Recognizing the danger, he slipped behind his line. Leaping over their spears, I latched on to the throat of one soldier and cast him aside, then took down another, wreaking havoc in the line as they compressed to protect Liam.

Gathered around him, they retreated, warding me off with the tips of their spears as I growled and snarled, looking for an opening. A wave of Samuel's magic blew past me, ruffling my fur as it struck the elven formation. A gap appeared, revealing the Elysian twins.

The gap in the elven line also left Liam vulnerable. As much as I wanted to kill him, I turned my attention to the more immediate threat. I charged into the gap, racing toward the twins. Just before a soldier intercepted me, his spear discarded for a sword, the female twin flung electricity toward the shop. I heard Samuel cry out.

Two more soldiers joined the first. Slipping behind one soldier's guard, I nipped his ankle to bring him down. Lunging for his throat, I was forced to turn aside to avoid another soldier's spear. The blade grazed my fur, drawing blood.

Marcia appeared between the twins, an invocation on her

lips. At her gesture, rain turned to a punishing hail. Fist-sized balls of ice pummeled my sides and head, driving me back toward the Sky and Josh.

Where is Sebastian? Had Liam caught them by surprise before we'd emerged from the shop?

Squinting through the storm, I saw the rest of the Creed appear behind Marcia, gesticulating in unison.

The shimmer of Josh's protective field materialized in front of me, shielding me from the storm. I glanced back to see Josh working his magic to strengthen the field while Sky stood next to him. Behind them, Samuel struggled to his feet.

A sudden flash of light blinded me. Hail pummeled me once more, indicating that Josh's field had collapsed. Just as my sight cleared, a new field appeared, stronger than the first. Despite the combined power of Josh and Samuel, the field wavered beneath the full weight of the Creed's magic. Sparks glittered and burst along the translucent barrier as it was pummeled by hail, lightning, fire, and bolts of energy.

It was only a matter of time before Josh and Samuel were overwhelmed, and Sebastian was nowhere in sight. I couldn't believe that Marcia, even with Liam's help, could defeat the pack.

Glaring through the field, I bared my teeth at Marcia and growled. Once the field collapsed, she would be my first target. I'd kill her and as many of the witches as I could, buying time for Josh and Sky to escape.

Sebastian, in wolf form, appeared charging from the east end of the alley. Gavin, Winter, and Marko, in human form, followed. As they struck Liam's guard, Sebastian burst through their line to crash into the elven twins, tearing them apart. The lightning strikes ceased, but the Creed continued to pummel the field. Ignoring the chaos behind her, Marcia confidently walked toward me. A knife was in her hand, the knife she'd used to cast the peace spell on Samuel.

The field buckled, showering us both in gold and purple

sparks. Before I could leap, an elven soldier thrust a spear at me, driving me back. Snapping and snarling, I tried to get past his guard, but the elf was determined, and skilled.

Behind him, I saw Samuel raise a hand to Marcia, the start of an invocation on his lips, then hesitate. His face darkened. He took awkward, spastic steps backward, as if propelled against his will, until he stumbled into the wall and remained there.

The peace spell.

Marcia acknowledged his plight with a twisted smile as she continued toward Sky. Taking one step back, Sky reached into her bag and drew out the glowing Aufero. A powerful field formed around her, only to fall a moment later from the combined invocation of the Creed.

Marcia gasped as the knife leapt from her hand to Josh's. Raising it, he charged. With a wave of her hand, he was flung back against the wall and pinned there. His eyes melted into black as he called upon his most powerful magic to free himself.

A contest of magic followed, spells and counterspells, as Josh tried to free himself. But Marcia had the advantage. The Creed beside her, they locked hands, combining their power.

I growled in frustration, unable to break from my fight to help him.

Marcia raised one finger, her attention fixed on the knife in Josh's hand as it slowly began to rise toward his throat. Grunting, panting, he strained for self-control. His hand shook violently, but continued rising until the blade cut the skin of his throat like paper.

I pivoted, trying to put the soldier off balance to dash around him. The tip of his spear sliced my right hip, forcing me to spin around to avoid a deeper cut.

Josh released a fierce, primitive roar that struck the witches like a shock wave. All but Marcia tumbled to the concrete. She screamed at the now knife embedded in her arm and fell to her knees.

The Creed vanished.

Struck by the fringe of Josh's shock wave, the elven soldier lost his balance. I clamped my jaws around his throat and shook. Bones crunched and the soldier's body went limp. I dropped it and ran back to Josh and Sky, relieved to find them safe. He remained lost in his rage, blasting magic at the few remaining soldiers in the alley.

Samuel nodded to me and moved closer to Sky.

The battle was nearly over. Steven and the rest of the pack had come in from the west, attacking the elves from behind. Liam had disappeared and most of his soldiers were dead, but the survivors were putting up a valiant fight. As Winter swung her katana, I saw a soldier slip in behind her, raise his spear. I struck him from the side, knocking the spear from his hands as I took him to the ground and tore out his throat.

"Skylar!" Gavin shouted.

The urgency in his voice turned me around just in time to see Samuel wrap an arm around her waist. They disappeared.

CHAPTER 20

*J*osh had only just realized that Sky was gone when I changed into human form.

"Where did they go?" I demanded.

He spun about, confused.

"Josh! He transported her. Where?"

"Not far," he said. "He's weakened. He'll take her somewhere close, where he can rest and get his power back."

Sebastian and Winter were at my side, leaving the last of the fight under Steven's direction.

"I should've never trusted him," I growled.

Even if they were close, the chances of finding them were slim. Our only hope was that Sky used the Aufero to escape. If she managed to free herself, she'd go somewhere public. If he took her out of the city, she'd look for a major road and follow it until she picked up a ride or found a phone to borrow. The best we could do was split up and hope to get lucky.

"I'll take west," Sebastian said. "Josh, go east. Winter, south. Ethan, north. Go twenty miles out, main roads only, then circle back."

On the way to our cars, I told Josh on a hunch, "I'll take east."

The little hope I held of finding Sky faded with each mile. As I drove out of the suburbs to an increasingly barren landscape, I felt a sense of dread. On the few occasions in my life where I'd felt hopeless, I'd always been able to substitute anger; I'd always been able to defy the odds through sheer will. There was nothing I could do now. Sky's safety was entirely out of my hands, and I felt empty. Powerless.

I let Samuel get closer to her.

If she were harmed, I doubted I'd ever recover from the guilt.

As I drove, my eyes shifted from the road to my phone beside me to the odometer. I was nearly at the twenty-mile mark when I caught a flash of someone on the other side of the road. I slowed, crossed the median.

Sky raised her arm to shield her eyes from the glare of the headlights. Relief rushed through me as I flicked off the high beams and brought the car to a stop next to her. Looking in her frazzled eyes, I nearly couldn't breathe.

The odds were almost impossible.

Looking inside to be certain it was me, she sighed and opened the door. She practically collapsed into the seat, exhausted, but she appeared unharmed.

I turned the BMW back toward the city and called Sebastian. The relief in his voice was palpable and nearly matched his surprise.

We were quiet for a few miles. I couldn't stop glancing at her, wondering how she'd found me. What was it that made me change directions with Josh?

"Why did you head east?" I asked.

She shrugged. "I don't know."

"That's twice."

"What?"

I smiled, watching her expression as she recalled stumbling upon me in New York. She nodded, not sure what to say. She glanced at her bag and a look of concern came over her.

"Something is wrong with the Aufero. Using it to draw out the dark elf magic seems to have corrupted it, made it darker."

I'd seen the change, but there was another possibility: Maya. Logan had warned us that eventually Maya might try to wield more of her power through Sky. "Are you sure it is the magic pulled from me?" Her lips pursed as she considered the possibility, but neither of us had an answer. "For now, don't use it until we can figure it out."

We were quiet, lost in our own thoughts, until I turned into her neighborhood.

"When did Marcia align with Liam?" Sky asked.

"I am trying to figure it out. There's something at hand and I think it is directed toward us." Whatever they were up to didn't bode well for the pack.

As I turned the BMW into her driveway, the headlights swept over a tall figure waiting on her porch. He stood straight, still, his lavender eyes narrowed as he fixated his attention on Sky. Unaware of his presence, she started out of the car.

"Sky," I said.

She paused, gasped when she saw Logan staring at her.

In removing Sky's curse, we'd removed his as well. Already, the consequences of our choices had come to haunt me.

MESSAGE TO THE READER

Thank you for choosing *Darkness Unveiled* from the many titles available to you. Our goal is to create an engaging world, compelling characters, and an interesting experience for you. We hope we've accomplished that. Reviews are very important to authors and help other readers discover our books. Please take a moment to leave a review. We'd love to know your thoughts about the book.

For notifications about new releases, *exclusive* contests and giveaways, and cover reveals, please sign up for our mailing lists at McKenzieHunter.com.